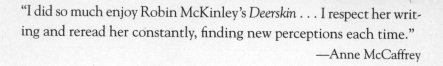
"I did so much enjoy Robin McKinley's *Deerskin* . . . I respect her writing and reread her constantly, finding new perceptions each time."

—Anne McCaffrey

"Fine, deftly told . . . [McKinley] has invented a wonderful story and told it in a wonderful manner . . . If McKinley doesn't melt your heart with her dogs, she'll tear you up with the plain, down-to-earth prince who falls for Deerskin . . . A wonderful story, wonderfully told."

—*The San Diego Union-Tribune*

"A classic journey-tale and a parable for modern times . . . McKinley turns her storytelling acumen and stylistic grace toward an adult audience, handling incest and rape with unflinching honesty while at the same time building a case for hope and renewal." —*Library Journal*

"*Deerskin* is a subversive fairytale with an element of myth, but most of all it is a psychological novel of great depth and power, using fantasy in the service of truth."

—*Locus*

"Well-chosen details, characterization is superlative." —*Booklist*

"McKinley's writing is amazing, dreamlike, gut-wrenching, and heartwarming . . . A very uplifting story of triumph and love."

—*Under the Covers*

Books by Robin McKinley

BEAUTY:
A RETELLING OF THE STORY OF BEAUTY AND THE BEAST

THE DOOR IN THE HEDGE

THE BLUE SWORD

THE HERO AND THE CROWN

THE OUTLAWS OF SHERWOOD

IMAGINARY LANDS

DEERSKIN

ROSE DAUGHTER

SPINDLE'S END

WATER:
TALES OF ELEMENTAL SPIRITS
(*with Peter Dickinson*)

SUNSHINE

Deerskin

ROBIN McKINLEY

ACE BOOKS, NEW YORK

THE BERKLEY PUBLISHING GROUP
Published by the Penguin Group
Penguin Group (USA) Inc.
375 Hudson Street, New York, New York 10014, USA
Penguin Group (Canada), 10 Alcorn Avenue, Toronto, Ontario M4V 3B2, Canada
(a division of Pearson Penguin Canada Inc.)
Penguin Books Ltd., 80 Strand, London WC2R 0RL, England
Penguin Group Ireland, 25 St. Stephen's Green, Dublin 2, Ireland (a division of Penguin Books Ltd.)
Penguin Group (Australia), 250 Camberwell Road, Camberwell, Victoria 3124, Australia
(a division of Pearson Australia Group Pty. Ltd.)
Penguin Books India Pvt. Ltd., 11 Community Centre, Panchsheel Park, New Delhi—110 017, India
Penguin Group (NZ), Cnr. Airborne and Rosedale Roads, Albany, Auckland 1310, New Zealand
(a division of Pearson New Zealand Ltd.)
Penguin Books (South Africa) (Pty.) Ltd., 24 Sturdee Avenue, Rosebank, Johannesburg 2196,
South Africa

Penguin Books Ltd., Registered Offices: 80 Strand, London, WC2R 0RL, England

This is a work of fiction. Names, characters, places, and incidents either are the product of the author's imagination or are used fictitiously, and any resemblance to actual persons, living or dead, business establishments, events, or locales is entirely coincidental.

Copyright © 1993 by Robin McKinley.
Moon image courtesy NASA/JPL-Caltech.
Cover design by Judith Lagerman.
Text design by Stacy Irwin.

PRINTING HISTORY
Ace hardcover edition / June 1993
Ace mass market edition / July 1994
Ace trade paperback edition / May 2005

Library of Congress Cataloging-in-Publication Data

McKinley, Robin.
    Deerskin / Robin McKinley.
      p.   cm.
    ISBN 0-441-01239-6
      1. Princesses—Fiction. 2. Conflict of generations—Fiction. 3. Fathers and
daughters—Fiction. 4. Women dog owners—Fiction. 5. Dogs—Fiction.   I. Title.

PS3563.C3816D4 2005
813'.54—dc22
                                                                2004062706

PRINTED IN THE UNITED STATES OF AMERICA

10 9 8 7 6 5 4 3 2 1

To Mary, Mary, Barbara, Susan, Alex, Steve, Andrea and George: thanks.

Author's Note:

There is a story by Charles Perrault called *Donkeyskin* which, because of its subject matter, is often not included in collections of Perrault's fairy tales. Or, if it does appear, it does so in a bowdlerized state. The original *Donkeyskin* is where *Deerskin* began.

PART ONE

One

Many years later she remembered how her parents had looked to her when she was a small child: her father as tall as a tree, and merry and bright and golden, with her beautiful black-haired mother at his side. She saw them, remembered them, as if she were looking at a painting; they were too splendid to be real, and always they seemed at some little distance from her, from all onlookers. They were always standing close together as she remembered them, often gazing into each other's eyes, often handclasped, often smiling; and always there was a radiance like sunlight flung around them.

Her mother had been the most beautiful woman in seven kingdoms, and seven kings had each wanted her for himself; but her father had won the priceless prize, even though he had been only a prince then, and his father hale and strong.

When the old king fell from his horse only a year after his son married, and died of the blow, everyone was shocked and surprised, and mourned the old king exceedingly. But he was forgotten soon enough in the brilliance of the young king's reign, and in the even brighter light of his queen's beauty. When the worst grief was spent, and such a joke could be made, some people laughed, and said that the most beautiful woman in seven kingdoms had the luck of seven kingdoms as well, for she was now queen of the richest, and for a mere year's wait.

It was the princess's nursemaid who told her this story, and told it often. It was the nursemaid's favorite, and became the little girl's, the long story containing many stories, of her parents' courtship and marriage. This story was better than anything read draggingly out of a storybook—for the nursemaid was uneasy with her letters, but as the ability to read was one of the requirements of her post, she was extremely anxious that no one should find this out. She told the princess that there was no need for dull stories out of heavy hard books, and as she made the storybook stories dull and the stories she herself told interesting, the princess came readily to agree, perhaps because her parents were only a little more real to her than the characters in the storybooks.

"Your lovely mother cast her eyes down when her new people said such things to her, for she was a modest girl then as she is a modest woman now; but everyone knew that she would have chosen your father over the other six kings even had he been a goat-boy with naught but a bell and a shepherd's stick to his name."

"Tell me about the task he was set," said the little princess.

"Ah, it was a terrible task," said the nursemaid, cuddling her close on her lap. "Each of the seven kings—six kings and one prince—was given a task, and each task was more difficult than the one before, as your lovely mother's father began to comprehend the setting of tasks; for such a joy was the daily presence of your lovely mother that her father was not eager to part with her. And so he looked to drive her suitors away, or to lose them on topless mountains and in bottomless valleys or upon endless seas. But who could blame him? For she is the most beautiful woman in seven kingdoms, and he died of a broken heart eight months after she married your father and left him, and even your uncle, who is now lord of those lands, says the country, the earth itself, is sad without her."

"The *task*," said the princess.

"I was coming to it," said the nursemaid reprovingly. "So your father was the seventh suitor after the six kings, because his father thought he was young to marry, and had heard besides that your lovely mother's father was setting such tasks that might lose him his only son. But in the end he did his son no favors, for his son—your father—would go, and so it was he who had the last and hardest task."

"And what was it?" said the princess, though she had heard this story many times.

"I am coming to it. The task was to bring a leaf plucked and unfallen from the tree of joy, which grows at the farthest eastern edge of the world, and an apple plucked and unfallen from the tree of sorrow, that grows at the farthest western end of the world.

"And when your lovely mother's father said the words of the task, he smiled, for he knew that no living man could accomplish it; and so at worst his daughter had but six suitors left.

"But he did not see the look that passed between his daughter and her seventh suitor, the look that said, *I will do this thing*, and was answered, *I know you will, and I will wait for you.*

"And wait she did; four of the six kings returned successfully from their adventures, bearing what they had been ordered to bring. The word came that the fifth king had been killed, and that the sixth had thought better of his third cousin twice removed, and went home and married her—and I've always heard that they're very happy," the nursemaid added, doubtfully, to herself. "And she such a plain girl, with a heavy jaw and thick legs. They all says she's kind, and loves her husband, but if you're king 'twould be easy to find plain girls with thick legs to love you, a penny the dozen, and any such who was made queen would be sure to be kind from . . . from surprise. It would be easy!" said the nursemaid, fiercely, pleating the edge of her apron with her fingers.

The princess fidgeted. "The task!"

The nursemaid started, and smoothed her apron, and put her arm again around the princess. "Oh, yes, my love, his task. So your lovely mother refused to choose among the four kings who had completed their tasks, saying that she would wait for the return of the last, which was only fair.

"The four kings grumbled—particularly since it was only a prince they were waiting for, and his father the king young yet—but your lovely mother's father smiled and smiled, because he began to suspect that some such a look as had passed between his daughter and her seventh suitor must have done so, and that his daughter waited for some reason other than fairness. He was well pleased, because he knew that no living man could bring back a leaf plucked and unfallen from the tree of joy, as well as an apple plucked and unfallen from the tree of sorrow. It might take a lifetime to do just the one or the other; and then the man who came at last within the shade of either of those great trees, did he once let those branches' immortal shadows touch him, might lift a sere and curled leaf or a bruised and half-rotted apple from the ground, and think his life well spent to do so much." The nursemaid was not easy with her letters, but she listened closely to every minstrel who sang in the king's halls, and she knew how a story should be told.

"So the father of the most beautiful woman in seven kingdoms smiled, for he foresaw that he would not need to set further tasks for the four kings, now sitting at his board, glowering and restless, because his daughter would refuse them all, waiting for the one who never came. And such was the love that he bore for his only daughter, and the desire for her presence, that he did not begrudge the entertainment of those four kings, however long they sat at table, however expensive their serving and stabling.

"But what he did not know was the strength of that look that had passed between the prince and the lady; for the strength between them of wanting and of need was greater than what one mortal man could do in one mortal lifetime. And so it was but a year and a day from your father's setting out on his quest, not caring that it was a hopeless one so long as he carried the look your mother had given him deep in his heart, that he returned. Because he loved her beyond life itself, and because he knew she loved him equally, he knew he must return; that knowing was greater than time and mortality.

"The old lord's health began to fail as soon as he set eyes on your father, striding into the court of his beloved's father, his face alight with happiness and hope; but I doubt your father noticed, for he had eyes only for the raven-haired lady sitting at her father's side. But everyone else noticed, and everyone remembered that your lovely mother's father had threatened to set a second task for any suitor she favored, so terribly did he want to keep her.

"But they said that when he saw the strength of the bond between them shining in your father's face, he did not have the heart to set any more challenges, for the strength of his own love made him recognize what he saw. Certainly he gave them his blessing when they turned to him and asked for it; but he gave it to them in the creaking voice of an old, old man, and when he passed his hands over their heads, the hands were thin and gnarled."

The princess, who did not care for old people, said, "But what of the leaf and the apple?"

"Ah, that was an amazement among amazing things. They thought the old king would defy his last successful suitor by saying that the leaf and the apple were not what they must be, but any shining leaf and any bright, round apple, for how is anyone to tell if something no mortal hands has touched before be that thing or no? But when your father took his tokens out of his pack and held them up for all to see, a strange blindness struck the company, as if their eyes had for the moment forgotten their work, or fled from the task of seeing. And they were dazed with this, with the betrayal of their own vision, and sank to their knees, and trembled, and did not know what had come to them, and only wished to return to their ordinary lives, and deal no more with marvels.

"But from out of their mazing they heard your father's laugh, and then there was a burst of flame that everyone saw, like a bonfire at Midsummer, blinding indeed if you look too closely, but a familiar kind of astonishment this was, one you understand and can turn away from. Everyone blinked, and in blinking their vision returned to them; and they looked around. The fire in the great fireplace had gone out; and it and the walls around it were blackened as by some great explosion, and the prince and the lady stood before that blackened hearth, now locked in each other's arms. And yet they had stood half across the wide court from each other before the blindness struck all those who watched."

"He had thrown them in the fire, the leaf and the apple," said the child.

"Aye, that he had," agreed the nursemaid. "Tokens worth the finest treasure in this world or any other, tokens no living man should be able to bear; and he threw them into the fire for the love of your mother, and felt no regret. For, he said, all the joy he needed was in your mother's eyes; and he could withstand any sorrow so long as he had once known that joy."

"And so they were married."

"Aye, they were married. The four kings came, and danced with your mother, and drank to your father's health; and went away sadly but politely, for they were all true kings. The successor of the fifth king was twelve years old, but he knew what was expected of him, or had ministers to tell him what to do, and he sent a handsome young lord who brought a golden casket full of pearls as a wedding gift. The sixth king . . . sent his regrets by herald, with but a second herald to accompany him, and they also brought a gift, a quilt, a patchwork quilt, made by his heavy-jawed queen and her ladies, in shades of blue, embroidered with stars . . . as well send an ostler with a horse blanket!" The nurse-maid sniffed. "It cannot be imagined what your lovely mother's life could have been, with such a husband.

"The other kings have all since married too, and each of their queens has borne a son, and"—the nursemaid lifted the child off her lap, and gave her a little, intense, gleeful shake—"in twelve or fourteen years, your father will be setting tasks for them!"

THE PRINCESS FELL ASLEEP NIGHTS THINKING OF the tree of joy and the tree of sorrow, and sometimes she dreamed of the sound of leaves rustling, and of the sweet, sharp, poignant smell of ripe apples. And she woke to another day bright with the presence of her parents, for they lit their world as the sun lights the great world, and every one of their subjects loved them and was grateful.

It was a favorite joke among their people that the way to be certain that it did not rain on any fair or harvest was to invite the royal couple to it. The sun himself, it was said, could not resist the queen's beauty, and loved nothing better than to tease the hidden red fires from deep within her glossy black hair.

There were no wars, nor even threat or thought of war, for the people were all too contented. It was said that any foreign danger, any officer from a rival king, would be so bewitched by the queen that he would charm his own master into renouncing his claim. The queen said nothing to this, neither yea nor nay, but smiled her secret smile, and cast her eyes down, as she had done when she was teased for her luck in her father-in-law's early death. The queen spoke little, but few words of her were necessary, for the wonder of her presence was enough.

When the king and queen made processions through their king-dom, the princess came too; and people were kind to her. They were kind to her when they noticed her, for all eyes were upon the king and queen, and she was but a child, and small, and shy; and during those early years of her life she worshipped her parents more than anyone, except, perhaps, her nursemaid.

Even her dancing-master, her riding instructor, and her mistress of deportment seemed able to think of teaching her only in terms of the queen's gifts and graces; and so the princess, who was only a child, thought little of her own talents, because by that standard she could not be said to succeed. And because she was a child, it did not occur to her to wonder why neither her nursemaid, nor her dancing-master, nor her riding instructor, nor her mistress of deportment ever said to her, "My dear, you are but a child yet, and the queen a woman in the fullness of her prime; you stand and step and move very prettily, you take instruction graciously, and I am well content to be your teacher." Her father and mother never suggested such things to her either; but then they never saw her practice dancing or riding, or sewing or singing. There were always so many other things for so popular a king and so beautiful a queen to do.

On the princess's twelfth birthday there was a grand party just for her, and all the lords and ladies came, and one of the sons of the once-rival kings, who was thirteen, and stood almost invisible among the tall figures of his guardsmen. There were musicians, and dancing, and talk and laughter, and the banqueting tables were piled high with beautiful savory food, and she could not bear it, that so many eyes should think to turn upon her as the cause of all this magnificence, and she ran and hid in the nursery.

When her old nursemaid found her at last, and washed her face free of tear-stains, and pressed her crumpled dress, and tidied her dark hair, and took her downstairs again, the queen was sitting at the head of the table, in the chair the princess had fled. The king sat at her right hand, and they were feeding each other bits of cake and sweetmeats, looking into each other's face, utterly absorbed in these things. The thirteen-year-old prince sat near them, watching, his mouth hanging a little agape.

The princess slipped away from her nursemaid, who would have wished to make her present herself formally. But even a royal nursemaid's jurisdictions end at the ballroom door. The princess found a chair standing next to a curtain and shadowed by the column at its back, and set herself silently down.

When the princess's return was noticed, and the dancing started again, one or two young men approached the princess hopefully. But she disliked her dancing lessons, and disliked being touched and held so by strangers, and she drew back in her chair and shook her head emphatically at her would-be partners. They went away, and after a little time no more came. She curled up on her gilt chair and rested her head softly on one of its velvet arms, and watched her mother and father dancing, their footsteps as light and graceful as the dainty steps of the royal deer.

Two

It was two years later that the queen fell ill, and no doctor could help her; and at first no one thought it was serious. Indeed, some went so far as to hint that nothing at all was wrong; that the queen merely needed taking out of herself—or perhaps putting back into herself, for she gave of her presence and her beauty too freely, and was wearied by the adoration of her people. At first it was only that she rose late and retired early; but the weeks passed, and she rose later and later, and was seen outside her rooms less and less; and then the news came that she no longer left her bed, and then that she could not leave her bed.

And then it was said that she was dying.

The doctors shook their heads, and murmured long words to each other. The people wept, and prayed to their gods, and told themselves and each other many stories, till the real story sounded no truer than

the rest. The story that contained the most truth, although it was not
the story that was listened to the most often, was that the queen need
not die, except that her illness, the strange invisible illness with no
name, had robbed her of the tiniest fraction of her beauty. Her brilliant
hair was just a little dulled, her enormous eyes just a little shadowed;
and when she guessed she might no longer be the most beautiful woman
in seven kingdoms she lost her will to live.

She had the window curtains drawn first, that the sun might not
find her out; she did not care that he might miss her, even as her people
did, or that his warmth might be less cruel than her own eyes in the mirror were. Nor would she listen to her doctors, that sunlight might mend
her; for she heard behind their voices that they knew nothing of what
was wrong with her and therefore nothing of what might heal. She sank
deeper into her pillows, and had her bed-curtains drawn as well.

The king was frantic, for after a time she refused to see him either;
but she was convinced to yield to her husband in this thing after all, for
he grew so wild at her denial that his ministers feared he would do himself an injury. So the queen drew a scarf over her head and a veil across
her face, and gloves upon her hands, and permitted one candle only to
be lit in her dim chamber; and it was held at some distance from the
queen's bed, and shaded by a waiting-woman's hand.

The king threw himself across the queen's bed in a paroxysm of
weeping, and tore at the bedclothes with his finger-nails, and cried
aloud; and the waiting-women all trembled, and the candle flickered in
the hands that held it, for they all thought the king had gone mad. But
it could be seen that, through the veil, the queen smiled; and one hand,
in its lacy, fragile glove, reached out and stroked his shoulder. At this he
looked up at her, with a great snarl of bedclothes in his big hands, pressing them to his face like a child.

"There is something I would have you do for me," she said in the
whisper that was all her voice now.

"Anything," he said, and his voice was no stronger than hers.

"I want you to commission a painter," she said, in her perfectly controlled whisper, "and he must be the finest painter in this or any other land. I want him to paint a portrait of me as I was, for you to remember me by."

"Remember you by!" screamed the king; and some time passed before even the queen could calm him. But in the end he agreed, because it was true that he would do anything for her, and she knew it.

Now every painter in the seven kingdoms considered long when the news of this commission came to them; although very few painters responded from the kingdom of the sixth king, who had married the girl with thick legs. It was said, scornfully, that this was because, in that kingdom, there was no beauty to inspire the painter's art. But very many other painters came from the other five kingdoms. Most of all, however, painters came from the queen's own country, from the towns where the king and queen had brought sunshine to harvests and celebrations. All brought drawings they had made over the years of the most beautiful woman in seven kingdoms, for they all had found her an irresistible subject. The highest number of painters from the smallest area, however, came from her uncle's, now her brother's, little fiefdom, and they brought drawings of a raven-haired child and young girl who would obviously grow up to be the most beautiful woman in seven kingdoms.

It was originally assumed that the king would attend the interviews and make the decision, but this was swiftly proven false, for the king did nothing but crouch by the queen's bed, clinging to her hand, and wetting it with his tears, until, sometimes, the queen tired of him, and sent him away. When he first tried to stand after the long hours of his vigil, he could barely walk for his grief, and without aid would have crawled like a beast. The burdens of the queen's desire thus fell upon his ministers, and they shared among themselves, some staying near the king, some hearing the most pressing matters of statecraft, some leafing through portfolios and sending away the most conspicuously inept. The other artists were made to wait, day after weary unbroken day—while their work was shown to the queen herself. And she did not hurry to make her decision.

She ordered the king to leave her while she looked at unfinished sketches and finished portraits; he grew so distraught, she said, that he distracted her. At first he was banished merely to the next room, but the queen could hear him, pacing, muttering brokenly to himself, and she said that even this fatigued her, and that she needed all her small remaining strength for the task at hand. And so the king was sent, stumbling, to a far wing of the palace, till she sent word that he might return.

The queen studied every painting, every fragment, every chalky shred, brought to her; and every one was beautiful, for even awkward artists could not fail to capture some beauty when they set out to portray her. She lay in her bed and stared at paintings till her attendants were exhausted by the intensity of her purpose.

After the first few days, every day or so thereafter she would discard one or another painter; and he would have his work returned to him, be given a coin for his trouble (everyone thought this royally generous, since none of the painters had been under any obligation to answer the invitation), and sent on his way. No one, apparently, thought to remark on the fact that all the artists hoping to paint the queen's portrait were men; although one maid-servant, who worked in the king's kitchens and was rarely allowed upstairs, and who had cousins who lived in every one of the seven kingdoms, did comment that the sixth king's official court painter was a woman. But she was only a maid-servant, and no one found this statement interesting.

The waiting painters began to dread the sight of the majordomo. He would appear with canvas and sketchbook-sized bundles under his arms, or in the arms of an attending footman, and beckon some unfortunate, waiting in the receiving-hall, or in what had been the receiving-hall when the queen had been well and the king had done any receiving. Occasionally, and worse, the majordomo paused in the grand arched doorway with the carved vines twining round and round the bordering columns twice as high as a man's head, and framed by this grandeur sonorously pronounced some name. And then the poor artist had to cross the long shining floor (for the house-maids were kept severely up to the mark however preoccupied the king was) under the eyes of all the other painters, and admit that the work thus displayed as a failure was his.

The selection was down to three at last. Three paintings stood on three easels at some little distance from the queen's bed in the queen's chamber; and downstairs, very far away, three painters nibbled at the food the impassive servants brought, and fidgeted, and could not speak to each other. Even farther away the king ignored the food his closest, most anxiously loyal attendants brought, and cursed them, and cursed his ministers too when they tried to encourage him to eat, or to engage him in the ruling of his country. He paced, and tore his hair, and cried aloud.

In the queen's chamber something extraordinary happened. She asked her attendants to move the three paintings to stand directly in front of the closely curtained windows; and then she dismissed the footmen who had done the moving, and all her serving-women but one. That one she told to draw the curtains—open; let the sunlight in, to fall upon the faces of the portraits. But the woman was to stand, facing out the window, with her back to the room; and she was not to stir till she was told. This woman knew her mistress well, as the queen knew; and would do exactly as she was told, as the queen also knew.

But the woman could hear. And what she heard was the sound of the queen turning back her bedclothes, and setting her feet upon the floor. She had lain there among her pillows for so many weeks that her steps were feeble and uncertain, and the waiting-woman trembled where she stood, for all her training told her she should rush to support her queen. But her training also told her that she must obey a command; and the command was that she remain where she was; and so she did not stir a foot, though her muscles shivered.

The queen stumbled—fell; "Mistress!" cried the woman, half turning—"*Stay where you are!*" said the queen in a voice as sharp and strong and unflinching as the fall of the executioner's axe. The woman burst into tears and covered her face with her hands, and so did not hear the queen pull herself to her feet and resume her slow progress toward the windows.

When the woman dropped her hands and sniffed, she could see, out of the corner of her eye as she looked straight ahead of her, the dark narrow bulk of the queen's body, leaning on the back of a chair. The queen moved the chair a little, her hands groping either at her own weakness or at the unfamiliarity of such a task, so its back was perfectly opposed to the waiting-woman's tiny peripheral glimpse of it. Slowly the queen sat down in the chair, facing the last three portraits of the most beautiful woman in seven kingdoms, lit as they were now by golden afternoon sunlight, till they were almost as glorious as the woman herself had been. The waiting-woman saw the shadow of a gesture, and knew that the queen was raising her veil.

THE FINAL SELECTION WAS MADE, AND THE OTHER two painters sent on their way—with three coins each, and a silver necklace and a ring with a stone in it, because they had been good enough almost to have been chosen. Although they would not have admitted it, they were at the last relieved that their work had not found favor in the queen's eyes, and that they could go home, and return to painting bowls of flowers for rich young men courting, and dragons the size of palaces being dispatched by solitary knights in gleaming armor for city council chambers, and fat old merchants spilling over their collars and waistbands for their counting-houses and inheriting sons. For they did not like the smell of the place where the queen lay dying of her own will, who had once been the most beautiful woman in seven kingdoms; and they had heard that the king was mad.

The young man who remained behind grimaced at his paint-stained fingers, and wondered if those fingers, of which he had long been proud, had betrayed him.

He never saw the queen. The painting that had won him his commission was returned to him, and he and it—now standing on a jewelled easel—were established in a large sunny chamber with windows on three sides and a curtained bed pushed up against the fourth. He was asked what he wanted; he wanted very little. He wanted a plain easel—plain, he emphasized—to set up his new canvas; and enough food to keep him on his feet. No wine, he said, only water; and food as plain as his painting-frame.

He had been so sure he would win the commission—so sure of his talent—that he had brought a fresh canvas with him, and all his best brushes and colors, for he was very particular about these things, and knew that to paint the most beautiful woman in seven kingdoms he must be more particular than he had even guessed at, thus far in his risky career. And so he had spent all his last commission—which might otherwise have kept him through the winter, so that he need not paint portraits of ugly arrogant people with money for some months—to hire a horse, to carry his exactingly stretched canvas and his paint-boxes and his beautifully tipped and pointed brushes, because this was going to be the commission, and the painting, of his life, and after this he would be able to pick and choose who hired him. He would even be able to sell paintings—large paintings—of his own composition, including the several already completed during the occasional months that he was enough ahead, for he lived frugally at all times, to paint what he wished, and not what people who did not know how to spend their money thought they wanted.

In the first days of waiting he had set up his beautiful naked canvas and begun the first sketching strokes of the portrait he would make of the queen, for he had the kind of armored single-mindedness that enabled him to work even when other, possibly rival, painters peered over his shoulder. This was a useful talent, and one that had earned him more than one winter's rent and food at harvest festivals. But this was no quick study to be thrown off in an hour; this was a masterpiece, and he felt it tingling in his fingers, till he had no need of concentration to ignore the other painters around him, for he forgot their existence.

The queen would be standing, looking a little over her shoulder toward her audience, and her royal robes would be so gorgeous that only paint could render them, for no mere dyed and woven cloth could have produced such drapes and billows, such tints, such highlights and fine-edged hues. And yet she would be lovelier, far lovelier, than all. It hurt his heart, standing before his empty canvas, his hand poised to make the first mark, how beautiful she would be.

But he stood now in the wide, light-filled chamber, having succeeded in winning the commission that would change his life, staring at the canvas with the few graceful lines on it, and his hand shook, and his mind's eye was full of shadows, and the velvets and silks and the soft gloss of skin and sparkle of eye would not come to him. He had put the canvas away very soon in that great receiving-hall, although it was not the waiting that preyed upon him. He stared at his canvas now, and felt as mad as the king.

The word went round that the young painter never slept; he called for lamps and candles at twilight, and, as the queen had ordered that he have everything he wanted, lamps and candles were brought. More! he shouted. More! And more were brought, till the room was brighter than daylight, and the chamber was a sea, and its rippled surface was the fragile points of hundreds of burning candles and oil-soaked wicks, and the painter gasped a little as he worked, keeping his head above that sea. He pulled down the curtains that hung round his bed, and told the servants to bear them away. The chamber pot he kept not under the bed but beside it, that he need not reach into even the small vague grey shadows of a well-swept floor under a high-framed bed.

In the morning, said the servants, the candles had burnt to their ends and even some of the lamps—full the night before—were empty for they had burnt through the night; and the painter was still working. Each evening he called again for candles, and fresh candles were brought, round and sweet-smelling; and the lamps, refilled, were again set alight. And in the morning, when the servants brought him breakfast, all were still burning, or guttering, or entirely consumed, and the painter still lashed his canvas.

It was not true that he never slept; it was true that he slept little, lying down for a few minutes or half an hour, till the light flickering against his eyelids brought him awake again, rested enough to work a little longer. But the underlying truth was that he hated the dark, hated it here, in this palace, hated and feared it, which he had never done before; some of his best studies had been done of twilight, or of Moon's image across dark water. But all that seemed to belong to another life, and here if any shadow fell undisturbed by light he would move a candle or call for another one, till there was nowhere he could stand, near his new portrait of the most beautiful woman in seven kingdoms, that did not have many tiny tongues of light flicking across his shadow, the canvas's, and that of the paintbrush that he held in his hand. It was true furthermore that he could not sleep with the queen's brilliant painted eyes upon him; no matter how he set the frame, he felt her eyes, felt her command, her passion, her presence; and so after a very few minutes' sleep he found himself pulled to his feet again, staggering toward the canvas, groping for a brush.

It was done in barely a fortnight. When the servants came in one morning they found him collapsed at the new painting's feet, and they rushed forward, full of dread that his heart had burst from overwork—or from the queen's gruelling beauty—and that the painting would remain unfinished.

But as they came up behind him they saw the painting itself for the first time, for he had guarded it from them before, fiercely, almost savagely. They cried out as they looked at it, and fell to their knees. At the sound, the painter stirred and sat up; and they did not notice it, but he carefully looked away from the painting himself, his masterwork, and looked at them instead; and he appeared to be satisfied with what he saw, and heard. She was, they said, the most beautiful woman not only in seven kingdoms, but in the kingdoms of the world. What none dared say aloud was: she, this splendid, immortal woman on the canvas, is more beautiful than the queen ever was. Or perhaps they had only forgotten, for it had been so long since the queen had walked among them.

The servants seized the painting. The painter might have protested their handling, but they treated it with the reverence they treated the queen herself with; and someone ran for a bolt of silk to swathe it in. Already they had forgotten the painter, who had not moved from where he sat on the floor after recovering from his swoon; but he did not care.

Dimly it occurred to him that he should wonder if the paint might still be damp enough to smear; dimly it occurred to him that he might wish to protect his masterwork, for himself, or, more, from the wrath of she who had commissioned it, for he feared the queen as much as he feared the darkness in this place where the king was mad. But he did not care. When they had wrapped his painting and borne it away, he stood up with a sigh, and packed his paints and his brushes, walking carefully, for he was more tired than he could ever remember being, tired, he thought, almost unto death.

He walked very carefully around the tall, wide-raking arms of the guttering candles in their candelabra, and the slim shining globes of the oil lamps, none of whose light he disturbed, for all that the morning sun was now pouring through the windows; for even the possibility of shadows in this place was more than he could bear, especially now, as his own fatigue claimed him. Almost it was as if the painting itself had been some kind of charm, even if a malign one, a demon holding off imps by its presence, and he now felt exposed and vulnerable. He rolled up his breakfast in a napkin and made to leave the room he had not left for a fortnight.

He paused to look at the other portrait, that which had won him the commission he knew he had executed better than any other painter could have done it; very rough it looked to him now, rough and yet real, real and warm and joyous. He looked at it, and thought of the canvas under it, that he might lay bare and paint again; but he left it.

He went downstairs with his two bundles under his arms, and his cloak and his extra shirt in a third bundle on his back, and he found his way unassisted to the stables. There he took the horse he had hired weeks ago, scrambled onto it among the harness that had held his canvases, and pointed its nose for home. No one stopped him, for the word had already gone out that the painting was done and that it was a masterwork; but no one stopped him either to praise him for his genius. He rode out through the court gates, and down the road, and at the first river he had a very long bathe, and then lay on the shore for a while and let the sun bake into his skin, while the horse browsed peacefully nearby.

Then he clambered on it again, grateful that he had a horse to ride, for he was too exhausted to walk, though he knew he could not have stayed in that palace another hour; and they kept on, for the horse seemed to be glad to be going home too, or perhaps it were merely bored from standing too long in its stable, however large the box and generous the feed. And though the way was a long one, and the journey back made in a haze of weariness so profound as to be pain, he was not sorry that it was no step shorter, and he was glad that his own country shared no border with that queen and king's.

But the painter lost nothing for having left his masterwork so cavalierly, for the minister of finance sent six horses with panniers full of gold across their backs after him. And so he never painted another fat merchant again, although it was observed that he never painted a beautiful woman again either, but often chose to paint the old, the poor, the kind, and the simple. But because he was the artist who had painted the most famous portrait in the world, of the most beautiful woman in seven kingdoms, everything he set his name to now and ever after sold easily; and soon he had not only a horse (for the first thing he did when the twelve panniers of gold caught up with him was to buy the horse he had ridden home) but a saddle. And then a house, and a wife, and then children, and he loved his family very much; and so he believed it had been worth it. But it was a long time before he could sleep without leaving a candle lit; and he never ventured across the borders of his own land again.

Three

The queen, who had been the most beautiful woman in seven king-doms, had her new portrait set by her bed, still wrapped in silk; and she called for the king her husband. And he came, and everyone no-ticed that while he was thinner, and his face was grey and haggard, he was no longer mad; and he sat down quite gently at the queen's side, and took her hand.

"I am dying," she said, through her veil, and the light cloth rippled with her breathing. The king shivered, and clasped her hand tighter, but he said nothing.

"I want you to promise me something," she said, and he nodded, a stiff, tortured little jerk of the head; and he never took his eyes from where her face was, under the veil. "After I die, you will want to marry again—"

"No," said the king in a cracked whisper, and now his trembling grew worse, and his voice sounded like no human voice, but the cry of a beast or bird. *"No."*

"Yes," said the queen, and held up her free hand to silence him: or rather lifted her fingers for a moment from their place on her coverlet, for she had little strength left for movement. "I want you to promise me this: that you will only marry someone as beautiful as I—was," she said, "so that you will not always be comparing the poor girl to me in your memory, and be cruel to her for it." There was a strange tone in the queen's voice; were it not so sad an occasion and were she not so weak, it might have been thought that the tone was of triumph.

The king, his head hanging, and his knees drawn up like a little boy's who is being scolded, said nothing.

"Promise!" hissed the queen.

The king laughed a little wildly. "I promise! I will marry no one less beautiful than you. I swear it."

And the queen sighed, a long, deep, satisfied sigh, and gestured for the servants to display the painting. They slowly, respectfully unwrapped the long folds, but the silk was thin, so while there were still several turns of cloth over it, the splendor of the painting burned through its swaddling. When its final, perfect glory was revealed the queen stared at it—or so everyone thought, as her face-veil was turned unmoving toward it. Then she turned her head away on her pillow and gave another great sigh, a sigh so vast and profound that it seemed impossible that a figure so slight and wasted as the queen's could have made it; and with that sigh she died.

The king remained with his back to the painting, crouched over his queen's hand; and for a long time the servants dared not disturb him, dared not try to discover whether he knew that he was holding the hand of a corpse.

.   .   .

THE FUNERAL WAS THREE DAYS LATER, AS SHE HAD wished it; and as she had wished it, her body was not washed and dressed and laid out for burial. Still in her veil, her long gown, gloves and slippers, she was wrapped in layers and layers of silk and brocade, and thus laid in her satin-lined coffin. And the first stuff which they lay over her, set next to her still-warm figure, was the thin white bolt that had wrapped her portrait.

But the mourning went on for weeks after that. The whole country dressed in black, and many people dyed their horses' harnesses black, painted their oxen's horns black, the doors of their houses, their wagon wheels, even their own hair, though their blackened hair never fired red in the sunlight the way the queen's had. The king was quiet and polite, but his eyes were blank, and his ministers steered him through his days.

Expressions of grief and condolences came from far around; the receiving-hall grew crowded with gifts bearing black ribbons, and ministers' aides hired aides of their own to do the list-making and write the acknowledgements, which the king himself never signed, his hands limply on his lap and his eyes turned to empty space. One king, their nearest neighbor, sent four matched black horses, without a white hair on them; another king sent a black carriage that gleamed like a mirror. The third king sent a heavy rope of black opals, and the fourth sent a cape of the feathers of the ebony bird, the cost of one of whose feathers would feed a peasant family half a year. The fifth king, who had been twelve years old when the dead queen had married her true love, sent the same lord as had attended the wedding, older now, and the casket he bore this time contained black pearls.

One day two heralds and three horses arrived, all bearing black stripes on their gear (although some noticed that the stripes were of the sort that could be taken off again), and this was an embassy from the sixth king of the queen's seven suitors.

Their own black-robed king was in his receiving-hall that day, for his ministers had determined that it would be good for him to go through the motions of governing, even though each motion had to be prompted by the ministers themselves. He could not even be trusted to feed himself, these days, but someone must sit next to him and tell him to put food in his mouth for every bite. But he was docile now, unlike the first weeks of the queen's illness; and the harassed ministers wished to believe this an improvement. And so it was the king who welcomed the heralds from the sixth king, or, more accurately, it was his ministers who welcomed them and, when prodded, not very subtly, the king who nodded slowly in an acknowledgement he did not feel.

The heralds noticed that his eyes were steady, if dazed, and they thought that if the rumors heard in their kingdom of his madness had been true, they were true no longer; for here was a man made weak and simple by his grief. So they made the correct obeyances, and were graciously granted leave (by the ministers) to demonstrate what gifts they had brought; and so they opened their baskets, displaying sparkling jars of preserves that the queen and her ladies had put up themselves; and some meltingly supple leather from a deer that the king and his huntsmen had themselves shot, dressed out, skinned and tanned, and dyed a flawless black. And, last, there was a small woven basket-pannier, and the herald who handled it touched it with particular gentleness, and when he set it down, and knelt beside it to lift the loop from the pin that held it closed, it seemed to move of itself, to stir where it sat.

When he opened it he reached in to lift something out: and there was a small silver-fawn-colored fleethound puppy who trembled, and struggled to be set down, and as soon as the herald had done so tried to climb into his kneeling lap, and hide her small slender face under his arm.

"The prince's favorite bitch whelped two months ago," said the herald, while the fleethound presented her rear parts to the court and dug her head farther under his arm. "When he heard of your loss, he begged his parents to let him send the princess one of the puppies."

It was the first time anyone of the court had thought of the princess since the queen fell ill.

·   ·   ·

HER NURSEMAID HAD SEEN TO IT THAT THEY WATCHED the long days in and out of the queen's long decline; and the nursemaid sank deeper and deeper into her grief, and the girl herself grew more and more silent and withdrawn, for her nursemaid had been her only lasting companion for as long as she could remember. And when the queen died, the nursemaid saw to it that the princess had a black dress to wear to her mother's funeral, and a black scarf to tie up her dark soft hair, and black boots for her feet, black stockings for her legs, and black gloves for her hands; and a black cap, gloves, and overskirt for herself. For even in her grief she knew what was required, just as she had seen to it that both she and the princess bathed every day, and had enough to eat, and proper clothing as the season changed. But it did not seem to her strange that the court forgot the princess in its preoccupation with the queen, for she would have forgotten the princess herself, had it not been her job to take care of her. There was no hauteur in her when she made sure of the necessities for herself and the princess.

The two of them had gone to the funeral, quietly, like any other mourners from the vast royal household; and if any recognized them as perhaps having a special place in the affair, no mention was made nor notice taken. The king and queen had absorbed all their people's attention for as long as they had been king and queen; there had never been anything left for the princess. That there might be something odd about this, even wrong, occurred to no one; their king, their queen, were too glorious, too luminous, too superb, for there to be anything wrong with them. That they forgot their child themselves, and distracted their people into forgetting her also, was merely a natural result of their perfections, as was the fact that the princess had no place and no purpose. No one of their people could imagine the country without this king and this queen. The idea that this child of theirs was their heir was incomprehensible; as if someone had suggested that a tadpole might inherit the sea upon the death of water. At the queen's funeral no one was capable of thinking beyond the fact that this was the end of their world.

The nursemaid and the princess stood with the two house-maids who most often attended to their simple needs, and who had helped in making up the princess's mourning clothes. The princess looked around quietly into the faces of her parents' people, last of all looking in her nursemaid's face, who was as dazed as anyone else in the kingdom—as the king himself. She had worshipped the queen with every breath she took, and had sought the position of caring for her daughter because she was her daughter.

The princess was in a daze also, but her confusion had more to do with perplexity than with sorrow. For what she realized was that her mother's death had no effect on her, but only on those around her. But this was so amazing to her that her amazement looked like grief, had there been anyone to notice.

She had grown up understanding that almost all those around her, chiefly her nursemaid but also the maids and the occasional courtier or minister who thought it politic to visit her, and certainly her parents, on those rare occasions that she was summoned into their presence, desired her to be biddable. For the most part she had acquiesced in this. She knew no other children, and never guessed the noisy games that most children play; and she learned very young that when she cried or was cross she was likely to be left alone; and as she had so little companionship she was unwilling to risk the little. She could not remember her babyhood; her first memories were of her nursemaid telling her stories, stories about her mother and father in the years before she was born; her second memories were of asking for those stories to be retold.

Her first rebellion, although she did not know it, was in learning to read. She learned rather easily, which was remarkable, for the nursemaid was an even worse teacher than she was a scholar. With the curious stark comprehension of children, she knew that her nursemaid's reluctance to read stories from books was because she was not good at it, and that it would be as well not to tell her that it was otherwise with herself. But the princess had seized on this thing not commanded of her, unlike dancing and riding and deportment, and soon came to treasure it; for books were companionable.

Somehow the occasional ladies who wished to pet her—either for her own sake, or for the sake, as they hoped, of their husbands' careers—rarely came to see her more than a few times. The queen, the nursemaid told the princess reprovingly, when she showed signs of missing a very young and playful lady who had contrived to visit her nearly a dozen times before being banished as mysteriously as the rest, was very strict about who might be permitted to cultivate her only child. The young and playful lady had not only taught the princess games that involved running and shouting, but had brought her fresh new storybooks, and helped her to hide them from the nursemaid; and although the princess noticed that this seemed to make the lady unhappy, she refused to tell the little girl why. But the princess had let herself be consoled for this loss, for she was still very young, when the nursemaid took her on her lap and told again their favorite story.

She thought of that lady now; it had been years before she had quite given up the hope that she would see her again (though she never told her nursemaid this) and had looked around her, shyly but eagerly, on such state occasions as she attended on her parents, seeking one face among the many faces in the crowds gathered to pay her parents homage. But it was all so long ago now the princess doubted she would recognize the lady's face even if she did see her again; and she would be older now, and perhaps no longer playful. Then she surprised herself by thinking that if she could remember the lady's name, she might ask for her. The surprise was so severe that any chance that she might recall the name she wished fled forever; and she sat very still, as if she might be caught out at something.

But she knew her mother's death had changed her position in the royal household, though she did not know how. It was enough, for the moment, that she no longer believed in the shining figures of her nurse-maid's stories, though she dared not think why.

Something had happened to her the evening of her twelfth birth-day, three years ago now, when she sat on the glittering chair and watched her parents dance. Some time during that long evening, after she had sent her prospective dancing-partners away, she had looked thought-fully at her hands, with their clean nails and soft palms, and at her legs, hidden beneath their long skirt, and she had wondered, as a hero might wonder before stepping across the threshold of a great Dragon's lair, what these hands and legs might be capable of.

It was a question that had returned to her a number of times over the next weeks, making her restless and peevish; but when her nurse-maid spoke to her sharply, she subsided, as she had always subsided, for she had no words for what she felt was trying to express itself. There was no outlet for the wondering, nor for the emotions that it caused; and her life did not change, nor had she any idea of how she might make a change, or what she might like that change to be. And so while she was aware of some quiet evolution going on in her heart and brain, she did not know what it was and, to a great extent, did not seek to know, for she could imagine no good coming of it. What the first twelve years of her life had taught her chiefly was patience, and so she held patience to her like a friend, and went on being quiet and biddable. One new plea-sure she gave herself, and that was to observe what went on around her; and she began to have thoughts about the palace and the people in it that would have surprised her nursemaid very much.

But then the queen's illness overshadowed all else, and any idea, faint as it had been at its best, of trying to explain to her nursemaid what she was thinking about, what made her uneasy, faded to nothing, and she tried not to pursue these thoughts while the queen lay dying, for it seemed to her that it was disloyal. The fact that it did not feel disloyal to be anxious and preoccupied with her own thoughts while her mother lay dying distressed her; and the distress was real enough, and she clung to it.

She was sitting in a window seat, as she often sat, staring out of the window as she often stared, turning over her bewildering and possibly traitorous idea, and the even more bewildering ideas that fell from it, like sparks from a burning stake, all of which seemed somehow connected with that earlier wondering of what she might be capable of. She still could not imagine uttering any of her musings aloud; and she glanced down at her mourning clothes. The nursemaid sat by the cold hearth, hugging and rocking herself, absorbed in her own grief; dimly aware of the creature comfort of the presence of another human being, assuming that the princess was as mazed by grief as she was—no more and no less. That the princess was the queen's daughter left no special mark on her; all the nursemaid knew was that her own grief was overwhelming, and that she had no attention to spare from it.

The knock on the door surprised them both, for it was not time for a meal or a bath or a ladylike walk in the formal gardens; and they both started in their seats. The door was flung open after a minute of silence, and a footman stood there. The nursemaid fell out of her chair to curtsey, for this was an upper footman, and he did not look at all pleased with his commission. "Her highness's presence is requested in the receiving-hall. At once." He turned and left immediately. He did not close the door.

"Oh! Oh!" cried the nursemaid. The princess stepped down from her perch and let the maid flutter around her, still murmuring, "Oh—oh—oh." The princess herself combed her hair, and asked her maid, in a clear, careful voice, to press her black ribbons for her, and shine the toes of her black boots, while she washed her face and put on her new black stockings. She was perfectly composed as she walked out of her chamber, the nursemaid still bobbing after her and murmuring, "Oh!"

The princess walked down the stairs, her boot-heels clicking to the first landing, for the final flight to the nursery was uncarpeted. She had consciously to recall the way to the receiving-hall, for she went there so rarely, and it was down and down long twisting corridors and more flights of stairs. The footman had, of course, not waited to escort her.

She paused, hesitating, at a final corner, and looked round, and knew she had come the right way after all, for at the door of the receiving-hall the upper footman stood, still stiff with outrage at having to climb to a region of the palace where the stairs were uncarpeted, and with him were two lower footmen and two pages.

The upper footman flung open the door for her without ever looking at her, and entered, and bowed, and stood aside; then the lower footmen entered as a pair, and parted, and faced each other across the doorway. The princess paused, waiting, but decided that perhaps it was her turn next, so she entered, with her chin up, and her steps were quite steady. The pause after the squad of footmen had prepared her entrance had done her no harm in the court's eyes; what she knew was the feeling of their gaze upon her, a feeling not unlike the prickly cling of cloth before a thunderstorm. She felt their awakening curiosity; they were wondering about her for the first time, she thought, wondering who she was and what she was worth. She wondered too. She was just fifteen years old; even her nursemaid had forgotten her birthday in grief for the dead queen.

One herald stood beside the dais where her father and his ministers sat, and one crouched at its foot with something, some pale lumpish bundle, in his lap. She walked calmly forward, not knowing what else to do, nor where the summons had come from, nor to what purpose. She went up to the dais and curtseyed to the floor, to her father; and looked up, and met his eyes. The blankness there parted for a moment, and she saw—she did not know what she saw, but it made her cold all over, suddenly, so cold that the sweat of terror broke out on her body. She stood up from her curtsey too hastily, and had to catch her balance with an awkward side-step. There was a whisper behind her, among the court: a pity she is not more graceful. Who has had the teaching of her? Such a drab little thing, such an odd child of such parents.

One of the ministers addressed her. "These heralds are come from King Goldhouse and Queen Clementina to offer their sorrow to us in our . . . loss. And their son, the prince Ossin, has sent you a gift."

The standing herald came forward, and bowed to her, and handed her a piece of stiff paper, folded and sealed. She looked at the herald on the floor, and realized that what was on his lap was the rear parts of a dog; the head and forequarters were wedged under his arm. She took the paper and broke the seal.

"To the princess Lissla Lissar, from the prince Ossin, I give you greeting. I have heard of your great grief and I am very unhappy for it. I do not know how I could bear it if my mother died. My favorite bitch had her puppies a few weeks ago and I am sending you the best one. Her name is Ash, for her coat is the color of the bark of that tree. There are many ash trees here. She will love you and I hope you will be glad of her. My highest regards and duty to you and your father. Ossin."

She looked up. She did not quite know what to do. The herald with the dog, who had children (and dogs) of his own, stood up, tucking the puppy firmly under the arm she was trying to disappear beneath. Her legs began a frantic paddling. He supported them with his other arm and slowly drew her out from hiding, turning her round to face the princess. The puppy bobbed in his grasp for a moment, but the princess had, as if involuntarily, taken a step forward, and reached out a hand.

The puppy caught the gesture, and large brown silvery-lashed eyes caught the glance of large dark-fringed amber-hazel eyes, and then the puppy began bobbing in good earnest, her ears flattening, her tail going like a whirlwind. The princess held out her arms, and the herald, smiling, lay the puppy in them, and the puppy thumped and paddled and kicked, and banged her nose against the princess's breastbone, licked her chin, and made tiny urgent noises deep in her throat.

The princess looked up: hazel eyes met blue, and the princess saw kindness, and the herald saw that the puppy would have a good home, and he was pleased, both because he loved dogs and because he loved his prince; and because he felt sorry for this young girl who had lost her mother. The herald bowed, deeply, and the princess smiled down at her armful. (Which made a dive at her face again, and this time succeeded in grazing the princess's nose with a puppy fang.) The court noticed the smile, and found themselves interested again, despite the clumsy curt-sey. "She's a pretty little thing," they murmured to each other. "I had never noticed. She might even grow up to be a beauty; don't forget who her mother was. How old is she now?"

But the princess had forgotten all about the court. She curseyed again to her father—without raising her eyes from her new friend's face—and requested permission to withdraw, in a voice as steady as her steps had been, before she met her father's eyes. There was a pause, and her smile disappeared, and she stared fixedly downward—she would not look up, remembering without remembering why she had not liked look-ing at her father before—but the puppy made her smile again and the waiting was no longer onerous. As the court began to wonder if the father was seeing something in the daughter that he, like they, had perhaps overlooked, he moved abruptly in his chair, and without any prompting from his ministers, spoke aloud, giving his leave for her to go.

As she turned away, the herald who had handed her the letter (which was presently being beaten to death by the puppy's tail) stooped to one knee before her. "I have also instructions for your splendor's new dog's feeding and care," he said. "May I give them to your waiting-women?"

She had no waiting-women, but she now had a dog; and she thought her old nursemaid would never notice the existence of a dog, let alone remember the necessities of caring for it. Then it occurred to her that she did not want anyone caring for her dog but herself: and this thought pleased her, and banished, for the moment, the memory of her father's eyes. "No, I thank you, you may give them to me," she said. Both the heralds remembered this, to take home and tell the prince, for he too took personal care of his dogs. It never occurred to them that the princess of this great state, much richer and vaster than their own and their king's and queen's and prince's, had no one to give instructions to.

Four

Then began the happiest two years of the princess's life. It was as if Ash crystallized, or gave meaning to, the princess's tumbled thoughts about who she herself was, and what she might do about it. Being a princess, she recognized, was a decisive thing about her, though it had meant little thus far; perhaps it would mean more if she tried to make it mean more. She did not know for certain about this, and for herself she might have hesitated to try. But now there was Ash, and nothing was too good or wonderful for Ash.

First she had her rooms moved to the ground floor. She had no appetite for breakfast on the day she steeled herself to tell the under-maid who brought them their morning meal that she wished to speak to a footman; and she was glad that she had eaten no breakfast when the under-footman presented himself to her and she informed him that she desired to change her rooms.

He disappeared, and an upper footman appeared, and she repeated her declaration, but more firmly this time, for she was growing accustomed to speaking; and because the first footman had bowed, just as the under-maid had. He disappeared in turn, and three more servants with increasing amounts of gold braid on their collars and lace about their wrists appeared and disappeared, and the parade climaxed with the arrival of one of her father's ministers—and not, she thought frowning a little, one of the most insignificant of them either. She preferred speaking to servants; the effects of asserting herself were developing a little too quickly. But she kept her face smooth, and nodded to the man as if she were accustomed to such visits at the top of the flight of uncarpeted stairs.

He had come to look her over. He wanted a closer look at her after her appearance in the receiving-hall. "By the locks on the treasury door," he thought, "she *is* going to grow up to be a beauty. All she needs now is a little more countenance—and some finer clothing." Mentally he rubbed his hands together at the prospect of this exciting new pawn venturing onto the gameboard, for he was a mighty player; and it suited him that she should have made the first move, that it should not be quite so conspicuous that he thought of the princess now that the queen was dead and the king showed no sign of recovering his former vitality.

He smiled, showing all of his teeth. "Of course, princess. Your rooms shall be seen to today. You are growing up, and your new status should be honored." He cast a quick glance around the shabby nursery and gloated: the girl was young and naive, and would be marvelously grateful to him for the glamorous new chambers he would provide her with—careful that she should understand that this was the hand that provided. Some token from his own house, he thought, something that he could point to that had conspicuously not been produced from her father's coffers, should have a prominent place. He congratulated himself on his foresight in bribing the upper footman to bring him any news of interesting goings-on in the king's household; for it was by this means that he stood here now.

He was very slightly discomfited by the faint smile the princess was wearing when he looked at her again after his perusal of her room; she should, he thought, be looking timid and embarrassed, tucked away here like a poor relation, like a distant cousin-by-marriage taken in out of charity. He did not know that she was thinking, Because I am growing up! I want rooms on the ground floor because I don't want to run up and down four flights of stairs every time Ash must go out; how can I ever train her about *outdoors*, if she has forgotten, by the time we get there, what she was scolded about when we began trying to leave *indoors*?

Again the minister demonstrated all of his teeth, and then bowing low, he backed through the door he had entered by, and left her.

Ash was in her lap, eating one of the black ribbons on her dress. Ash did not fit in her lap very well, for already her length of leg spoke of the dog she would become; but she did not care about that, and neither did the princess. As one or another dangling leg began to drag the rest of the puppy floorward after it, the princess scooped it back into her lap, whereupon some other dog-end inevitably spilled off in some other direction. "Did you see him?" Lissar murmured. "He backed out of my presence—just as if I were . . ." She stopped. She had been going to say "as if I were my father," but she found that she did not want to align herself with her father about this or any other thing.

To distract herself, she concentrated on the silky fur along Ash's back. The ribbon on her dress was beginning to look rather the worse for wear. Lissar thought she should probably remove it from the puppy's joyful attentions. But she didn't. She didn't care about mourning or about mourning clothes; all she cared about was Ash.

. . .

THE CHAMBERS THAT THE IMPORTANT MINISTER arranged for her were very grand indeed. There were seven individual rooms opening off a great central room like a smaller version of the royal receiving-hall; and not, to her startled eyes, enough smaller. Squarely in the center of the big room was a sculpture, that of a woman festooned with a great deal of tumultuous drapery, which appeared to be trying to strangle her. Lissar stopped dead in front of it, momentarily transfixed; and then the minister with the teeth appeared as if from nowhere, very pleased at the effect his chosen art object appeared to be making. The princess, who was growing accustomed to the surprising things her intuition told her since the first profound shock of knowing that she did not care about her mother's death, looked at him, knew what he was thinking, and let him go on thinking it.

Her bed-chamber was almost as large as the room with the alarming statue in it, and the bed itself was large enough for several princesses and a whole litter of long-legged puppies. She discarded it instantly, behind the unbroken calm of her expression, and explored further. In the last of her over-furnished rooms there was a large purple couch which Ash leaped on immediately, and rolled over, gaily, digging her shoulder and hipbone and long sharp spine into its cushions, leaving a mist of little silver-fawn dog hairs behind her. The princess, all of whose black clothing was now covered in little fawn-silver dog hairs, laughed.

To the right of the couch was a door; a rather plain door, after all the princess had recently seen, which she therefore opened hopefully. There was a key-hole in the door, and as she opened it, there was a clatter on the stone flags beyond, where the key, which had been left loosely in the far side of the door, fell out. She picked it up without thinking, and pocketed it.

There was a flight of three shallow stone steps and then a little round room, and she realized she was standing at the bottom of one of the palace's many towers. The wall, immediately above the ceiling of this little room, began to flare out, to support a much vaster tower above; the walls of this little ground-level room were subsequently very thick.

There was another door, which she again opened. This time she looked for a key in the key-hole, but there was none; perhaps the key to the inner door opened both, for the shape of the lock looked the same. She did not greatly care, and did not pause to try the key she had picked up in this second lock. She stepped through the door and found herself in what once had been a garden, though it had obviously been left to go wild for some years. The official door to the out-of-doors, from a short but magnificent hall off the princess's receiving room, and through which therefore she would have to take Ash several times a day, led into a formal courtyard with raked gravel paths and low pruned hedges; simple grass was not to be got at for some distance, grass being too ordinary for the feet of a princess who was abruptly being acknowledged as possessing the usual prerequisistes of royal rank.

She had looked out over the clipped and regulated expanse and thought that this was not a great deal better than the four flights of stairs she was seeking to escape. And, standing on the wide shallow marble steps, she had wondered what the high wall to the left was, with ivy and clematis creeping up it so prettily; but she had not cared much, for she was already rejecting the minister's exotic suite in her mind. When she had gone back indoors through the receiving-room, past the statue, she had begun, between the sixth and seventh rooms, to arrange what she would need to say to the minister to get what she wanted. That was before she found the tower room, and the wild garden.

But now she was changing her decision, standing on the other side of the high mysterious wall. Great ragged leaves on thick stalks stood shoulder-high on that side; yellow sunbursts of flowers erupted from them, and shorter spikes of pink and lavender flowers spilled out in front of them. A small graceful tree stood against the wall, over which rioted the ivy and clematis so tidily cut back on the other side. In the center she could see where paths had once been laid out, to demarcate, she thought, an herb garden; she could smell some of the herbs growing still, green and gentle or spicy and vivid, though she could not give names to them. One path looked as if it led to the small tree; perhaps there was a door in the wall there, buried under the tiny grasping hands of ivy and the small curling stems of clematis seeking purchase. The garden was walled all around; against the wall opposite the one she had seen from the other side a tangle of roses stood, leggy as fleethound puppies, sadly in need of some knowledgeable pruning.

Perhaps this was something she could learn: to prune roses, to recognize herbs from weeds and cultivate the one and pull up the other. Between the herb garden and the flower beds there was plenty of room for rolling and leaping and the chasing of balls, even for a dog as large and quick as Ash was becoming; Lissar wondered why such a lovely garden had been neglected for so long. But it did not matter.

For the moment she looked at the high wall around her garden with satisfaction; Ash was no more than half grown and already she could leap higher than Lissar's head. The little round room, for her, and the big walled garden, for Ash, made her new chambers perfect. The other rooms mattered little, but . . . it would probably be wise not to ask that the statue be removed; she could learn to ignore it. And perhaps a few pillows could stun the purple of that couch.

The minister had been trying to break into her reflections for several minutes; she'd heard a grunt of suppressed protest when her hand had first touched the plain door next to the extravagant sofa. She turned to him gravely as Ash disappeared into the undergrowth, waving stems marking her passage. She was now willing to hear, and to pretend to listen, to what he might have to say, now that she had found what she was looking for.

"I am terribly sorry, princess," said the minister. "I wished you to see your new rooms at once, and so the work of preparation was not complete; the door to this place was to have been closed off."

"I am very glad it was not," said Lissar. "I will want the little round chamber set up as my bedroom, and this garden is perfect for Ash. It is for Ash that I wished to move to the ground floor, you understand," she explained, kindly, as he had obviously not taken this in the first time she spoke to him. "Ash is only a puppy, and it will make her training much easier."

The minister's jaw dropped. He looked toward Ash, who had re-emerged from the shrubbery, and was defecating politely by the side of one of the overgrown paths, flagged with the same rough-surfaced stone as the three small stairs down to the base of the tower. He jerked his eyes away from this edifying sight, and worked his lips once or twice before any words emerged.

"But—princess—" he said, or gabbled, "the tower chamber will—it is very small, and it will be damp, and there is only the one window, and the ceiling is so very low, and the walls are not smooth, and enormously thick, they will be very oppressive, and surely one of your waiting-women can—er—attend your dog out-of-doors?"

Lissar refrained from laughing. She had, it was true, acquired waiting-women with her new rooms, or so it—or rather they—appeared; and the minister wished delicately to claim their assignment also. But Lissar knew that he had not been the only one looking her over, and knew also that he would not have been able to arrange for her new rooms entirely by himself and in secret. Some of the waiting-women were ladies, and had assigned themselves; some had been maneuvered into position by other ministers. Since the presence, and hypothetical usefulness, of waiting-women appealed to Lissar about as strongly as did the statue in the hall, it was not a point she felt compelled to dwell on.

"The bed-chamber you so beautifully set up for me is too large," said Lissar firmly, "and while I thank you very much"—here she dropped a

tiny curtsey—"the round room will suit me much better. I want a bed
only so wide that my hands can touch either side simultaneously. And
the rough walls can be hung over with rugs and drapes, pink, I think,
because I like pink, which will also brighten it despite the one window
and thick walls. These, with the fire that will be in the grate, will take
care of the dampness. My waiting-women, perhaps, can make use of the
bed-chamber."

The minister swallowed hard. He had little experience of dealing
with anyone so apparently unmotivated by greed. He could not think
what to do in this instance, and so in confusion and dismay he acquiesced, assuming he could regain lost ground—for he felt sure that somehow he had lost ground—later. He was too good a player to withdraw;
this was but a pause to recoup.

In this he was mistaken, for in awakening to the fact that she had a
mind to use, Lissar was discovering the pleasure of using it. And by using it, she came to know it. Had Ash not come to her, she might have
discovered greed instead, for her world as she understood it had ended
with her mother's death; and what she had learned by that death was
that she was alone, and had always been alone, and had grown accustomed to it without knowing what she was accustoming herself to.

With the knowledge of her aloneness came the rush of self-
declaration: *I will not be nothing.* She was fortunate, for Ash happened to
her before the minister or his kind did. She understood that she was fortunate, but not for years would she understand how fortunate; she did
not see, because she already had Ash, the threat that the minister really
was, behind the machinations she saw quite well enough to wish to
avoid.

The little tower room was furnished as she wished; and she herself began the work of reclaiming the garden, although she was frustrated in this
for some time, since she could only guess at how to do what needed to be
done. There was no one to ask; her muddy fingers and green-stained skirt-
knees and hems horrified the waiting-women, whose ideas of gardening

began and ended with baskets full of cut flowers and graceful pairs of shears specially made for a lady's soft delicate hands. Lissar, indeed, proved so odd in so many ways that one or two of the waiting-women decided at once that the game was not worth the candle, and disappeared as mysteriously as they had come. Some of the others stayed for the pleasure of a turn in the bed-chamber that had been outfitted for a princess.

A few of the waiting-women and one or two of the ministers (not including the one whose statue continued to grace the princess's receiving-room) had enough common sense to recognize what was under their noses, and cultivated relationships with Ash. Lissar, who was learning many things, rapidly formed a working definition of *expediency*, but could nonetheless not quite harden her heart against anyone who smiled at her dog. Ash, who thought that people existed to be playmates for puppies, was only too happy to be cultivated.

Lissar became friends with one of her ladies, not a great many years older than herself, who obviously was not pretending her affection for Ash, nor her admiration for a fleethound's beauty. It was novel and interesting to have a human friend, Lissar found, although a little alarming; she was never quite sure what she could say to Viaka. Viaka laughed, sometimes, at the things Lissar said, and although her laughter was never unkind, Lissar was puzzled that she had laughed at all, and thought it was perhaps because she, Lissar, had had so comparatively little practice talking to other people. But when she suggested this to Viaka, Viaka became so distressed that Lissar stopped in the middle of what she was saying. There was an unhappy little pause, and then Viaka patted Lissar's cheek and said, "You mustn't mind my laughing; I am a very frivolous person. Everyone knows that." But her eyes were sad as she said it, and not frivolous at all.

Viaka was kind and good-natured, and pleasant to have around, and Lissar began to rely on her without, at first, intending to, or even realizing what she was doing. It became Viaka who went with Lissar once a week to visit her old nursemaid, who now lived in a little comfortable room not far from where the old nursery was. The nursery itself had become something of a boxroom, and was mostly shut up, but the room Hurra now occupied was brighter and cosier than the nursery had ever been, and when Lissar suggested, quite gently, that the last flight of stairs might be carpeted, it was done.

Hurra sat rocking in her favorite chair, knitting, sometimes, her yarns almost always some shade of blue, which had been the queen's favorite color. Sometimes she only sat and rocked and stared at her hands. Often she talked to herself: The most beautiful woman in seven kingdoms, she murmured. The most beautiful . . . She would seize the hands of anyone who came too near her, and tell stories of the dead queen, of her beauty and charm, of how the king loved her, how neither he nor his kingdom would ever be the same again.

Lissar sat and stared out the window that Hurra never seemed to notice, and endured the stories of her mother; but it was Viaka's hands that Hurra held, Viaka's eyes she fixed her bright mad gaze on. Lissar tucked her own hands under Ash's ears, as if to protect her dog from the tales; she wished she could protect herself. Ash sat with her head in Lissar's lap (which was all that would fit any more), and waited till it was time to leave. Lissar did not realize how much Viaka learned of what Lissar's life had been by listening to Hurra's stories.

Lissar could not stop the visits to her old nursemaid; she was the only visitor the old woman had, barring the maid who opened and closed the curtains, and made up the bed, and brought food and clean water and linen and took away what was dirty and discarded. Only Lissar and Viaka and an under-maid cared that the last flight of stairs was now carpeted. But Lissar could not forget that Hurra had been all that she had had for all the years of her life till the death of her mother. She understood, now, what Hurra had really been to her, all those years, and she to Hurra; but that did not change the fact that it was Hurra who had fed and dressed and looked after her. And Lissar listened to the low stumbling intense syllables of Hurra's endless, repetitive tales, and felt herself ground like wheat between stones.

But there were many things that even her now unshackled mind could not tell her, for it had no knowledge to work with; and Viaka could tell her some of these, gently, as if it were not surprising that Lissar did not know them. And Viaka was wise enough to know that it was indeed not surprising. Viaka knew about family; and it was from this knowledge, and not merely because of her own mad Aunt Rcho, that she could visit Hurra, and hold the old hands, and let the stories wash over her.

It was near Ash's first birthday that the Moon woke Lissar's body to its womanhood for the first time; Viaka, suppressing her misgivings that Lissar had come to it so late, told her what the blood meant, and that it was no wound—or that it was a wound without cure. Lissar grew in stature as well, as if catching up for the years pent in the nursery, when she should have been learning to be a young woman; and then came the first days when some of the grand visitors to her father's hall brought gifts to curry the princess's favor as well.

Five

L issar saw little of her father during this time; little because she wished it so and he did not require otherwise. By the time of the first anniversary of his wife's death, the king was going out among his people again and his ministers no longer ruled the country alone. One or two of them who were inclined to resist this change found themselves rewarded for their deep devotion to their land and their king by the gift of country estates that urgently needed setting in order, which happened to lie at some considerable remove from the king's court.

The king was thinner than he had been, and at first, when his people saw him, he walked a little stooped, like an old man. But as the months passed he began to take on his old strength, though the deep lines on his face remained, and he wore few colors, even for festivals appearing in black and grey and white.

By the time Lissar was almost seventeen and her mother had been dead for two years, the kingdom was speaking more and more openly of the hope that their king would marry again, a strong man in his prime as he was, and with, many said, a new, ethereal beauty from the great grief he had suffered and survived.

Lissar began to be obliged occasionally to attend royal dinners, when either some visiting dignitary wished to see her, or some of her father's ministers wished such a dignitary to see her. The summons never seemed to come from the king himself, or so the phrasing led her to guess, and wonder: "The greetings and deep respects of Lord Someone Important, who wishes the princess Lissla Lissar to understand that her father the King requests and commands her attendance upon him for the occasion of the dinner to honor the arrival of Significant Personage Someone, from the county or country of Wherever."

The court banqueting tables were very long, and she rarely sat near the king; he sat at the head while she often sat at the foot, or rather at the right hand of the foot, next to the dignitary not quite so fortunate as to sit at her father's right or left hand. Since the minister whose compliments had been delivered with the summons invariably sat opposite her at the dignitary's left, she had little to do but not spill her soup and, now and again, respond, briefly, and without too great a show of personality, to some remark addressed to her by either the dignitary or the minister. She did not understand how it was that she had immediately known that no one who addressed the princess on these occasions was speaking to any portion of her but the part epitomized by her being her father's daughter; but she had never been tempted to make any mistake about this. Perhaps it was another result of the long years of invisibility in the nursery with her single maid; but the effect was that her brevity of speech, in a princess of such tender years, was accounted modesty, and applauded.

About one thing the princess was stubborn. Ash lay under or beside her chair, no matter how lofty and formal the event. Ash developed her own legend, and people began to speak of the grace of the pair of them, the princess entering hall or chamber not on anyone's arm, but with her hand resting gently on the head or back of her tall dog; both moved elegantly, and were inclined to silence. The people, who liked a little mystery, began to sigh over the half-orphaned princess, and how it was the loss of her mother that made her so grave.

Lissar was grave and silent because it had never occurred to her to be otherwise—not with people. And she entered every room with her hand on Ash's back that she might be observed to have a habit of entering alone with her dog; that it might therefore be that much less likely she need ever enter any room on her father's arm.

She had not forgotten the look on his face when she had entered the receiving-hall on the day that Ash was given to her—although she wanted to, although she blamed herself and was angry at her failure to forget, as if it were something she could or should control. She could not remember when, before that day, she had last seen him; she could not remember his ever looking at her. She remembered that, on a few occasions, when she was very small, her father carried her in his arms; but he seemed always to be looking over her head, at his queen, at his people. She could not remember, before that day in the receiving-hall, ever having seen her father without her mother at his side.

She tried not to look at him after that day; she tried to make not looking as much of a habit as entering rooms with her dog at her side was a habit, so that she need not think about it, need not remember its origin. But this too she failed at: she knew why she did not look. She did not want to see that expression again; and she believed that if she looked, it was that she would see. She knew what his people saw in his face, the grief and the nobility; she could not forget that she had seen neither. She woke from nightmares, seeing his eyes bent on her again. It was that much worse that she had no name for what she saw and what she feared; and this she spoke of to no one, not even Ash. It was that much worse that she could not see what sought her down the long tunnels of dream, could not see nor hear nor smell it, could not escape it, neither its seeking nor simply the knowledge of its existence.

Those dreams were the worst; but she had nightmares as well that the painting of the most beautiful woman in seven kingdoms, which now dominated the receiving-hall, came to life, stepping down from its frame to press a tiny, shapely foot into the cushion of her husband's throne, alone now on its dais, her own great chair having been removed; and her foot left no dint. But the look she bent upon her daughter was only slightly less terrible than the king's. Six months after the queen's death the painting had been hung behind the king's throne (this too had been specified by the queen, both the space of time and the location), and since the day of its unveiling Lissar had avoided the receiving-hall almost as assiduously as she avoided meeting her father's gaze.

But Lissar was young, and he was her father, and the king; there was little she could do but try to avoid her avoidance being noticed. She would have cultivated a fondness for the company of her ladies, if it had come more easily to her; her shyness in the company of ministers and courtiers came very easily indeed. She played tag and hide-and-seek with Ash in the garden; and she went for walks with Viaka. There was for a time some jealousy from the other ladies about Viaka's ascendence over them; but when they found that Lissar gave her preferred companion no rich presents, nor insisted on her being seated at the high table with her during banquets, the jealousy ebbed. It disappeared for good when they learned—for Viaka, who was rather cleverer than she pretended, told them—that Lissar gossipped not at all and, indeed, at times barely spoke. If all Viaka gained in her congress with the princess was the loss of time that might have been more gainfully expended elsewhere, well then, there was little to be said after all for being the princess's apparent confidante. And the waiting-women all nodded together, and argued over whose turn it was to sleep in the royal bedchamber that Lissar never set foot in.

The maid-servant who raked out the old embers and lit the fire in Lissar's bedroom (which was kept burning even in the summer, against the damp) more than once found the princess in her wild garden at an unfashionably early hour. The maid-servant had initially been alarmed by this, because it might mean the princess would require her to get up even earlier, and mend her fire before she arose. But the princess never made any such suggestion, and the maid-servant, cautiously, went on as she had begun, without telling anyone what she saw.

Once Lissar was stepping back indoors as the maid entered the little rose-colored room, and impulsively Lissar held out the twig she had between her fingers. She had bruised the leaves, and from her hand arose a wonderful smell, both sweet and pungent. "Do you know what this is?" she asked.

"No, splendor," the maid said; but she was caught for a moment by the wonderful scent and stood quite still, her bundle of sticks for the fire dangling unregarded from her hands. She remembered herself in a moment and ducked her head before the princess could have a chance to notice that she was not attending to her business; for the palace housekeeping was run under a stern eye.

The princess was having no such thoughts, but stood with her head a little bowed, twirling the little sweet leaves in her fingers. The maid, who had come to like her a little, in a wary and disbelieving way, said, on her knees by the hearth, "My aunt would know—splendor," and then crouched lower in the ashes, fearful that she had been too bold. The fact that Lissar never asked her to do anything was almost as alarming as if she asked her to do too much. She heard the stories from some of the other maids about some of the other palace ladies, and worried that perhaps when the blow came it would be stunning. Ash ambled up behind her and licked the back of her neck, and she started.

"Your aunt?" said Lissar. "It's only Ash," she added, as Ash did it again. "Do you mind it?" she said, not thinking that her maid would

never tell her "no" but only in amazement that anyone might wish to
reject Ash's advances. Lissar forgot to wear her cynicism about court life
all the time, and she saw everything Ash did through a haze of devotion. The maid was saved from having to frame any reply by Ash's ceas-
ing her attentions and climbing on the bed for a nap, having first
scrabbled the coverlet into a twist to her shape and liking. The maid
did not mind Ash licking the back of her neck—she'd grown up with
dogs—but was braced against the possibility that her volunteering a
comment might be counted too forward.

"Could I meet your aunt?" said Lissar, taking the maid's breath
away.

"You can do anything, splendor," said the maid without irony, stat-
ing the truth as she saw it.

"Will you ask her to come to me, then?" said Lissar, equally without
irony. She did know that she was asking something a little out of the
way, but she did not know how the world looked to a young maid in a
new job, especially a job involving royalty. The maid was silent for a
moment, at the enormity of the breach of courtly order she was about
to commit in response to this mildly spoken command, and wondered
what Layith, who was mistress to all the maids, would say if she found
out. "Yes, splendor," she said, accepting her fate.

The maid, who was young and simple and came from a simple family, merely appeared one morning about a fortnight later with a small
woman, wearing a great many shawls, at her side. This was Rinnol; and
Rinnol was a gardener, an herbalist, a midwife. Rinnol had never been
to court, nor wanted to, and was very cross with her younger sister's girl,
and inclined to refuse the summons. But Lissar's maid, panic-stricken at
what might happen to her if she did not fulfill the princess's orders,
talked her into it, she and her mother both, who thought that she had
done a good thing for her daughter by sending her up to the palace.

So Rinnol came, prepared grudgingly to be polite but little else, for
she had as little understanding of the breach of court etiquette as Lissar

herself did. She found, to her surprise, a girl the age of her niece who was perfectly willing to get down on her knees and dig in the dirt with her fingers, despite the possibility of damp soft earthworms and small jointed things with many legs, and getting smudges on one's face and clothing. So Rinnol began to teach the princess which green things were weeds to pull out and which were things to be kind to, and she taught her the names of many and the uses of some, returning to the palace every few days for another lesson, without any words of any such arrangement ever passing between herself and Lissar. After that first day she simply stumped in, up the grand sweep of low stairs from the grand smooth garden that lay on the other side of the wall, through the marble hallway, behind the statue with the homicidal draperies, and through to Lissar's tower room; and the waiting-women learned to bear her indifference because they had to, although she was one more mark against the princess in their minds. But Rinnol had found that she enjoyed the lessons, for Lissar was a good pupil.

Lissar surprised herself in this, since she had been given so few lessons to learn in her life she did not know that she was quite able to learn, and was further surprised to find that she could like learning besides. Hurra had taught her her letters, but those lessons had been given her grudgingly, and that she learned them seemed almost cause for shame. She knew how to ride a horse, so long as the horse was reasonably cooperative, and how to curtsey, and how to dance, which she believed she disliked, for she had never danced with a friend. But these things had not engaged her. She was stiff with Rinnol at first, and Rinnol with her, and Rinnol was not a cheerful personality, as Viaka was. Viaka, after one or two meetings, avoided Rinnol; plantlore did not interest her, and Rinnol was herself so dour. But Rinnol, like many people who follow a vocation and know they do well by it, was won over by Lissar's attention.

Their unlikely friendship blossomed to the point that Lissar visited her at home several times, in her little house an hour's brisk walk from the palace; for the odd erratic attention that her father's ministers paid her was such that she could absent herself even overnight occasionally with no one to tell her nay. There was indeed no one in a position to tell her anything but her father, and he seemed willing to let her avoid him, and live out her young girlhood with few adult restraints and admonitions.

Lissar then filled her days with Ash and Viaka and Rinnol, and they were enough. She bore with state dinners, and with the occasional attempts by some member or other of the court to cultivate her. The seasons passed, and she watched them with greater attention than she had before Rinnol had come into her life, and she found that everything in nature interested her, and that she was happy to spend entire days walking the wide lands beyond the court gardens with no companion but her dog. And almost she managed to convince herself that she took no thought for the future.

Six

For Lissar's seventeenth birthday there was to be a grand ball. Lissar did not know who made the decision; she was informed of it by one of the oldest and grandest court ladies, who occasionally embarrassed Lissar by trying, in her orotund and inflexible way, to mother her. Lissar received the news in silence and waited on events.

The portrait of the queen, which had hung in terrible splendor in the receiving-hall for the last year and a half, was to be moved, hung in the ballroom for this event. Its placement seemed to be the first and most important decision to be made, and everything else was arranged from that first priority. It was impossible to say whether the haunted portrait was assumed to be casting its blessing on its human child, or making sure that that child could never compete with its beauty; no one, afterwards, could remember where the initial idea of moving the

portrait originated, although everyone vaguely, or hastily, guessed that
it must have been upon the king's orders. Because the curious thing
was that it was not only Lissar who found the portrait's magnificence
oppressive, or eerie, or . . . no one was willing to pursue this thought
because everyone insisted on grieving for the queen and loving her
memory; but even the servants no longer went in the receiving-hall
alone, when it was not in use, but always at least in pairs. No one ever
remarked on this or made it difficult to accomplish; the feeling was too
general. And so the beautiful queen stared down, glittering, and her
people scuttled by her.

   Lissar did not look forward to her birthday banquet and ball. There
would be many foreign lords and princes there, as well as all the more
local lords, and she knew she was now old enough to be auctioned off in
marriage to the alliance best for her country. She knew because her
waiting-women had kept her apprised of this, all through her seventeenth year, till the birthday at its climactic end began to look as dreadful as the thought of dancing, gracefully and gaily, before her mother's
portrait was. When she heard, not that the portrait was to be moved,
because she was rarely told anything directly, but of the moving of it, it
was like the last blow of a long and tiring joust; this one knocked her
out of the saddle at last, and she lay on the ground gasping for her lost
breath. She did not look forward to her inevitable marriage, but she
thought of it in terms of being sent away from her father, and this she
found hopeful. In the meanwhile there was the ball to be got through.

Another very great lady, and one that brooked no nonsense about
motherliness, attended to the production of Lissar's first real ball-gown.
Everyone who might be expected to have the price of a ball-gown was
invited to this royal birthday-party, and so the seamstresses and tailors
had instantly been swamped; the very great lady, having been assigned
this task a little late, merely plucked the seamstresses she wished to
patronize from whatever other commitments they had (neither giving
birth nor dying would have been sufficient excuse), as, perhaps, a farmwife

might choose a chicken or two from the flock for the evening's supper. The chicken does not argue.

Lissar's gown was to have a vast skirt, and to be covered with so many tiny glinting stones as to be blinding to look upon. The grand lady thought privately that the princess was a washed-out little thing, and that to make her visible at all, drastic measures were required. The lady granted that there were points to work with; Lissar's hair had left off being mousy, and had darkened to black, except when the light struck it, when it gave off red sparks, just like her mother's. And she was tall and slender, as her mother had been, and could stand well, although she was still inclined to move awkwardly (the lady had only seen her in court situations), particularly if startled. Her tendency, indeed, to look like a trapped wild creature was the greatest difference between her and her mother; her mother had had all the poise and graciousness in the world. The very grand lady had the unexpected thought that perhaps this had been as much a part of her reputation as the anatomical facts of her beauty; for Lissar, upon close inspection, physically resembled her mother a great deal. If only she were less timid! Even her complexion was pale, and she looked at the grand lady as if the grand lady were a judge about to pronounce her sentence.

The grand lady was not much given to thought, and this one thought she had about the resemblance between the late queen and her daughter became so unsettling, as she began to follow it to its logical conclusion, that she banished thought altogether (as she had banished acknowledging her faint uneasiness about the rather overwhelming portrait that had been moved to the ballroom), and began treating Lissar with a kind of impatient briskness, as if Lissar herself were an obstacle to be got round.

Lissar bore this without protest; she had found that she did not want to think about her prospective marriage after all, because it would take away Rinnol and Viaka and her garden. It did not occur to her that she might request Viaka, at least, to go with her as her companion; but it did not occur to her either that any husband she might have could object to Ash.

On the day of the ball Lissar's hair was dressed very early, and then she was told to behave herself and not disturb any of the coils so delicately arranged, nor the golden filigree woven through it, to hold the fresh flowers that would be thrust among its tiny links at the very last moment that evening. Lissar felt as if she were carrying a castle on her head, and it made her scalp itch. Ash was put off by the perfumes of the hair oils, although nothing would keep Ash away from Lissar for long.

So Lissar took Viaka and went up the long stairs and down the long halls to visit Hurra, for Hurra liked to hear of grand doings at the palace, which would remind her of the grander doings in the queen's day, which would then be her opportunity, eagerly seized, to retell these at length. Lissar could sit at her usual place next to the (closed) window, and not get herself or her hair into any impetuous draughts.

Hurra told the story of the first ball that the old king had given to honor his son's new bride, and how lovely the bride had been; Hurra herself had been there, in one of the trains of one of the grand ladies. She lost herself in the telling, as she always did; but on some days her mad gaze softened and looked inward, and even Lissar could sit near her and be untroubled. When Hurra's voice fell into silence, Lissar stood up and came to stand behind Viaka's chair. Some shadow of her movement disturbed Hurra's reverie, and she looked up, blinking through tears, at Lissar's face.

A look of puzzlement passed over her face, and with it a look Lissar had not seen in two years: recognition. "Why, Lissla Lissar, child, is that you? You're all grown up. How can I not have noticed? I almost didn't recognize you, you have such a look of your mother. My dear, how much you do look like your mother!"

Lissar's hands clamped down on the back of Viaka's chair. "Thank you, Hurra," she said in a voice she could barely hear through the ring-ing in her ears, "but you do me too much honor. It is the headdress merely."

But Hurra shook her old head stubbornly, staring with bright, curiously fierce eyes at the young woman who had once been her charge. As Viaka stood up to join the princess in leave-taking, Hurra took a firmer grip on the young hands she held. "She looks like the queen! She *does*. Can't you see it?" She gave Viaka's hands a shake. "Look! Don't you see it?"

Viaka turned awkwardly, her hands still imprisoned, to look over her shoulder at the princess; what she saw was the princess, looking white and frightened. Because she was the princess's friend she said: "I see Lissar in a splendid headdress for her first ball."

Hurra dropped her hands, and the bright fierce look faded from her face, and she began to work her empty hands in her lap, and to rock, and murmur, "the most beautiful woman in seven kingdoms."

Lissar, without another word, turned and fled, Ash, her ears flat with worry, crowding into her side. Viaka paused only long enough to pat the old woman's hand and say, with the distinctness she reserved for her own old and wits'-wandering relatives, "Good-bye, Hurra, we'll tell you all about the ball when we come next," and then hurried after her friend.

"I don't look like my mother," said Lissar, as Viaka caught up with her. She stopped, whirled around, seized Viaka by the shoulders. "Do I?"

Viaka shook her head, not knowing what to say, for Hurra was right. But Lissar had none of the manner of her mother, as the very grand lady had already noted, none of the regal graciousness, the consciousness of her own perfection, which was why Viaka herself had not observed the growing resemblance; that, and the fact that the queen had been dead for two years and the memory of the most beautiful woman in seven kingdoms begins over time to adapt somewhat to the rememberer's personal preferences in beauty.

Viaka went into the receiving-hall no oftener than Lissar did and so did not have her memory—or her awe—freshened by the scintillant example of the master painter's art. She did remember that when she was younger, and her parents had a few times taken their flock of children to some grand event where the king and queen were present, Viaka had been more frightened than drawn by the king's grandeur and the queen's exquisiteness, which qualities seemed to stand out around them like a mist that it would be dangerous for more ordinary mortals to breathe. Viaka remembered one occasion vividly, when a very pretty young woman had collapsed, sobbing, at the queen's feet, and Viaka had taken her breath in in a little jerk of fear when the queen bent down to the girl. She had been surprised, and then wondered at the strength of that surprise, both at the gentleness of the queen's touch and at the look of passionate adoration on the girl's face as she permitted herself to be lifted up.

All these thoughts went confusedly and fragmentarily through Viaka's head; they produced no useful possibilities for soothing remarks. "Your—your hair is a little like," stammered poor Viaka at last, quailing under the princess's eyes. "It is only old Hurra, you know, and she is easily confused."

"My hair is brown!" cried Lissar. "The queen's hair was black!" Viaka said nothing, but the spell had been broken, and Lissar felt a little relieved; she dropped her hands from her friend's shoulders and charged off down the hall, her skirts whipping around her, making Ash half-invisible amid them and, from the weight of her grandly arranged and decorated hair, holding her chin much higher than usual. Viaka had to look up at her, as she hurried beside her; Viaka had been the taller a year ago, but Lissar had grown.

Perhaps it was the unusual angle, or the unusual expression on Lissar's face—unlike the very grand lady, Viaka knew Lissar's face often bore high color and animation; but the very grand lady had never seen the princess playing with her dog. This was nothing like the beaming face she daily turned to Ash—and to Viaka; this was an obsessed intensity that—Viaka thought suddenly—made her indeed resemble the queen.

Lissar parted her lips a little and flared her nostrils, and Viaka remembered something her parents had said of the queen: "When she lets her lower lip drop a little, and her chin comes up and her nostrils flare—get out of the way! If she notices you, you'll be sorry."

"Lissar—" Viaka began, hesitatingly.

Lissar stopped. Viaka stumbled several more steps before she caught her balance to stop and turn; her friend was still staring straight ahead with that queer glassy fierce look. But then Ash, re-emerging from the quieting froth of petticoats, put her nose under her mistress's hand, and Lissar's gaze came back into ordinary focus. Her chin dropped, and as it did so her headdress overbalanced her, and she put her free hand up to it with a little grimace of irritation. With that grimace Lissar was herself again. She looked at Viaka and smiled, if a little wryly.

"Well, I am not my mother, of course," she said. "Even if I am wearing too much hair and too many petticoats today. And that's all that really matters, isn't it?" She ran a thoughtful finger down the delicate ridge in the center of Ash's skull. "You know they've rehung the—the portrait"—Viaka did not have to ask what portrait—"in the ballroom, don't you?" Viaka nodded. Lissar tried to laugh, and failed. "That should stop everyone from thinking I look like my mother. I'll try to be grateful. Come, help me dress, will you?"

"Oh yes," said Viaka, whose own toilette would be much simpler. "Yes, I would like to."

"Thank you. You can protect me from Lady Undgersim," Lissar said; Lady Undgersim was the very grand lady. "Shall we go to your rooms first, and get you in your dress: it will be practice for all the buttons and laces and nonsense on mine."

Viaka laughed, for her own dress was very pretty, and both of them knew that Viaka did not envy Lissar her splendid dress nor the position that went with it. "Yes, let's."

Seven

The princess's first ball was as grand as any proud and domineering lady could want. Lissar, watching from the corner of her eye, could see Lady Undgersim swell with gratified vanity at the immediate attention, the reverberent bustle involving many servants and lesser notables, that their entrance produced.

Lady Undgersim, indeed, had visible difficulty not pushing herself forward into the center of events; Lissar, on the other hand, would have been delighted to permit her to do so, and wished it were possible. She, Lissar, would be overlooked in Lady Undgersim's large shadow—or, better yet, her invisibility could have been such that she could have remained quietly in her little round room, keeping Ash company. Ash, who hated to be parted from her princess, was capable on such occasions (said the maids, and there were the shredded bedding and seat covers as proof) of actual, incontrovertible bad temper. Lissar guessed there would be some marks of chaos when she got back. She wished she could shred a blanket herself, or rip a pillow apart, and throw the feathers into all these staring eyes.

Without warning, her father, resplendent in sapphire blue, was at her side, offering her his arm. Too suddenly: for she did not have time to compose herself, to prevent her body's automatic recoil from his nearness; and she knew by the tiny ripple of stillness around her that her involuntary step back had not been unnoticed. She swallowed, laid a suddenly cold, reluctant hand on his arm, and said, in a voice she did not recognize, "Forgive me my surprise. My eyes are dazzled by the lights, and I did not at once understand the great blue shadow that stooped over me." She thought that the courtiers would accept this— for how else to explain an only daughter, especially one so richly taken care of, cringing away from the touch of her father's hand? How indeed?

She looked briefly into his face and saw there the look she had spent the last two years eluding; the look she found treacherous but with no word for the treachery. She had the sudden thought that these last two years of her life had been pointless, that she had learned nothing that was of any use to her, if she still could not escape that look in her father's eyes. It was all she could do not to snatch her hand away again, and the palm felt damp against the hot blue velvet.

The crowd parted as the king led the princess down the length of the huge hall; at the far end hung the painting of the dead queen. Lissar felt that she watched them come, but she dared not look into the queen's blazing face for fear of what she would find there: not treachery but understanding of treachery, and from that understanding, hatred. She kept her eyes fixed on the bottom of the frame, upon the small plaque, too small to read at a distance, that stated the queen's name and the artist's. "How beautiful she is!" Lissar heard, and her first thought was that they spoke of the queen.

"How beautiful she has grown!"

"How handsome he is!"

"What a beautiful couple they make!"

No, no! Lissar wanted to cry out; we do not make a beautiful couple! He is my father!

"It is almost like seeing the king and queen when he first brought her home! She looks so like her mother! And see how proud he is of her! He is young again in his pride; he might not be a day over twenty himself, with the queen at his side!"

There was a wide clear space in front of the painting of the queen, for this was where the dancing was to be held. To one side the musicians sat, and she felt their eyes piercing her; their gaze felt like nails, and she felt dizzy, as if from loss of blood.

Her father swept her around, to face back the way they had come; her full white skirts whirled as she turned, and twinkled in the light. She raised her chin to look out steadily over the heads of her father's people, and she heard a collective sigh as they stared at her. Then she felt her father's big heavy hand clamp down over the fingers that rested so gingerly on his sleeve, and she felt as if his hand were a gaoler's bracelet of iron, and as she caught her breath in a gasp she heard, like a chorus with an echo, "How like her mother she is!" "She is the perfect image of her mother!"

She found herself trembling, and her father's hand weighed on her more and more till she thought she would go mad, and there before all the people staring at her, try to gnaw her hand off at the wrist, like an animal in a trap. Her mouth fell open a little and she panted, like a trapped animal. Her headdress was as heavy as a mountain, and she could not keep her chin up; it was pushing her down, down to the floor, through it to the cold implacable earth, and she could feel her father's body heat, standing next to him, standing too close to him.

"She is just as her mother was!"

"How proud he must be!"

"How proud he is! You can see it in his eyes!"

"I give you," said the king, and at his side the princess trembled, "the princess Lissla Lissar, my daughter, who is seventeen years old today!"

The applause and cheers filled the room like thunder. She took the occasion to snatch her hand free; to bury both hands in her flooding skirts, and curtsey low to the people who hailed her. They loved this, and the cheers grew as enthusiastic as courtiers, well aware of their own dignity, ever permit themselves to become. The king raised his hands for silence, and the princess rose gracefully, tipping her chin up again in just the way her mother had, the white flowers in her headdress framing her young regal face. The king gestured to the musicians and caught the princess around the waist.

Perhaps a few of the onlookers noticed how stiffly the princess responded, how awkward she seemed to find it, held so in her father's arms. But the occasion was grand and dizzying, and she was known to be a modest girl. The light flickered as if the air itself were the breeze-ruffled surface of some great bright lake. There were thousands of candles hung in the great chandeliers of silver and gold, and thousands of clear drops and icicles of crystal that reflected each candleflame thousands upon thousands of times. The saner, more sober oil lamps that stood at all times at intervals around the huge room were lit, and, as always, polished till they were almost as bright as the crystals on the chandeliers, and the light they reflected was golden. But for grand occasions there were also heavy gem-studded rings hung round their throats, and these on this night flashed and sparkled as well.

The costumes the courtiers wore were the grandest thing of all, grander even than the tapestries that hung on the walls, that were worth the fortunes of many generations of kings. All the colors and fabrics that were the finest and richest shone and gleamed upon arms and shoulders, backs and breasts. Local seamstresses and tailors had outdone themselves, and when even this surpassing splendor was not enough, messengers had been sent far away for strange rare decorations heretofore

unseen in this country; for Lissar's father's courtiers were very conscious
that they were the richest of the seven kingdoms and must not be out-
shone by any visitors, however lofty and important. All the jewellry
that present wealth could buy or past victories bestow upon its heirs was
on display.

It is unlikely that anyone there was entirely undazzled, entirely
themselves, or much inclined to see anything that they had not already
decided beforehand that they would see. Almost everyone decided that
the young princess looked just like her mother, and looked no further.
Only two sets of eyes saw anything different: Viaka watched anxiously,
but from such a distance, as she was not an important person, that she
could not say for sure that the princess's frozen look was anything but
the grandness of the occasion and the gorgeous dishonesty of thousands
of candles reflected in thousands of gems and crystal drops. And the
queen's eyes knew the truth, and hated it, but she was only paint on
canvas, and could do nothing but watch.

And within her costume, her magnificence, her heritage, Lissar
moved, invisible to the crowd. The music howled in her ears; it sounded
no different to her, no more like music, than had the cheers of the
crowd earlier. She went as her father guided her, and had no need to listen to the music, for this was the easiest thing she did that whole long
desperate night, moving as quickly as possible away from her father's
lightest touch, that he might not touch her any more firmly. As the king
was an excellent dancer, Lissar stepped here and there as if she were an
accomplished dancer herself, as if the music itself moved her feet.

And so the royal couple passed, magnificent, as dazzling as any
chandelier, with the shining medals and golden chains upon the king's
breast, and the gleaming tiny colored stones sewn upon Lissar's white
dress, down the long hall they had walked up. And then the first dance
was over, and most people stopped looking at the king and princess so
that they might look for a partner, and seized upon whom they would or
could; and the dancing became general.

The king courted the princess as assiduously as a young lover might; rarely and reluctantly, it seemed, did he release her into another man's arms. One foreign prince took offense, for he had understood that the purpose of the ball had been to introduce the princess to possible suitors, and he saw the king's reluctance as an insult to his eligibility. He and his courtiers left early, watched in dismay by the king's ministers, for he was a very wealthy prince. Two of the ministers then bore down upon the king; one took Lissar's hand and presented her to a duke who was looking for a young wife, and could afford to pay for one that suited him.

Lissar took the proffered arm in a daze, and danced away with the duke, the size of whose midsection necessitated a somewhat awkward arrangement; Lissar's hand reached only as far as the duke's large, soft upper arm. Lissar danced lightly with this partner too, her body reflexively glancing away from the guiding hand at her waist. "How ethereal she looks!" murmured the onlookers. "Even with that great clumsy brute she moves like flower petals on the wind."

"How modest she is!" thought the duke. "She would do."

But the king would not listen to his ministers. After but the one dance with the duke he took his daughter away again for himself, and so the long night wore on. Occasionally she was permitted to stop, to rest, to sit down on some tall padded chair, to drink something cool and sweet. When it was once Viaka who brought her her glass, she barely recognized her friend; Viaka, looking into her face, thought she looked like one in a fever, her eyes too bright and unfocussed, but she dared not say anything. She dropped a curtsey to the king without looking into his face, where her friendship for the princess might have given her the same knowledge that glittered in the queen's eyes; but then perhaps not, for she loved her own parents, and they loved their children, as parents and as children. She went away again, swearing to herself that she would stay up however late she had to, to see the princess to bed herself.

Lissar drank what was brought to her, for her throat was dry with fear; but she thought little of what she drank, for her father stood near her, and she could think of nothing else. When he offered to share a plate of food with her, she refused, and averted her eyes as he lifted a tiny biscuit ornamented with pâté in the shape of a fish, and set it between his red lips.

There was an enormous mahogany and gilt clock, its face starred with rubies, that crouched on a silver table near the door Lissar had entered by, a clock grand and glorious enough to overlook a royal ball. From a distance she could not always read the hands against the jewelled and enamelled face, but she could make out the dancing figures that moved around its circumference as the hours passed; she looked at it as often as she could without noticeably turning her head. As she was harried through the figures of the dance she raised her eyes when she faced the door, to let her gaze sweep across the clock, and lowered them again before she must face her mother's face. The tiny dancing figures did not seem to her to dance, but to creep.

At midnight she begged to be excused; but the king said that the party had barely begun, and did her feet hurt so soon? Her other dancing-partners must be careless boors, and had trodden on her; he would have to keep her all to himself. The ministers, hovering around, agreed with the king's initial sentiments, for they wanted the princess on public view for as long as possible, but were twittering in alarm and frustration by the end of their master's short speech.

"But the princess must meet—"

"But the duke is very taken with—"

"But the baron came specially to—"

"Nonsense!" said the king, throwing out his chest, and tossing back his heavy hair, still as yellow and as thick as it had been in his youth. Many female eyes were fixed upon him, and not merely for his rank. "This is her birthday-party, and she is here to enjoy herself. She does not wish to meet all your old men."

"They are not all old!" protested one minister, misunderstanding, for he was young himself, and had not held his position long. The king looked at him with a look that said he would not keep his post much longer.

"Who would make her happier than her own father?" he said, looking down from his magnificent height upon the unfortunate young minister, who was small and slender.

"But—" began the minister whose statue stood in Lissar's antechamber, silently cursing the young minister's bluntness.

"And," said the king, fixing this minister with his brilliant eyes, "she is my daughter, and I can do with her as I please. As I please tonight is to dance with her!" He seized the princess's shrinking hand once more, and they joined the dance.

It was not Lissar's feet merely that hurt; it was her whole body. She felt that her spirit had come loose from its webbing deep within her bones and muscles, had slid from beneath its center behind her heart, and was being tossed about inside her fragile skin, lost in the dark. It was hard to keep herself in her body, conscious of the need to keep it upright, its feet moving in specific patterns, its arms raised, a faint stiff smile on its face; conscious of the thick male arm crushing her ever nearer to the immense male breast opposite her. She smelled warm clean velvet, and perfume; and she smelled him. She thought he stank.

Panic whispered to her; he would smash her against him soon; it grew harder and harder to see over his high broad shoulder; he would hold her so tightly that she would smother, her face in warm velvet, her lips and forehead cut by medals and gems. She thought that if she could not see over his shoulder, see that there was more of the world than his encircling arm, she would yet go mad.

At one o'clock, all but weeping, she insisted that she was exhausted, and must go to her . . . she stumbled over the word "bed" and altered it to chamber. To rest, she said. She was used to going to . . . sleep early, and rising early; the people, the music, the myriad flickering lights, all were overwhelming her; she was very sorry, but she was at the end of her strength. She sank down in a chair as she said this, leaving her arm in her father's grip like a hostage. She blinked her eyes, and the heavy head-dress remorselessly bent her head forward.

The ministers re-formed around them, as they did any time the king paused. One of them, the oldest, the one who seemed the least inclined to press the duke's or the prince's or the baron's suit, said, "Of course, my dear, your splendor, such an evening is a great strain on one's resources when one is not—er—accustomed to it." Lissar could feel the ministers' eyes withdraw from her and refocus on the king, who stood beside them, tall and handsome and strong and unwearied. The king laughed, a rich full sound, and when he spoke to the princess, his tone was caressing.

"Go back to your soft narrow bed, then, my lovely, and rest well, that beauty may blossom again on the morrow. Sleep sweetly," he said, and he raised her hand to his lips, "in your white child's bed, with your lace pillows and your smooth cool sheets." After he kissed her hand he kissed her cheek; she closed her eyes.

When he released her it was only her own weariness that prevented her from fleeing him headlong; slowly instead, and with the half-helpless grace of someone near the point of collapse, she stood, and tipped her chin up; and found herself on the arm of the old minister—the first arm in the whole long evening she had been glad to lean on.

He escorted her to the door she had entered so many centuries ago, murmuring small nothings that neither of them paid attention to; but she recognized that he was attempting to be kind to her, not only preventing the princess, the king's daughter, from making an awkward exit. At the door she dropped her hand and turned to face the old man, to thank him. He bowed to her and, upon straightening, looked into her face as if looking for a sign. He opened his mouth, hesitated, closed it again, bowed a second time and turned away silently.

Viaka had been watching, and was waiting for her at the door. She looked into her friend's face and then put an arm around her waist, expecting to have to support her; but as soon as Lissar was free of the ball-room and walking down the hall full of none but ordinary serving folk and occasional lords and ladies—no kings, no painted queens—her strength began to return, and soon they were walking so quickly that Viaka, with her shorter legs, had to half trot to keep up.

Lissar paused once to pull off her shoes—"Oh, don't run," pleaded Viaka, recognizing what this meant; "I am much too tired." Lissar laughed, not a light-hearted sound, but one not devoid of humor either, and they went in a somewhat more leisurely fashion the rest of the way to Lissar's round tower room.

Her bed had, as it turned out, to be remade, down through to the top mattress, for when Ash had finished flinging the blankets all over the room (including one into the fireplace, where the banked fire scorched it beyond recovery, and, as Lissar said severely to Ash, who knew she was in disgrace but did not care, it was fortunate she had not set the palace on fire or at least the room and herself) she began digging a hole, causing a considerable rain of feathers.

Lissar, although she attempted to give Ash the scolding she deserved, at heart cared for this as little as Ash cared for the burnt blanket. She tore off her ball-gown, to the dismay of the other ladies who had appeared to assist and, as they hoped, to hear from the princess's own lips how she had enjoyed her ball. They were all of them envious that the king had danced with none but his daughter; but Lissar would not speak, and she dropped her ball-gown on the floor as if it were no more than a rag. Her high-heeled shoes, embedded with diamond chips, had been left in the receiving-room, like an offering at the feet of the statue. Her stockings followed her dress, and then she wrapped herself in an old woolen dressing-gown and began tearing at her hair. Viaka took her hands away and began to take it down herself, gently.

The other ladies were dismissed, somewhat abruptly, but since the princess would not play the game with them of what a lovely ball it had been, how beautiful she (and they) had looked, and how splendid her father was, they were not all that unwilling to go, and talk among themselves about how unsatisfactory a princess Lissar was, even on an occasion like this one. They had thought that her very own ball would have had an effect, even on her.

Lissar and Viaka and Ash went to sit in the cold garden; Lissar loaned Viaka another dressing-gown, so that she would not harm her own ball-gown.

After Ash's initial transports, including suitable but absentminded grovellings when she was scolded, were over, followed by racing around the perimeter of the garden at a speed that made her only a vague fawn-grey blur in the starlight, she came and wrapped as much of her long leggy self as would fit around and over Lissar's lap. Autumn was passing and winter would be there soon; the three of them huddled together for warmth. Viaka kept looking into her friend's face, a narrow line of worry between her own brows; but for once she had nothing to say, and they sat in silence, Lissar combing her released hair through her fingers as if reassuring herself it was her own.

Rinnol's niece came out in a little while to tell Lissar that the bath she had ordered was ready. Even in Fichit's voice was some consternation that Lissar should wish instantly to divest herself by washing of so delicious an event as the evening's ball. But Lissar at once disentangled herself from Ash's legs and tail and came indoors. Viaka, who was happy to keep her fancy clothes on a little longer, for the only shadow cast on her evening was by watching her friend, came indoors too. She carefully took the protective dressing-gown off, so that she might float around the little round room, humming gently to herself, pretending still to be in the arms of young Rantnir, son of her parents' friends. She was anxious about Lissar, but willing to set that anxiety aside; being a princess, she thought, was doubtless a difficult business in ways she had no guess of.

She recollected herself enough from the sweet dream of Rantnir's eyes, when Fichit emerged from the bath-room to ask if Viaka had any

orders for her, to ask if Lissar had ordered dinner; and upon the nega-
tive, commanded some herself. She had eaten with Rantnir, but she
could guess that Lissar had eaten nothing, and perhaps after her bath
she would be relaxed enough to be ravenous—which Viaka felt that by
rights she should be. Viaka herself, who did not chase a fleethound
around a garden on a daily basis, nor go for long plant-gathering walks
with the indefatigable Rinnol, was often astonished at the amount of
food Lissar could eat.

One of the other maids was still creeping about the round edges of
the tower room in search of escaped feathers.

Lissar rubbed herself all over with the soap, and washed her hair
vigorously. Over and over again she scrubbed at her cheek, as if her father's kiss had left an indelible mark. The bath was so hot as almost to
be scalding, for she had added even more hot water from the ewer after
Fichit had left; and yet beneath the soap and the hot water she still
smelled warm velvet. . . . She stayed in the water till it cooled, and
when she came out, rubbing at her hair, she found Viaka asleep in a
chair by the fire, her face in her hand, smiling happily in her sleep, with
a tray of covered dishes next to her on the round table.

Lissar tucked a blanket around her and climbed into bed herself,
with no inclination to discover what was under the dish-covers, her wet
hair still wrapped in towels. Her last waking memory was of Ash's long
length stretching out beside her.

Eight

Lissar awoke late, and muzzy-headed, with a heavy, dragging sense of
dread, but without at first remembering any cause. She recalled
vague oppressive dreams; remembered one in which someone was shouting at her, though she could not remember the words spoken, nor if they
were uttered in joy or wrath. In another, a distant figure waved at her, in
a gesture like a farmer scaring crows from cropland. His sleeves gleamed:
blue velvet.

Even after she recalled the evening before she felt confused; the ball
was over with, the new morning wanted to tell her. She had disliked the
night before very much, but . . . her thoughts tailed away, and morning
became an evanescent thing, with no comfort to give. It wasn't over
with. Last night, the ball, had been a beginning, not an ending.

There had been many lords present; she had known they were there, though she had been introduced to few of them, by their heraldry. She had seen them conferring with her father's ministers, as her gaze wheeled through the room and her father drew her through the long dances. She sought out the ministers to focus on, to keep her feet when the ground seemed too uncertain; to eliminate the possibility of accidentally meeting the eyes of her mother's sovereign portrait. Only her mother and the ministers, in all the huge ball-room, were not dancing; even the servants seemed almost to dance, as they made their ways through the guests; even the musicians moved and swayed as they bent over their instruments. Only her mother, and the ministers, were quiet enough that she could look at them without making herself dizzy; and looking at her mother made her more than dizzy.

The lords danced with other ladies; but some of the lords stood a while and spoke to the ministers, and when they did this she saw how often their eyes looked toward her. What if one of them bid for her? What if the fat duke were to offer his best price for her?

Why did these thoughts seem less horrible than others that remained wordless?

She sat up suddenly, dislodging Ash, who muttered to herself and burrowed farther under the bedclothes without ever opening her eyes. What if—? She could not bear the *what ifs*. She would not let herself think of them.

Viaka had gone; but someone had come in and quietly made up the fire while she slept, and taken away the supper she had not touched. There was water that had been hot but was still warm in a basin with fresh towels laid out beside her toothbrush; and a fresh dressing-gown lay over the back of a chair. She stood up slowly, feeling old, as old as Hurra, as old as Viaka's tiny bent grandmother, who was carried from her bed to her chair by the hearth every day, and back again every night; as old as the stones in her round tower room.

She picked up the dressing-gown, gratefully inhaling its ordinary, quilted-cotton-with-a-whiff-of-laundry-soap aroma, ignoring the creaking of her joints. There was nothing of balls, perfume . . . velvet . . . about the dressing-gown. She put it on and opened the door to the garden.

After the warmth of the bed, and of Ash, who radiated heat like a hairy, long-legged stove, the autumn wind cut through her, cut through her skin, and tugged, as if it were peeling back a layer of . . . what? . . . left by the ball: of a gummy film deposited by the touch of all those eyes, of warm blue velvet, that her bath the night before had not dissolved. She went outdoors, feeling the wind on her face, blasting through the seams of her nightgown and up the sleeves of the dressing-gown; she paused, shivering, at the mint patch, not yet frost-killed, and pulled up several stems. She bruised them in her hands and put her face down among the sharp-smelling leaves, breathing thankfully in—till she coughed from the sting at the back of her throat.

She looked up, at the blue sky; it was a beautiful day. She would take Ash for a long walk—they would go to see Rinnol—and after that she would feel much better. Absently she put a few mint leaves in her mouth and dropped the rest in the pocket of her robe. She rubbed her mint-sticky hands through her hair, banishing the last whiff of perfume. It was a beautiful day, and it was going to be all right. She would think no further than this fragile splendid morning, and the wind on her face.

She went back indoors to drag Ash out of bed, where she would stay, so far as Lissar could tell, till her bladder burst, if no one disturbed her. Once or twice Lissar had been a little late, and Ash had left a small yellow trail in her wake, just the few steps from the bed to the garden's threshold. Lissar was careful that no rugs were laid at the edge of the cold stone floor, and she cleaned up herself, and soaked the towel afterwards in her bath when she was done with it.

"Ash," she said. Nothing. "Ash," she repeated. Faint rustling, then silence. She walked to the bed and ripped the bedclothes off. Ash opened one eye, every graceful line of her body expressing outrage and indignation. "It's time to go *out*," said Lissar. "You will go, or I will pull you out of bed by your tail."

Ash yawned hugely, displaying several ells of pink tongue, daintily stepped out of bed and stretched elaborately (this absorbed most of the floor space of the small round room; Lissar retreated to the doorway) and then bounded for the open door. After she relieved herself Lissar chased her around for a few minutes—or Ash let her think she was chasing her—and when they came back in again they were both in quite a good humor and ready for breakfast.

Lissar brushed her dark hair, separating by hand the strands that the mint-sap had matted, relishing still the smell of it, glad that she need not have her hair imprisoned in a headdress or herself in a ball on this day. She banished the knowledge that last night was a beginning, not an ending, from her mind; she concentrated on thoughts of breakfast, and on what Rinnol was likely to be looking for, this late in the season. Fichit should be here soon, to see if she was awake yet, to see if she wanted anything. She had missed dinner last night; she was very hungry. She would make an excellent breakfast. Lissar hummed to herself while Ash chewed on her current favorite stick, leaving wet, gooey wood fragments on the carpet.

Fichit came in almost immediately with the breakfast, but Lissar's eyes had barely rested on the well-burdened tray when she noticed that on Fichit's heels came Lady Gorginvala. Lissar could not remember her ever having penetrated so far as to the little room before; the receiving-room with the statue was much more her usual habitat. She was a friend, insofar as such ladies had friends, of Lady Undgersim. Gorginvala was wearing a gown so elaborate that only someone who had seen her in a ball-dress could imagine it as ordinary day wear; she had some trouble getting through the door. Lissar paused, hairbrush still in her hand.

Lady Gorginvala cleared her throat and said, as if announcing to a multitude, "Your father wishes you to attend him in the receiving-hall, as soon as you are . . ." She paused, and her eyes travelled briefly over Lissar, still in her nightdress, its hem muddy from running through the garden. ". . . Ready." She turned, stately as a docking ship, and went back up the few low stairs as if they were the steps to a throne, and disappeared. The odor of her perfume lingered, an almost visible cloud. Ash sneezed.

Lissar laid down her hairbrush and felt the weight of the evening before shut down over her again. She forgot that it was a beautiful blue day with a wide bright sky, a perfect day for visiting Rinnol and petitioning for another lesson in plantlore. She felt trapped, squeezed; she felt . . . She took a deep breath. She tapped her fingers against the back of her hairbrush, shook her hair back over her shoulders. She was imagining things. She didn't even know what the things she was imagining were. But when she picked the hairbrush up again, her hand trembled.

There was no reason for her to have hated the ball as much as she did. . . . The word *hated* just slipped into her thoughts; she had not meant to use it. How could she have hated her seventeenth-birthday ball? No reason, no reason. No reason to hate and fear her father. No reason.

Ash ate Lissar's breakfast for her, licking the jam-jar clean and leaving the porridge. Lissar dressed herself as if she were still going for a walk in the woods: a plain shirt, with a green tunic and long dark skirt over it, and plain dark boots. She wore no jewellry, and tied her hair with a green ribbon not quite the shade of the tunic. She did not look like a princess. Her hair was pulled severely away from her face; she fastened the shirt closed up to her throat, and the sleeves came down nearly over her hands. The heavy skirt gave no hint to the curve of hip and leg beneath it, and the boots hid her ankles.

The upper footman who was doorkeeper to the receiving-hall that day looked at the princess's clothing with something like alarm, but he knew his place, and made no comment. He stepped past the doors and announced, Her young greatness, the princess Lissla Lissar.

Lissar, her hand on Ash's back, stepped forward. The receiving-hall was alight with lamps and candelabra and the flashing of jewels; there were windows in the room, but they seemed very small and distant, muffled by the heavy grand curtains that framed them. Daylight did not seem to enter the room gladly, as it did most rooms, but hesitated at the sills, kept at bay by the gaudier glare of the royal court. Lissar thought it looked as if everyone from the ball had simply stayed up through the night and into the morning, and now had moved from the ballroom into the smaller receiving-hall and throne room, bringing the night-time with them. In the smaller room there were too many bodies, and too many shadows, tossed and flung and set against each other by the tyranny of too many candleflames, too many gestures by too many jewelled hands.

Involuntarily Lissar's eyes went to the place where her mother's portrait usually hung, expecting to see bare wall; to her dismay the portrait had already been returned to its place, and the painted eyes caught at hers like claws. Lissar blinked, and in tearing her gaze loose again two tears, hot as blood, fell from under her eyelids.

Why were so many people present? She knew that her father's court had grown over the last year, and as she avoided its occupations as much as possible, perhaps she did not know if this was an unusual gathering or not. But there was a quality of expectancy about these people that she did not like, too eager an inquiry as they turned to look at her. She had nothing for them, nothing to do with them. Nothing! This thought wanted to burst out of her, she wanted to shout *Nothing* aloud, and let the sound of it push the peering faces away. But she knew that the word was not true, nor had it any charm to save her.

Last night was a beginning, not an ending.

But she still did not exactly know, beginning of what; she did not want to have to know yet. She wanted to go for a walk in the woods with her dog. She wanted not to return. Her hand on Ash's back quivered, and the tall dog turned her head to gaze up at her person's face. Whatever it is, I'm here too, her eyes said.

"My daughter!" said her father, and swept regally toward her, his handsome face shining and his tunic perfectly fitted to his wide shoulders and slim hips. Lissar registered that he was not wearing the glittering costume of the ball the night before; then his hand seized hers, and her mind went blank.

The three moved down the length of the room slowly. The princess looked dazed, as if she was having difficulty setting one foot after the other. (It is just like last night, she thought. No, it is not just like last night; Ash is here.) She seemed to cling more to her dog than to her father's hand. What an odd creature she was! And she was dressed so plainly; had she not sufficient warning that she was to wait upon her father and her father's court? But why would a princess ever dress as plainly as this? What matter to be a princess? She looked like a wood-cutter's daughter, not a king's.

Many people remembered how blank and bewitched she had looked the night before, and frowned; could she not remember what was due her rank, due her father; her father who was royal in all things, all ways, as her mother had been, whom she resembled so much in face and figure? How could this daughter do nothing but stumble, this daughter of such a king, such a queen, how could she refuse to meet the eyes of her own people?

But the king was resplendent enough for them both, and the people's eyes left the unsatisfactory princess and returned to linger upon the king. More than one of the older courtiers murmured to their neighbors that they had not seen him look so strong and happy since the first days of his marriage; one would never know that he was thirty years older than the young woman at his side; he looked young enough to be her lover.

Murmured the older courtiers' neighbors: the princess's physical resemblance to her mother is astonishing to us all, and makes us recall how it was when we had both a king and a queen, and how happiness radiated from them like heat from a sun, and warmed the entire country. Briefly their eyes touched the unsatisfactory princess again: how pale she was; there was no heat there, to warm her people's hearts.

What a thousand pities that the princess has not more presence!

When the king reached the dais where his throne now stood alone, he swung the princess around, or he would have, had she not moved so stiffly, like a wooden doll with too few joints. The tall dog at her side was more graceful. Princess Lissla Lissar looked down at the dog, who looked up at her, and the court saw her lips move briefly; the dog sat, and curled its long tail around its feet, like a cat.

"I have an announcement!" cried the king; and all the court smiled and were happy to see him so joyful. It will be about the princess's marriage, they said wisely to each other; the king of Smisily must have made the offer after all; or perhaps our duke Mendaline fell so in love with her last night. . . .

"I have an announcement!" the king repeated, gleefully, as if keeping them in suspense for another few minutes brought as much pleasure to him as the announcement itself.

"The princess Lissla Lissar is of an age, now, to marry." He turned to look at her, moving to arm's length, as if to display her to best advantage to his audience, perhaps to the future husband, while he admired her with a connoisseur's vision. One or two of the ministers—the ones who had tried the hardest the night before to present the princess to different dancing-partners—looked faintly uneasy. The pale princess closed her eyes.

"Is she not beautiful? Look at her, my friends, my lords and ladies, my vassals, servants, bondsfolk, ministers, and all of my court. Is she not the loveliest thing your eyes have ever beheld?"

The two or three ministers who were feeling vaguely uneasy exchanged even more vaguely uneasy glances.

In fact the princess was not the most beautiful thing the court of the king who had been married to the most beautiful woman in seven kingdoms had ever beheld, and had they any moment of doubt they need only raise their eyes to the portrait of that queen which hung behind the very dais where the king stood and spoke of his princess. The painting seemed to be presiding over the magnificent room, the drama being enacted at its feet. Never had the painted face seemed fiercer or more compelling, or more alive; certainly it seemed more alive than the drooping princess, dangling from her father's hand, leaning upon her dog. She swayed a little, and looked ill.

The uneasiness of the ministers became a little more general, but the uneasiness had yet to take definite shape or name. It began to occur to the court that they had seen very little of the princess for the whole of the seventeen years of her existence, and was that not very odd, for a princess, and an only child of so grand a personage as their king, as well? It was true that she had been a little more visible the last two years, but she rarely spoke, and seemed to prefer the company of her dog; there were rumors of a dirty, uncouth old woman, some herb-hag, that the princess was mysteriously attached to; no one knew why.

Was it not possible therefore that there was . . . something amiss about the princess?

The smiles began to fade off the faces of the courtiers. She looked, as they thought about it, haggard. Did she have a wasting illness? (What had, finally, her mother died of? The doctors never said.) Suddenly the king's over-jovial words struck on them harshly. Could he not see that there was something wrong with her? Although perhaps he could not. She was his daughter and his only child, and he could not look at her but with eyes of love. But . . . they did not want to think it, but they did . . . perhaps there was a sinister reason for her habitual absence from her father's court, for her reluctance to take up her birthright, her royalty—why did she shrink from the eyes of her people?

The court shook itself, and decided to be impatient with the princess, impatient so that they need think no worse.

But the king—did he not speak a little wildly? Was it completely . . . proper . . . even in a king, to praise his daughter so extra-
vagantly? Some of the courtiers remembered his madness upon the
queen's death, and the long months he had remained locked up in his
rooms during her decline, seeing almost no one, state affairs attended to
by a featureless collection of ministers with ponderous voices. Those
had been bad times for the country.

But that was all over . . . so everyone had hoped. He had been fit
and capable again now for over a year—surely there was nothing really
wrong now (with him or with the princess)—it would be a good thing
when the princess was married and gone—he would settle down again
then. He praised her extremely because she so obviously did not deserve
it; with a father's love he wished her shortcomings to be overlooked;
which meant that he was aware of her shortcomings.

It was really not surprising that any man should be a little over-
anxious, over-thoughtful of his only daughter, particularly when that
daughter was also his only child. And this girl has grown up so distract-
ingly like and yet unlike her mother—it is not to be wondered at, that
the king does not know quite how to behave toward her.

He still misses his wife, of course, for he has not remarried. That is
probably the girl's doing. Every girl wants her father to herself. Look at
her now, pretending to be so bashful, so shy that she cannot open her
eyes, as if she did not like being the center of attention. Look at her,
half-swooning, making sure by her weakness that her father will stand
close, will hold her, protect her, not take his eyes off her. She probably
has a hundred little petting, luring ways with him when they're alone
together. And he, poor man, thinks the sun rises and sets in her. Just see
the way he looks at her.

It will be better when she is married and gone.

"The princess, as I say, is to be married!" And the king gave a high-
pitched giggle as he said it; and then all the court truly was uneasy.
"It is high time she was married, for she is a woman grown!" And he

stroked her arm in a way that made many members of the court look away, although they would not have admitted why, even to themselves.

"The princess, furthermore, is to be married very soon; the sooner the better." The king's voice, too loud, boomed out over the heads of his people. The candles flickered, as if in response; people's gazes flickered, the expressions on their faces flickered. "I have set a great machinery in motion today, this morning, to have all this great land in readiness for the most magnificent celebration any of us has ever seen! I decided upon this thing last night, at the ball, as I beheld the princess for what seemed to be the first time; and I realized there was no time to waste. And so I set about the work this morning before dawn."

A sense of dread had settled on the company no less profound than that which lay upon the princess, who still stood silent, facing her father's people, suffering his hand upon her arm.

"For in the princess's face I have seen a thing more glorious than any I have looked on before in the long years of my life: I have seen my youth returned to me, something no man ever thinks to behold, something no man—ere now—has ever been granted. In three days' time we shall celebrate the wedding of our beautiful, beloved princess, Lissla Lissar—but it is not only your princess's wedding you shall celebrate, but your king's as well—for I shall be her bridegroom!"

Lissar fainted. She swam back toward the light again, fleeing from the roaring of invisible monsters who seemed to press close around her. She thought briefly that one of them had seized her right arm—the arm her father had held—which ached fiercely. But as she opened her eyes she realized that it was only that she had fallen on that side, and bent the arm painfully under her; and she noticed further that her shoulder ached, as if wrenched, and she guessed that her father had not wanted to let her go.

For a moment she could not move. It seemed her trapped arm held the rest of her captive; she was twisted in such a way that for a moment there seemed no way to begin the untwisting. She lay, blinking, her mind, still confused by the roaring of the monsters, failing to make sense of what she saw; the rippling of hems and the strange, abrupt, un-connected motions of shoes and boots bewildered her.

Very near her eyes was a narrow dark shape with a slightly irregular outline, like a table-leg, perhaps; she had the sense of something sus-pended over her, something not too high or far away, and of the pres-ence of more legs similar to the first. But they could not be table-legs after all, for the one directly in the line of her slowly clearing sight was . . . hairy. And then the rest of her consciousness returned to her in a rush, and she perceived, at the same moment as she understood that it was a living leg braced in front of her face, that it was Ash's leg, and Ash who was standing over her, that she was lying on the floor of the dais, and that the roaring in her ears was not of invisible monsters any longer, but her father's shouting voice:

"Kill the damned dog! Where are the archers? Kill it! Oh, my dar-ling, my darling! And I not wearing a sword!"

Beneath his voice, another sound, much nearer her ear: the sound of Ash's growl, echoing through the deep fleethound chest.

She sat up at once and grabbed Ash around the neck; no one would dare harm her with the princess clinging to her—said a tiny voice in the back of her head, but it did not sound certain. Or perhaps the archers will come, and will dare to shoot, and perhaps their arrow-points will fall away just the width of a thread, just at the moment of release. . . .

And then her father's voice drowned out the tiny voice. "I will not have a dog about me that behaves so! Kill it! I care not for what you say! I am the king!"

"No!" Lissar climbed shakily to her feet, leaning on Ash, who had stopped growling. Almost. But her ears were still pinned back, and her usual gentle expression was replaced by an intent, almost longing look that every hunter in the room might have recognized; and perhaps every-one but Lissar recalled that the prince Ossin's hounds were renowned for their hunting prowess—and for their loyalty to the person they ac-cept as their master.

"Ash is my best friend! You will *not* take her away from me!"

The court was startled again, in this morning full of shocks, by the strength of the princess's voice, that little weak creature who could barely stand on her feet, saying such words, and about a *dog*. . . . They noticed too that for the moment she was not pale either; her cheeks were flushed and her hazel eyes flashed.

The king, blustering, reached out to lay possessive hold upon his daughter again, but Lissar shied away from his touch, and the tall dog moved not a whit, nor shifted her steady, baleful regard, and the king's hands dropped to his sides again, empty.

"You have three days to say good-bye to your childhood pet, then," said he at last, and there was no love nor gentleness in his voice. "For you shall have it no longer, after the wedding—after *our* wedding!" He cried the last words like a herald declaring a victory, and struck himself on the chest with a blow so fierce it must have hurt.

"For with the wedding, you shall set aside all childish things and enter into your womanhood, and the devotion you have learnt—and I do not say it was ill learnt—shall now be centered upon me. Upon only *me*!" And again he smote himself on the chest.

"No," whispered Lissar, and the color drained away from her face again. The roaring returned to her ears, and she staggered a little, but her watchful dog was as still and steady as a marble dog might be. The tall slim fleethound with ankles more slender than the princess's own wrists, and a chest barely more than the princess's hand's-breadth wide, stood as unshakeably as a round stone tower, and Lissar clutched to her, and stood, and did not lose consciousness again.

Beleaguered as she was, Lissar was slow to comprehend the reaction of the court to the events that overwhelmed her. What finally attracted her attention was the lack of archers nocking arrows to strings, should the king change his mind once more and reject a foolish leniency. He had been shouting for archers when she came out of her faint, and the king's commands were acted upon immediately.

Kneeling beside her, she leaned across Ash's silken shoulders as she looked, that she might dispose herself best for her dog's protection. The king had changed his mind; but he had called for archers, and archers should have appeared, if only to be dismissed. But no archers had come. Even his body-guardsmen had failed to draw their swords.

She drew a sharp breath and risked a more complete look around her, turning her head away from her father for the first time, but warily, as if in certain knowledge that she did a foolish thing, that her father was the sort of enemy to attack if watchfulness failed. But because she was herself again now, she recognized what she was seeing: the court was paralyzed in horror. Their faces were blank with shock; but as her eyes sought to catch theirs, their eyes slid away, and horror began to separate itself from indeterminate shock. She saw them begin to decide what to think, and she did not dare to watch any longer; for she feared their decision.

She turned her eyes back to her father in time to hear him say, "Do you understand me, Lissla Lissar? Three days. On the morning of our wedding, the dog goes into the kennel with the other hounds—where she should have been all along. I have been lax. If there are any complaints of her before or after—then I will have her shot after all. You should not be distracted by a *dog* on the eve of the most important day of your life."

"No," said Lissar. It was hard to talk at all; harder still to bring out this one word—this word that acknowledged, in the saying, that it needed to be said, that what was happening was not mere nightmare, when a word spoken aloud by the dreamer into the dark will awaken her to her real life. "No. F-father, you cannot mean to do this. You cannot mean to m-marry me."

With these words from Lissar, the court stirred at last. "Marry! The princess marry her own father! It will be the death of the country. The country must rot, go to ruin and decay under such a coupling. The princess marry her father! What spell is this! We have thought her so weak and timid! We cannot understand it! He has been so fit and well; his justice and judgements have been faultless. What has she done to him, this witch-daughter, that he should desire to devastate his country and his people this way? The other kings will know that he has gone mad; we shall be invaded before the year is out. How can this have happened to us? Oh, that her mother should have lived! Then this could not have happened."

"Mean to?" thundered the king. "Of course I mean to marry you. I have proclaimed it—you have heard me proclaim it—" He flung his arms out to either side, as if he would embrace the entire court; the court which was shrinking away from the man and woman standing on the dais, with the dog standing between, and the painting blazing impotently over their heads. "I will marry you, three days hence, in the great courtyard, and everyone shall attend upon us!

"It will be a glorious day—and a glorious night," and as he said this the pupils of his eyes suddenly expanded, so that they looked like bottomless black pools, like the lightless, lifeless place she had found herself drowning in when she fainted; and these pools seemed all of his face, and his face was no longer human. She threw up a hand as if to ward off a blow.

"It is terrible!" muttered the court. "Do you believe it? Hear what he says. It is terrible. How evil the girl must be, to have brought her own father to this pass; how can we never have noticed? She has always been such a quiet little thing. What can we do? There is nothing we can do; it is too late. We can only hope the fit passes, and our good king returns to us unharmed. Three days! There is no hope for the marriage; we will have to play this vile thing to its close. Perhaps we can prevent news of this—wedding—from leaving the kingdom. Perhaps there will be a way to spirit the girl away after a little while, send her far away, where she can be no further trouble, and our king's own will may return to him, and he become himself again. What a terrible thing this is!"

"Go now," said the king to his daughter. "Go, and begin your preparations; and remember that in three days we shall be wed, with all re-
joicing. Remember!" In his mouth, *remember* was a word that had
nothing to do with joy.

Lissar stumbled down from the dais, still leaning on her dog, who
pressed against her side; pressed against her as the people pressed away.
Once she raised her eyes, despairingly, pleadingly, seeking any eyes that
might meet hers; but none did. And so she made her slow way to the
door, her dog placing one steady foot after the other, that her person
might walk safely; and when the princess went through the doors of the
receiving-hall the doorkeeper shied away from her as from a curse, or
contamination by disease; and as soon as she was fairly through, he hastened to the other side of the doors, and slammed them shut behind her.

The sound reverberated through the hall, through Lissar's body and
the soles of her feet; she shuddered. The receiving-hall doors were
never closed; it was the purpose of the king's attendance in that room,
that by making himself thus available, anyone who wished to address
the king might approach through the open door, and lay the matter before him. Even when he was not there, the doors remained open, and a
secretary awaited any who might come with a message. The doors were
never closed.

Ash took a step forward, suggesting that they go on; Lissar had
stopped when the doors were closed, and stood staring at them as if at
the end of her world, as if at the appearance of a fabulous beast, something out of a storybook. Lissar felt Ash's movement, and a bolt of
courage or despair shot through her, and she picked up her skirts and
fled, Ash bounding at her side.

They ran till they reached the princess's rooms, and through all the
great, solemn, over-furnished chambers, to the little round rose-colored
room that Lissar felt was the one room that was truly hers; and she
buried her face in her pillow, tearing her fingernails with the strength of

her grasp upon the bedframe; and she moaned. The horror was too deep for tears or cries; even to think of it—to try to think of it—only made her numb, made her feel as if some portion of herself were being split off from the rest, some portion of herself must move to some distance away from the rest even to contemplate something so alien, so abominable, as marriage to her father.

It could not be so. It was the worst, utterly the worst, of all nightmares; the nightmare that had lived with her, hiding in the shadows, since that day the heralds had brought her a puppy from a kind young prince from far away, and she had looked up, her arms full of Ash, and met her father's eyes. She had feared him since then, without naming her fear; and last night, last night at the ball, when he would not yield her to any of the lordly suitors who had attended the ball for her sake, the nightmare had begun to take shape, but a shape then still made of shadow. . . .

Had there been a ball last night, or was that a part of this nightmare?

Had she a father?

Who was she?

She moved slightly, raised her head. She knew who she was, for there was Ash, and she knew who Ash was, Ash was her dog and her best friend.

It occurred to her to notice that there was no one else around, and that this was odd. There were always the waiting-women, the latest court ladies, murmuring and rustling in the outer rooms, occasionally breaching the princess's small sanctum, speaking of ribbons and satin, pearls and lace, and of balls, and lovers, and . . . weddings.

But word of the king's announcement had penetrated the entire palace as if instantly, as his voice had penetrated the ears of the audience in the receiving-hall, and the court ladies had responded as everyone else had responded.

Lissar guessed this, dully, without putting it to words; dully she wondered if she would ever see Viaka again; and if she did not, if Viaka had been kept away, or had stayed away voluntarily. Dully she wondered who would be assigned to see to her wedding-dress. She thought that the king's people would not dare defy him openly; shun her they might—and would—but if he declared that she was to be adorned for her wedding, then adorned, bedecked and bedighted, she would be.

Ash was sitting by the side of the bed, looking at her gravely. Her person did not lie on the bed in the middle of the day; whatever was wrong, whatever she had tried to protect her from just now, was going on being wrong. . . . She leaned toward Lissar, and licked her face. Lissar began to weep then, the stunned, uncomprehending tears of hopelessness: of a truth too appalling to be contained by nightmare breaking into reality, that the body one inhabits is about to be used in a way one would rather die than undergo.

But it was part of the horror that Lissar knew she had not even the strength to kill herself, that the unspeakable might be avoided at the last. That kind of courage required that all the parts of her, body and mind, flesh and spirit, be united enough to take decisive action; and instead she was a handful of dead leaves in a high wind. She could not even sit up, or stop crying.

"Oh, Ash," she groaned, and cupped her hands under her dog's silky, whiskery chin. Ash delicately climbed up on the bed and curled up next to her; she rested her long sleek head on her person's neck, and Lissar clasped her hands around Ash's shoulders, and so they spent the day.

Nine

Lissar drifted in and out of consciousness. She could not have said what she dreamed and what she saw with open eyes in the physical world.

At some point, near twilight, she rose, and let Ash out into the garden to relieve herself; and while she was alone, she went to a small drawer in the desk that stood in one cornerless corner of the round room, and from it she took a key. With the key she locked the door that led into the palace, into the chambers for a princess. When Ash returned, she tried to fit the key into the lock of the garden door, but it would not go.

She looked at it, at first in dismay, and then in rising panic; and she had to sit down abruptly, and press her hands to the back of her head. As she sat thus—with Ash's nose anxiously inquiring over the backs of both hands—she thought, It does not matter. The other garden door, the one to the rest of the out-of-doors, has a hundred years of ivy growing over it; the key to it must no longer exist. From the outside, from the other side, one cannot see that there is a door at all; I only know from this side because of the old path. . . . I have looked, from the other side. I *know* the door cannot be found. It does not matter.

She stood up, and brushed herself off, and fed Ash some of the cold cooked eggs from her breakfast, which had never been cleared away; and she drank a little of the water that had been left in the big pitcher, which had been hot twelve hours ago, for her washing, before the summons had come, before her world had ended; and she gave Ash water as well.

She thought she did not sleep that night, although it was hard for her to tell, for her life now felt like sleeping, only a sleeping from which she could not wake. She lay curled upon the bed, feeling her limbs pressing into the mattress, feeling them too heavy to shift; and Ash curled around her. As the dark grew thicker, her eyes seemed to open wider, her body become more torpid. She could not count the passage of time, but she knew that it did pass; and she felt the essence of herself poised, perched, at the edge of some great effort, some bright hard diamond-spark of self burning deep within her slack flesh; but she knew too that this was a dream of respite only, and that she had not the strength to win free. And she lay on her bed, imprisoned by the languor of her own body, and listened to herself breathe, felt the dampness of the air as it returned from its dark passage of her lungs, and watched the night-time with her open eyes.

She knew that midnight had come and gone when a hand was laid upon the latch of the inner door, and the latch lifted. But the lock held. The door was shaken, and she heard anger in the shaking, and felt anger, and something more, seeping through the pores of the ancient wood, a miasma that filled her room as the person on the other side of the door shook it and hammered upon it in his rage and desire.

She buried her face deeper in the hard muscle of Ash's shoulder and breathed in the warm sweet clean smell of her. And at last the person, having said no word, went away. Lissar could not bear the dark when silence returned, and sat up, and lit a candle that lay on a table near her bed, though it took her many tries to kindle fire, for her hands shook. And she sat up, wrapping the blankets closely around her, for she was numb with cold, and felt the miasma seep away; but it left a stain upon the walls, which were no longer rosy, but dark, like dried blood.

IN THE MORNING LISSAR ROSE AND LET LET ASH out, and fed her the end of yesterday's breakfast bread. Then she unlocked the inner door, and ventured through it, that she might relieve herself like a human being instead of a dog; and she met no one on her way. But she found a tray bearing a pitcher of fresh water, a loaf of bread, and butter and cheese and apples, on a small table usually reserved for ladies' gloves, near the door from the anteroom with the statue, leading into the hallway of the palace; as if the person who left it could not risk coming any farther inside. Lissar did not know why she had come so far through her rooms herself; but when she saw the tray, and picked it up, she thought, Viaka.

She carried it back to her round room with the darkened hangings on the walls, and the ivy creeping around the window, and gave Ash some bread and cheese although she herself drank only water. Her mind was vague and wandering; it had focussed, for a moment, on the memory of Viaka; but there was nowhere to go from that thought, and it fled from the memory of yesterday, and the knowledge of the day after tomorrow.

Lissar sat on the bed, and rocked, and hummed to herself, and thought about nothing, and once or twice when Ash thrust her nose under her person's arm for attention, Lissar had to make an effort to remember not only who Ash was, but what: a living creature. Another living creature. A living creature known as a dog. This dog: Ash. Her dog. But then her mind wandered away again.

THAT EVENING AGAIN AS TWILIGHT FELL SHE AROSE from the bed where she and Ash had spent a second day, and locked the inner door again; and again she lay wakeful, and her mind cleared a little, for it was waiting for something, and it hovered around the waiting and eluded the knowledge of the thing awaited.

She listened to the soft sound of the dog's breathing, and of her own, and heard the hours pass, though she did not count them.

And again at some time past midnight she heard a hand upon the latch, and this time when the person beat upon the door that would not open it made a noise louder than thunder, and Ash turned to marble under Lissar's hands again, as hard and still as marble, except for the reverberant buzz that Lissar could feel though not hear, which was her growl. And this time too the person went away without a word, though the attack upon the door, this second night, had gone on for longer, as if the person could not believe that by mere force of will it could not be made to open.

AND IN THE MORNING LISSAR AGAIN AROSE, AND unlocked the inner door, and went out, and this time there was meat as well as bread upon the tray, pears instead of apples, with another pitcher of water, and a bottle of wine, and a deep bowl of green leaves, some sharp and some sweet, in a dressing smelling of sesame. And Lissar built a small fire with the remains of the kindling from two days ago, and heated the rest of the water from yesterday, and washed herself.

Tomorrow was her wedding day.

She would not think of it.

She had seen and spoken to no one but Ash since the king's pro-
nouncement. What of the ladies to make her dress, and the maid-servants
to bring her flowers, flowers for her and for those special friends who
would stand behind her in gorgeous dresses of their own, to weave the
maiden's crown? And because she was a princess, the form the flowers
were woven into was not basketry, but the finest, lightest, purest golden
wire, not easily found at any village market, which had to be ordered
from a jeweller familiar with such rare and dainty work. What of the
preparations for her wedding?

But perhaps the preparations did proceed; perhaps she only did not
remember, as she did not—would not—remember that tomorrow was
her wedding day. Her wounded mind flared up a little, and declared that
it was no wedding that would occur on the morrow, but a murder; it was
not that she feared her wedding, but that she grieved her execution. But
her mind could not hold that thought long, either, any more than it
could hold any other thought.

And perhaps the preparations were going on. Perhaps the last two
days had been full of ladies talking and laughing, full of bolts of cloth so
light that when unrolled too quickly they floated, waveringly, in the air,
like streamers of sparkling mist; full of laces so fine as to be translucent,
that they might shine with the maiden's own blushing beauty when laid
over her innocent shoulders; full of ribbons so gossamer that they could
not be sewn with ordinary needle but must be worked through the
weave of the fabric itself. Perhaps even now her maiden's crown lay in
the next room, in a shallow crystal bowl of scented water, to keep the
flowers fresh till the morrow.

Perhaps this all had occured, and she only forgot. Perhaps even now
she was not standing alone in her round room with only her dog for
company, drying herself from her awkward bath on three-day-old towels, but surrounded by seamstresses adding the last twinkling gem-stars
and gay flounces. She could not feel her own body under her hands; her

body did not feel the texture of the towel against it; she neither knew where she was, nor why, nor what was happening to her.

SHE WOKE, STILL WRAPPED IN A TOWEL, IN A HEAP in front of the cold hearth. Ash had lain next to her and kept her warm; she sat up and shivered, for the parts of her not next to Ash were bitterly cold. It was almost full dark—she jumped to her feet in alarm, seized the key, and locked the inner door.

She took a fresh shift from her wardrobe, leaving the clothing she had worn for the last two days folded over the chair beside the bowl she had used for her bath water. She put the shift on, and then stood staring into her wardrobe, not knowing what to put over it. It was dark, she could wear a nightgown, go to bed; in which case she should take the shift off again. Or did she mean to escape, put on dark clothing, find some way over the garden wall, two stories high as it was, escape from what was happening tomorrow.

But what was happening tomorrow? She could not remember. Why was she standing, in her shift, in front of her wardrobe? It was too much trouble to take the shift off, to put a nightgown on. . . . She turned away and went back to bed, curling up on her side, as she had done the last two days and nights; and Ash came and lay down beside her again, and nosed her all over, and finally laid her head down with a sigh, and shut her eyes.

THIS NIGHT LISSAR SLEPT, AND IF SHE DREAMED she did not remember. But she knew she woke to reality, to eyes and ears, and breathing, and the feel of her shift against her skin, and of the furry angular warmth of Ash, when there was a terrible noise from the garden.

THE GARDEN GATE WAS OPENING.

IT CREAKED, IT SCREAMED, IT CRIED TO THE HEAVENS, and the ivy and late-blooming clematis were pulled away and lay shattered and trampled upon the path; the little tree that lay just inside was broken down as if a giant had stepped upon it. But the ancient key had been found for the ancient lock, and the key remembered its business and the lock remembered its master; and so the gate was ravished open.

Lissar heard the heavy footsteps on the path, and she could not move; and as the possibility of motion fled, so too did reason. A little, fluttering, weak, frightened fragment of reason remained behind, in some kind of helpless loyalty, like the loyalty that left bread and water by the antechamber door, like the loyalty of the relatives who take away what the executioner has left. And this flickering morsel of reason knew that it could not bear what was to happen; and the princess, dimly, observed this, and observed the observing, and observed the sounds of footsteps on the path, and did not, could not, move.

But Lissar remembered herself after all when the door of her small round room was flung violently open, because Ash, in one beautiful, superb, futile movement, launched herself from the bed at the invader in the door.

It was the best of Ash, that she be willing without thought to spend her life in defense of her person; and yet it was the worst of Ash too because it brought the scattered fragments of her person into a single, thinking, self-reflective, self-aware human being again, who saw and recognized what was happening, and her part in it.

As Ash leaped, Lissar sat up and cried, "No!" for she saw the gigantic hands of the invader reach out for her dog, like a hunter loosing a hawk in the hunt, with that swift, eager, decisive, predatory movement. And she saw the one huge hand seize the forelegs of her dog, and for all the power of that leap, that threw the both of them around by the force of it, the invader kept his arm stiff, keeping that snarling face well away from him, where she could waste her fury only on his armored forearm. And in a blink, as the leap was completed, he seized Ash's hind legs with his second hand, and as she sank her teeth uselessly into his wrist, with the momentum of her leap, he grasped her legs and hurled her against the wall.

It was an extraordinary feat of strength and timing; almost a superhuman one. But it was not only the wall Ash struck, but the protruding frame of the door, and her head caught a pane of window-glass, and Lissar heard the sickening *crack* her dog's body made beneath the shrillness of breaking glass; and she screamed and screamed and screamed, her throat flayed with screaming in the merest few heartbeats of time, till her father stripped off his great gauntlets and left them on the floor beside the broken body of her dog, and strode the few steps to her bedside, and seized her.

She could not stop screaming, although she no longer knew why she screamed, for grief or for terror, for herself or for Ash, or for the searing heat of her father's hands which burnt into her like brands. Unconsciousness was reaching out for her, that bleak nothingness that she knew and should now welcome. But she had no volition in this or in any other thing, and she went on screaming, till her father hit her, only a little at first, and then harder, and harder still, beating her, knocking her back and forth across the bed, first holding her with one hand as he struck her with the other, first with an open hand, then with a fist, then striking her evenly with both hands, and she flopped between them, driven by the blows, still screaming.

But her voice betrayed her at last, as her body had already done, and while her mouth still opened, no sound emerged; and at that her father was satisfied, and he ripped off the remaining rags of her shift, and did what he had come to do; and Lissar was already so hurt that she could not differentiate the blood running down her face, her throat, her breasts, her body, from the blood that now ran between her legs.

And then he left her, naked, on her bloody bed, the body of her dog at the foot of the broken window; and he left the chamber door open, and the garden gate as well. The whole had taken no more time as clocks tell it than a quarter hour; and in that time he had spoken no word.

Lissar lay as he had left her, sprawled, her limbs bent awkwardly, her face turned so that one cheek touched the torn bedding; she could feel something curling stickily down her cheek, and the taste of blood was in her mouth. She knew where she was, and who, and what had happened to her, because her eyes could not stop looking at Ash's motionless body; starlight and Moonlight glanced off the shards of broken glass, as if she lay in state upon a bed of jewels.

Lissar went on breathing as she looked, because she did not know how to stop; but as time passed she felt the cold upon her body, feeling it like a soft inquisitive touch, like the feet of tiny animals. She did not recognize pain as present experience, for such a distinction was too subtle for her now; rather it was that pain was what there was left of her, as screaming had been her existence some little time before. The creeping cold was a change, or a further refinement, upon her existence. But the cold was not content to pat at her skin and then grasp her feet, her hands, her belly and thighs and face. It wormed its way inside her; but she could resist it no more than she had been able to resist her father. Nor, she found, did she now want to, for the cold brought oblivion, the cessation of pain.

And then she saw its face, and it was not an animal at all, but Death, and then she welcomed it. Almost she made her split lips work to give it greeting; but her voice had fled away some time before.

I am dying, she thought, in the guttering of consciousness, I am dying, she thought, in the encroaching cold stillness. I am dying, and I am glad, for Ash is already dead, and it will all be over soon.

PART TWO

Ten

She opened her eyes reluctantly. She had been called back from a very long way away. The coming back had been hard, and she had not wanted to do it; the leaving had been bearable only because she believed she would not return. She could not imagine what thing could have such urgency as to convince her to return—to permit herself to return, to make the choice to return—to her body. She had left it sadly, wearily, with a knowledge of failure, a consciousness of having given up; but also with a relief that flared out so bright and marvelous that as she fled from the battered flesh that had been her home for seventeen years, it shone more and more, till it looked not like relief at all, but joy. Joy! She wondered if she had ever known joy; she could not remember it. But if she had not, how could she know to put a name to it?

It was then that she felt the need to return from the bright, weight-less, untroubled place where she found herself; it was then she knew someone was calling her, calling her from the old unhappy place she had just left. She was astonished—and then angry—that there was enough of her still attached to her life to listen: immediately to listen and, worse, to respond. In that bodiless, peaceful place there was that in her that moved in reaction to that call: like the needle floating freely in its bath choosing to acknowledge north. Did any other bits of that needle resist the pull; were there bits that did not understand it, that were themselves bent and shaped as their stronger sisters aligned them-selves, pointing strongly, single-mindedly, north?

She remembered where she had learned about joy: she had learned from her dog, Ash. She and Ash had loved each other, played with each other, grown up together, been each other's dearest companion. It had been Ash only who had not left her, there at the very end of things, at the end of the princess Lissla Lissar.

And, for her loyalty and love, Ash had been killed. Lissar had no need to go back, because Ash was dead; and no one else had the right to demand she return.

But Ash was not dead. Ash was crouched by her person's bed, shiv-ering, whining a tiny, almost subvocal whine, very deep in her throat, licking her person's bloody, swollen face, licking her wounded, bleeding body, licking, licking, licking, anxiously, lovingly, desperately; she was saying, Come back, please come back, don't leave me, I love you, don't die, please don't die, come back, come back, come back.

Lissar opened her eyes. Ash flattened her ears, began licking Lissar's face so wildly and eagerly that it was hard to breathe through her min-istrations; the dog was trembling now more than ever, and her tiny whine, readily audible now, had risen in pitch.

Lissar found herself slowly fitting back into the rest of her body, as if consciousness were a fluid, as if the pitcher had been upturned at the tiny spot behind her eyes, and was now flooding downward and outward, from her eyes to her ears and mouth, then down her throat; again she knew her heart beat in her breast, again she knew she breathed . . . again she knew that she hurt.

She became aware of how her arms and legs lay, of how her body was twisted, one leg bent under her, her head painfully forced to one side. And then, suddenly, she began to shiver; the numbness rolled back, and she was cold, freezing cold, paralyzingly cold. She discovered that she could make at least one hand move to her will, and so she moved it; she unclenched the trembling fingers, unbent the elbow, flexed the shoulder . . . reached up to touch Ash's face. Ash made a little "ow!"—not quite a bark, not quite a whimper—and climbed up on the ruined bed, and pressed herself again against her person.

Her warmth made Lissar colder yet, as the last fragments of numbness shook themselves loose and left her, finally and absolutely, stranded in her body again; and, worse, lying passively on her bed with Ash next to her, lying fearfully and hopelessly and furturelessly, reminding her of . . .

She felt consciousness begin to curl up around the edges—her edges—and retreat, leaving a thick, terrifying line of nothing dividing her mind from her body. She took a great gulp of air, hissing through her teeth, and the shock of the sudden necessary expansion of her lungs, and the pain this caused her, jolted her mind and body back together again, though they met ill, as if two badly prepared surfaces ground together, not matching but clashing. She felt nauseated and weaker than ever, and very much afraid of the nothingness's next assault. She had decided to live. If she could not think of certain things, she would not think of them. There were other things to think of, immediate things.

She touched Ash's back, and her hand came away bloody; but she could not tell if the blood was her own or her dog's. How badly were they hurt? She did not know. She feared to find out.

She lay quietly, another minute or two, trying to gather her strength despite the dictatorial cold that shook her. She listened to the sound of two creatures breathing, a sound that, with the feat of listening, she thought she had given up, just a little time ago. The sound interested her from this new perspective, as it never had before.

Lissar knew they dared not stay where they were. They dared not because . . . no, they simply dared not. She need not remember why; the instant choking crush of panic told her as much as she needed to know. And then there was the wind; there was a cold wind—the door must be open, the outside door to the garden—and she was naked and bloody on a bed that no longer had any comfort to give.

Ash was still shivering as well, and had thrust her nose, in a trick she had had as a puppy, as far under Lissar's shoulder and arm as she could get it; she made little determined, rootling motions now, as if, if only she could quite disappear under that arm, everything would be all right again. She made tiny distressed noises as she dug her nose farther under.

Lissar's shoulder hurt where Ash was joggling her with her excavations; but then her other shoulder hurt, and her head hurt, and her breast hurt, and her belly hurt, and her . . . no, she would not think about it . . . though that hurt worst of all. Slowly, slowly, slowly, she brought the elbow belonging to the shoulder Ash was not burrowing under to a place that enabled her to sit up halfway.

The door to the garden was open, as she had guessed from the wind; but beyond that the door in the garden wall was also open. She had never seen that door open before; how strange. She had thought it buried under generations of ivy that held it shut with thousands of tiny clinging fingers. If it was open, then the tower room was no longer safe, for someone could come straight through the garden door, and then to the tower door; anyone . . . no, she would not think of it.

But there was something about the door she did need to think about, although it was hard . . . so hard . . . her mind would not settle to the task, but kept trying to run away, threatening to escape into the strength-sapping nothingness again; what was it she needed to remember?

That she was cold. She could remember that. That the open door was letting cold, late-autumn air into her bedroom. She struggled to sit up all the way, her mind settling gingerly on this single, straightforward problem. Nothingness retreated.

There was a violent, white-hot pain through one hip that shot through her body and seemed to explode under her breastbone; and her headache—had she remembered the headache?—struck her heavily behind one eye. The combined pain made her dizzy; and then she began feeling her bruises. When she opened her mouth a little to gasp, her crusted lips cracked, and the metallic taste of blood was fresh again on her tongue; but she realized simultaneously that the rusty taste of old blood had been there already, since . . . no. Her mind began to fragment again. But then she found an acceptable form for memory to take, that her mind agreed to coalesce around: since she had opened her eyes to Ash's licking her face.

She looked down at her dog. Ash's knobbly backbone was skinned and bleeding, like human knuckles, except that it was impossible to conceive what blow could have done . . . no. This time her mind only quivered, expecting to be brought back, accepting that the thoughts that could not be looked at would be snatched away and hidden in time.

Ash had rusty brown contusions down one side of her ribcage, and a lump just over and beyond the last rib; and a dark, wet swollen place to one side of the back of her neck. Although she no longer had Lissar's shoulder to press herself under, her eyes were tightly shut, and she lay tensely, not at her graceful ease as she usually did.

Lissar looked down at herself and . . . could not. Her mind bucked and bolted, and she almost lost the struggle; but she hung on. She raised her eyes to the door again. If she shut it, she would be warmer. Could she stand up?

It wasn't easy. She had to think about things she hadn't thought about since she had learned to walk; she had to cling to support as fiercely as any two-year-old. But unlike the fortunate two-year-old, Lissar hurt all over, and her head spun. Her hip sent a jolt through her that made her gasp with every movement; she found that she could only hold on with one hand, and her eyes would not focus together. She found that she was better off it she closed one eye and looked only through the other; meanwhile her headache continued, bang, bang, bang, bang.

There was a tired moaning in the bed behind her. As she stood bent over a chair, panting, hoping to regain enough strength to stagger the rest of the way toward the door, Ash crept off the bed to join her. Lissar let one hand drop too quickly, and Ash flinched, although she did not move away from the touch.

Lissar looked toward the open door and the night sky beyond; she thought the night was old rather than young, and that thought aroused some feeble urgency in her; yet she could not understand what the urgency wished to tell her. She feared to investigate; nothingness curled close behind her; she could feel its teasing fingers against her back.

She stood, leaning on her chair with her good hand, the weaker one resting lightly on Ash's back, panting, shivering. She looked down at herself again, accidentally, because her head was too heavy and aching to hold up; but she was nonetheless shaken by another gust of panic; had Ash not been supporting her as well as the chair she might have fallen.

She shut her eyes, but the spinning was much worse in the dark. She raised her head, painfully, opened her eyes, closed one, opened it and closed the other. The world steadied slightly; she was once again conscious of her heartbeat, and it seemed to her surprisingly strong and steady. Timidly, sadly, a thought formed, a thought expecting to be banished instantly: If I put on some clothes, I wouldn't have to risk seeing myself.

She managed to hold the thought despite the immediate tumult in her mind (Don't look! Don't look! Don't even think about looking or not looking! Just do it!). She turned her head, feeling that her spine was grating against her skull. The wardrobe would require a detour on the way to the door. She couldn't do it. But clothes would also be . . . warmer. And wasn't that why she'd decided to stand up in the first place? She couldn't remember.

Clothing, she said to herself. I can remember that I want to go to the wardrobe and put clothes on. Half an era of the earth's history passed during that journey; but she arrived. She remembered, after staring at the wardrobe door for a moment, how to lift the latch; but then the door swung open, surprising her, striking her. She grabbed the edge of it, but could not hold it, and she slid slowly, frantically, to the floor.

She must have lost consciousness again, for again it was Ash's tongue that recalled her from wherever she had gone; but this time there had been no brightness, nothing, only that, nothing. She had decided to live, she was resigned to this side of the abyss—if she could stay here. The bright place was beyond the abyss, and she no longer had the strength to cross it; she was expending all her little remaining energy in clinging to her decision to stay alive. There was irony in the thought, but she was too confused for irony.

She regained her feet, made a grab with her good hand at one of the old wardrobe's shelves; it was an enormous, heavy piece of furniture, and stood solidly as she hung from it. After a moment she groped into the darkness of the shelves. Her hand found something thick and soft; she pulled it out. She was in luck; a heavy flannel petticoat unfolded itself, and a long-sleeved flannel under-shirt fell after it. She could not get her weak arm through the sleeve, but the shirt was cut generously, and there was room for it to hang next to her body. The petticoat was harder, for she could not tie the drawstrings, and the button went stiffly through the buttonhole; but she pushed it through at last. Sweat had broken out on her face, and stung her.

Ash left her as she dressed herself, and stood by the door, looking out. Lissar looked at her as she rested from the labor of clothing herself, and the attitude of Ash's body suggested something to her. She raised her eyes to the patch of sky visible over Ash's head, over the garden wall: it was definitely paler than it had been, and this frightened her. She did not want to meet anyone else—she had trouble with this concept, with the idea of the existence of other people. She knew, dimly, that other people existed, must exist, but she could not quite bring a vision of their being into her clouded mind—but she knew she did not want to meet anyone else. Her eyes drew themselves to that open door in the wall and she studied it; she closed one eye again so the door would stand still. What did the door make her think of?

Ash stepped down, slowly, stiffly, into the garden, walked toward the other door, and then turned her head, slowly, moving her shoulder a little so that she did not have to bend her neck so far, and looked back at her person.

Leave, came the thought to Lissar's bruised mind. We must leave; before dawn, before there are many people about; before . . . her mind would permit no more, but it was enough.

Lissar took a step forward, and another; and bumped into the table where there lay three half-eaten loaves of bread, some shreds of meat and crumbs of cheese; two apples and a pear. Food. She tried to focus her eyes on the food. She would have use for food some time, she thought; and put out her good hand, and picked up the first thing it touched, and put it in a pocket. Then she took up a second thing, and put it in another pocket; and a third; and a fourth. The petticoat had enormous pockets; she had a dim recollection of owning so unfashionable a garment because she used to go for long walks in the wood with . . . with . . . and they used to collect . . . she could not remember. Plants? Why would one pull the leaves off plants and put them in one's petticoat pocket? And what matter was it if a petticoat was fashionable or not? Why did it matter if *her* petticoat was fashionable?

But her mind began to shiver and pull away again, and by then her pockets were full. She made her slow, uncertain way to the open tower door.

The flannel's warmth, and the unexamined comfort of being clothed, and a plan, even so simple a plan as to walk through one door and then another door and then on somewhere else, cleared her head a little. She paused on the first threshold to take a deep breath; it hurt; but the strength it provided was greater than the pain, and she took a second breath. She opened both eyes, blinked, looked at the garden door, and willed her eyes to focus together.

For a tiny flicker of a moment, they did; and heartened by this, she took a step forward, outside; and the full strength of the wind struck her, and she stumbled; pain stabbed her hip. She took a step backwards, facing into the room she had just left, her hand on the doorframe to steady herself.

She saw several articles of clothing lying over the back of one of the chairs beside the table that bore the food. She fumbled through them, and drew out a long, heavy length of dark green stuff with a . . . collar. She recognized the purpose of the narrow little roll of material in the wide sweep of the thing: a cloak. Awkwardly she hung it over her shoulders.

Then she stepped outdoors again, and followed in her dog's wake.

Eleven

Since she knew neither from what they fled nor where they were going, it was an odd and frustrating journey, and frequently a terrifying one. Two things lodged in her mind, and she allowed herself to be guided by them as she might have been guided by two fixed stars by which she could determine her bearings, and choose a line to take.

The first fixed point was: away. Away from where she had been when she was first recalled to herself by Ash's soft, frantic tongue. This first point she had mostly to leave to Ash, however; for she wandered in and out of full consciousness. Occasionally she awoke lying on the ground, without any recollection of halting to rest; sometimes she merely awoke to the knowledge that her limping feet had gone on taking one slow step after another while her mind had been elsewhere.

Once she awoke like this standing in a stream from which Ash was drinking eagerly; and she was glad to bend cautiously down and do like-wise. Sometimes she awoke to the realization that her eyes had set themselves upon a tree she was making her way toward; for she had found early on that this was the steadiest way for her to proceed, to sight at some distance some landmark and work her way toward it, and then, upon gaining it, choose another. Her balance and her vision were still too erratic to risk much looking around in the ordinary way of walking; and watching the jogging, swinging form of Ash was not to be con-sidered.

Or at least she guessed that her landmark-by-landmark form of travel, like a messenger riding from one road-stone to the next, was not the usual method of the healthy. She was not sure of this as she was not sure of almost everything. Was she, then, not healthy? Her hip hurt her all the time. She knew she did not like this, and guessed that it should not be that way. But should both her eyes be able to focus on a single thing? Then why had she two eyes?

The one external fixed point in her universe was Ash, for all that she could only look at her directly when one or the other of them, and preferably both, were standing still. The one word she had said aloud since she had first opened her eyes in answer to Ash's calling her back, was Ash's name. She could not remember her own. She stopped trying, after a while, because it frightened her too much; both the trying to re-member and the not remembering.

Most of what they saw was trees, and, fortunately, frequent streams. Sometimes there was a trail, perhaps a deer track; sometimes there wasn't; but luckily the woods were old and thick, and there was not too much low undergrowth to bar human passage, although Lissar had sometimes to duck under low limbs. This was lucky in another way, that the tree cover, even this late in the season, was heavy enough that rain did not often soak through. She was often thirsty but rarely hungry. She ate a bit of bread occasionally, when she thought of it, and fed a little to Ash, who ate it with a manner similar to her own: a sort of bemused dutifulness, nothing more.

Ash occasionally snapped up and swallowed leaves, grass, insects, and small scuttling creatures Lissar sometimes recognized as mice and sometimes recognized as not-mice and sometimes did not see at all. As Lissar watched, another memory tried to surface: edible plants.

She had learned—not long ago, she thought, though she could not remember why she thought so—quite a bit about edible plants. Her good hand reached out, traced the shape of a leaf . . . something . . . she remembered. She pulled the leaf off and bit into it. Sharp; it made her eyes water. But she held it in her mouth a moment, and it began to taste good to her; it began to taste as if it would do her good.

She pulled a few more leaves off the tall bush and gave them to her other hand to hold. She had finally worked that arm through its sleeve; that had been one long evening's work. They did mostly halt—she remembered this from day to day, and it comforted her, this bit of continuity, this memory she could grasp any time she wished—when it grew too dark for her to see Ash easily, even glimmering as she did in shadow.

She stood, holding leaves in one hand, thinking about what to do next; and then she brushed the edge of her cloak back so that her hand could find her pocket, and she deposited the leaves there, with the last dry-but-sticky, unpleasantly homogenous bits of their food-store. The cloak got twisted a bit too far around her throat during this process, and she had to spend a little more time to tug it awkwardly back into place. Then she hastened, in a kind of limping scuttle, after Ash; though Ash had already noticed her absence, and had stopped to wait for her.

She had learned to fasten the hook through its catch upon the cloak a little more securely; she unfastened it when Ash and she lay down to sleep together, so she could more easily spread it around them both. But her left arm was still difficult to move, and its range of motion was very small. Her hip hurt the worst, though she had grown somewhat accustomed even to this; her headache came and went, as did her dizzy spells. And her lapses of consciousness.

At some point she washed Ash's back, and the bump at the base of her skull, with a corner of her petticoat, as they stood in one of the frequent streams. Her own wounds had clotted and in some places her clothing was stuck to her skin; she did not think about it. When she needed to relieve herself she did it where she was, standing or squatting, wherever she happened to be, and when she was finished she moved on.

She noticed that the weather was growing colder. The ground, and worse, running water, when there were no stones for a bridge (and even when there were, rarely could she keep her balance for an entire crossing dry-footed), hurt her bare feet increasingly. She often left bloody footprints, and her limping grew so severe that sometimes her damaged hip could not bear it, and she had to stop, even when the sun was high.

She noticed that the skin was sunken between Ash's ribs, and that her eyes seemed to take up her entire face. She did not know what her own ribs looked like, and she never touched herself if she could help it. She knew she stank, but she did not care; pain and weakness took up too much of her wavering awareness, pain and weakness and fear and the need to keep following Ash as she trotted, more and more slowly, ahead of her.

She knew that they were not going very far, each day; but they kept going, kept putting one aching foot in front of the other. They had eaten everything in Lissar's pockets—some time; she remembered eating, a little, but she did not remember the end of eating. She ate late-clinging berries off bushes she thought she recognized. Often she forgot that the pain in her belly was a specific pain with a specific origin; pain was so general a condition of her life. She was accustomed to dizziness too, and did not think that part of it was due to lack of food.

At night she and Ash huddled on the ground, and the cloak covered them both; and Lissar slept, or at least the dark hours passed without her awareness; and she did not dream.

The nights grew longer and the days colder, and Lissar shivered even with the cloak clutched closely around her, walking as swiftly as she could. She thought that they had been climbing for some time, though she could not have said how long—days? weeks? She had no idea how long they had been travelling, how long it had been since she had dragged on a flannel petticoat and shirt and walked through a door and a gate and kept on going. But she was sure that she had noticed the ground gently rising underfoot for some time past; to be setting the next foot a little higher than the last felt familiar, as if it had been going on for some while. They never saw another human being.

But the ground grew steeper, and Lissar was near the end of her last strength.

One night it snowed. At first Lissar had no idea what the soft white shreds drifting down might be; at first she thought that her vision was playing some new trick on her. The white fragments were pretty, mysterious, rather magical. Lissar lifted her face to them; but they were also cold. Perhaps they were happening around her, and not just in the lingering fog before her eyes. She felt their coldness on her face first, but they grew thicker, and in a short while they made walking agony. Usually she and Ash halted as soon as it was too dark for Lissar to see clearly; it hurt too much to blunder into a tree or a thorn bush. Tonight they kept on. Ash seemed to be going toward something with a purposefulness Lissar thought was unusual; but Lissar no longer gave much credibility to anything she thought.

But Lissar had another thought, and this made her willing to keep on, despite the chance of a brutal encounter with a tree: she thought, somehow, that if they stopped, while this white stuff (*snow*, came the term for it, very distantly) was falling, they would not start again. This thought was not without its attraction, but she had chosen not to give up again till she had no other choice. In the meanwhile she trudged on, following Ash.

And so together they blundered into a small clearing among the trees through which they had been weaving their pathless way; and there was a dark bulk at one end of the clearing, much lower and wider than any tree. Ash made straight for it, Lissar coming haltingly behind.

It was a tiny cabin, not much more than a shack, with the roof built out on two sides, one to protect the wood-pile, which covered the entire wall, up to the rough plank awning; one overhung the door and the narrow strip of outside floor, a little wider than a step, that ran the length of that wall. Lissar had one brief, terrible moment upon first recognition of human habitation; but she saw almost at once that this tiny hut stood empty, probably had for a long time, and, she let herself think, therefore likely to remain so. When she drew near she could see cobwebs over the wood-pile and hanging, snow-spangled, from the roof over the door.

If Ash's and her luck was so bad after all that some other travellers were to come here during this same storm, then so be it. For the moment the hut would save their lives, and that was enough. She stepped, dragging one foot behind her, up to the low threshold, lifted the latch, and went in.

The smell of the room was musty, shut-up-for-long, many-families-of-mice smelling. Lissar stood for a moment, waiting for her eyes to adjust. By the dim light of the open door, and the memory of the shape and placement of a rough stone chimney on the rear wall visible over the roof of the wood-pile, she saw the fireplace opposite the door. Perhaps the cold and the imminence of death helped her, for there were no long blank pauses in her thoughts after deciding that seeking this shelter was worth the risk.

She recognized the use of the fireplace, and went over to it, and felt that there was a fire laid; then she calmly and patiently went about the business of feeling for a tinder box. Later she would wonder at her certainty of its existence; the person who had laid the first might have been expected to carry so precious a thing as a tinder box on his or her person. But it was there for her to find, and she found it after not too many minutes, to one side of the hearth, where there was a small pile of extra wood as well. She braced her weak hand, struck a spark, and lit the fire. It flared up with a smell of mouse nests.

She knelt by it long enough to be sure it would catch, and then stood up and went back to the still-open door, and stared out at the falling snow, feeling more peaceful than she had for weeks; since before she and Ash had gone on their journey. Since before she had begun to fear whatever it was that had happened, that had sent them away. She could remember no more of it than that, but she remembered that much without any gaps, and without any rush of panic. She had come to this small peace within herself, that she would not try to remember, and that therefore her memory's guardians need not drain her small energy store by leaping to defense, leaving her sick with weakness.

This was her life now; it had begun with this journey. "My name is Lissar," she said to the quiet snow; and then she shut the door.

Twelve

She and Ash slept for a very long time. She woke to add wood to the fire, and then slept again. They both had fallen down in front of the fire, a luxury so unheard-of that no further questions about their new shelter's possibilities could arise in their minds at first. The floor was hard, and cold, but neither so cold nor so hard (at least not so mercilessly irregularly hard) as the ground they had slept on for many days past.

Lissar dreamed she was melting, that her hair ran in rivers, her fingers and toes were rushing streams, her eyes overflowing pools. And as the sound of water grew wilder and wilder she heard something wilder yet behind it: joy, she thought, the joy of being alive, and she moved in her wet earthy bed to embrace it; but when it came to her it was neither joy nor life but . . . she woke, screaming. Ash had sprung to her feet and was looking dazedly around, looking for the bear or the panther, her poor staring ribs pumping her breath like a bellows.

"I'm sorry," said Lissar. "It was only . . . a dream." It was slipping away even as she spoke; she could no longer remember what it was about, only that it had been horrible. The horror welled up again, but no images accompanied it; just blank, unthinking terror and revulsion. She shuddered with the strength of it, and put out a hand to seize a stick of wood, felt the dull prick of its bark against her palm gratefully. She tossed it into the fire and thrust her face so near that her eyes wept with the heat.

Ash sat down again and snuggled up against Lissar's back, with her head on her shoulder, as she had done before the hearth in their old . . . "No!" said Lissar. "Whatever it is—it is over with. Ash and I have escaped, and are free." Her words sounded hollow, but the defiance in them drove the horror back a few paces, and she lay down again and fell again into sleep.

It was daylight for a while, and then dark, and then daylight again. And then Lissar began to recognize that she was waking up for good, that she was desperately thirsty, that she was so hungry that her head hurt and there was a bitter taste in her mouth, and that she needed to relieve herself. She dragged herself reluctantly to a sitting position. Ash lay in a tiny round knot beside her, near enough that Lissar could feel the heat rising off her fine-haired body, and watch the short hairs gently separate and then lie softly together again with the rise and fall of her breathing. Lissar was never quite unsurprised at how small a sleeping creature Ash could make of herself when she was curled up her tightest, with her long limbs folded expertly into the hollow of her belly and her flexible spine curved almost into a circle.

Lissar staggered upright, wakened with dreadful thoroughness by the pain in her hip, went to the door and opened it. A little heap of snow immediately fell in on the floor. Snow lay, in a beautiful, smooth sweep of eye-bewildering white (she blinked, closed one eye), across the little clearing that the hut stood in, and disappeared into the blue shadows under the trees. The sun was shining, the view was mesmerizing, the more so by her own exhaustion and the knowledge that she and Ash would not have survived the first night of the blizzard if Ash had not found this haven for them. The weight of this knowledge seemed to hold her in place like the stiff, resisting weight of ceremonial robes . . . she frowned. What an odd thought: ceremonial robes. Heavy with gold braid they had been, with glints of colored stones.

She looked down at her filthy, flannel-clad self, and wished to laugh, but could not. Pain and hunger had stolen her lucidity; and she an herbalist's apprentice. Almost she could remember her master's name: R . . . Rinnol. That was it. Lissar had been lucky, for she had not wanted an apprentice; but Lissar was a friend of her niece, and Rinnol had agreed, very grudgingly at first, to take her on.

The snow was over her knees beyond the lip of roof that sheltered the hut's door and narrow wooden porch. She waded, barefoot, only just past the corner of the hut before she squatted; she would have to see if the hut yielded anything she could use for boots. Ash emerged and bore her company at the hut-corner; when she was standing again her ears and tail came up and for a moment Lissar thought she would go bounding through the snow like a puppy. But then the tail and the head dropped again, and she sighed, and almost crept back inside the little house. Only then did Lissar notice how dull and flat her once-shining coat looked in the sunlight.

A memory came to her, of chasing her beautiful dog around a walled garden; she was herself running freely, neither hip hurt, her eyes focussed easily, adaptably, without thought, and she stretched out both whole, strong arms to make a snatch at Ash as she spun around a corner and leaped entirely over her person. Lissar let the memory fade. She did not wish to remember more; the guardian panic hovered, watchful, in one corner of her mind; she did not want it disturbed.

She went back indoors. Ash was sitting, unhappy head hanging, by the dying fire. She opened and closed her mouth, almost thoughtfully, as if trying to remember something—or trying to rid herself of a memory of something. She looked at Lissar beseechingly.

Lissar looked around the tiny room. A table stood against one wall with a tiny shuttered window over it; a bed was shoved against the wall the wood-pile stood on the other side of. The door and the fireplace took the other two walls. Next to the door were cupboards. Under the table stood a bucket. Lissar took it outdoors and began shovelling snow into it. She had to stop often, because her fingers burned and turned red, and her feet went almost instantly burning-cold, without the comfort of numbness.

A bucket of snow warmed by the hearth yielded a depth of water about equal to the length of one finger-joint. She drank one sip—lowering the bucket after just the one sip was one of the hardest things she had ever done—and gave the rest to Ash. Then she went outdoors and began digging up more snow.

She was trembling with weariness by the time neither she nor Ash was thirsty any more. She had tried eating snow, but it hurt her throat and made her head and stomach ache. There was a little water left in the bucket when she sat down in front of the fire and almost fell asleep again, but she knew she did not dare to, not yet. She needed to investigate the cupboard by the door. Fearfully she opened it, for she knew that their lives lay within it, and she dreaded to find it empty.

Stale brown flour. Some kind of meal, spotted with small dark flecks, with legs. Dried meat, old and black and lightly fuzzed over with a greenish fungus. Some tiny, wizened, almost black roundish items she recognized by smell as onions and apples. Some squashy potatoes bristling with pale dry sprouts with brownish tips. Tears of relief blurred her eyes. It occurred to her to wonder whom the hut was for, and whether its usual occupant—or the person who had stocked it, perhaps for just such an occasion as being snowbound—might return and be angry at the trespassers. But she could not think about imaginary owners for long. Her head swam; she gripped the cupboard door and rested her throbbing head against it, feeling the hot tears creep slowly down her face, tasting the salt on her lips. She stood just breathing in the amazing aroma of *food*. Of life continuing.

Ash stood up slowly and stiffly and walked over to stand beside her, her nose pointed hopefully at the cupboard, and a new light was in her eyes.

Lissar's meat-broth was dull, the broth watery and the meat tough, her flatbread a soggy, crumbly, burnt disaster; but she and Ash ate every scrap and drank every drop, and fell asleep again. Lissar woke up suddenly and violently in the middle of the night, when her abused bowels declared that they could no longer cope; but she *ran* for the door with better strength than she had had since . . . before her life began.

She knew that she was not accustomed to much snow, but as she did not think of her old life or of her future she did not think about the snow either, beyond the fact that it was there. It was there, and it went on not only being there but adding to itself, till it lay halfway up the window over the table in their hut, which was the direction of the prevailing wind; Lissar opened the door very cautiously each morning till she could see how much of it was going immediately to fall in on her.

She never did move her latrine farther than the corner of the hut because she could not shovel very far or very effectively with only one fully useful arm and an aching hip. Fortunately the hut had produced a shovel—and a broom, for sweeping what fell indoors upon the opening of the door back out again—and boots, mittens, hat and coat, all of the latter enormous.

The clothing had been in a bin beneath the bed, along with several blankets and pillows. The bedframe itself bore nothing but a straw mattress, smelling rather strongly of a small wild animal. The bed troubled Lissar, though she did not know why, and she had only to recall the existence of the shadowy, never-quite-motionless panic-monster in the corner of her mind to decide not to investigate why this, or the other things that namelessly disturbed her, might be so. She kept the pillows and blankets tidily rolled up in the bin, and at night she took them out and spread them in front of the fireplace.

Ash occasionally slept in the bed for a little while, but usually she woke herself up by rootling little hollows in the canvas-covered mousiness with her nose, and when she decided she actually wanted to go to sleep she joined Lissar on the floor. She also caught several of the resident mice and one squirrel.

She ate the first one or two—Lissar heard the crack of her jaws and then the brisk, immediate sound of swallowing—but one evening when she left Lissar's side in a leap, Lissar heard the sound of pounce-and-snap but no ensuing *gulp*. Missed, she thought, not moving from her place facing the fire; but then a long pointed face thrust itself over her shoulder, a long pointed face with a little furry morsel dangling from its jaws.

"Thank you," Lissar said gravely, taking it by the tail a little hesitantly. At least it was already dead, she thought. She had never cleaned or dressed out anything; she was aware she had some idea how it was done, but not a very large or very clear idea. . . . Did dressing out apply to something as small as a mouse? She didn't know. Perhaps it would be good practice. Good for what?

She stood up, still carrying Ash's contribution to their food supply, and took it over to the table. She picked up the smaller of the two knives that were another of the hut's valuable resources. The knife was so old, and had been sharpened so often, that the blade was barely wider than a finger, and curved abruptly in from the use-dark horn handle. Their onion and potato broth that night had splintered mouse fragments in it.

After a certain inevitable amount of experimentation, both Lissar's soup and her bread improved. She had found herbs in the food cupboard upon further exploration, as musty as everything else was, but still capable of imparting flavor; and she set her bread-sponge out for a day to catch the wild yeast before she kneaded it and baked it; Rinnol had taught her about this.

There were also further shapes and smells in the bins where she had first found apples and onions and potatoes that were undoubtedly other vegetables, and while she and Ash ate them, she never did know what most of them were. Some grew recognizable upon scrubbing clean, like carrots, even old wrinkly rusty-orange ones. But there was a carrot-shaped thing that, when cut, was creamy-colored inside, and which disintegrated in the soup-bucket much more quickly than carrots, which she did not know, although the taste seemed vaguely familiar. Some things, like a long round brown root that had to stew most of a day before it was soft enough to eat, she had never met before. There were also a few bags of astonishingly dry and rot-free grains of various sizes and shapes, round or oval or folded, tiny or not so tiny, all of which she and Ash ate, although the husks of some of them caught unpleasantly in the teeth and the throat. And, best of all, there was a big rough sack of salt: salt for bread and salt for soup, salt for any and everything, lots of it, more than she could imagine using. The salt-sack made her feel rich.

They had been in their cabin for several days or perhaps several weeks when Lissar woke up one morning and thought, What is that smell? There must be something rotting in the vegetable bin after all. She would attend to it later—she wasn't going to get up yet. She curled up more snugly on her side, drawing her knees up and tucking her chin down over her crossed hands; and a breath of warm air slipped up from beneath the blankets, beneath her flannel petticoat and addressed her nose. . . . Oh, she thought. It isn't the vegetable bin. It's me.

Taking a bath was an arduous process. There was only the one bucket and a few bowls of varying sizes and depths to hold water. She tore another strip from the blanket that had already yielded floor-scrubbing and dish-washing and hot-bucket-of-soup-holding cloths, to wash herself with. Her clothing had . . . adhered to her skin in several places where the . . . wounds were the worst; and here her mind began blanking out on her again. But by then she had begun to remember what it was like to feel *clean*; even though that required a clearer memory of what it was like to live in her body than she usually permitted herself. She found that she wanted to feel clean again.

Grimly she soaked the crusted flannel free; sometimes she wept with pain suddenly awoken from uneasy quiescence; sometimes she gasped from the reek. She heated the water over the fire; but she no longer let the fire burn as high and hot as she had at first, as she realized how quickly they might use up their wood-pile, and going back outdoors for more snow to melt made her shiver the worse from her ablutions with luke-warm water. Furthermore she was impatient. She had learned to put their supper on early in the day that it might be cooked by evening; but she wanted to be clean *now*.

Finally she could peel her shirt off; bent over, her filthy hair tied back to keep it out of her way till its turn came, she saw her breasts for the first time in . . . she did not remember, but a howling darkness sprang up from nowhere and struck her down. When she climbed to her feet again, grabbing for the table edge to support herself, she twisted her body, and one soft breast brushed against her upper arm. And with that gentle touch she fell again, and retched with great force. There was little in her stomach to lose, but it felt as if her body were turning inside out to get away from itself; as if her flesh, her inner organs, could not bear the neighborhood of the demon that ate at her, that by exposing her body the demon became visible too.

She came to herself again slowly, taking great heaving breaths. She lay on her side, the arm beneath her stretched out in front of her; she could feel the weight of that breast against that arm, and she dared not move. Slowly, slowly, slowly, she made her other hand approach her body and . . . touch it, touch her own body, stroke her own skin, as if it were some wild beast she hoped to tame, or some once-domesticated beast whom she could no longer trust. She touched her side; even after a good deal of soup and bread, each rib stood up individually from its sister, stabbing up through her skin. And I have not even a coat of fur for disguise, she thought, caressing the thin, shivering side. I have less charity for you, my own poor flesh, than I do for Ash.

Her fingers crawled upward and touched the outer curve of her breast, and the fingers paused, quaking in fear; but after a moment, despite the panic trying to break out of its shadows and seize her mind, she told her fingers, Go on. This is my body. I reclaim my own body for myself: for my use, for my understanding, for my kindness and care. Go on. And the fingers walked cautiously on, over the curiously muscleless, faintly ridged flesh, cooler than the rest of the body, across the tender nipple, into the deep cleft between, and out onto the breast that lay limp and helpless and hardly recognizable as round, lying like a hunting trophy over her other arm. Mine, she thought. My body. It lives on the breaths I breathe and the food I eat; the blood my heart pumps reaches all of me, into all my hidden crevices, from my scalp to my heels.

She sat up, and began slowly and dizzily to wash her body; then she mopped the floor, and hauled the dirty water outdoors, to spill it over the latrine-corner; it would be frozen by the time she brought the next bucket of dirty water out.

The private places between her legs were still sore, and some old scab cracked open and began bleeding anew. She knelt by the fire, her arms wrapped over her clean belly, and her hand holding the bloody cloth, and wept for the loss of whatever she had lost, for whatever it was that had brought her here, to a tiny one-room hut with snow lying waist-deep around it, and a too-rapidly diminishing store of wood and food, alone with her dog, and afraid of herself—afraid of the touch of her own flesh, afraid to give herself a bath, afraid to do what she wished to do; afraid to be clean, afraid to relish being clean, which would be a new, more complete reinhabiting of the bruised and humiliated body she feared and tried to ignore.

She wrapped herself in the cleanest of the blankets when she was through, and Ash came and nuzzled her, and sniffed and licked some of the bits of her that were exposed to view. Lissar stared at the sodden, streaky grey-brown heap of her clothing, and wondered if she could ever get it clean, even if she had proper soap, instead of the soft, crumbly eye-and-nose-burning stuff she had found in a small lidded bowl. There wasn't much of it, but it burnt her hands as well till it was mixed with a great deal of water, so she did not worry about this, at least, running out; though they could not eat soap. She sacrificed the biggest bowl, the shallow one she used for making bread, to put her clothing in to soak for a while.

But her bath had cleaned some window or mirror in her mind as it had cleaned her skin, and she began to have visions, sleeping and waking, that came between her and the simple time-consuming tasks that were now her life. She saw the faces of people that were no longer around her, but that she knew had once been a part of her ordinary days; and always, just out of sight, was the monster who haunted her, who still entered her dreams at night and woke her with her own screams.

Even in daylight its looming, oppressive presence was near her, just out of sight, just out of reach; she found herself looking over her shoulder for it, and not believing that it hadn't been there the second before she turned her head. She felt more vulnerable to it, whatever it was, now that her skin was clean, as if the dirt and the half-healed wounds, the sores that by some miracle were not infected, had been protection. Now that she could feel the air on her skin, she could feel her oppressor's presence more clearly too.

She was also, now, often faintly nauseated. She did not vomit again—because she did not let herself. She set her will to this, and her will responded. She and Ash did not have any food to waste, and so she did not waste it. But what this meant in practice was that her meals often took a very long time, as she had to eat mouthful by slow mouthful and dared swallow again only after the last bit declared its intention to

remain quietly in her belly, and her belly declared itself willing to cooperate. Even so, twice or three times, she miscalculated, and found
herself on her knees, her mouth clamped shut and her hands tight over
both nose and mouth, while her stomach tried to heave its contents out
and away from her. I *will* not, she thought fiercely, eyes and nose streaming and throat raw. I *will* not. And she didn't.

Ash's eyes grew bright and her coat again shone. "Rotten meat and
moldy onions agree with you," said Lissar affectionately, and Ash rose
gracefully on her hind legs and kissed her on the nose. Ash now spent
some time outdoors every day; Lissar loved to watch her.

Ash would pause at the edge of the porch, looking around her, as if
for bears or toro; and then she would bound joyously out into the open
ground. She disappeared to her high-held head when she sank into the
deepest drifts of snow over hidden concavities, but she emerged again
with each astonishing kick of her muscular hind legs, the snow falling
off her like stars, and seemed to fly, her legs outstretched in her next
bound, much farther than any simple physical effort, however powerful,
could be responsible for; till she came gracefully down again, her front
feet pointed as perfectly as a dancer's. And she sank into the snow
again, only to leap out.

Lissar had made herself a very rough dress by cutting a hole in the
lightest of the blankets, and poking her head through it. Her own clothing had largely disintegrated under the stress of washing; some flannel
strips she salvaged, and some bigger swatches of the cloak, but no more.
One of the strips she now used as a belt. With the coat, mittens and hat,
the latter tied with another flannel strip in such a way that it could not
swallow her entire head and blind and smother her, Lissar ventured at
last out into the meadow. Her hip was a little better, or perhaps it was
that the walls of the little cabin seemed to press in around a shrinking
space. The boots were so large that she could not pick her feet up, but
had to shuffle, or wade, sliding one foot after the other, even though
she padded them somewhat with more of the ubiquitous flannel strips.

Awkwardly she dug a path all the way around the hut with the shovel, but left the meadow for Ash.

The hut was set at one end of the clearing, and the snow was much less under the trees; in places the ground was almost bare, and Lissar could walk, or could have walked if the boots had let her. She followed a curve of ground downhill one day into a cleft and found a stream, not quite frozen; followed the stream a little way till it emerged from the cleft and wandered out into a clear space that Lissar could recognize from the patchy look of the snow-cover as a swamp. Here she found cattails still standing, and another of the lessons she had learned from Rinnol came back to her. But it had been a long walk—too long—and she was limping badly by the time she got back to the meadow.

Ash met her on the porch that day, tail high and waving proudly back and forth—and a rabbit in her mouth. As Lissar waded up to her, she laid it at Lissar's amazed feet.

She watched hopefully as Lissar wrestled, messily and only somewhat effectively, with disembowelling and then skinning it. Lissar gave her the entrails, which disappeared in one gulp, and then Lissar had to sit down with her head between her knees for a few minutes. The mouse had not prepared her enough.

The soup that night was almost stew; and while it tasted a little odd, Lissar didn't know whether this had to do with her lack of hunterly skills or with the fact that she had forgotten what fresh meat tasted like. Ash made no complaints. Ash seemed to have a mysterious preference for cooked meat.

The next day, Lissar found her way back to the swamp, and came home with not only cattails, but a little borka root, which she had dug up where the boggy ground remained unfrozen, and a few stubborn illi berries that still held to their low pricky bushes. Her hip, and her shoulder and wrist of her weak arm, throbbed so that night that she found sleeping difficult; but it had been worth it.

Lissar's spirits began to lift, in spite of the nagging bouts of nausea. Her days and Ash's fell into almost a schedule. In the mornings, Lissar began the meal that would be their supper, putting bread dough together to rise, cutting up the solid bits that would go into the stew, melting snow for water, deciding if she could spare the bucket to make soup in or whether she needed to use the less reliable method of burying a lidded bowl in the ashes and hoping the contents would cook. Near noon, when the sun was as high and warm as it would get, Lissar would let Ash out, and when she disappeared into the trees Lissar waded, stiffly, around the house to fetch more wood, and to break up some of it, awkwardly and one-handed, for kindling. If the weather was fine and Lissar was feeling strong enough, she went foraging also, sometimes following Ash's tracks for a little way, sometimes returning to the marsh to see what she could scavenge. When she was feeling slow and sick, or when the sky was overcast and the wind blew, she stayed indoors, trying to piece the rags that had once been a flannel petticoat and shirt into something useful, or sewing the hems of her dress-blanket together that it might keep the wind out more effectively; or sweeping the floor; or, once a week, giving herself a bath. Since her first bath she had been making an effort to pay better, more thoughtful attention to her physical self, although it was still an odd discipline. She often thought of her body as a *thing*, as something other than herself, whose well-being and good intentions were necessary to her, but still apart from her essential self. But this distance was helpful more than it was alienating, or so she experienced it, for it helped her bear the pains of the lingering wounds she did not remember the origins of.

It occurred to her after a time that a sling might help her arm, and so she made a rough one, and her arm began to hurt less; at the least the sling reminded her to treat it gently. She did not know what to do for her hip, or for the sudden waves of nausea, or for one or two of the sores that never quite grew dangerously infected, but which went on being a little swollen, a little tender, a little oozy.

After her first rabbit, Ash brought rabbits, or squirrels, or ootag, or other small furry four-footed things Lissar did not have the name for, now and then, just often enough that one of Lissar's worst fears was assuaged, and she began to believe that they would not run out of food before the winter ended. The cattail flour, and the borka root, which was very filling when stewed, although it tasted rather the way Lissar imagined mud would taste, also helped. And she really didn't care what it tasted like. What mattered was that she and Ash were going to come through. The pleasure and satisfaction this thought gave surprised her. But pleasure was so rare an event for her that she returned to it often: that they would come through.

Thirteen

I f the winter ever ended. Lissar still could not think about the future. She knew in theory that winter came to an end, and was followed by spring, and the snow and ice would melt, and the world would be warm and green again, and she remembered that the green stems of the borka were delicious. But the idea of spring—of warmth, of an end to whiteness and silence—seemed distant to her, as distant as the life she must once have led, in seasons other than winter, that she now recollected so little of. She even feared spring a little, as if the turning of the seasons— her direct experience of the rolling year—would wheel that life back to her somehow, that she would have as little say in it as she had in the weather.

She wished winter would stay, forever. She brushed aside questions of food for themselves and the fire when she was in this mood. And perhaps it would stay. She had no idea how far Ash and she had come; how many days they had spent travelling, how many leagues they had crossed. Perhaps here in these woods, far from anywhere, perhaps they had wandered into the forest of the farthest north, where winter stayed all the year around but for the brief vast burst of flowers and small stubborn fruits of high summer, before the first blizzard of autumn covered the blinking, sun-dazed earth once again.

She had found a pair of snow-shoes lying under the blankets at the bottom of the bed-bin. They fitted the too-large boots, but for a long time she did not think of trying them, because she knew her hip would not bear the added strain of splay-legged walking. But as she grew stronger, she thought she would try; by then she had grown fairly clever at wrapping her feet in enough blanket and cloak strips to wedge them firmly into the boots.

She had never worn snow-shoes before, but they were reasonably self-explanatory, and after walking out of them a few times from misreading how the straps went, and then falling down a few times by misguessing how to walk in them, she grew adept. She trudged along sometimes in Ash's wild wake; she, lightly staying on top of the snow like a web-footed bird, yet had nothing of the aerial grace of the long-legged dog. And Ash, particularly once she entered the trees, with their lesser snow-cover, could disappear in a few bounds.

Lissar worried about bears and dragons, but she had seen signs of neither (didn't they sleep in the winter? Well then, but what about wolves and iruku and toro?) and tried to leave all such questions to fate, which had brought them to their haven in the first place—or Ash had, which came back to Ash again. But the conclusion then was perhaps the more comforting—that Ash could take care of herself.

Ash never stayed out so long that Lissar's will not to worry was tried too hard. Ash—Lissar remembered, in the hazy, fenced-off way that memories of her former life presented themselves to her—had never liked the cold much, even in that gentler weather they had once been used to. She could think about the weather, she found, so long as she was careful not to press out from it too far. So she remembered wearing heavy clothes and shivering, but she thought that the sort of cold that sealed the nose and froze the throat was new to her. Lissar did know snow; knew she knew it. And she had heard rumors of things like snow-shoes, which was how she recognized the great, round, funny-looking platters of woven leather in the first place; for she knew also that she had never seen such things before, nor had any need of them. Cautiously she thought about why she had never had need of them: because she never had cause to go walking in deep snow, or because she was un-accustomed to deep snow?

The latter, she thought. But—this was troubling—the former kept obtruding. She kept having odd fragments of almost-memory, like her vision of ceremonial robes, of being waited upon; but she was an herbal-ist's apprentice, and herbalist's apprentices are waited on by nothing but ants and spiders and their own imaginations . . . apparently she had once had a vivid imagination.

Rumor and half-memory told her other things too, and hesitantly she greased, with the rendered fat of Ash's kills, little enough as it was, the webbing on the snow-shoes, which in the long term may have been a good thing, but in the short term what she produced was a sticky mess. The neat, even-stretched weave became somewhat less neat and a good deal less tightly stretched, and the whole affair became infinitely less easy and more frustrating to handle. But Lissar persevered; perseverance was the central lesson of all she had learned since . . . since Ash and she had first set out on their journey.

Lissar followed Ash slowly on her snow-shoes, each time wonder-ing again at the vast space between the leaping pawprints and the de-scending pawprints. She began picking up dropped branches from the trees, and dragging them back to the hut; if she wanted winter never to end, she had to solve their second most pressing problem, their wood-store. Ash was doing her part; Lissar would try to do hers. As she looked for dead wood, peering at branches, a little more of her apprenticeship came back to her, and she recognized a few more edible plants available to her even in the winter. There were the dry, crumbly, tasteless but edible, shelf-like tree mushrooms. She painstakingly peeled bits of bark off young birch and caradal trees—not too much, not to kill the tree—and dug more roots along the occasional wet spots near the stream, although this always made her hip and shoulder ache. Tea she made from erengard leaves, and the bitter brew gave her strength.

Even without the added stress of digging her hip still hurt and prevented her from straying very far, although she found to her surprise that once she was accustomed to it, the odd tiptoe-and-slide motion necessary in the snow-shoes was gentler than ordinary walking, in spite of having to move wide-legged. Her arm now hurt only if she used it too strenuously, so she took it back out of its sling, though its range of motion remained very limited.

She had begun to keep track of each seven days as it passed. But as she did not know how much time she had lost in coming to this place, and in the first exhausted days after, it was a rather whimsical exercise. But it gave her some few standards that her old habits of mind found comforting: she wore her sling for four spans of seven days, for example, before she took it off; and every seven days she treated herself to another bath.

As the weeks passed her wounds did appear to heal, and her skin grew smooth again, although some scars remained, and there was a tightness down the skin of her back and along one side of her neck that she assumed was also scars, though she could see neither, and the sensations under her fingers were inconclusive. The part of her back that her stiff shoulder would not let her touch remained unexplored, and there was a space down her jaw and throat that had no feeling at all, which was confusing, and she could not there read what fingers told her. She was not sorry for the lack of any looking-glass.

She and Ash did not eat so well—or perhaps it was that they worked so hard—that their ribs ever disappeared under a layer of flesh which, in winter weather, might have been a pleasant thing to have. But Lissar noticed that her arms and legs, even the weak shoulder and painful flank, developed a new kind of wiry roundedness, that of muscle; and she was both pleased and puzzled by this, for she knew that this, too, was new to her. Had she led so lazy a life before then? Perhaps picking herbs, and bundling them to dry (and brushing away the ants and spiders), and learning their names, was not such arduous work. Perhaps someone else had chopped the wood for Rinnol's stove.

Ash's wounds disappeared completely; even ruffling the fur down her back, Lissar could not see exactly where her hurts had been. The one reminder of her ordeal was a knot to one side of the base of her skull, a small knot, much smaller than the original swelling, and much less tender. But it was still there, and still sore to the touch. Ash winced away when Lissar's hand found it.

But something troubled Lissar still, something beyond all the shadows in her mind: something real, tactile, immediate. Her own ribs still showed, and the new solidity of her limbs was muscle; but her belly grew bloated, till the skin stretched tight over it. Each week for several weeks now she had rubbed her belly when she took her bath, and wondered, and she looked at herself again on this particular afternoon and wondered again. At first she had been able to ignore it, to suppose she was imagining it, but that was no longer possible. The bulge was bigger than it had been, and unmistakable, and her body seemed to have rearranged itself somehow around it. Her ribcage was a different shape, and the slope of breasts seemed changed. The wondering was not easy or comfortable, and the uneasiness moved into her stomach, and she felt dizzy and ill.

Had she worms, perhaps? But she had examined her own feces, and Ash's as well, and found no signs of worms; and the dubious meat she cooked for them was boiled very well before they ate it. Perhaps her distended belly was caused by some form of malnutrition; she had heard of such things, as Rinnol's apprentice, of herbs and green leaves to banish such afflictions. Ash's needs as a dog were different; perhaps some human need was being overlooked.

She remembered what she could, but it was winter, and there was little green to be had; nor had Rinnol time to teach her everything, and Lissar could remember nothing specific of an antidote to this odd sort of belly-bloat . . . she tried to remember what she did know of the causes of any kind of belly-bloat . . . Rinnol had not had time to teach her everything . . . it would have taken years, and Lissar had been her student only some months, and an unofficial student at that . . . reasons for belly-bloat, and a sudden image of blood flowing between her legs; her Moon-blood, which she had not seen since she and Ash had begun the journey that had brought them here; but it was not Moon-blood that ran down her legs . . . Lissar's breath came short, and the words fell into her mind like blades, like flaming arrows, and there were none on the walls to defend her, the guardians were dumb, dead, escaped, banished, crippled . . . an unofficial student, for Rinnol never quite forgot that she was telling her king's daughter what to do. . . .

Rinnol.

King's daughter.

Her swollen belly . . .

The panic roared at her, a red mouth opening, a monster with jaws gaping wide enough to swallow her, and within its gullet the sight of her father's face as he turned from Ash's body, no longer human as he loomed over her, his striking hands larger than boulders, his body huge as a mountain, blackening the sky and the white snow, tearing the vision from her eyes, smashing her to the floor with the weight of an avalanche.

What brought her back to animal wakefulness was a terrible, seizing cramp in her belly. There was blood on the floor beside her, pooling beneath her outflung legs. The pain came again, doubling her over; her breath came out with a jolt, jerking from her half a grunt, half a cry.

There was a noise at the door. . . .

But it was Ash; Ash had returned.

Lissar struggled up off the floor, seizing her blanket-towel to wrap around her against the cold, and opened the door. Ash leaped in and flung a squirrel at her feet, and then nosed at her anxiously, smelling blood, perhaps feeling the tremor of another spasm passing through the body of her person. Lissar, without thinking, let her desperate fingers claw down beneath Ash's chin, and cling there.

She sank slowly to her knees, her hands still clinging around Ash's neck, and pressed her face against Ash's breast, feeling Ash's wet nose against her cheek, and suddenly loud whuffly breathing in her ear, thinking, Ash has adapted to this life. So can I. So can I. And a pang ripped through her so sharply that she screamed.

She slipped into timelessness, into a space where she bore what she did because choice had withdrawn itself from her. She did not think in terms of living and dying because she was beyond thought. She paced when she could not lie still, and lay still when she could not move. But she did not sleep, and lay down seldom, and the earth's evening and night passed, and by dawn she was exhausted; exhausted enough that she no longer knew the difference between her private visions and the snow and trees and the hard blood-stained floor of the cabin.

She saw a tall man who stood laughing beside her, a man she feared with all her heart and soul, despite the great crowd surrounding them that insisted he was her friend, insisted in a susurration of voices that sounded like the pleas of the damned. As she cowered away from the man, he opened his mouth to laugh the louder, for it seemed that her fear amused him, and she saw that he had the fangs of a wild animal, and the long curling fiery tongue of a dragon.

She turned and fled, flinging herself through the door of the hut,

into the snow and the icy light of fading stars and rising sun. Her staring eyes saw only the vision her terrified mind could not dislodge, and
her ears heard the roaring that was her heartbeat, but which she believed
to be the man-dragon, and the screams she believed were the crowd, but
were from her own dry throat.

The snow hampered her, and that part of her body that still wished
to live ignored the ravings of her mind and began desperately to shiver;
for she had run outdoors naked, and she would not last long in this cold,
if nothing brought her back to her ordinary senses.

What she saw instead of snow and trees and the cold dawn sky as
she ran from the man-dragon, looking fearfully over her shoulder as she
stumbled and wavered and dragged herself along, was a great woman's
face rising up even higher than the man's tall figure; and the woman was
laughing too, and her headdress was made all of fire, as were her scarlet
finger-nails, as she reached out around the man-dragon, toward Lissar,
her arms longer than any human being's, as long as the flight of an
arrow from a strongly stretched bow, and they came on as rapidly as arrows: her scarlet fingernails were tiny worms of flame, with glittering
eyes, and mouths that opened and hissed; and each mouth was as large
as one of Lissar's hands, and there were words in the hisses, and the
words were *At last*.

The earth, Lissar believed, quaked under her, as her feet stumbled
over the writing backs of more fire-worms, but these were large, their
rounded backs wider than her hopeless feet, and now the long fire-
tipped arms had reached past her, and the wrists bent inward, and the
fingers stretched back toward her as she ran, so close that she could feel
the hot breath of the tiny hissing mouths on her fevered face; and she
slowed to a halt, appalled, for she could not run toward or away any
longer. She recognized she was trapped, and as she began to turn, to
look back behind her, the vivid backs of the fire-worms still heaving beneath her feet, she felt the man-dragon's hand on her shoulder, and she
knew she felt her death.

But then a strange calm coolness banished the fire and the pain; and then it was coolness no more, but warmth, a beautiful warmth with a beautiful silence; and then it was silence no longer either, but a sound like bells, or not quite like bells, but something like the sound that trees might make if they tried to speak with human voices, for the sound had a good deal of the sweet murmur of running water about it.

Lissar knew that she lay curled up on something soft, but she did not open her eyes, for her eyes would see nothing of what she was seeing now, a tall, black-skinned, black-haired woman who sat beside her, with one cool-warm hand on Lissar's cheek. But no, the hand was white, and the woman's skin was white, as was her hair; and then as she turned her face toward Lissar she was both black and white, shadowed and unshadowed, a blackness with a light upon it and a whiteness shining from the dark.

"My poor daughter," she said, and her voice was like bells and running water, and Lissar saw that both her white-black skin and hair had green gleams, and her slender fingers had a translucence almost like the first leaves of spring. Her hair was the white of apple-blossom, and the black of a deep hollow in an old tree; and she wore a long robe which was both black and white, and it shimmered with an iridescent green, like water in sunlight. She raised her hand gently from Lissar's face, and as she spread her fingers, Lissar could see through the flesh between her thumb and first finger, as if a candle were burning just behind her hand, as if her hand were itself the sun.

"My poor daughter," she said again. "But rest you now with a quiet mind and heart, for this short story within this life's journey has an ending you may call happy, which makes you one of the fortunate ones. Rarely does fate's wheel turn so quickly for any soul." She paused, and stroked Lissar's hair, and Lissar thought she had never experienced anything so wonderful as the woman's touch.

"Or perhaps my hand has given the wheel a spin; for I do not, sometimes, see that suffering to break any creature's spirit is so excellent a thing. My world is a small one, I know, and like to remain so, for I spend perhaps too much time and strength pitting myself against the great wheel." She laughed a small chiming laugh, and Lissar nestled down more contentedly, for the woman's words stroked her as gently as did her hand, and while she did not understand the meaning of the words, they soothed her, like a mother's bedtime story to a child too young to know language.

"But my world shall thus stay small, for I will go on so pitting myself, and spending such power as I have, and will never, perhaps, be willing to accept that simplicity—that lonely simplicity—that would lift me out of this world forever. . . ." She laughed again. "And why, then, do I tell you this? I recognize something of myself in you, perhaps: the obstinacy, perhaps; or perhaps I know the one who keeps you company. Wake, my child, for someone who loves you wants comforting."

But Lissar's eyes stayed tightly closed. She did not want to wake. She knew too much about waking, for she had been called away from peace back into pain before, and she did not want to go through that again. She wanted to stay just where she was, and sleep forever.

But the woman would not let her. "Wake up, my child. I have given you several gifts, and the world is not as you have feared it, or not wholly so, and I would give you to see the things that are good and kind, for I think you have seen enough of the other. I have given you the gift of time, first; but I have given you other gifts, one that you must discover and one that you must seek. But wake you shall, for I will not have my gifts wasted." And Lissar accepted that the woman knew her better than she knew herself, and that since she believed Lissar would wake, then wake Lissar must.

She opened her eyes as reluctantly as she had ever done anything; she knew that as soon as she opened her eyes she would be . . . where? Memory returned to her cautiously, forming at some little distance from her, that she should glance at it only, not feel it, not let it sink through her, spoiling her peace and comfort: she remembered her last bath, the blood between her legs, leaping out into the snow to escape the man-dragon . . . the memory blurred and fell away from her even as she thought it, crumbling to nothingness like the mysterious contents of an ancient box or trunk or cupboard, opened at last and exposed to sunlight: for a moment the relics stand sharp and clear, but at a touch they fall to ashes, impalpable to the surprised hand, lingering only long enough to make the seeker sneeze.

What remained was a sense of the Lady, of her voice, the touch of her fingers, the calm of knowing that the Lady had intervened on Lissar's behalf. The peacefulness was a part of the intervention; Lissar knew she was grateful, beyond grateful, for having been plucked up from her old fate and set down again, facing some new direction, leading to some new fate; but the memory of why she had needed the intervention was an empty, battered trunk or box or cupboard.

No, Lissar thought very quietly. It is not empty; but I can close it for now, and put it away. I will draw it down later, and open it again; but the Lady has given me time and healing, time for healing. I will be strong again when I open that box; strong enough to open it. My strength now is to set it aside.

And she opened her eyes, blinking.

Fourteen

Ash lay, nose on paws, so near to her that as Lissar opened her eyes she recognized that her cheek was being tickled by Ash's whiskers, where the Lady's hand had touched her; and Ash was lying where the Lady had sat. And as she opened her eyes, Ash looked into hers, and a great shudder of relief and excitement went through her, and she leaped to her feet and gave one short, wild, delirious bark; and she never barked.

Then she stood, her newly plumed tail whisking madly back and forth. For the first thing that met Lissar's gaze and understanding was that the silk-furred Ash, whose belly had once shown pink through the light soft down there, had grown a rich, curling coat like one of the great mad-eyed wolf-hounds of the far north. She was still silver-fawn; but as she moved her coat rippled, and when she flung her head back her long fur fanned out like a horse's mane. Lissar stared, astonished, thinking, This is the Lady's doing; this is one of the Lady's gifts. . . .

Lissar sat up. She lay on a little grassy—*grassy* mound, surrounded by violets; their perfume was in her nostrils. She had thought it was the smell of the Lady. Around her there were still a few patches of snow, and melt-water ran in rivulets everywhere she looked, though where she lay was quite dry and warm.

As she turned her head to look around her in her amazement, something brushed against her face, and she recognized a wisp of her own hair only after a moment's startled thought. For her hair was soft to the touch, cleaner than a bucket of tepid snow-water and a little harsh soap could make it; and, furthermore, it was combed and smooth and bound up on her head, and there was nothing in the hut for a comb but her own fingers. There was another surprise for her: she reached up to stroke her own hair wonderingly and as she drew her hand down again let her fingers trail against the side and back of her neck, and found there no numb places, but only smooth, yielding, feeling skin.

She climbed to her feet, her brain dazedly acknowledging that her hip no longer hurt and each arm swung as freely as the other—suddenly remembering that she had touched the top of her head, investigating the way her hair was twisted in place, with both hands, and yet the one she had not been able to raise above waist level since she and Ash had escaped into the mountains.

As she moved she noticed the dress she wore, made of the supplest deerskin, white as snow, or as the Lady's gown, though her own plainer, more mortal clothing gave no green light, held no impenetrable black of pure shadow. And as she looked down to her bare feet she saw that the little hollow where she had lain was quite bare of grass, and that the outline of the curve of her body, and of Ash's, was sharply etched by green leaves and violets.

She turned completely around. Ash bounded around her, springing as high as if she imagined she still had snow-drifts to overcome; and briefly Lissar quailed, fearing that what she saw was only a beautiful dream, and that she would blink once or twice more and winter would return, and physical pain.

But she blinked many times, and the warm breeze still moved around her, her limbs were still whole; and her eyes saw clearly, and together, and without dizziness, no matter how often she blinked and how quickly she turned her head. She saw that she and Ash were at one end of the little clearing—now a meadow, full of white and yellow flowers, tall buttercups on stalks, ragged bright dandelions, young white erengard—and that their hut lay at the end opposite where she stood. When Lissar's head stopped spinning, she moved toward the hut, whose door hung wide open as if still from the strength of her own arm when she bolted out into the snow.

The few steps toward the cabin were a little shadowed by her memory of the winter; firmly she remembered that it was this hut that had saved her life, that she had accepted her return to life there, that she had made some of her own peace there, before the Lady came to save her from something beyond her capacity to save herself from. But the shadows lay lightly, for Lissar remembered the Lady, and remembered that she had been granted time to leave the box that contained her past in some attic for now; and for the simple, glorious pleasure of being young and healthy and unhurt, feeling the easy way her legs worked, her arms swung, her feet pressed the ground, her head moved back and forth on her neck, her eyes focussed.

The hut stank and was filthy. Methodically Lissar noticed this, and then, methodically, began setting it to rights. First she hauled all the blankets outdoors, following the loudest sound of running water, and dumped them in the stream, weighing them down with rocks that they might not escape her. Then she began hauling water, bucket by bucket, back to the hut. At first she merely poured it across the floor, and swept it back out again; later she scrubbed, the floor, the walls, the table, the cupboard and the bedframe. It astonished her, and dismayed her a little, how very dirty the hut was; for she remembered that she had done the best she could cleaning with tepid snow-water and rough soap. Yet everything was dark with grime, and the blankets smelled strangely musty and sour, and had unbent stiffly, and seemed more dilapidated then she remembered; and the walls and furniture seemed to bear the dark accumulation of years.

The stain on the floor would not fade, however much she scrubbed and soaked and scrubbed again.

The straw mattress she dragged outdoors and let lie in the sun. First she thumped it all over with the handle end of her broom, and was gratified by several tiny grey bodies bolting out of several holes in the cover, and disappearing into the grass. The holes she sewed up, and then she flung the mattress over the edge of the porch roof—far enough up that its edge only dangled over the roof edge, and the entire mattress did not slide off again—that its ex-inhabitants might find the way home a little more difficult, and that the sun could bake the dankness out of it.

Ash, meanwhile, was equally busy; there was a heap of small furry dead bodies next to the wood-pile when twilight began closing in and Lissar began to recognize that she was tired and hungry—and to comprehend that this tiredness and hunger felt good, simple and straightforward and earned. She took the bucket one more time to the stream and filled it, and built up the fire, and threw in chunks of meat and some of the fresh green things her nose had found for her as she hauled water back and forth. And while the soup boiled she skinned and cleaned the rest of Ash's kill, and laid out the strips she made to wait till the fire had died down enough that she could hang them in the chimney; for she wanted to make some return for all the cabin had given her this winter, and there was a great deal she could not replace.

Then she sat outside for a while; even with the fire burning higher than she had dared build it when the snow was still deep and she too weak to hunt far for wood, it would take some little time for the soup to cook to her (and Ash's) satisfaction. It grew cold as the sun set, too cold to sit, but spring was in the air, and she had been indoors for so long; she felt that she had been penned indoors all her life. . . . She sprang to her feet and pulled the white deerskin dress over her head, dropping it on the grass, and ran to the stream, which was only a few steps beyond the edge of the clearing, and leaped in.

The water was *cold,* and this time there was no gap or distortion between her body's reaction and her mind's awareness of it. *Cold!* she thought. So cold it makes my teeth ache!

But it was a wonderful kind of coldness, or maybe it was the awareness itself that was wonderful; and she rubbed herself all over, feeling the day's hard labor swept sweetly away from her. This was better than baths out of a bucket, even though they had been performed beside the heat of the fire. Speaking of the fire—she burst out of the stream again, one plait of her hair tumbling against her naked back like a whiplash of ice, her body iced with gooseflesh, and shot back to the hut, where Ash was considering trying to drink the boiling broth out of the suspended bucket. The stripped carcasses of the other small beasts lay in easy reach on the table, but Ash was, as usual, intent on cooked food. Lissar tucked her hair up again, one plait under another, pulled her dress on again, and gave them dinner.

They spent most of another week at the hut. Lissar gathered what herbs she could find this early in the season and hung them in bunches from the low ceiling; there were hooks there already, and thread came from the unraveling of the ubiquitous washing-cloth blanket; and Lissar hoped that the meat she had smoked would keep.

The hut blazed with cleanness; she had very nearly replenished the wood-pile, although her wood was neither of as good a quality, being only what she could pick up from the floor of the forest, or cut where it lay fallen with her small hatchet and bring back, nor was it stacked as competently. She had buried the remains of her winter latrine, or at least she dug and turned over the earth where she remembered the latrine had been, for the melt-water seemed to have taken care of it surprisingly efficiently already; and now she went far from the hut to do her business, as Ash had done automatically since they both woke on the grassy hillock.

There was nothing left for her to do—except, perhaps, hope to find someone to thank, some day, and possibly put into their hands the things she had not been able to replace: apples, onions, potatoes, flour, grain, two blankets. And she would add: a comb, good soap, a second bucket, an axe. A second bucket would have been a finer luxury than fresh vegetables and silk underwear.

She had already found that her white deerskin dress did not get dirty. She, inside it, did; but it remained as unperturbed by use and wear as Ash's new curly coat was—although Ash now required brushing, which Lissar did as best she could with her fingers and the broom, nightly, by the fire, so that mats she would not be able to deal with would not have a chance to form. But her dress did not require even this much care; if a little mud adhered to a hem, a knee, an elbow, Lissar waited till it dried and flicked it off. It fit her as well as Ash's coat fit Ash; it almost surprised her that she could take it off. It was as if it, too, had grown out of her skin. It wasn't much more improbable than that a fleethound should grow the thick shaggy fur of a northland wolf-hound. The dress seemed as well to be proof against the jabs and slashes of Lissar's vigorous outdoor life, and took no damage, no matter how dense the twigs and thorns; and Lissar's own feet and hands grew tough, till she hardly looked where to put her palm when she reached to grab a branch, till she could walk swiftly and easily even upon the streambed, which was sharp with rocks.

The morning they set out Lissar felt a pang of parting. She could not say she had been happy here, but she had lived, and that was a great deal—she knew just how much. And while the hut—and Ash—had given her the means, still she had taken those means and used them, chosen to use them, known that she had so chosen.

She still knew nothing of her future; she did not know where to go or what to do. She had one white deerskin dress and one tall curly-haired dog; she did not know what fate these might lead her to, what fate she might seek. She thought, I must remember that I possess also myself; but what this self is, after all, I still know little about. What can I say that it does, what can I say that makes predicting my future any more explicit? I who—still, again, for now—remember so little of my past? She paused in her thinking, and looked around her, at the meadow, at the small bald hollow where she and Ash had awakened after the Lady had spoken to them; and she felt the Lady's peace.

I know I am Lissar, and that I have escaped . . . something. I know that I once had a friend named Viaka who fed me, and once I had a friend named Rinnol who taught me plantcraft. And I know I once wore ceremonial robes, and that people cried my name. . . . "They called me princess," she murmured aloud; Ash's head turned at the sound of her voice. I was not Rinnol's apprentice, but a princess; and it was as princess I escaped. . . . She took a deep breath, remembering the Lady's voice; remembering that it was not the time to take down the old worn box from the attic. I cannot remember my father's name, or my mother's, or even my country's. It hurts when I try. Therefore I will not try. The past is past, and I face now the future, a future the Lady gave me.

She had made a rough attempt to scrape and tan the hide of one of the rabbits Ash brought home, soaking it in ashes and water and then stretching and pegging it. She had learned to skin Ash's small kills neatly by this time, and she wanted to leave a message for the owner of the hut, whoever he or she was who had saved her life; and she worried that what she had taken or used might risk the life of whoever came to the hut next. Besides the things she could not replace, she was taking the bigger knife and the flint with her.

She laid the skin on the table, weighing its corners with stones, and wrote on it in charcoal: *Thank you for saving my life.* She wanted to say something about how she would try to return, try to repay in the coin she had spent. But she did not think it was likely enough that she would be able to find this place again, even had she anything to bring; and so she wrote no more. Furthermore, the skin was small, and her charcoal lump large and clumsy.

She paused at the table a moment, rereading her unsatisfactory message. The flint was in the small leather pocket-bag sewn into the bodice of the deerskin dress; the knife, sheathed, hung in a loop at her hip, a loop made for just such a knife. She carried nothing else. "We're off," she said to her dog. "Can you tell me where we're going?"

Ash turned and trotted away under the trees: trotted downhill, across the little stream, opposite the way they had come at the beginning of the winter, as if the long months at the hut were but a pause on a preordained journey. Lissar turned her face away from the little, solitary, silent house, and followed her.

Fifteen

Very quickly travelling became as familiar, as beginningless and endless, as the long snowbound time in the hut had been. At first Lissar followed Ash, as blindly as she had done during the long dreadful days before they found the cabin, but then she found that she too seemed to know where they were going—though she knew nothing more of it than in what direction it lay.

It was like following the direction of the wind beating in her face: if she fell off the point, she could feel the change at once; if the wind shifted, she felt that at once also; but where the wind blew from she did not know. Indeed, she thought, orienting herself to the—smell? sound? touch of air against her cheek?—of that directionless direction, wind would carry more messages of its source. Wind would be warm or cold; wet or dry; smelling of flowers or trees or fire or barnyard. This sensing was a trembling of the nerves, and she might not therefore have believed in it, except that she needed some direction to set her feet and this was at least as good as any other: better, then, because it was there, and it spoke to her. More significantly, it seemed Ash's nose pointed the same way.

She remembered something of the journey to the hut, and the sense of going forward to she knew not what aroused those older memories, of when she had dumbly followed Ash, sick and weak and stumbling. Now it was as though with every step, every touch of her bare tough feet to the ground, she grew stronger. Soon she trotted side by side with her hunting hound when the way was wide enough, a stride almost as leggy and tireless as Ash's.

She began to practice throwing stones; she found as if by some further magic a little detachable pocket in her deerskin dress that was just the right place for small stones to come easily to her hand; the pocket was there just as she began to think of carrying small stones. And with that discovery the stones seemed indeed to come more easily to her hand, and her wrist and shoulder seemed to know better how to twist and flick to set the stones where her eyes had sighted. She felt that she was the ruler of all the kingdoms of the world the first time that a stone of hers knocked down dinner for her and Ash, though there were none but the two of them to celebrate, and Ash took it quite calmly. She slept sweetly that night, believing now in some new way that she would win through; she would reclaim her life—she would find a life to claim.

They travelled one Moon through and into a second. One day each of those months Lissar did no travelling, but lay curled up in what haven she could find, while her mind gave her red dreams and her body sent red blood into the air of the world from a small opening between her legs. She drowsed through those days, Ash close beside her, seeing red water and red sky and red Moon and sun in her mind's eye, and yet finding the visions strangely comforting, like the hand of the Lady upon her cheek. On the second day, each month, she tied sweet grass between her legs, that she might not leave a blood trail; and she found that the white deerskin dress took no stain from blood any more than it did from dirt or sap or sweat.

Lissar began to feel that perhaps this travelling was what her life was, and was to be about; travelling in this wilderness of trees and rocks, and peaks and valleys, for she thought they walked among mountains, although she never had a long enough view to be sure. At last this occurred to her as odd, that she should not know, or seek to find out; and so one day she struck straight uphill—away from the breath of direction on her skin—away from the complex of faint trails made by wild creatures through the trees, leading to the next stream, the next nook to creep into against the weather, the next sighting of something for Ash or for a quick-thrown rock to bring down.

She felt like a wild creature herself, breaking her own trail. But it was an odd goal for any such, not to food or water or even a lookout for danger, but for the satisfaction of simple inquisitiveness: what was this place she and Ash wandered through?

She had picked herself a steep climb. They came up above the trees in some little time, and a little while after that she began to notice that her breath hurt her throat; and then her eyes began to burn, and her head felt light. The ground began to seem almost a wall, rising abruptly up before her, so that it was as logical to grasp with her hands as to tread with her feet. Once or twice she had to stop and give Ash a boost.

It was a good day for seeing distances, however; the sky was blue and clear, and as she looked around she saw the mountain tops stretching out around her. . . . For the first time she thought of how long it had been since she'd seen another human being, heard a human voice other than her own. And she looked around her, thoughtfully, and noticed that in one direction the mountains sank away and became hills, and the forests covered their rounded tops. As she faced that way, she felt the faint tingle of *direction*. We will go that way, she thought. This is the way we are going.

It was still a long time that they were in the mountains, for all that Lissar now felt and understood that they were going slowly downhill. They saw more creatures as they descended; there was more game for them—and a less devastating sense of loss if either of them missed—but more competition for prey as well, and Lissar began to build a fire in the evening for its warding properties as well as for heat and cooking.

Spring wore on, and the last buds burst into leaf. The rabbits and ootag she and Ash ate were plump now, and there was sometimes enough for breakfast even after they had eaten till their stomachs felt tight at dinner—there was breakfast, that is, if they had hidden the remains of dinner well enough before they went to sleep.

Lissar's hair grew long; she thought, vaguely, that in her previous life she must have cut it sometimes, for she could not remember its ever being so long before, and it felt somehow odd under her fingers, thicker or softer or wirier or stronger, but she thought that if Ash's hair could undergo such an odd change then she should not be troubled with her own. She kept it braided, since she still had no way to comb it, and dreaded tangles; she found a way to weave a bit of vine into the braids, which gave her something to tie it off with; only fresh vines were flexible enough, and the sap made her hair sticky, but it had a fresh, sharp, pleasant smell, and she did not mind.

She was washing sap out of her hair one day in a pond. They were well into the round hills by now, and the air seemed gentler, and the water moved more slowly. It was no longer always rushing downstream, whipping itself over drop-offs and into chasms. A swimming-bath was an extraordinary luxury; she and Ash both paddled back and forth, amazed and delighted with this new game. She had stood up in the shallows to work her fingers through her long hair. Usually she stood up straight as she did this, combing it back from her face and over her shoulders, persuading it to lie in the direction she wanted it to dry in, so that it would be as easy as possible to braid later. She wasn't conscious of deciding to do anything different today; had she thought of it, she would have been as wary of anything that might do for a looking-glass as she had ever been, now, in her new life. But today, she pulled the long tail of her hair forward, to hang down her breast, and, musingly, her eyes slid downward to the surface of the water: and the quiet pond reflected what it saw.

It took her a moment to register what she was looking at. The long white thighs meeting in a nest of curly dark reddish-brown hair, up across the smooth belly to her hands working familiarly at the hair falling from her bent head . . . her hair was white, as white as the deer-skin dress, as white as a birch tree.

Her fingers stopped moving. Her hair had been . . . had been . . . when had it turned white? She knew it had not always been white. How could she not have noticed? And yet she looked at herself as little as possible. A memory-flash, no more, of her first bath in the hut . . . but when had she last looked at her hair, as she washed and braided it? She kept her eyes closed, mostly from the habit of protecting them from the fierce soap left at the cabin; but against memory as well, against paying too great attention to herself, anything about herself, that might disturb the Lady's peace. She had faith in the Lady, but not in herself; how could anything to do with herself, who knew so little of her past and less yet of her future, not be precarious?

She bent over the pool. She had a sudden memory that her eyes were green, amber-hazel. But they were not. They were black, as black as despair, as opaque as windowless rooms; pupil and iris alike were in-distinguishable, unfathomable.

She raised her head and watched the slim silver shape of long-haired dog's head; Ash was still swimming, now in circles, as if this were the most fun she'd ever had, biting at leaves and water bugs as they crossed her path, or as she altered her path to cross theirs.

Good, said a voice in her head. They will never recognize either of you.

Recognize me? she answered the voice. If no one recognizes me, how will I learn who I am? But her heart quailed even as she asked the question, and she was relieved when the voice had an answer to this.

Be glad of your curly dog and your white hair and black eyes. Be glad, and go boldly into human lands, and find a new self to be.

THAT NIGHT A BEAR STOLE THEIR BREAKFAST; ASH growled, but Lissar grabbed a handful of her chest hair, and pulled down. "No," said Lissar, "It is not worth it." Once or twice they had met wolves, which terrified Lissar; but the wolves had only looked at them with their level yellow eyes, and trotted away. Both times Lissar knew she had seen them only because they moved, and she wondered how many times she had not seen them because they had not moved, and this thought was ice down her back.

But the only thing that offered to attack them was a small dragon.

Ash had been increasingly unhappy about the route Lissar was insisting on, Lissar having fallen into the habit of believing that the only advice she need take was the intangible pointer in her mind, telling her her direction. Lissar was stubbornly following a trail that went in the direction she wanted; a trail that it was just beginning to occur to her was strangely worn, dusty or ashy . . . she just caught a whiff of something both acrid and rotten when the creature itself came bolting out of the undergrowth at them.

Fortunately it was a small one; but big enough for all that. It stood no higher than Ash's shoulders, but its body was almost as big and solid as a pony's, its small crooked legs thrusting out at awkward-looking angles from its heavy, ungainly body. It paused, briefly confused by the fact that there were two of them, and swung its ugly, smoke-leaking head back and forth for a moment—and then chose Lissar.

"Ash, no!" Lissar said, just in time, and Ash hesitated in her spring, and Lissar grabbed an overhead branch and pulled, just missing the thin, stinking stream of fire the dragon spat at her.

"*Ash, run!*" she shouted, almost in tears. Dragons are stupid creatures. When she pulled herself into the tree it lost her, forgot about her. But its short legs could move its bulk at astonishing speed; in short bursts it might even be as swift as a fleethound. The dragon was turning toward Ash when, at the sound of her voice, it stopped again and looked up at her with its little, deep-set eyes, red with malice. She thought that if it spouted fire at her again she would not be able to get out of the way in time. The branches were close-set, and she was not an agile climber. And she was afraid to climb higher because she was afraid of what Ash would do—for Ash had not run away.

She fumbled in her pocket for a stone as the dragon opened its mouth—as Ash began her charge; and such was the swiftness of a fleethound of impeccable breeding when she is protecting someone she loves, Ash *outran* the dragon's fire as it swung its aim away from Lissar and toward her dog.

Ash bowled it over, but she was bred to pull down long-legged deer by grasping the nose, and letting the weight of her leaping body do the rest; or to snatch a rabbit mid-spring as she outmatched its speed. She did not know what to do with a dragon. Its thick hide gave her teeth no purchase, and it was too bulky to bowl over very effectively, or for very long. Lissar's heart nearly stopped her breath, it thundered so mightily. She flung her stone—and by good luck struck the dragon squarely in the eye. The eye was much protected by its horny socket, but the dragon was at least confused, for it fell again as it tried to stumble to its feet after Ash's attack; and when it parted its scummy jaws again, it was only to pant.

Lissar threw herself down from the tree, clapped Ash on the shoulder as she hurled herself into her best running stride—feeling the heat of the dragon's skin as she swept by it—and said "Come on!"—and Ash did, although she refused to run any faster than Lissar.

They ran for a long time, for as long as it took the panic to sweat out through Lissar's pores; as long it took for what she knew of dragons to recall itself to her mind: that they were dismayingly, fatally swift, but only over short distances. She and Ash had left this one behind long ago.

Lissar did not sleep well that night. The brief battle with the dragon brought other images to her mind; glimpses of—she knew not what. It was as if a door had opened and closed again too quickly for her eyes to recognize anything behind it; a brief stab of horror assailed her, like a clap of thunder might strike her ears. While it shook her, as lightning striking too near may throw someone to the ground, she could not see where the horror came from, nor what were its dimensions or its name.

At the earliest greying of the sky she roused Ash and they went on.

ONE DAY THEY STRUCK A ROAD.

It was really not more than a path, a track; but it had been worn by human feet in leather, pounded by the iron shoes of domestic horses and rutted by the narrow strike of wheels.

Lissar stood, a little back from it, still hidden in the trees, and looked. Ash sat down and let her tongue unroll; she scratched an ear, investigated a flank, and, when her companion still showed no sign of moving, sprawled down full length on the ground for a nap, her head on Lissar's foot for safekeeping. Long months of life in the wild had not eradicated Ash's belief that her person was the chief mover of the world; on the other hand, Lissar, looking down, saw the cocked ear, and knew that Ash's nap was more apparent than real.

Lissar found herself willing to go on standing still simply because Ash's head was resting on one of her feet. It was not as though Ash had not leaned against or collapsed upon all portions of Lissar's anatomy many times before, had been unloaded as many times with protesting groans, and instantly did it again as soon as an opportunity presented itself—thus proving no hard feelings, nor any intention of altering her behavior. But in this particular case Lissar knew she had come to what she had decided, weeks ago, on a mountaintop, she wished to look for—signs of humanity. Having found what she sought, she was grateful for anything, even a dog's resting head, that might be held to be preventing her from acting on her discovery.

When Ash raised her head in response to a crackle in the undergrowth (which might be dinner), Lissar slowly, stiffly, lifted her freed foot and set it down in front of the other one. Then she raised that one and set it down in front of the first; then—then a silvery-fawn streak blasted silently past her, and across the portentous road. There was a brief rustle and squeak, and Ash reappeared at a more moderate gait. She crossed the road once more as if roads were nothing to her, something hairy and mottled brown dangling from her jaws.

Lissar stopped, still several steps away from the road. "We'll camp here tonight," she said aloud, to Ash, who twitched her ears. It was rare any more that Lissar needed words to communicate with her dog. She used them occasionally to remind herself she could, to remember what her voice sounded like.

They moved far enough back from the road that Lissar felt relatively safe from discovery, even with a small fire burning. She knew that the road was not heavily used; not only was it narrow, but she had seen no sign of human habitation—inns, she thought tentatively; rest houses for wayfarers, their gear and their beasts—and there were grass and weeds striking up through old ruts and hoofprints. But that the road existed at all meant someone used it; and the weather had been dry, so there was no mud to tell any tales of recent travellers, nor any recent piles of dung to tell of their beasts. All that meant to her, in her anxious frame of mind, was that it was the more likely that travellers would come soon. She stared through the trees toward the road; she felt as if she could smell it, as she had—belatedly—smelled the dragon. As if a miasma or a magic hung over it, a magic derived from the simple friction of human feet against the wild ground.

She drifted off to sleep with her head on Ash's flank, the curly hair tickling her cheek and getting sucked occasionally into the corner of her mouth or her nose as she breathed, so she made little snorting noises in her sleep. She woke up to a sound of roaring; Ash had curled around her, and put her nose in her ear. They rearranged themselves, and fell asleep again.

Lissar gave herself no time to think the next morning. She rolled to her feet, rubbed her face, pulled the white deerskin dress to order, and trotted off to the road, her muscles (and bladder) protesting such rough usage so immediately on arising. Ash, grumbling and out of sorts at such abrupt behavior during her least favorite time of day, followed her, and they struck the road together, although Ash had set foot on it already and had not noticed this as a significant act. Lissar felt a tingle up through the bottoms of her callused feet as she ran along the road; a tingle she was willing to believe was imaginary, and yet no less important—no less felt—to her for that.

They ran till the sound of water distracted them; and then they halted for some brief ablutions. And then ran on. Lissar had chosen downhill, not because it was faster—though there were moments when running upon the particular angle of slope felt like flying—but because she thought she remembered that *cities* were more likely to occur on flat plains and meadows beyond the feet of mountains; and it was cities that contained the most people.

But did she want so many people at once? a little voice, scared, whispered to her. Her direction-pointer had disappeared as soon as she first recognized a human-used trail, as if the pointer were a guide through a limited territory, and, having brought her to the edge of its own land, left her there. She was a human being; presumably she belonged in human landscapes. But its desertion made her feel lost, more tentative about her decision; it had helped to keep her back among the trees, with Ash's head on her foot. Perhaps, she thought, the words of her thinking coming in the same rhythm as her running footsteps, perhaps what she wanted was a village, something a little smaller than a city.

No, whispered the same voice she'd heard on the mountain-top. *City*.

She shook her head. There was already too much that was peculiar about what did and did not go on in her mind. She would have preferred simple memories, like other people had . . . like she supposed other people had . . . But perhaps other people had voices in their heads too, voices that told them what to do, or not to do. She remembered the Lady's voice, the sound of running water and bells.

She and Ash ran on, looking for a city.

Sixteen

When they broke out of the trees Lissar stumbled and almost fell. Her horizons had opened too suddenly; her vision could not take it all in, and her feet faltered. She slowed to an uneven walk, and great shuddering breaths shook her that had nothing to do with the pace they had been keeping. She kept spinning to look behind her, behind her, always behind her; the wind whispered strangely out here in the open. . . . She wanted a tree to hide behind, a rock to put her back against. She stood still—turned a quarter circumference—paused—another quarter turn—paused—another. Her breath refused to steady.

Ash had initially wandered off on her own errands when they had come out from the forest, but now she trotted up and looked at Lissar inquiringly. Ash was a sighthound; open ground with long plain vision in all directions must be her heart's delight—or at worst a situation no stranger or more alarming than any other. Lissar lowered her hands to her dog's silky head and stood so—facing the same direction—for several long moments, till her heart and her breathing had slowed. Then they went on, but walking now, Lissar looking to left and right as far as her neck would stretch.

She had noticed, a day or two since, that the trees were thinning, the road almost imperceptibly widening, though the surface grew no better; and there had been clearings that took half a hundred running strides to cross, and much longer spaces that were not forest at all but fields with scattered trees in them. In one the grass and willowherb stood higher than her head, and as she swam through it she came unexpectedly upon three crushed circles where some creatures had briefly nested; a tuft of brownish-grey fur remained on a sharp stem-elbow.

But this was something different. When the afternoon light was turning the world soft and gold-edged she turned and looked back, and saw the mountains looming up over her, and knew that they had reached the flat land she sought. They slept that night at the edge of a meadow full of daisies and vetch, and clouds of lavender-pink trollbane.

There was a further development about this flat land with its scarce trees the next day: she recognized the regular rows of planting set among clean smooth earth, and knew this for human farming. She knew at the same time that she had not remembered "farmland" one day before, but now that it was before her eyes she had a name for it, and memories of farmers, male and female, behind ploughs pulled by horses or oxen, or even pulling the ploughs themselves; and the rhythmic flash of the scythes at harvest, and the tidy-wild, great round heaps of gold-brown grain. She even remembered, with the smell of tilled earth in her nostrils, the smell of cows and chickens, of milk in a pail; she remembered Rinnol astonished at how little a . . . a . . . at how little she, Lissar, knew, because she was a . . .

It was like a great rock, holding her memory down, or the door of it closed; as if she camped uneasily at a barricaded gate, afraid to leave, afraid not to leave; as if occasionally words were shouted to her over the barrier, which sometimes she understood and sometimes did not. Perhaps her memory was merely very small; perhaps this is the way memory is, tight and sporadic and unreliable; perhaps everyone could remember some things one day and not another day. Perhaps everyone saw the Lady. She stared at the tall grasses and the flower-spangled banks that ran along the road. Was it only that she was far from her home that she could put names to so few things? Rinnol had been a good teacher.

Ash and Lissar walked on. As twilight came on again, Lissar broke into a trot, and they went on so till the Moon rose and sank. And then Lissar found a stream that ran though a hedgerow, and a little hollow on one bank just large enough for a woman and a dog to sleep curled up together; and there they stopped. The sun rose over them and spattered them with light, for the leaves of spring had not gained their full growth; but they slept on. It was late afternoon when Lissar woke, and shook Ash (who, as usual, protested).

Lissar slipped out of the white deerskin dress and stepped into a quiet place in the stream, lined with reeds, where the water bulged into the same soft place in the earth where she and Ash had slept; and she stood there long enough for the fish to decide she was some strange new kind of flotsam; and she flipped their breakfast, flapping and scaly, up on dry ground. Ash was still the best at rabbits, but only she could catch fish. The water was cold; after the necessity for standing perfectly still was over with the sudden plunge and dip for her prey, her body broke into violent trembling, and gooseflesh ridged her all over. It was some minutes of dancing around and waving her arms before she was warm enough to hold tinder steadily and make fire. It had occurred to her more than once that the reason Ash did not learn fishing was because she did not like standing in cold water; and streambanks were rarely a suitable shape for fishing dry-shod.

It took Lissar two or three days to notice that she had switched them over to travelling at night—travelling from shadow to shadow like ootag giving wide berth to the scent of yerig. I'm frightened of facing human beings again, she thought. I don't know where I am; I do not know even if I speak the language of this place . . . I do not know the name of the language that I do speak. I do not know who I am or where I come from; I do not know why and how I know that there are different human tongues. I am frightened of the things I cannot explain.

She thought: I long for another human face just as I fear it.

She paused and looked out over the Moon-silvered landscape. This looked much like the farms she remembered—but how did she understand what she remembered? She had not remembered *farming* till she had seen fresh-sown cropland and the green coming growth of the early crops laid out in front of her. Perhaps she did not recognize the difference between these lands and where she had lived before because . . . she had thought, sometimes, that the bits of her memory she could clearly recall felt stretched, as if they were obliged to cover more territory than they could or should. . . . Perhaps she had come back to the place she had left . . . escaped from. Her heart began beating in her throat, and she put her hands up to hold it in: she could feel it against her palms, as if it would burst through her skin.

No, said the voice in her head. *This is a different place. You have come a long way from where you left. That place is far from here.* I will believe you, she thought, slowly, in the voice she thought of as her own, because I want to. She and Ash walked on.

That morning, as dawn slowly warmed the countryside, Lissar did not look for a place to sleep, to hide, but kept on—walking, but slowly, for it had been a long night, down the rough, endless road. And so that morning, at last, she saw another human being; and that human being spoke to her.

He was leaning on his gate, watching her. She had seen him emerge from his house—a thin curl of smoke from its chimney had suggested to her that its occupants were awake—with harness over one shoulder and a fierce-looking rake over the other. She watched him move, and thought how strange he looked, how unwieldly, reared up on his hind legs like that; utterly without the grace of dogs, deer, of everything she had seen moving during her long solitude in the mountains, even the dragon. How very oddly human beings were made; and she wondered how she looked in Ash's eyes.

The man paused at the roadside before putting his hand to the gate-latch, looking up and down the road as he did every morning, expecting to see, perhaps, that damned dog of Bel's out getting up to mischief again, or maybe someone getting an early start for a trip into town. And what he saw was a Moon-haired woman in a Moon-colored dress with a tall Moon-colored dog at her side. She was barefoot, and her hair hung down her back in a single long plait. Her dress was so white it almost hurt the eyes, while the dog's long curly coat was softer, silver-grey, almost fawn, like the Moon in a summer fog. He paused, waiting, his hand on the latch.

"Good morrow to you," he said as she drew near.

She started, though he had seen her looking back at him, had known he was there. She started, and stood still. She was close enough for him to see her eyes, black as her hair was white. The dog paused too, looking up into her lady's face, then glanced at him and gave one brief, polite wave of her plumy tail.

"Good morrow," she said, with a long pause between the two short words; but he heard nonetheless that she spoke with an accent he did not know. This did not surprise him; it was her existence that surprised him. He had seen no one the least like her before; given that she existed, that she stood before him at the gate of his farm, she must speak unlike his neighbors. It was reassuring that she did so; had she not, she must be a dream, and he was not given to dreams, or a ghost. He wondered if his language was strange to her; and then, even in the thought wondering that he should think such a thing, him, a farmer, who occupied his days with seeds and crops, and mending harness and sharpening tools, and the wiles and whims of beasts both wild and tame—wondered if perhaps this woman spoke a language belonging only to her, that she spoke it aloud only to hear the sound of her own voice, for only her ears recognized the meaning of the words. Even if she were not a ghost or a dream there was some magic about her; he moved uneasily, and then thought, No. If she bears magic, there is no evil in it.

She looked around, taking in his farm, the harness, his hand on the latch. He saw her understanding what these things meant, and was almost disappointed that such mundane matters were decipherable to her.

"Is it far to the city?" she said.

"The city?" he echoed, himself now startled; what could this woman want with the city, with her shadow eyes and her naked feet? "Oh, aye, it is a long way."

She nodded, and made to pass on.

"Your dog, now," he said, surprising himself by speaking his thought aloud before he had come to the end of it in his own mind: "Your dog has a bit of the look of the prince's dogs." This was perhaps her reason for venturing down from her mountains—from the wild land beyond the farmland that was his life and his home—to go to the city. Something about her dog.

She nodded again although whether in agreement or merely acknowledgement that he had spoken, he could not tell; and then she went on. Her footfalls were as silent as her dog's. The farmer stared after them, relieved that their feet displaced the dust in the road.

THE NEXT MORNING LISSAR HAD TWO RABBITS FLUNG over her shoulder; this morning she met a man trudging toward her with a mysterious bit of ironwork over his shoulder. She guessed he was on his way to the smithy she had seen as they trotted through a village in the dark hour just before dawn. *Smithy*, her mind had told her, the mountaintop voice had told her; she listened. She had been emboldened by her first conversation with the man at his gate, and was almost sorry to be passing through her first village while everyone was sleeping. Not one glimpse of candlelight did she see, not one person waiting up for a birth or a death, or putting the last stitches in a wedding-dress or a shroud.

This man had his head bent, his back bowed with the weight of his load. "Good morrow," she said as she approached; he looked up in surprise, for he had not heard her footsteps, and she further knew and was glad for the relief the knowledge brought her that her accent branded her a stranger.

"Good morrow," he said, politely, the curiosity in his face open but not unkind.

"Do you know anyone hereabout who would be willing to trade a fresh-killed rabbit for a loaf of bread?" She had thought of doing this just after she had left the man with his hand on his gate-latch, and the hope of its success made her mouth water. She had not eaten any bread since she had left the hut, and remembered further that not all bread was necessarily slightly gritty and musty-tasting.

A flash of white teeth. "Ask for two loaves," he said, "which is more nearly a fair trade. Your catch looks plump, and the skins are worth something besides. Ask for some of last year's apples too, or maybe a pumpkin that wintered over."

She smiled back at him. It was an involuntary gesture, his smile begetting hers; yet she found the sense of contact pleasant, and she saw that he was pleased that she smiled. "My wife would give you bread," he went on; "she did her baking yesterday. And we've still a few turnips and pumpkins in the barn. You ask her. My name is Barley. The house isn't far; there's a red post out front, you'll see it. Her name is Ammy. There are chickens in the yard. 'Ware the black and white hen; she's a devil. Dog's tied up out back, won't trouble yours." Any other dog he might have questioned the manners of, in a yard full of chickens; somehow he did not question this dog any more than he felt the need to question the woman. His own dog was a more ordinary breed; he and his wife were as well.

"I am grateful for your hospitality," Lissar said gravely, and they parted.

She found the red post without difficulty; and the black and white hen took one look at Ash and retired from the field. The house door opened before they arrived at the step, and a smiling woman looked out at them, a curiosity a little touched with awe, much like her husband's, bright in her eyes.

"B-Barley said you might trade us a loaf of bread for my rabbits," said Lissar. As soon as she had really to ask barter of a person who could say *yes* or *no*, she lost all faith that her offer was a reasonable one; forgot what Barley had said, forgot that this was his wife and that he had already bargained with her for a better price than she asked. She found, too, that it was hard to pronounce his name, to say to his wife, I know this person well enough to have his name to use.

The woman's eyes moved to the limp, furry forms dangling from Lissar's shoulder. "I can do better than that," said she, "and shame to him if he did not tell you so. Come in. I'll give you breakfast. And I'll cook both rabbits, and you can take one away with you, and two loaves of bread."

"I thank you," said Lissar shyly, and ducked her head under the low lintel. "He—he did say that one loaf was too little."

"I'm glad to hear it." The woman glanced again at Lissar, measuringly, this time, and said, hesitantly, "I mean no offense, but I think you have been on the road a long time. Is there anything an ordinary house and an ordinary house-woman might offer you?"

"Soap," breathed Lissar in a long sigh, only just realizing she was saying it, not conscious of the thought that must have preceded it. "And hot water."

The woman laughed, and was more comfortable at once, for her visitor's exotic looks had made her wonder . . . well, it was no matter what she had wondered, for this woman's answer was just what she would herself have answered in similar circumstances. "I can give you a bath by the fire. Barley won't return before sundown, there are only the two of us."

It seemed the greatest luxury Lissar could imagine, a bath, hot water in a tub big enough to sit in, beside a hearth with a fire burning. She watched in a haze of happiness as the great kettle she had helped fill from a well-spout in the yard came to a slow trickle of steam over the fire. She ate breakfast while the water heated; Ammy declared that she had eaten already, but she fried eggs and bread and slabs of smoked meat, and long thin spicy greens and short frilly mild ones, and Lissar ate it all. Ammy, watching her narrowly, then did it all over again. She had much experience of farm appetites, and Lissar ate like a harvester at the end of a long sennight. By the time Lissar had eaten her second enormous meal she had slowed down a good deal and Ammy did not threaten her with a third.

Ash, meanwhile, had swallowed three bowlsful—tureensful—of a mixture not wholly unlike what was more neatly arranged on Lissar's plate, and then flopped down where she was—in the middle of the floor, so that Ammy and Lissar then had constantly to step over her—and soon began snoring gently.

"And here is your bread," Ammy said, plunking down two great swollen loaves on the table that Lissar felt amost too full to push herself away from.

She shook her head. "You made a very bad bargain. I will leave you both rabbits for breakfast alone."

"You may leave me both rabbits and I will make a stew which you may have some of for dinner or supper, after your bath and a nap. When you leave I will give you something to carry the bread in," said Ammy briskly.

There was enough room in the tub that with her knees drawn up Lissar could sink down till her whole head disappeared underwater. The water was so hot even her uncovered knees throbbed with it, and the feeling of the warmth beating against her closed eyes was delicious. She felt her skin relaxing, as if even the hairs on the backs of her arms, at the nape of her neck, had been on watch these long months past, and felt easy at last. She sat up again, partly to breathe, partly because her full stomach protested being folded up so snugly.

"You're as red as winter flannel," said Ammy, laying down towels. "I'll leave you alone now; soak as long as you like."

But Lissar, leaning her head back against the lip of the tub, found herself growing uncomfortable. As her body relaxed, something that the tension of the long travel-stained weeks had held prisoner threatened to break out of its weakened bonds. A bath by the fire, she thought . . . In the wintertime, her mind went on, slowly, when the big grand stone-walled bathroom was too cold. . . . The stone stood in tall narrow panels, black, white, black, all veined with gold and grey, and polished so smooth that fingers were briefly deluded into thinking it was soft. . . . What . . . ? And, unbidden, the memory of a small round room came to her, its walls hung with tapestries and rose-colored silk, and a bath drawn up by the fire, and a table with a meal for one person and one dog stood beside it. As she sat in the tub, the bed would be just behind her, there—

She stood up and spun around, spraying the room with water. Ash, who had been struck in the face with a hot wet wave, opened one eye and registered a complaint; but Lissar was standing, staring at nothing—nothing but a table with shelves beyond it bearing ordinary kitchen things, bowls, plates, a spare pot, a cleaver, a grinder, several spoons—and shivering as if she stood naked in a blizzard.

Slowly she recollected herself, turned her head to where the door into the garden did not stand in this room, and slowly this other room re-formed itself around her, becoming lower, long, rectangular, plainer. Slowest of all she sat down again.

I have given you the gift of time, the Lady said.

The little round room vanished, along with whatever other memory it might have given her; but it left a shadow, and Lissar's bath was spoiled. She soaped herself thoroughly, particularly relishing working it into her long white hair, and then rinsed, and stepped out of the bath at once. She bailed enough of the water into the channel in the corner that would carry it outdoors that she could tip the bath up on one end and empty it.

Ammy, in the kitchen garden, was surprised to see her so soon. She stood up, her apron full of weeds. "Would you like to sleep now? We've a spare mattress in the attic. I haven't made it up yet, but we can do that now."

Lissar shook her head. She was tired, her feet did not wish to move, and her stomach did not wish them to move either because it was still concentrating on digestion; but she was anxious, restless and fidgety now, and there was something wrong with the shape of the homely, welcoming kitchen, and knew that she would not lie easily on a mattress on the floor above it.

"What's the matter?" said Ammy quickly, having forgotten, for the moment, that she was a little in awe of her visitor, that the sadness in her face seemed an acceptable excuse for not offering any name to her host. Courtesy prevented Ammy from asking; but there was no harm in noting none given. Ammy saw in her face now that some old pain or fear had risen somehow, suddenly, to the surface; and Ammy had raised eight children and loved them all, and missed having them around now that they were grown and gone. "You—you look like you've seen a dragon." She knew that was not what she meant, but knew that she dared not say what she did mean. She reached out to touch Lissar's arm and then paused at the last moment and did not. Lissar was not one of her own daughters, after all, and it seemed too much a familiarity to this young white-haired woman with the black eyes full of grief and secrets.

Lissar smiled faintly. "We did once, up in the mountains."

All of Ammy's first thoughts about the identity of this woman came rushing back. Very few people walked away from a solitary encounter with a dragon. "What happened?"

"We ran—and it wasn't very hungry."

Ammy stood looking at her guest for a moment, and then said, shrewdly, but in her early hesitating manner, still thinking about the dragon: "Would you be more comfortable sleeping in the barn? The hay's still sweet and dry, not at all musty; Barley turns it so it will stay good."

It was Lissar's turn to look at the other woman in surprise. "Yes . . . I think I would. I thank you. That's very . . . thoughtful." She touched her grateful stomach. "I would rather sleep than go on walking."

"Do you—know your direction?" said Ammy cautiously, a little afraid that Lissar might read *Where are you from?* and *Where are you going?* plain in her eyes.

"How far is the city?" said Lissar.

"The city?" Ammy said, frowning. "Do you mean the king's city?"

The king's city. The *king's* city. Was this what she wanted? Did she know her direction? She wished again for the breath of direction against her cheek, that she had not felt since she first saw the road; and the voice from the mountaintop was silent. "Yes," she said.

"It's a way," said Ammy doubtfully. "I've not been there. Barley was, once, when he was a young man; the roads are better now." Ammy added, allowing herself a twinkle, "If you stay for supper you can ask him about it."

Lissar smiled, and felt her face muscles awkward again in the gesture. "Oh," she said with a sigh, as what felt like several months' exhaustion fell on her all at once; "I do feel I could sleep till suppertime twice over." She thought: No wonder wild animals live such short lives. This is what it feels like, never being quite sure that that crackle in the underbrush isn't something that wants to eat you. She felt suddenly unable to bear all that watchfulness.

Ammy said: "Stew only gets better for waiting. I'll keep you some for tomorrow night, if you oversleep."

At that Lissar laughed out loud; and the sound frightened her in the first moment that it broke out of her. Ammy saw the fear, and her friendly heart was shaken by the knowledge that any human creature could fear her own laughter. Without time for thought she reached out and took both Lissar's hands in hers, and said, "My dear . . ."

Lissar grasped those hands firmly for a moment, and they stood in silence. "I have been, perhaps, too long in the mountains," she said quietly. And then Ammy took her out to the barn, and Lissar and Ash burrowed deep in the clean sweet-smelling hay and were asleep before Ammy finished pulling the heavy door shut behind her.

But the habits of the last months were still strong in Lissar; furthermore all the noises she heard here were unfamiliar and therefore suspicious. She half-woke when the rooster crowed, which he did at intervals, without any reference to the position of the sun in the sky; half-woke when Ammy went in and out of the house-door, when she called the chickens for their food, when she answered a friend's greeting from the road. The farm dog barked once, perhaps at some whiff of Ash's presence; Ash bristled and growled briefly in her sleep.

One noise in particular disturbed her, dredged her up farther than half-sleep, almost to waking, till she recognized it: the crunch and creak of wagon wheels. She had not heard that sound for a long time, and its echoes rang off other memories she did not want disturbed. She dozed and drifted, and then came fully awake on the instant when Barley came home and entered the barn to hang up his mended tool.

She slid down from her crackly perch, pulling hay-stems from the neck of her dress. "Ah," said Barley. "Ammy said you were here." He was smiling at her, but there was a puzzlement, almost a wistfulness, in his eyes similar to the way his wife had looked at her. "I thought perhaps you would have slipped out the back way and gone on—to save the trouble of talking to them old folks again. Old folks can be real meddlesome."

She surprised herself by saying almost angrily: "I would not have left without saying good-bye. I am grateful for your help and kindness and welcome. I do not see you as meddling."

The half-anxious, half-curious look faded, and he said, "Never mind me. Ammy's always telling me I talk before I think. Since you're awake now, come in for supper—it's rabbit stew. Isn't that something?"

The stew was better than anything Lissar had made last winter in their hut; the onions and herbs were fresh, and obviously added by a hand that knew what it was doing. They ate by firelight; Lissar listened to Barley's story of his day's adventure without paying attention to the meaning of the words. It was fascinating to her merely to hear language spoken again, to listen to the rise and fall of a voice speaking intelligibly, hands gesturing now and then to support or illustrate a point. It did not matter what the point was. It was enough—more than enough—that this sort of communication went on; that there were sounds that were not creaks in the bushes, however meaningful, or the fussing of chickens, however meaningless. She noticed that Barley used a word now and then that was unknown to her, but she felt no desire to ask him to explain, whether from a gentle indifference to unnecessary particulars, or from a fear of exposing too much of the extent of her own strangeness, she did not know.

She came back to full attention when Ammy said, "Our guest was asking about the yellow city— how far it is. I couldn't tell her."

"The yellow city?" said Barley. And he repeated what his wife had said earlier: "The king's city?" And again the word *king* made Lissar want to look behind her, throw pebbles in the shadows to see what would be flushed out.

Barley ran his hand over his head. "I haven't been there in thirty years. There isn't enough grass there, and too many people, and the vegetables ain't really fresh, even in summer. What do you want with the city?—Wait," he added hastily, "I'm not asking, it's just my way of talking. I ain't used to anybody who ain't used to me. It took us, well, near a month to get there; but the wheel-horse threw a shoe and went lame with it, and we lost a few days. The roads are better now; it's one of Cofta's pet projects, the road system."

"Cofta?" said Lissar before she thought to stop herself.

The other two stared at her. "King Cofta," Barley said, after a moment. "It's his city you're wanting." Lissar looked up from the table,
through the unshuttered window, where sunset still kept the darkness at
bay. The entire world was rose-colored with this day's end, the same
rose color as the hangings of a small round room.

"Ah, well," Barley went on, "both of us know from listening to you
that you ain't from around here." The pause this time was anxious, trying not to be expectant and failing.

"No," said Lissar. "I'm from . . . a place beyond the mountains."

Barley hastened into the pause that followed this statement. "You
might never have heard of our king as Cofta anyway, for he's King Goldhouse the Seventeenth; but they've all been Goldhouses, all seventeen
of them in a row, and Ossin will be Goldhouse the Eighteenth when his
time comes.

"Their great house is yellow brick, and the door is covered with
gold leaf, and the creatures carved into the arch of it have golden claws
and eyes and tail-tips. Most of the town is built of the same brick, so it's
called the yellow city, although there ain't any other gold except the
door-handle of the guild hall, where there's always a doorkeeper, just
like at the king's door."

LISSAR DECLINED HER HOSTS' REPEATED OFFER OF THE
mattress, or a return to the warm haystack. She was tempted, for the weariness the bath had awoken deep in her bones was still strong. But she felt
that she had lost the knack for sleeping under a roof, and that, now she
knew the name of the place she had chosen as her goal—the king's city,
the yellow city—she wanted to keep on toward it as steadily as she could.

"Come see us if you come back this way," Ammy said hopefully.

"I will," Lissar said, surprising herself by meaning it.

It was full dark as she and Ash stepped onto the road again—with two loaves of bread, tied up in a kerchief, under one arm, for Ammy had won that argument—and fell into their familiar loping pace, Ash silent at her left side. The weariness, strangely, dropped from her as they ran, as she breathed deeply of the cool night air.

Seventeen

L issar was more warmed and shaken by her encounter with Ammy
and Barley than at first she realized. She often remembered the
sound of their voices, the words they used, words a little different from
the ones she or Rinnol would have chosen, and differently pronounced.
But she rolled the sound of their voices around in her head like coins in
the hand. And she decided, without ever deciding, that she would continue travelling by night. It was too important a matter, this talking to
people, and listening to them, to do it lightly or often.

The weather grew warmer, both, she thought, as they came farther
and farther from the mountains, and as spring progressed toward summer. There were the first pale shoots of witchgreen growing by the
streams they camped by, tender and sweet, and nothing like the huge
dark intensely bitter leaves the same plant would have produced by

midsummer. Lissar risked tastes of plants she did not know but that looked and smelled plausible; one of her guesses gave her a day of belly cramps, but the rest were good, and provided some welcome variety. Nothing was as good as Ammy's rabbit stew however, and her bread was gone far too soon.

But the morning came when they could find no wildness to retreat to, not even any semi-cultivated hedgerow to sleep under. The road had grown wider and wider yet, and there was traffic on it sometimes even at night, though when anyone hailed her she merely raised a hand in acknowledgement and kept on. At night, usually, other travellers were in a hurry, bent too urgently on their own business to take much note of who shared the road with them. Once, one twilight, someone's dog leaped off a wagon and tore after them, barking briefly in a businesslike manner that Lissar did not like; it was big and black and it ran like it was nobody's fool. But before she had done anything but touch her stone-pocket, Ash had turned and hurled herself silently on their pursuer. Something happened, very quickly, and the other dog fled, howling like a puppy. Lissar barely had had time to break stride. She paused, but Ash gave her a look as if to say: why do you bother?—and Lissar thought perhaps she did not want to enter into a conversation with the men on the wagon who were—she glanced at them—staring at her and Ash with their jaws visibly hanging. So they ran on.

As the days grew longer it was no longer possible only to travel in the dark hours; she would waste too much time, and she was impatient to reach the city she had chosen as her destination. Farmers' dogs occasionally chased them but were careful not to get close: I am merely, they barked, announcing that this is my territory; I have no quarrel with you so long as you continue on your way.

She had not expected to come to the city so soon. Perhaps it had, in the last thirty years, since Barley's journey, reached out to meet him—and got her instead. Dawn was growing, pink and yellow and long streaks of pale orange, and she and Ash were tired, but she saw nowhere for them to rest in hiding. She had been careless; she had grown accustomed to running along a straight and easy road every night, with no decisions to make but which field looked a likely place to find dinner. She had grown accustomed to the steady increase of houses, and the occasional village spilling out from the road like groundwater filling a footprint. But the villages had been small and farmland began again on their other side, and with farmland, small wild groves and un-tilled meadows.

The first time they came to a town center where there were no fields at all, and the buildings were all attached to each other, as if the road had high thatched walls with shuttered windows in them, she had stopped in amazement. She felt she had run into another world, where the people must be visibly alien, with mouths at the top of their faces, or eight fingers on each hand. But that piece of the road was quite short—she paused to peer down a side-road, similarly lined with unbroken wood and stone—and they soon ran through it and out into the open land again. She realized that farmland now looked almost as familiar to her as unbroken forest once had.

Maze, she thought, thinking about the building-walled town. There was a maze, once, in a garden where I walked, with hedges high and clipped close. You were supposed to find your way into the center and back out again. I went there with Viaka. But with the name *Viaka*, her memory shut down again, and she thought no more about the town.

Dawn was now morning, and there were more and more other people on the road. She and Ash had to slow to a walk, partly because it would be too awkward, and partly too conspicuous to thread their way through the throng at a more rapid pace; people on foot walked. Horses and carriages moved more quickly. But partly also it was from weariness. They had noth-ing to eat; it was not unusual to miss a meal, but to have the prospect of neither food nor sleep was hard. Ash's tongue was hanging out.

At least we can find water, thought Lissar. Somehow. I hope. But Lissar had not taken into account town hospitality; soon they came to a wide low watering-trough by the roadside, set next to a well. A woman was there already, watering her horses by pouring bucket after bucket into the cistern. Ash stepped up beside her and lowered her head.

The woman turned, startled. Her horses were tall and handsome, both pairs dark bay, wearing glittering harness; the woman was short and drably dressed, and her horses' tails had been more recently combed than her hair, which had been bundled erratically into a braid. "I thought I'd missed one," she said to Ash. "You're almost big enough to be a horse, although you don't drink like one." Ash was lapping noisily. The woman dropped the empty bucket into the well; when she pulled it up again, she offered the dipper, attached to the side of the well by a thin chain in case of accidents, to Lissar.

"I thank you," said Lissar, and drained it, and offered it back to the horse-woman.

"You've come a long way," said the woman. Lissar wondered if she was referring to her accent, her thirst, her dishevelled appearance, or her obvious weariness; and she smiled a little. Her thoughts were tired too, and inclined to wander. "Yes." She looked at the ground, and then down the road, the way they were going, toward the yellow city, which must be very near now. Many of the buildings around them were of yellow brick. Perhaps they were already in it and she had not noticed when they crossed from outlying town to the city itself. Was there a gate? Was there a reason she expected there to be one? So, here they were. Now what? The voice in her head remained obstinately silent.

"I don't mean to be rude," said the woman, "but you look like you might be able to use some advice. I am not very good with the kind of advice my mother used to give out—which is why I don't live at home any more"—the woman grinned—"but I've lived here longer than you have, I think, so maybe I can help."

Lissar looked at her. She was still smiling, and it was a nice smile; and her four horses all looked shiny and content. When she made a quick gesture to wave a wasp away from the nearest horse's head it did not startle away from her.

"I—it's hard to say," Lissar began finally. "I do need—advice, as you say. But I don't know what to ask for." Ash sat down in the middle of the road and began digging at the back of her neck with one hind foot, her lips pulled back in the canine rictus of joy that scratching inspires. Lissar looked up again. "I decided to come to the city—but, oh, I forget! And now that I'm here I don't know what to do."

The woman laughed. "You sound like me—although I did remember why: to get away from my mother. But I was still a farm girl—still am—but I was lucky, and they could use a horsewalker. Indeed they need another one for a few weeks, because Jed fell and broke an ankle, the chump. Usually we pick up the post-horses in pairs. These four"—she patted a shoulder—"are very good-natured—well, all Cofta's horses are good-natured, just like he is; if you want the kind of idiocy that equally idiotic people like to think of as spirit, the Count Mayagim has 'em. Horses that have been let think rearing is cute . . . sorry. I mean, one person for four horses isn't enough. Would you like to come with me? It's not far now, but it'll get more crowded, particularly once we're in through the gates, and I'd appreciate the help.

"There's a meal at the end of it, and a bed, and you can talk to Redthorn, who hired me; he knows everything that goes on in the city. And, you know, the king offers a meal and one night's bed to anyone who asks, so now that's two days—how can you lose? Something'll turn up. Besides . . ." She paused at last, and looked at Ash, who was whuffling in the road-dust after a beetle. "The prince'll like your dog, and the king and queen like anything Ossin likes."

"The prince likes dogs?"

"You really aren't from anywhere, are you? The prince is almost a dog himself. You never saw anyone so miserable as him in the reception-hall—he looks so much like a dog about to have a bath you expect to

see his ears droop. But then you see him out charging over the landscape with his dogs, or in the kennels covered with puppies—and puppy
dung—and you wouldn't know him from the under-shoveller. Normal
people *mind* getting dog dung on them. I think actually the king and
queen wish sometimes that he liked someone other than anyone with a
nice dog."

"You know him?" Lissar said, fascinated.

"Nah. I mean, no more than anybody does. I'm kind of one of the
under-shovellers in the barn, but horse dung isn't so bad. Bringing post-
horses back is a big promotion for me. I've only been here a few months
myself. But Ossin is always outdoors except when his parents nail his
feet to the floor to do the receiving with 'em. You'll see him too—the
price of the king's meal is that you go present yourself to him and ask for
work. Sometimes he has some to give you. Usually it's just a formality.
Redthorn got to me first—or I found the stables first. You know, the
prince's dogs look a lot like yours except they're short-haired.

"So are you lot ready to be off yet?" she addressed her horses. The
bridles were looped together in pairs; she twitched one leading rein up
and offered it to Lissar. "Do you know anything about horses?" she said.

I don't know, Lissar wanted to answer; but the supple leather strap
felt familiar in her hand, and the great dark eye turned toward her
looked familiar as well, as was the warm smell in her nostrils. She raised
her other hand to stroke one flat cheek, and then an inquisitive nose as
the far horse presented himself for introductions. "A little," she said.

"Not much to this, so long as you're not one of those who're automatically frightened of something bigger'n they are," said the woman.
"Follow along behind me; keep close. I'll have an eye back for you.
Shout if you get stuck behind a wagon—not that I'll hear you," and she
grinned again. "You can't get too lost—stay on the main road, it ends at
the Gold House's doors, and then you follow the horse droppings to the
barn. That's not true. Redthorn will sweep up himself if there's no one
else, but Jed's really missed. If you get to the Gold House doors the horses

will take you the rest of the way; they'll be thinking of dinner. That one's Tessa, and the pushy one is Blackear. Oh," she said in an obvious afterthought, "my name's Lilac. What's yours?"

There was a longish pause. "Call me Deerskin. She's Ash."

BLACKEAR HAD A SLIGHT TENDENCY TO WALK ON her heels, but in general the horses were a lot less upset by the city bustle than she was. It was midmorning by the time they passed the city gates, and the traffic was so heavy that they were sometimes jostled by the simple press of too many bodies in too little space. The horses bore it patiently, though Blackear shook his head up and down and flattened his nostrils and looked fierce; but Lissar found her breath coming hard and her heat beating too fast.

Ash stuck to her so closely it was as if they were tied together; the big dog had often to take a quick leap forward to avoid being stepped on by one horse or another— once directly between Lissar's legs, which was almost a disaster, since she was too tall to fit through. But the horses stopped, and Tessa watched mildly and Blackear interestedly while the two smaller creatures sorted themselves out; and then they had to hurry to avoid being swept too far away from Lilac and her charges, going steadily before them.

Lissar realized eventually that, far from being unduly crowded, most of the other people on the road were giving her and Lilac extra berth; in recognition, she assumed, of the king's horses. She was wryly grateful, and stayed as well between Tessa and Blackear as possible; if they were accustomed to it, let them take the bumps and blunders.

They stopped twice to water the horses and let them rest; once at an inn, where an ostler came out with hay and grain and a girl with a plate of sandwiches. "You're not Jed," she said, accusingly, to Lissar.

"Give that girl a medal," said Lilac. "Jed's got a broken ankle. It'll heal; what about your brain? If she knows which end of a bridle to hang onto, why do you care?" The girl blushed angrily, and disappeared inside. "Jed's already got a girl-friend," said Lilac cheerfully.

Lissar ate three sandwiches and fed two to Ash. Lilac wandered away presently in what looked like an aimless fashion, but a second plate of sandwiches—this one brought by a young boy—appeared shortly after. Lissar ate another one, and fed two more to Ash.

Afternoon was drawing toward evening, and Lissar's head was spinning with exhaustion and noise and strangeness and smells and crowding by the time she woke up enough to stop before she ran into the hindquarters of Lilac's pair. Tessa and Blackear had prudently halted a step or two before, and it was the drag against her shoulders that awoke her to her surroundings. They were halted at another gate, where a doorkeeper flicked a glance at Lissar and at Ash, tried to suppress his obviously lively curiosity, smiled, and nodded them through.

"You look worse than I feel," said Lilac a few minutes later. They had brought their horses to their stalls, unhooked the leadlines, and let them loose. Lissar was in the stall with Tessa, trying to decide which of the many buckles on the headstall she needed to unfasten to get it off without merely taking it to bits. Two, she saw, as Lilac did it. It was hard to focus her eyes, and she couldn't stand still without leaning against somthing. "D'you want to skip supper? You can talk to Redthorn in the morning, and eat breakfast twice."

Lissar nodded dumbly. Lilac led her up what felt like several thousand stairs to a little room with . . . all she saw was the mattress. She didn't care where it was. She lay down on it and was asleep before Ash was finished curling up next to her and propping her chin on her side.

Eighteen

There was a window, because she awoke in daylight. Ash had her neck cramped at an impossible angle and was snoring vigorously. Lissar staggered upright and leaned out the window. It was still early; she could tell by the light and the taste of the air and the silence. She was in a small bare corner of a long attic-looking room full of boxes and dusty, more mysterious shapes. She looked around for a moment, let her eyes linger on the snoring Ash, and then left quietly, closing the door behind her. In the unlikely event of Ash's waking up voluntarily, she didn't want her wandering around; she didn't know what the rules of this new place were. She'd come back in a little while to let her out-doors.

She met a young man at the foot of the stairs (which were still long, even going down them after a night's sleep) who stared at her blankly for a moment. His face cleared, and he said, "You must be Deerskin. I'll show you where the women's washroom is. Breakfast's in an hour. You want to clean some stalls?" he said hopefully; but his gaze rested on the white deerskin dress and his expression said, I doubt it.

She washed, let Ash out, and cleaned two stalls before breakfast, Testor having demonstrated one first. "It's not like it takes skill. You heave the dung out with your pitchfork"—he did so—"leaving as much of the bedding behind as possible. Then you sort of poke around"—he did so—"looking for a wet spot. Then," he said, each word punctuated by stab-and-lift, "you fluff everything up." He cleaned six stalls to her two. "May the gods be listening," said Lilac, when she saw. "Testor, you pig, couldn't you have found her a pair of boots? Nobody should have to muck stalls barefoot."

"I never noticed," said Testor sheepishly.

Ash, released from the attic (or rather reawakened and hauled forth), made herself implausibly small and fitted under Lissar's chair at breakfast, although her waving tail, which uncurled itself as soon as Lissar began dropping toast and sausages under the table, made walking behind her treacherous. There were eighteen of them at the table, including the limping Jed; and Redthorn sat at the head.

Everyone wanted to know where Lissar and Ash had come from; but these questions evaporated so quickly when Lissar showed some distress that she guessed there must be other secrets among the company, and she felt hopeful that perhaps here they would let you become yourself in the present if you wished to leave your history behind. She felt the hope and wondered at it, because she knew it meant that she wished to find a place here in the yellow city, where she was uncomfortably walking the streets and alarmed by the number of people, wished to find a place so that she could stay. Stay for what purpose? Stay for how long?

Redthorn did ask her bluntly if she had any particular skills; but he looked at her kindly even when she said in a small voice that she did not. I can run thirty miles in a day and then thirty miles the day after that; I can hit a rabbit five times out of seven with a flung stone; I can survive a winter in a mountain hut; I can survive. . . . The thought faltered, and she looked down at her white deerskin dress, and rubbed her fingers across her lap. Her fingers, which had just introduced another sausage under her chair, left no grease-mark on the white surface.

She looked up sharply for no reason but that the movement might break the thread of her thoughts; and saw a dozen pairs of eyes instantly averted. The expressions on the faces varied, and she did not identify them all before courtesy blanked them out again. Curiosity she understood, and wariness, for the stranger in their midst and no mutual acquaintance to ease the introduction. She was startled by some of the other things she saw: wistfulness . . . longing . . . hope. A glimpse of some other story she saw in one pair of eyes; a story she did not know if she wished to know more of or not.

She moved her own eyes to look at Lilac, spearing a slab of bread with her thov, and Lilac glanced up at just that moment, meeting her eyes straightforwardly. There was nothing in her gaze but herself; no shadows, nor shards of broken stories; nothing she wanted to make Lissar a part of; the smile that went with the look was similarly kind and plain and open. Lissar was Lissar—or rather she was Deerskin—Lilac was willing to wait on the rest. Lissar smiled back.

The consensus was that while Redthorn could find work for her, at least till Jed was active again, she should present herself to the court first. Everyone agreed that the prince would like Ash.

"It's, you know, polite," said Lilac. "I went myself, after about a sennight; I was just curious, if nothing else, there's a king and a queen and a prince and a princess a stone's throw away from you—a stone's throw if you don't mind braining a doorkeeper and breaking a few windows— it's a waste not to go look at 'em, you know? So I did. Got a real bad impression of the prince, though—I told you, he looks eight kinds of vegetable slouched down in some chair of state, covered with dog hair, he's always got a few of the dogs themselves with him and they look better than he does. I keep wondering what he must be like at formal banquets and so on; I know they have 'em. Cofta is easy-going but he still remembers he's a king. But that's no mind really. You'll end up liking him—Ossin—too after you've seen him coming in from running the young hounds for the first time, with burrs in his hair. Clementina's the practical one—that's the queen—lots of people would rather go to her with their problems than the king because she understands things at once and starts thinking what to do about them. Cofta's dreamier, although his dreams are usually true."

"There's a saying," broke in Jed, "that Cofta can't see the trees for the forest, and Clem the forest for the trees."

"Camilla's the beauty," continued Lilac. "It's so unexpected that that family should produce a beauty—the Goldhouses have been squat and dreary-looking for centuries, you can see it in the portraits, and Clem's just another branch of the same family; she and Cofta are some kind of cousins—that they're all struck rather dumb by it. By Camilla. And she's so young that being beautiful absorbs her attention pretty thoroughly. She may grow up to be something; she may not. I don't think anyone knows if she's bright or stupid."

Breakfast was over by then, and Lilac and Lissar were leaning on a post outside the barn, and Lissar was watching out of the corner of her eye, while listening with most of her attention, the bustle of the morning's work at the king's stables. Jed paused beside them when he needed to rest his ankle. "She's probably not even beautiful, you know," he said. "It's just that she's a stunner next to the rest of them. Besides, she's ours, so we like her," and he grinned. He was himself good-looking, and knew it.

"Except for that Dorl," said Lilac. "Since Camilla got old enough, he's started hanging around."

Lissar knew that while Redthorn might well find work for her, she did not belong at the stables. She knew little of horses, though this she might learn, and less, she thought, of getting along with other people; that she feared to learn, although she remembered the hope she felt at the idea of finding a place for herself in the yellow city, which was so very full of people. Choices were choices; that did not mean they were simple ones. But she had not liked the eyes around the breakfast-table.

So she borrowed a brush and comb, and took turns working on her own hair and Ash's. When either of them whined and ducked away too miserably she switched over to the other for a while. Finger-combing was frustrating and time-consuming and she had neglected both of them in the last weeks.

Cofta's general receiving was this afternoon; the sooner she got it over with the better. It would be another three days to wait if she missed today. There were voices in her head again, and not the quiet voice from the mountaintop. These voices were . . . "The king was very handsome and grand, but the queen was the most beautiful woman in seven kingdoms." It was a story she had heard somewhere, but she could not remember where; and trying to remember made her feel tired and weak and confused.

In her mind's eye she was wearing another white dress, not of deerskin, but of silk; and Ash was beside her, but the Ash she was remembering, as her fingers lost themselves in the long cool waves of the skirt, had short fine hair instead of thick curls. Ash? No, she did remember, Ash had grown her heavy coat this last winter, when they had been snowbound for so long. But Ash was not a young dog, a puppy reaching her adulthood and growing her adult coat; she could remember holding the puppy Ash had been in her arms for the first time, and she had been smaller then herself. She remembered the kind look of the man who handed the puppy to her; and she remembered there were a great many other people around. . . .

Perhaps it was a market day, and she had come to town with Rinnol, to whom she had been apprenticed. She opened her hands, laying
the brush down for a moment.

I give you the gift of time, the Lady said.

Her winter sickness had robbed her of so much. What did she even
remember surely that she once had known how to do? Something to
give her some direction to pursue, to seek, a door to open? What did she
know how to do? Nothing. This morning she had discovered that while
she understood the theory and purpose of stall-mucking, the pitchfork
did not feel familiar in her hand, as the leather rein had. But neither the
familiarity nor the unfamiliarity led to anything more.

I give the gift of time, the Lady said.

Even the memory of the Lady was fading, and Lissar thought perhaps she had been only a fever dream, the dream following the breaking
of the fever, her own body telling her she would live. What was the gift
of time worth?

As she stared at her hands she saw the white dress again, and there
were bright, flickering lights around her, so many that they made her head
swim, and the noise and perfumes of many splendidly dressed people. . . .

No.

The thought ended, and all thoughts blanked out. She was sitting,
feeling tired and weak and confused, in the small mattress-furnished
end of a long attic room with a steeply pitched roof over one end of the
king's stables. She had only the memory of a memory of when she had
first held Ash in her arms, and the only white dress she remembered
wearing was the one she wore now; and Rinnol was only a name, and
she was not sure if she had been real.

A bad fever it was, it had killed . . .

She could not remember what it had killed, nor did she understand
why her lack of memory seemed more like a wall than an empty space.

But she remembered the touch of the Lady's fingers on her cheek,
and the sound of her voice, bells and running water. She looked down

at her lap, her anxious hands. And there was the deerskin dress. If the Lady had been a dream, then some dreams were true.

She picked up the hairbrush again. Ash, watching the brush, re-tired into the shadows of the opposite end of the room and tried to look like dust and old wooden beams.

Nineteen

L ilac went with her far enough to ensure that she would not get lost. There was a stream of people, narrow but steady, going the same way they were. Lilac knew the doorkeepers and had a friendly word for each of them, accompanied by the same clear, straightforward look that had rescued Lissar that morning at breakfast—and, she thought, had first weighed and considered her at the water cistern.

"I'll leave you here," Lilac said at last, at the end of one hall. "You can't miss it from here. Straight through those silly-looking doors"— they were carved as if the open entry were a monster's roaring mouth— "and then look around. There'll be a group of ordinary-looking folk off to one side, and a lot of unordinary folk wandering around trying to look important. You go stand with the first lot." She grinned. "I'd stay with you a little and watch the show, but I've skipped enough work for one day. Redthorn is a good fellow, but you put your hours in or he won't keep you."

Lissar was finding it hard to see; she blinked, but as soon as her eyes were open, she saw . . . two different pictures, one superimposed upon the other. She could see the monster-mouth doorway, and the friendly, casual doorkeepers, who seemed not to lose nor fear losing any of their dignity by speaking to all the mixture of people that passed in and out. Through this scene or over it she saw another, taller, plainer doorway, with guards standing by it, dressed in golden uniforms with breastplates bright enough to be mirrors; and a doorkeeper so haughty that he seemed grander than most of the stately, expensively dressed people he permitted to pass through the doors; two flunkies stood at his elbows, tense with watching for his orders.

"Thank you," she said to Lilac, blinking again. "I'm sure I'll find the way from here."

"Are you feeling quite well?" Lilac asked abruptly. "You've gone pale." She touched Lissar's arm. "Did you get a touch of heatstroke yesterday? Or maybe Cala's sausages don't agree with you. Gods only know what all she puts into them."

Lissar shook her head—gingerly, still blinking. "No. I'm just—still not accustomed to so many people."

Lilac looked at her a moment longer, and dropped her hand. "I still wish you'd let me loan you some shoes. Barefoot before the king and queen!" She shook her head, but she was smiling again.

Lissar murmured, "I like to know where I'm walking. In shoes I'm always walking on shoes."

"Well, it identifies you as a stranger, anyway, and strangers are often exotic. But it makes you look like you have no friends. Now remember, come back to the stables tonight, whatever happens. We won't keep you in the boxroom forever."

Lissar nodded, and Lilac, after looking at her anxiously a moment longer, turned away.

"Lilac—"

Lilac, who had moved a few steps away, stopped at once and turned back.

"What do you call them, the king and queen, I mean? Your— your"—the word fell out of her mouth—"splendor?" It tasted ill, as if the name were an insult, and for a moment she braced herself for anger, but Lilac answered easily enough.

"You can, but it will brand you worse than your feet. Call them 'your greatness.' 'Splendor' is unfashionable here. Like lap-dogs."

Lissar nodded again, and made her way down the hall, to the yawning doors. One of the keepers said to her cordially, "Welcome. You are here for the general receiving?"

Lissar nodded, hoping it was not necessary to speak. Evidently it was not; the doorkeepers were accustomed to ordinary folks' stage fright upon the prospect of being introduced to royalty. "Go straight in; you will see there is a place to wait. You will have your turn; do not worry. The king and queen see everyone who comes. Not only the prince is here today, but the princess, and the Curn of Dorl," he added, as if she would be glad to hear this; she smiled a little at his tone.

With her smile, he seemed to focus on her at last, to forget his prepared announcement for a moment; and his eyes swept over her, her white hair, black eyes, deerskin dress, bare feet, silver-fawn dog; and something came into his face, something like what she had seen in the faces of Lilac's fellows, and again she did not want to understand, to guess at a name for it. She turned her own eyes away, and went through the door.

She was aware of a number of things simultaneously, too many things, and this confused her. She was still more accustomed to being among crowds of trees than crowds of people, and she was unaccustomed to the pointless (it seemed to her) movement and gestures, the purposeless chattering of human crowds. She remembered the forest, the mountains, with longing, where one day was much like the next, where the priorities were simple and plain: water, food, warmth, defense. Sound had meaning in the wild; as also did smell. She felt suffocated by the smells here, perfume and tobacco and too-rich food.

There was something else as well; with every breath and step she expected to see and hear . . . something other than what she saw and heard; yet her expectation was always a little before or behind her thought, and she could never identify it. It made her feel off-balance, as if she were walking on the swaying limb of a tree instead of on solid earth. Just now, for example, as she stepped through the door, she lifted her eyes to see the portrait at the end of the long room . . . and yet this was a square room, and there were no portraits; tapestries of hunting scenes hung on the walls, interspersed with sconces and niches. What portrait? And why was the absence of an imaginary portrait such a relief?

She did not know, and yet her eyes would not quite focus on what lay around her now, even as her mind could not quite bring into recognition what her eyes looked for.

She shook her head and moved cautiously to her left. The blaze of colors—the density of perfumes—on her right told her that this was not where the common supplicants waited. There was quite a little group of the latter, smelling reassuringly human, and so she had some time to look around her before it was her turn to present herself to the king and his family.

She found them first. The royal family sat on a dais near the center of the room—a little nearer the back wall, where tall doors opened and closed beneath the sconces and between the tapestries, than to the single huge door by which she had entered. A series of tall chairs stood on the dais, but she could identify the king and queen by their attitude as well as by the fact of their chairs being the tallest and most central. She identified the prince next, for his location at the king's right hand, and by the long narrow dog-face poking out from behind his chair. Without Lilac's description she might have guessed that the young man at the queen's left must be the prince, for he sat and looked about him in a

more princely manner. Between the queen and the young man sat a
young girl. Her cushioned chair was backless, and yet she sat straight
and still and poised; and there was a golden circlet upon her head,
which declared her the princess. The prince was bare-headed.

The receiving moved briskly. She believed that the king and queen
did listen to each of their subjects, however humble both in appearance
and in the tale each had to tell; even at this distance she could see the
expressiveness of their faces, hear the responsive tone of their voices
when they asked questions or made rulings. Mostly, she thought, the
rulings were popular; most sets of shoulders on the people leaving the
royal presence were square and relieved.

She wished the rumble of conversation around her would diminish
that she might hear what was said around the dais. It was not that the
voices of those she wanted to listen to were so far away or so soft; it was
that she could not distinguish one voice from the next. She could only
listen to all of them at once and therefore understand nothing. This was
a knack, she thought, one that she had perhaps had in her old life; it
would come back to her. Meanwhile she took in, without wanting to,
the tale of the old woman behind her and her sickly only son, and the
tale of the old woman with her, whose previous husband had come back
from the dead, as she had supposed, and not to wish ill upon the living
since it now seemed he was living, but she had liked him better dead, for
he was a ne'er-do-well and her second husband suited her much better,
and she wished to keep him. These voices fell the nearest upon her ear,
and she could not turn her listening away from them.

Ash had stayed quietly at her side, pressed up against her, her wide
brown eyes moving quickly, her fleethound's muscles vibrating faintly at
all the tempting or dubious shadows and sudden bursts of motion; but
she was no longer a puppy, and not only her own dignity but her person's demanded she stay where she was.

As the crowd before her thinned, Lissar could see the folk on the
dais more clearly. She liked the queen's brightness of eye, the king's

ready smile; she liked that both of them were quietly dressed (not all of their court were so modest); she liked that they seemed to speak no more than was necessary. She liked that neither of them was handsome.

The young man to the queen's left was handsome. His hair was thick and curly, his eyes large and brilliant, his lashes long, his hands slender and graceful. Lissar could see the women, young and old, look at him when they went to address the king and queen; and they looked long and longingly. The young man looked back, smiling, without arrogance, but with a kind of self-consciousness that Lissar did not like. He rarely spoke, and then only if the king or queen spoke to him first.

The princess was not beautiful in the common way, but she drew the eye and then held it. There was something about her, as if she were always poised on the brink of doing something surprising and wonderful; an air as if she too believed she were about to do something surprising and wonderful. Sitting so close to the beautiful young man neither put her out of her composure, nor put her in the shade of his more predictable beauty. She, too, spoke only when the queen or king addressed her first, but she looked searchingly at every supplicant, and her clear face said that she had opinions about everything she heard, and that it was her proud duty to think out those opinions, and make them responsible and coherent.

The prince spoke as little as possible, and there were long pauses before his answers, if a question was addressed to him. But she noticed that everyone, including the king and queen, paid sharp attention when he did speak, and her impression was that his words on more than one occasion had significant influence on the outcome of the particular situation under discussion. This was, she thought, reassuring, as there was so little at all princely in his demeanor.

He was probably tall, though it was difficult to be sure, for he hung in his chair as if he rested on the middle of his spine instead of his pelvis; and he sprawled over one arm of the chair as well, his head negligently propped on one fist. His hair, though thick, was inclined to be lank, his eyes were a little too small, his nose a little too square, his chin a little too large—as was his waistline. His hands were big and broad, and either of his boots looked long enough for a yerig to den in. As she was thinking this, he uncrossed one leg from the other and stomped that foot on the floor; she startled, as if he had known what she was thinking, and her involuntary movement, for some reason, among all the gaudy motion of the court, caught his eye.

It was almost her turn; perhaps he had been looking her way already, searching longingly for the end of the queue, the end of this afternoon's work. He looked, and his gaze paused. She knew what he saw: a black-eyed, white-haired woman in a white deerskin dress; she was an exotic figure, enough taller than the average that she stood out even before the oddity of her clothing (and bare feet) might be remarked. And she was growing accustomed to the way other people seemed to leave a little space around her; it was no different from her feeling separate from the rest of humanity, though she had no name for what the separation meant or was made of. And, whatever the truth of it was, she was glad to be spared the closest proximity of the crowd. Then the woman ahead of her stepped forward, and Lissar stood next in line, and the prince saw Ash.

He straightened up in his chair then, and she saw that he was tall; she also saw that he was capable of enthusiasm, and not so sluggish as she would have first guessed. His eyes brightened, and he shoved his hair back from his forehead. He was paying no attention whatsoever to the woman now telling her story.

With his motion, two long narrow heads rose from behind his chair; or rather, the one she had already noticed rose as the dog sat up, and a second head appeared around the shoulder of the first. One was fawn-colored, a little more golden than the silvery Ash; the other was brindle, with a white streak over its muzzle, continuing down its chin, throat and chest. The two looked first in response to their master's interest, and then they too saw Ash. Ash went rigid under Lissar's hand.

The king and queen said something to the woman before them, and she bowed, slowly and deeply, and made her way to the door all the supplicants left by, different from the one they had entered, a smaller and simpler door, as if exiting was a much easier, less complex and less dangerous matter than was the feat of going in in the first place. It was Lissar's turn, and she had heard nothing of what had just occurred between the woman next to her in line and the king and queen, for she had been distracted by the prince and his dogs. Now she had to go forward without the reassurance of seeing someone else do it first. She walked forward.

The prince's eyes were on her dog, the king's on her dress, and the queen's on her feet. She did not notice where the handsome young man's eyes rested, or the princess's, or if perhaps they might have found her too dismaying an object to look at straight at all. Her bare feet were silent on the glossy floors, against which even the softest shoes were liable to tap or click; Ash's nails were well worn down from the many leagues she had travelled with her person, and so she too made no sound. Lissar felt that the whole court had fallen silent though she knew this was not true; but a little bubble of silence did enclose the dais. The two dogs rose fully to their feet and came to stand by the prince's chair; an almost negligent wave of his big square hand, however, and they stopped where they were, although their tails and ears were up. Ash was Lissar's shadow, and she stopped when Lissar stopped, but Lissar kept her hand on her shoulder, just to reinforce her position. She bowed, still touching her dog.

"Welcome to the yellow city," said the king in a friendly voice. "I say welcome, for I have not seen you before, and I like to think that I see most of my subjects more than once in their lifetimes. New you are at least to this our city, I think."

"Yes, your greatness, and to your country as well; and so I thank you for your greeting." Lissar hesitated, uncertain how to proceed. "I—I was told that you would hear anyone who presented herself to you. I—have little to present. But I—think I would like to stay here, if I could, and so I need work."

"What can you do?" said the prince, not unkindly. The handsome young man laughed, just a little, gently, and at that moment Lissar decided she disliked him. Her eyes moved in his direction and she noticed the princess sitting straitly on her bench, and thought that for the moment she did not look poised, but stiff, as if her backbone had turned to iron. She thought, The princess does not like the handsome young Curn of Dorl either: but what does she think of her brother?

She looked at the prince as she answered honestly: "I do not know what I can do." She did not know what inspired her to add: "But I like dogs."

"Where is yours from?" said the prince. "If it were not for her long coat, I would say she is a line of my breeding."

"Ossin," said the king.

The prince smiled, unabashed, and shrugged, as if to say that a dog was a dog and he could not help himself. The Curn of Dorl made a little catlike wriggle in his chair, and for a moment his beautiful profile presented itself to Lissar, and out of the corner of her eye she caught the curl of his lip; but she remained facing the prince.

The humor faded from Ossin's face and now she realized that he looked tired and sad, and that the droop of his shoulders as he slumped forward again was of a weary burden. He said softly, "One of my best bitches died this morning. She left a litter of puppies a few hours old. The pups haven't a hope unless they are nursed most carefully; they probably haven't a hope even with nursing, but I dislike giving up without a struggle—and their mother was a very special dog. There are eight of them. If any survive it will have been worth almost any price to me. Would you care to play wet-nurse? It will be disgusting work, you know; they'll be sick at both ends right up through weaning time, most likely, if any should live so long, and you won't get much sleep at first."

"I will do it," said Lissar, "but you will have to teach me how."

Twenty

That was the end of her audience; she bowed, and if she did not include the Curn in her courtesy, she doubted that anyone noticed but herself. The prince spoke a few words to a servant, who came to Lissar, bowed himself, and said, "If the lady will follow me." Lissar thought to bow again to the dais because the servant did; somewhere she recalled that one always bows last thing before leaving the royal presence, even if one has already bowed several times previously. Somehow she remembered this from the wrong angle, as if she were sitting on the dais. . . . She followed the servant, leaning a little on Ash as a brief wash of dizziness assailed her.

The servant led her to a small antechamber off a vast hall similar to the one she had entered by. She sat down when the man bowed her to a chair, but she was not comfortable, and as soon as he left the room she stood up again, and paced back and forth. Ash remained sitting next to the chair with her chin propped on its seat; but she kept an eye and an ear toward Lissar. Lissar was thinking, I have been in the wilds too long, this great building oppresses me. Why do I remember sitting while some- one bows to me? I am an herbalist's apprentice—an herbalist's apprentice who has lost most of her memory to a fever she was not clever enough to cure herself of.

And yet her own thought rang strangely in her head, for a voice very like the one that had spoken to her on the mountain, the voice that had left her without guidance since she and Ash had come down from the wild lands, said, *It is not that you have been in the wilderness too long.* But this brought her no comfort; instead she felt angry, that she was permitted to understand so little; that even her own mind and memory spoke warily, behind barricades, to each other, without trust; that her guiding voice was not to be relied on, but spoke like an oracle, in riddles that she must spend her time and thought to unravel, to little effect.

She began to feel caged, began to feel that there was something searching for her; perhaps the creature whose gullet led to the royal receiving-room would tear itself free of its bondage and come looking for her. She heard a distant rumble like roaring, she heard a swift pant- ing breath.

She started violently when a long nose was thrust into her hand, but as she looked down into Ash's brown eyes she recognized the pant- ing breath as her own. Deliberately she slowed her breathing, and she had regained her self-possession when the servant re-entered the room, another servant on his heels, bearing a small table, and yet another ser- vant behind him, carrying a tray. Lissar, standing, still breathing a little too hard, barefoot, in the middle of the velvet-hung room, longing for her mountains, suddenly laughed, and then the roaring in her ears went away entirely. With the laugh she felt strangely whole and healthy again.

She looked with interest at the plate of fruit and small cakes on the tray, and was spilling crumbs down herself (which Ash swiftly removed as soon as they touched the floor) when the prince entered without warning.

She stopped chewing, and bowed, half a cake still in one hand. "By all the gods and goddesses, high, low, wandering or incarnate, never bow to me unless I'm pinned to that blasted chair in that blasted room," he said feelingly, "or, I suppose, if my parents are present, or my sister— she's suddenly gotten very conscious of her standing—that's Dorl's doing, drat him, and she doesn't even like him. Pardon me," he said, his voice a little calmer. "All my staff knows not to bow to me, that's my first instruction, but usually—I hope—handed out a little more graciously. It has not been a pleasant afternoon, and I was up all night. I didn't want to believe that Igli would let herself die on me.

"But today has been worth it—even with Dorl there—to have someone to take care of the puppies. My regular staff are all falling in each other's way to avoid it; they all have better sense than I do, and it's a grim business watching little creatures die when you're wearing yourself out trying to keep them alive."

He was not as tall as she had expected, looking up at him and his big booted feet on the dais from her place on the floor; but he was broad-shouldered and solid, and his feet were still big, even looking down at them from standing height instead of having them at chest level. "Come on, then, I'll introduce you to them."

He picked up a piece of fruit from the table and paused a moment, looking at Ash. He frowned, not an angry frown but a puzzled one. "It's true, I don't know northhounds much, but she looks so much like another bitch of mine who died a few years ago—never threw a bad pup, all her children are terrific. She was my first really top-quality dog, and when I was still a kid I gave too many of her get away to impress people—too dumb, or obsessed, to realize that most people, particularly the so-called nobility, who are, I suppose, obliged to have other things on their minds, don't know the difference between a great dog and an ordinary one. Even those who can tell a good dog from a bad one. I look at yours and I could swear . . ." He shook his head.

Lissar cast her mind back, but in the anxious, pleading, elusive way her fragmented memory now presented itself to her, she could not remember exactly how Ash had come to her. She remembered the kind man handing her an armful of eager puppy. . . . She remembered wearing a black-ribboned dress, as if she were in mourning. . . . She looked down at her dog, who, conscious of her person's gaze, moved her own from this interesting new person who smelled so fetchingly of other dogs, to meet Lissar's eyes. Her ears flattened fractionally. In public, on her dignity in the presence of a stranger, she was not going to do anything so obvious as wag her tail, or rear up on her hind legs, put her paws on Lissar's shoulders, and lick her face.

"She was a gift," Lissar said finally. "I do not know where she came from," she added truthfully. It was hard to think of her life before Ash, as if trying to remember life before walking or speech. She knew, theoretically, that such a period existed in her history, but it was very vague, as if it had happened to someone else. As if the rest of my life were not vague, she thought, in a little spasm of bitterness.

"Wherever she came from, she is obviously your dog now," said the prince, who could read dogs and their people, and knew what the look Ash was giving Lissar meant, even without tail-wagging.

He had idly eaten the remaining cakes on the tray, and now he went through the door. Lissar followed with Ash at her heels; just outside the two dogs that had sat behind the prince's chair sprang to attention. Ash stopped and the other two froze; heads and tails rose, toplines stiffened. Ossin looked from one to the next. "Nob, Tolly, relax," he said, and tapped the nearer on the skull with one gentle finger. "I hope yours isn't a great fighter," he added, as his two moved forward on only slightly stiff legs.

Lissar thought of the black dog that had chased them, and said nothing.

There was some milling about—Ash did some extremely swift end-to-end swapping when she felt the two strangers were taking unfair advantage of their number—and Lissar noticed with interest that Ash was standing a little ahead and the other two a little behind when all three chose to remember the presence of human beings. "Hmm," said the prince, doubtless noticing the same thing; and strode off. Lissar and the dogs followed.

They went down a dozen hallways, took two dozen left and right turns, and crossed half a dozen courtyards. Lissar gave up trying to remember the way, and gave herself instead to looking around her, at people and rooms and sky and paving stones, and horses and wagons, and feet and shoes and the size and shape of burdens and the faces of the people and beasts who carried them; and the end result was that she still felt hopeful about the place she had come to.

Many of the people hailed the prince, and many bowed to him, but she noticed that the ones whose greetings he answered the most heartily bowed the most cursorily. There were other dogs, but both Ash and the prince's dogs disdained to notice them.

The kennels smelled of warm dog, straw, and meat stew. Several tall silent dogs approached to investigate Ash; but Ash, apparently feeling that two at a time was enough, raised her hackles and showed a thin line of teeth, and growled a growl so low it was more audible through the soles of the feet than the ears. "Con, Polly, Aster, Corngold, away," said the prince, as carelessly as he had gestured at the two dogs behind his chair; and the dogs departed at once, though there was much glancing over shoulders as they trotted soundlessly back into the kennel hall.

The prince strode after them without pause; Nob and Tolly circled Ash carefully to stay at his heels. Lissar and Ash followed a little more warily. The floor was hard-packed earth, and well-swept; Lissar thought

of the double handful she had combed out of Ash that morning, and
wondered how often someone swept here, even with short-haired dogs.
The hall was lined with half-doors, the tops mostly open and the bottoms mostly shut. One wall by the wide doorway was covered with
hooks from which hung a wide assortment of dog-harness.

The roof was much higher on one side than the other, and the high
side held a line of windows, so that the entire area was flooded with
light (Lissar was faintly reassured to see a few short dog-hairs floating in
the sunbeams). The dogs that had come out to look them over were re-
tiring through one or two of the open half-door bottoms; one disappeared through a tall open arch, and Lissar heard: "It is not mealtime, as
you perfectly well know, Corngold! Get out of here or I'll lock you up."
Corngold, looking not the least abashed, trotted out again, exchanged
looks with Ash, and went off after the others.

Ossin paused and opened the top of one of the half-doors. Lissar
stepped forward and looked over the bottom half. There was a small, pa-
thetically small, rounded, lumpy pile in one corner of the small room,
which was ankle-deep in straw. A small window—this room was on the
low side of the hall, and the door ran up to the ceiling—let sunlight in,
a long yellow wedge falling across the floor and brightening the white-
and-brindle rumps of a couple of the tiny puppies in the pile. Lissar
could see blanket-ends protruding from under tiny heads and feet.

"There they are," said the prince sadly. "I thought of putting a bitch
in with them, but my two most reliable mothers have litters of their
own. By the time I found out if one of the others would accept them and
start producing milk, if the answer was no, it would probably be too late
to try again."

Lissar softly pulled the bolt on the lower half-door and stepped
inside. She knelt down beside them and touched a small back, ran a finger down the fragile spine. The puppy made a faint noise, half murmur,
half squeak, a minuscule wriggle, and subsided. She looked around. Ash
was standing in the doorway with a look of what Lissar guessed to be

consternation on her face; Nob and Tolly were nowhere to be seen. There was a water dish with a piece of straw floating in it, near the puppy-heap. The little run was very clean.

"That water dish is doing a lot of good," said the prince irritably. "Jobe—has anyone tried to feed Ilgi's litter?"

Lissar heard footsteps stop. "Hela tried, but I don't think she got too far." The voice was that of the messenger who is not completely sure that his message won't get him killed.

"Oh, get out of here, I'm not asking you to be wet-nurse," said the prince in the same tone. The footsteps began again, quicker this time, and then a pause, and a voice, as if thrown back over a shoulder, "There's six left."

"There were nine born, live and perfect," said Ossin, and there was both anger and grief in his voice. "While they're asleep, I'll show you where your room is—after I ask Berry what's available. Cory's old room, I expect."

Lissar shook her head. "I'll sleep here, if you don't mind, and I have no possessions to keep. Ash will stay with me." She looked up, sitting on her folded legs; the prince was looking at her with an expression she could not read. It might have been surprise, or relief. It was not wistfulness or longing; it might have been hope. "They will have to be fed every couple of hours anyway," she said. "And kept warm."

The prince shook himself, rather like a dog. "As you wish. Washrooms and baths are that way"—he raised an arm, the hand invisible behind the frame of the door. "Jobe and Hela and Berry can get you anything you need—milk, meal, rags and so on—you and the dogs get the same stew, most of the time, but my dogs eat very well, so it's not a hardship, and the baker is the same one providing bread for my father's table." The prince's smile reappeared, and fell away again immediately. "I have to go attend some devils-take-it banquet tonight, and I will probably be trapped till late. I'll come by when I can, to see how you are doing."

Lissar was aware that his anxiety was for the puppies, not for her, but she said sincerely, "I thank you."

He took a deep breath, and as he turned and the sunlight fell fully on his face, she saw how tired he was, remembering that he had said that he had been up all the night before with the bitch he could not save. "I hope I don't fall asleep in the middle of it," he added. "The count is the world's worst bore, and he always wants to tell me his hunting stories. I've heard most of them a dozen times."

After he left, she went out to find someone who would provide her with the requisites for her attempt at puppy care. Jobe was watching for her, and led her through the open archway that Corngold had been earlier turned away from, where he introduced her to Hela and to Berry, who left at once, several dogs in his wake. Jobe was lugubrious and Hela brisk, but they treated her as if she knew what she was doing, which she both appreciated and simultaneously rather wished they would condescend to her instead, if the condescension would provide her with any useful advice.

The puppies were beginning to stir and make small cheeping noises, bumbling blindly through the straw, when she returned, looking for someone who was not there. Twilight was falling; as she sat down cross-legged on the floor with her bowl of warm milk and rags, Jobe appeared with a lantern, which he hung on a hook in the wall inside the door to the puppies' stall. "There's an old fire-pot somewhere," he said. "Hela's gone to look. It would be easier if you could heat your milk here, during the nights, when our fire is banked." "Our" fire burnt in the common-room, where the staff—and most of the dogs, come evening—collected, and there was a pot of stew, firmly lidded in case of inquisitive dogs, simmering there now. "And it would give you a little extra warmth, too, as long as . . ."

"As long as I can prevent the puppies from frying themselves," Lissar answered, and saw the faint look of approval cross his long face as he nodded. "Thank you," said Lissar. "It would be helpful."

Jobe seemed inclined to linger, but hesitated over what he wished to say. "You'll do your best and all that, of course, my lady, but the prince isn't an unfair man. He knows as well as I do you've a hopeless task, and he won't fault you for it. None of us would take it, you know."

Lissar looked up at him, thinking of her bare feet and long plait of hair. "Why do you call me 'my lady'?"

Jobe's expression was of patience with someone who was asking a very old and silly riddle that everyone knows the answer to. "Well, you are one, ain't you? No more than yon bitch is a street cur. They don't generally let people bring livestock to the receiving-hall, you know." He smiled a little at his own joke, and left her.

Twenty-one

Silence fell after he left; she heard the occasional yip—these dogs all seemed to bark as little as Ash did—and the occasional crisp word from a human voice. My lady, she thought. I was only the apprentice to an herbalist. Perhaps this is why the title makes me uncomfortable; I am pretending to be what I am not. But am I not pretending worse than that, in being here at all?

She picked up the nearest puppy, who had blundered up against her foot and was nosing it hopefully. The sounds the puppies made were no louder than rustled straw. She dipped a rag in the milk, and offered it to the puppy, who ignored it, now exploring her fingers. Its squeaks began to sound more anxious and unhappy, and she noticed that the little belly was concave, and the tiny ribcage through the thin hair felt as delicate and unprotected as eggshell. She squeezed the tiny raw mouth open, and dropped the milky rag inside, but the puppy spat it out again immediately, in its uncoordinated, groping way, and would not suck.

She paused, cradling the pup in one hand. I cannot fail so immediately and absolutely, she thought. If the puppy will not suck, I must pour it down his throat somehow. I wonder what Jobe meant when he said Hela hadn't "gotten too far"? Had she gotten anywhere at all?

The pup was now lying flat on her open hand, as if it had given up its search; but its little mouth opened and closed, opened and closed. The other puppies were struggling among themselves, some of them falling over the edge of the blanket and trying to propel themselves on their stomachs with dim, swimming motions of their tiny legs.

One very bold one found Ash, and was making as much noise as it could, convinced that it had found what it was looking for, if only she would cooperate. It clambered at her front feet, mewing insistently, while poor Ash stood, her back arched as high as it would go and her four feet tightly together, pressing herself as far into the corner by the closed door as she would fit, desperately willing this importunate small being away, but too well-mannered to offer any force against anything so small and weak.

Lissar's eye fell on the straw that made up the puppies' bedding; or rather on the straws. She picked up a stout, hollow one, blew through it once, then stopped, sucked up a strawful of milk, held it by the pressure of her tongue over the end in her mouth, gently squeezed the puppy's jaws open again, placed the straw in his mouth, and released the stream. The puppy looked startled; several drops of milk dribbled out of the sides of his mouth, but Lissar saw him swallow. And, better yet, having swallowed, he lifted his little blind face toward the general direction the straw-and-milk had come from.

None of the puppies would suck the milky rag, but she squirted strawsful of milk down them all. Even with day-old puppies it took several squirts before Lissar was satisfied with the roundness of their small bellies. Her lips trembled with exhaustion and her tongue was sore by the end of their supper, and she'd worn out several hollow straws, but at least she had not failed her first attempt. The fed puppies were willing to lie more or less contentedly in her lap and around her knees, and Ash, having been rescued from that very dangerous puppy, had relented enough to sit down, although she would not go so far as to lie down. Her eyes were fixed unwaveringly on the puppies in case one should make threatening gestures at her again.

There was a little milk left in the bottom of the bowl, and quite a bit of it on, rather than in, the puppies, Lissar, and the surrounding straw; but there was no doubt that six little bellies were distended with the majority of it. The puppies bestirred themselves erratically to make the small vague gestures at one another that in a few weeks would be rowdy play, including growls, pounces, savage worrying, and squeals from the losers. At the moment they looked like mechanical toys whose springs were almost wound down, and since their eyes were not yet open, even the most daring of them kept losing track of what it was doing.

Lissar looked up to a small noise and saw Hela leaning over the half-door. "There's supper for you any time you want it. I congratulate you on your empty bowl; I didn't get so far."

Lissar held up her last straw, which looked rather the worse for wear. "Hollow," she said; her cheek muscles were stiff, and speaking was awkward. "Mostly they swallowed instead of spitting it up." She rubbed her face. "I'm sore."

"Clever," said Hela, but something in her voice made Lissar look up at her again, and there was that expression, much like what she had seen in so many of the faces she had looked at since she came down from the mountains: something like awe, something like wistfulness, something like wariness.

The prince had not looked at her like that. She wasn't sure, as she thought about it, that she had registered with him at all; he was more interested in Ash than in her human companion. Lilac hadn't looked at her that way either. She thought, Why should I care? I need not care. I have a purpose—these people have given me a purpose—and that is all that matters. I need only be grateful that they have welcomed a stranger. "I have to hope it went into their stomachs and not their lungs—but they wouldn't suck." She gestured at the rejected rag.

She dropped her gaze to the mostly now-sleeping puppies, and smiled. Tomorrow she would find out how to make her way back to the stables and tell Lilac what had become of her. One puppy was attempting to worry the hem of her dress. She touched its tiny blunt muzzle with a finger, and it turned its attention to her fingertip, chewing on it with soft naked gums. "They don't look anything like fleethounds," said Lissar. "You'd never know."

"They're always like that at first," said Hela. "All puppies look very much alike when they're just born, only bigger or smaller."

"It has no legs at all, or almost," said Lissar, picking up the one who was failing to make progress with her finger. She held it up, and its stubby legs waved feebly. "And its head is square."

"In a fortnight you'll start to see the head and the legs," said Hela. "Er—haven't you raised dogs before?"

"No," said Lissar. "I've only raised Ash, and she was weaned when I got her. She looked like what she was going to be, only smaller, except for her feet."

"Ah," said Hela. "That explains how Ossin convinced you to take this job—begging your pardon—none of us who knows better will do it."

Lissar nodded, setting the doomed puppy down to huddle among its equally doomed siblings. She was beginning to wish that people would stop reminding her quite so often that she had taken on a hopeless project. "I know. But I have no other job, and—and I like dogs," realizing as she said it that it was what she had said to the prince in the receiving-hall.

Several expressions crossed Hela's face; among them was a look that said that she expected not to understand, but the final look was one of sympathy. "All the more reason not to want to do it, but we're all glad you're here, so I'll be quiet. Do you know about rubbing their bellies to make their bowels work?"

"No," said Lissar.

"Yes," said Hela, with an inscrutable glance into Lissar's face. "Mum'd do it if she was here. We've lots of blankets—the royal kennels have better laundry service than my whole village back home—I brought you some more. Make it easier for cleaning up."

"Thank you," said Lissar.

"And—er—there's a room for you upstairs, when you want it, and I—er—laid out some clothes for you, a tunic and leggings and—er—boots. If they don't fit, we'll find other ones. Ossin's staff also dresses better than most of my village. We—I—er—thought you won't want to get your . . . dress dirty. That all comes with the job, the room and board and clothing."

"Thank you," said Lissar again, brushing at a milk-spot on her lap. It was still wet. It would bead up as it dried, she knew, and brush right off. A tunic might make her less conspicuous, however, which she would prefer; perhaps it would stop some of the strange looks that came to her; perhaps Hela's natural friendliness would win out over her imposed caution.

"Your bitch has never had puppies, has she?" said Hela.

"No."

"She has that look to her," said Hela, amused. "'What are these things? I don't care! Just take them away!'—How old is she?"

There was a pause. "I'm not sure," Lissar said at last. "I—I have trouble remembering certain things."

Hela flushed to the roots of her hair and dropped her head. "My lady, forgive me," she said in a voice very unlike the one she had used till then; and before Lissar could think of something to say in response, Hela went hastily away. Lissar could hear her quick steps down the main aisle, back toward the common-room.

. . .

WHEN LISSAR FOLLOWED HER A LITTLE LATER
(having produced nothing in response to the belly-rubbing; perhaps
there was a trick to it. It would not do to have succeeded at step one and
failed at step two; she adamently refused to let this happen, even if she
did not see, straight away, what to do about it), conversation stopped as
soon as she appeared, barefoot and silent, in the doorway. Yet she had
heard what they were discussing as she walked past the heaps of sleeping dogs, for whom she must already bear the correct smell of a fellow
pack-member, for none challenged her or Ash. The common-room discussion was of a recent hunt, during which one dog had done particularly well; nothing, Lissar thought, that they should have cared about
her, or anyone, overhearing, nor anything that, in a collection of dog
people, should have broken off upon the entry of another person.

Jobe stood up and served her a bowl of stew, and set another one
down on the floor for Ash. Lissar never quite got over her amazement at
how swiftly and delicately Ash could inhale large amounts of food; it
was like a magic trick, the mystic word is spoken, the hand gesture performed and presto! the food disappears, without a crumb or speck left
behind. Ash looked up hopefully at the bowl in Lissar's hands.

"Come and sit," said a man Lissar did not know. She went and sat,
but she did not stay long; the conversation tried to start up again around
her, but it lurched and stumbled—barely more deft than a day-old
puppy. She set her bowl on the floor for Ash to perform her magic on,
took a hunk of bread and a tall mug of malak—whose name drifted into
her mind as she tasted it for the first time, in, when?—said "good-
night," and left as silently as she had entered. A chorus of "good-night"
followed her, sounding both eager and sad, like a dog who is hoping for
a kind word but doubts its luck. She paused and looked back at them as
they looked at her; and realized that they were not anxious for her to

leave even if they were uneasy in her company. She smiled a little, not understanding, and returned to the puppies' pen.

Some of them in her absence had responded in the desired way to the belly-rubbing, and some cleaning up was in order, since they did not differentiate between one substance, like straw or sibling's body, and the next. Lissar thought, frowning, that she would have to keep track of who needed more belly-rubbing. She sighed; tiredness fell on her suddenly, with the arrival of food in her own belly. She would figure it all out tomorrow.

The fire-pot had arrived while she was at supper, and there was a low, heavy-bottomed jug of milk beside it.

The puppies were all asleep again in their heap, as soon as she set down the cleaned-up ones. She wondered how the ones on the bottom were managing to breathe. She laid out two more of the blankets Hela had brought, for a mattress, and lay down herself. Ash was standing by the closed door in alarm: You don't mean we're spending the night in here with—them?

"Come," said Lissar. "You can lie next to the wall, and I will protect you."

She fell asleep in some anxiety, not knowing how she would awaken to feed the puppies again. They could not be left all night, and she was too tired to remain awake. But her anxiety made her sleep lightly, and the first uncertain mumuring protests from the puppy-heap brought her awake at once, staring around a moment in fright, feeling the ceiling leaning down close to her, not able to remember where she was, or what it was that had awakened her. She staggered upright, the ceiling returning to its normal position, and went to warm the milk. Ash, who could ordinarily not be moved by force once she was comfortably asleep for the night, got up at once and perched near her. Ash had a lot to say about the whole situation, in a low rumbling mutter.

Lissar's cheek muscles were aching before the first puppy was fed; by the sixth she was balancing the pup on her knees because she needed her other hand to keep her lips clamped on the straw. Tomorrow, she told herself fuzzily, without moving her lips, I will find an alternative. The puppies were weaving themselves back into their pile; it became impossible in the dim light to differentiate one puppy from the next. The puppy-heap was one creature, fringed by tails and a surprising number of feet.

She stroked a nearby back. Two of the puppies were discernibly weaker than the other four. She remembered what everyone kept telling her about the pups' future, and the uselessness and duration of her temporary job; what she was doing was only to reassure the prince that his bitch's last litter hadn't automatically been given up on. But she wanted to succeed. She didn't want to be reasonable. She wanted the pups to live. She didn't even want four pups to live; she wanted all of the remaining six.

There was a sudden, surprising rush of heat like anger as she thought this; and, warmed and strengthened by it, she began lifting the puppies up again, one by one, and massaging their bellies. Tomorrow she would ask for an old glove, and cut the fingers off, and make a tiny hole in a fingertip, and pour milk down the puppies' throats that way.

Twenty-two

Lissar woke up very warm. One large dog was knotted up against her back and six tiny dogs who had, by some osmosis, slowly oozed their way the short distance across the floor during the night, were now piled up in a small irregular sausage from her breastbone to her thighs. There were various sounds of protest when she moved; a baritone grumble from behind her and a series of fairylike cheeps from before.

"It's morning," she whispered. "Is everybody still alive?" Everybody was. Her throat relaxed, and there was suddenly more room in her chest for her heart to beat. But the two weak pups had been joined by a third. The worst was a tiny grey bitch, who simply lay limp in Lissar's hand, without moving her head, without making the least fluttering movement with feet or tail. "Don't die," said Lissar, sadly, "don't die": and she was warmed by another swift blaze of anger. "You haven't been alive yet; what did you go and get born for if you're just going to die?"

It was so early there was almost no one else stirring; but Berry was in the common-room grumbling over a shortage of biscuit-meal to make dog breakfasts with, and he found her an old pair of gloves, and a pin to prick with. She took her new supplies back to the puppy pen, sawed off a glove-finger, and prepared to try out her invention. The little grey bitch lay exactly as Lissar had laid her down, looking almost more like a small grey puddle than a dog. She picked her up first.

The pup lay dully in her hand. She weighed so little Lissar felt that if she tossed her into the air, the puppy would float to the ground, whisking gently back and forth like a leaf. Lissar turned her over, cupped her in her hand, and wiggled the little mouth open till she could get the glove-tip inside. The jaw, once open, merely hung slack; the glove-tip would not go in far enough, nor stay once put. Lissar wrestled for a minute or two. The milk only leaked out of the puppy's indifferent mouth. She did not swallow, she did not resist; she did nothing. She lay in the position Lissar had pinned her among her own fingers, the tiny ribcage barely registering the tiniest of breaths.

Lissar lay the glove-finger down, picked up a straw, stared at it, sighed. She thrust the tip in the bowl of milk, sucked it full, thrust the straw down the pup's throat, and let the milk loose. The puppy gasped, coughed, choked—and kicked; the milk all came out again. But the pup was startled; she made a little mewling noise, her blind head trembled, her tiny paws twitched.

Lissar refilled the straw hastily, stuck it not quite as far down the puppy's throat, and released the milk. This time the puppy gasped, choked, kicked—and swallowed. Very little milk reappeared. The puppy swallowed several more strawsful without further complaint; her little belly had a faint new convexity of outline. Lissar laid her down very tenderly.

As predicted deprecatingly by Jobe and Hela, the puppies all developed diarrhea. The first night was the last real sleep Lissar had for ten days. Hela helped sometimes, but it was obvious her heart was not in it, and she avoided handling the puppies herself. She said it was because as few people as possible should handle puppies so young; but Lissar did not think that was the real reason. She was grateful for Hela's help in fetching milk and clean cloths, and cleaning up; but she knew that she and the puppies were still ostracized—and the puppies at least, condemned.

Ossin himself was a more valuable assistant. He had looked in and seen them all sleeping, that first night, and gone quietly away again; but after that he came every day. He had no qualms about touching the pups, although at first the little bodies were so dwarfed by his big hands that she wondered how he could cope with handling anything so small. But he fed them more easily than she did—and praised her ingenuity with straws and glove-fingers, although she knew that these ideas were not new, that her ingenuity was only that she was willing to think about how to keep the pups alive and then put her ideas into practice.

He never spoke a sharp or angry word himself, however sharp Lissar's exhaustion made her, and how much she forgot to whom she spoke, or rather, did not speak, for she was too tired for courtesy. He insisted instead that she not forget herself entirely; he brought her her meals occasionally, when those in the common-room suspected she had missed eating; he sent her off for a nap in the bathhouse ("just don't drown") saying that an hour there would do her more good than an entire night of unbroken sleep.

And once she woke with the horrid awareness that she had slept too long, and saw him with a puppy in one hand and a damp, distended glove-finger in the other; and straw in his hair. He had been there all night; she remembered him bringing her her supper, and how she had sunk down, her head on her arm, to rest for just a few minutes. And now there was early morning creeping through the window.

"All still alive?" she said. It was a reflex. She said these words more often than any others, even when her first words should have been, Your greatness, I am so sorry, why did you not awaken me?

He turned his face toward her, and there was no reproach in it; instead a tired smile curled the corners of his mouth. "Yes," he said, with evident satisfaction, as if her question were the correct response to his presence.

But she was not unaware, and she began to make her belated excuses, whereupon his face closed down and he turned away from her again. "I wish to make your impossible task as nearly possible as—as mortal flesh and blood can. It is I who wished it tried at all, and I who know, none better, that no one will help you but me. I am glad to do it. Here, you"—and he directed his attention to the puppy in his hand, who was attempting to play with the glove-finger instead of nurse from it.

Lissar pushed the hair out of her face, and crawled toward the puppies. Two or three of them now had narrow slits of eye showing between the lids, and most of them were swimming, belly to the floor, fairly actively; occasionally they took a few staggering almost-steps, their little legs crooked out at painful-looking angles, moving like turtles, as if they bore great unwieldy weights on their backs. But there were still two who moved very little, who moved only when they were lifted up for milk, whose heads hung over the palms of the hands that held them if they were not picked up carefully, as if their necks were nothing but bits of string; who would not nurse but needed straws thrust down their throats, who needed the most belly-rubbing and yet simultaneously had the most persistent diarrhea.

Lissar looked at the six of them—all still alive, against the odds—and her heart quailed; there were still long weeks ahead of her before her task could be declared accomplished, success or failure; and if it was over before then it was only because she had absolutely failed. She picked up one of the two smallest puppies, rolling its unprotesting body in her hand, feeling the butterfly heartbeat, and picked up a hollow straw.

Without speaking a word about it, Ossin fell into the habit of spending every other night in the puppy pen; and Lissar got a little more sleep that way, although never again did she embarrass herself by sleeping through the night. The prince stayed sitting up, snoring faintly sometimes as his head dropped to his chest; Lissar lay down, near the wall, with Ash stretched out behind her. Ossin never acknowledged his own regular presence by pressing Lissar to leave the puppies to him and go to her own room, the bed she had never yet slept in; and so Lissar never quite dared protest what he was doing. And at some dim distance she also knew that she appreciated his company, not only for the practical help and human reassurance he provided.

Over the course of every night, wherever the puppy-heap had begun, it rearranged itself to spill over Lissar's hands and feet, or to press against her belly. Ash mellowed to the point where she would not instantly leap to her feet on a puppy's coming in contact with her; but she never offered to let Lissar lie next to the wall either. Lissar woke up sometimes by the sensation of a puppy being gently lifted off her; which meant that the prince had already warmed the milk on the tiny fire-pot, rust-free and freshly blacked, that stood always in the corner of the stall. After this had happened two or three times Lissar woke once to a large shadowy figure reaching down to her, stooped over her, and she sat up with a gasp, throwing herself backwards, against Ash, who yelped.

Ossin straightened up and took a step backwards. "I'm sorry," he said. "It's only me, not a night-monster. We turn them away at the city gates, you know. You can sleep quietly here." He was standing perfectly still, his hands hanging loosely at his sides. She recognized the tone of voice even as it worked on her: he wished to soothe her as he might a frightened dog.

"I—forgive me. I—I must have been having a bad dream, although I . . . don't remember it."

The first three weeks were the worst. Not only was there the persistent fear of one of the weaker ones giving up entirely—and the need therefore to feed them oftener because they would swallow or keep down less, and used it less efficiently than the stronger ones—but as soon as they all seemed more or less thriving for half a day, that was a sure sign that one whose health she had begun to take for granted would suddenly reject its food, or cry and cry and refuse to defecate or to settle down to sleep. Lissar worried also that they would strangle on a broken straw, or a shred of blanket; that one of the bigger puppies would smother one of the weaker ones and she would not notice till too late; that she herself would crush one in her sleep, for none of them had any sense about where they disposed themselves around her. Every time one of the pups coughed she knew it was about to die: that due to her carelessness in thrusting straws down their throats, some milk had gone down the wrong way and produced pneumonia.

But none of them died.

By the end of the first fortnight she had grown accustomed to the sense of trying to climb an avalanche. She still had nightmare fragments during her fragments of sleep; but these nightmares were different from the ones she had had when she and Ash were still alone. These were not about her; and when she woke from them, she had something to do: check the puppies. When she found them all still breathing the sense of release and of peace was so extraordinary that sometimes she sat or lay for several minutes or a quarter hour, thinking of nothing but that her charges were well, and that she was . . . happy. She noticed, but did not pursue the thought, that she felt most content with her world on the nights that Ossin was snoring gently in his corner.

She remembered, as if she would remember a dream, that the first days of the Lady's peace had been much like this; but it was different as well, more complicated; this was a peace of wind or running water rather than a peace of solid rock or quiet ground. It was a contentment of motion, of occupation, instead of stillness: it was a contentment more like the Lady herself.

Sometimes it seemed her contentment was not that at all but a mere physical reaction to the numbness of exhaustion. She awakened when the puppies stirred, and her hands began their work while her brain was too tired to recognize what was going on. The little muffled squeaking noises they made, slowly evolving into recognizable canine yips, reassured her even as they woke her up. Sometimes puppy-noises were part of the nightmares, and then her sleeping self laughed and said, It's only the puppies, and she woke up calmly and sweetly.

These uneasy dreams and these awakenings were so very different from ones that she remembered . . . remembered . . . from before.

And none of the puppies died.

By the end of the third week several of them were almost plump, and walked on their feet instead of paddling on their bellies; and they all had their eyes open, and the grand sweep of breastbone and tucked-up stomach characteristic of all the sighthounds began to be apparent. Some of them were growing coordinated enough to begin knocking their brothers and sisters around. They were developing unmistakable personalities, and with their personalities inevitably came names.

Pur was the biggest, but Ob the most active. Fen and Meadowsweet were still the smallest and weakest. She had not meant to name them, but she could not help herself; and having done so she thought, Let their names be symbols that their lives are worth the keeping. Let them struggle a little the harder, to keep their names. Ferntongue yawned the most ecstatically, and Harefoot, to Lissar's eye, already had longer legs and a deeper girth than any of the rest. She named them, spoke to them using their names, as if the names were charms to keep them safe; she knew it wasn't over, they could still catch some wandering illness that would kill all six of them in a day or a sennight. But she began to have some real hope, irrational and stupid with sleeplessness as it was, that Ossin might have some reward for his stubbornness. She did not think in terms of rewarding her own.

As the weeks passed, and the puppies grew and thrived, the look of wistful awe in the faces of the rest of the kennel staff when they looked over the half-door into Lissar's little domain grew so clear and plain that Lissar stopped going into the common-room at all, except to fetch her meals, milk and mush for the puppies, or to ask questions, which were gravely answered. She thought: I have asked questions so ignorant they should shock you; why do you look at me as if I were setting you a trial that you are not sure you will master?

Her heart still hurt her when she looked at *her* puppies, and yet looking at them was a pleasure unlike any pleasure she could remember; raising Ash had been different, she thought, not only because Ash was a big strong puppy when they met, but because she and Ash had, it seemed to her, grown up together. But those memories were still vague, still hemmed round with walls she could not breach, as solid, it seemed, as real brick and stone. When she grew very tired, and hallucinations crept round the edges of her vision, she remembered that she was accustomed to hallucinations too. She did not remember why she had spent the last winter on the mountain, but she remembered what it had been like.

She also remembered that the most brutal dream she had had ended with the Lady, the Moonwoman, and that when she had awoken, the supple white dress that now lay folded away on a shelf in a bare little room over the kennels, had remained, as real as she was, as real as Ash's long coat was.

And Ossin was real; realer somehow than Hela or Jobe or Berry or Tig, perhaps because they had given up on the puppies when Ilgi died, and Ossin had not. Or because of the way they looked at her, and Ossin looked at her only as if she were another human being. But when he walked into the pen, it was as if the sunlight came with him.

She remembered him as if he dressed in bright colors: red and green and yellow and blue. And yet his clothing was usually the drab, practical sort one would want to wear in a kennel, when a puppy might vomit over your lap at any moment; although it was true that he often wore bright shirts under his tunics, or that the tunics themselves had bright cuffs or collars or hems. She also thought of his face and hair and eyes as bright, when in fact he was as drab as his clothing, and his hair and eyes were a dull brown. But his smile lit his dull square features as fire lightens darkness; and so when her memory of him startled her when she set her eyes again on the reality, his smile reminded her of what she chose to remember.

Sometimes they kept watch together in the small hours, too tired even to sleep; for while he did sleep in a bed every other night, he was still expected to keep up his other duties as the king's only son and his heir, and he was no less tired than she. "Fortunately I'm already known as less than a splendid conversationalist," he told her ruefully; "I'm now gaining a reputation as a total blockhead." They talked softly, the puppies clean and fed and asleep, and Lissar's long hairy head- or foot-rest snoring gently.

He talked more than she did, for she had only half a year's experience available to her, and much of it was about not remembering what went before—about fearing to remember what went before; and the rest was not particularly interesting, about hauling water and chopping wood, and walking down a mountain. She did not mean to tell him this, that she did not remember what her life had been, but at four o'clock in the morning, when the world is full of magic, things may be safely said that may not be uttered at any other time, so long as the person who listens believes in the same kind of magic as the person who speaks. Ossin and Lissar did believe in the same kinds of magic, and she told him more than she knew herself, for she was inside her crippled memory, and he was outside.

But one thing she always remembered not to tell him was her name. Since she remembered so little else, and since she had a name—Deerskin—this created no suspicion in his mind; but she wondered at it herself, that she should be so sure she dared not tell him this one fact—perhaps the only other fact she was sure of beyond Ash's name.

He in turn told her of his life in ordinary terms. There were no gaps in his memory, no secrets that he could remember nothing of but the fearful fact of their existence. He was the only son of his parents, who had been married four years before he was born; his sister was eight years younger. He could not remember a time when he had not spent most of his waking hours with dogs—except for the time he spent with horses—or a time in which he had not hated being dressed up in velvets and silk and plonked on a royal chair atop a royal dais, "like a statue on a pedestal, and about as useful, I often think. I think my brain stops as soon as brocade touches my skin."

"You should replace your throne with a plain chair then," said Lissar. "Or you could take one of the crates in the common-room with you."

"Yes," said Ossin, "one of the crates. And we could hire an artist to draw running dogs chasing each other all the way around it, as an indication of my state of mind."

Twenty-three

Spring had passed and the warmth now was of high summer. When Lissar paused on the way to the bathhouse and lifted her face to the sky, the heat of the sun struck her like the warmth of the fire in the little hut had struck her last winter, as a life-giving force, as a bolt of energy that sank through her flesh to her bones. She took a deep breath, as if welcoming her life back; as if the six small furry life-motes in the kennels behind her were . . . not of no consequence, but possessed of perfect security.

It was a pleasant sensation; she stood there some minutes, eyes closed, drinking the sun through her pores; and then Hela's voice at her shoulder, "There, you poor thing, you've fallen asleep on your feet." Lissar hadn't heard her approach. She opened her eyes and smiled.

Two days later she and Ossin took the pups outdoors for the first time. He carried the big wooden box that held all six of them, and she had occasion to observe that the bulk of his arms and shoulders, unlike that of his waistline, had nothing to do with how many sweet cakes he ate. She and Ash followed him, Lissar carrying blankets, as anxious as any nursemaid about her charges catching a chill.

The puppies tumbled out across the blankets. The bolder ones at once teetered out to the woolly edges and fell off, and began attacking blades of grass. They were adorable, they were alive, and she loved them; and she laughed out loud at their antics. Ossin turned to her, smiling. "I have never heard you laugh before."

She was silent.

"It is a nice sound. I like it. Pardon me if I have embarrassed you."

She shook her head; and at that moment Jobe came up to ask Ossin something, a huge, beautiful, silver-and-white beast pacing solemnly at his side. It and Ash threw measuring looks at each other, but both were too well-behaved to do any more: or simply too much on their dignity to initiate the first move. Lissar still had only the vaguest idea of the work that went on around her every day in the kennels; she heard dogs and people, the slap of leather and the jingle of metal rings, the shouts of gladness, command, correction—and frustration; smelled food cooking, and the aromas from the contents of the wheelbarrows the scrubbers carried out twice a day. The scrubbers were not lightly named; they did not merely clean, they scrubbed.

Lilac came to visit her occasionally, the first time the day after Lissar had gone to meet the king and queen in the receiving-hall. By the mysterious messenger service of a small community, word had reached her that evening of what had become of her foundling, and why Lissar had not returned as she had promised. "I knew you would land on your feet," she said cheerfully in greeting.

Lissar, after one nearly sleepless night, and weeks of them to come, and six small dog-morsels threatening to die at any moment, was not so certain of Lilac's estimation of her new position, and looked at her with some irony.

Lilac, who had dropped to her knees beside the puppies, did not see this. "They're so tiny," she whispered, as if speaking loudly might damage them. "I'm used to foals, who are born big enough that you know it if one stands on your foot."

"I'm supposed to keep them alive," Lissar said, as softly as Lilac.

"You will," said Lilac, looking up, and for just one moment Lissar saw a flash of that look she saw in almost everyone's face. Lilac's eyes rested briefly on the white dress Lissar had not yet changed for kennel clothes; and Lissar wondered, suddenly, for the first time, why Lilac had spoken to her at the water trough, what seemed a lifetime ago already, and was yet less than three days.

The glimpse left her speechless. "You will," said Lilac again, this time turning it into a croon to a puppy, who, waking up, began to crawl toward the large warm bulk near him, cheeping hopefully. This was the one Lissar would name Ob: he was growing adaptable already, and was realizing that more than one large warm bulk provided food.

As THE PUPS GREW AND BLOSSOMED, THE NAMES she had at first almost casually chosen, as a way of keeping them sorted out, instead of calling them "white with brindle spot on left ear," "small grey bitch," or "big golden-fawn," began to feel as if they belonged, that they did *name*; and she slipped, sometimes, and called them by their private names when someone else was near. At first it was only Lilac. Then, one day, Ossin.

"I—I am sorry, your greatness," she said, catching herself too late. "They're your pups; you have the naming of them. It is only that I—I am so accustomed to them."

Ossin shook his head. "No; they are yours, as they would tell you if we asked them. I am sure you have chosen good names for them." After a moment he added: "I am sure you are hearing their names aright."

She knew that he did not mean that the pups belonged to her, but she was more relieved than she liked to admit that he would let her names for them stand; she feared a little her own tendency to think of names as safety-charms, helping to anchor them more securely to their small tender lives. And the names did fit them; not entirely unlike, she thought, she was "hearing" them, in the prince's odd quaint phrase. "Thank you," she said.

He was smiling, reading in her face that she was not taking him as seriously as he meant what he was saying. "I have wondered a little that you have not named them before; pups around here have names sometimes before their eyes are open—although I admit the ones like 'Pigface' and 'Chaos' are changed later on. And I think you're imagining things about Harefoot, but that's your privilege; a good bit of money—and favors—pass from hand to hand here on just such questions.

"Mind you," he added, "the pups are yours, and if you win races with Harefoot the purses are yours, although I will think it a waste of a good hunting dog. But I shall want a litter or two out of the bitches, and some stud service from at least one of the dogs—Ob, isn't it?—I have plans for that line, depending on how they grow up."

If they grow up, she thought, but she did not say it aloud; she knew in her heart that she was no longer willing even to consider that she might lose so much as one of them, and she kept reminding herself "if they grow up" as if the gods might be listening, and take pity on her humility, and let her keep them. "Of course, your greatness," she said, humoring his teasing.

"And stop calling me 'your greatness.'"

"I'm sorry, y—Ossin."

"Thank you."

A day or so later, watching puppies wading through a shallow platter of milk with a little cereal mixed in, and offering a dripping finger to the ones who were slow to catch on (this was becoming dangerous, or at least painful, as their first, needlelike teeth were sprouting), she heard a brief conversation between the prince and Jobe, standing outside the common-room door. This was at some little distance from the puppies' pen, but conversations in the big central aisle carried.

"Tell them none of that litter is available."

"But it looks like they're all going to live," Jobe said, obviously surprised. "You can always change your mind if something knocks most of them off after all."

"You're not listening," said Ossin patiently. "Yes, they are all going to live, barring plague or famine. They *are* going to live. That's not the issue. He can offer me half his kingdom and his daughter's hand in marriage for all I care. None of Ilgi's last litter is available. Offer him one of Milli's; that line is just as strong, maybe stronger."

There was a pause, while Jobe digested his master's curious obstinacy—or was it sentimentality? Lissar wondered too. "I've heard the daughter isn't much anyway," said Jobe at last.

The prince's splendid laughter rang out. "Just so," he said. "She neither rides nor keeps hounds."

When did I start finding his laughter splendid? Lissar thought, as her fingers were half-kneaded, half-punctured by little gums that were developing thorns.

WHEN SHE WENT TO THE BATHHOUSE NOW, UPON HER return the puppies all fell on her, wagging their long tails, clambering up her ankles, scaling her lap as soon as she knelt among them. Even Ash now lowered her nose to them and occasionally waved her tail laconically while they greeted her. Her lack of enthusiasm for them never cured them of greeting her eagerly. She would still spring up, dramatically shedding small bodies, if they tried to play with her when she lay down; but if one or three curled up for a nap between her forelegs or

against her side, she permitted this. Lissar saw her lick them once or
twice, absently, as if her mind were not on what she was doing; but then
for all her reserve her restraint was also perfect, and she never, ever offered to bite or even looked like she was thinking about it, however tire-
somely the puppies were behaving.

Lissar was deeply grateful for this; she could not exile her best
friend for objecting to her new job. Perhaps Ash understood this. Perhaps she didn't mind puppies so much, it was more that she didn't know
what to do with them.

The puppies grew older; now they looked like what they were,
fleethounds, among the most beautiful creatures in the world; perhaps
the most graceful even among all the sighthound breeds. Though they
were puppies still, they lost the awkwardness, the loose-limbedness, of
most puppies while they were still very young. They seemed to dance as
they played with each other, they seemed to walk on the ground only
because they chose to. When they flattened their ears and wagged their
tails at her, it was like a gift.

She loved them all. She tried not to think about Ossin's teasing
about their being hers; she tried not to think of how they must leave her
soon, or she them. She knew they would be old enough soon to need
her no longer—indeed they no longer needed her now, but she supposed that the prince would let her remain with them to the end of
their childhood, and she was glad of the reprieve: to enjoy them for a
little while, after worrying about them for so long.

During the days now they wandered through the meadows beyond
the kennels, she and Ash and a low silky pool of puppies that flowed
and murmured around them. Even on most wet days they went out, for
by the time the puppies were two months old, getting soaked to the skin
was preferable to trying to cope with six young fleethounds' pent-up energy indoors. Even worrying that they might catch cold was better than
settling the civil wars that broke out if they stayed in their pen all day.

Lissar could by now leave them as she needed to, although the

tumultuousness with which they greeted her reappearance was a dis-
couragement to going away in the first place. She no longer slept every
night in the pen; but then neither did they. Her room was up two flights
of stairs, and even long-legged fleethound puppies need a little time to
learn to climb (and, more important, descend) stairs; and she had
assumed that as weaning progressed she ought to wean them of her presence as well. But the little bare room felt hollow, with just her and Ash
in it, and it recalled strongly to her mind her lingering dislike of sleeping under roofs. She thought about the fact that the prince's two
favorite dogs went almost everywhere with him (they slept by the door
of the puppies' pen on the nights he spent there), and that Jobe and
Hela and the others usually had a dog or three sleeping with them.

No one but Lissar had seven. She had crept up very late the first
night out of the pen, puppies padding and tumbling and occasionally
yelping behind her. She'd been practicing for this with some outside
steps conveniently located for such a purpose. The puppies were ready—
they were always ready—for anything that looked like a game; Climbing Stairs was fine with them. Harefoot was the cleverest at it straight
away; she and Pur were the two tallest, but she carried her size the more
easily. At first they only spent half the night upstairs; two flights were
simply too many to have to go up and down more than once, and the
puppies were learning that there was a difference between under-a-roof
and out-of-doors in terms of where they were allowed to relieve themselves. Fleethounds were tidy dogs, and quick to catch on; but infant
muscular control can do only so much. By the end of the first week of
the new system, they were waking Lissar up at midnight, and going to
stand by the pen door in an expectant manner; although Meadowsweet
and Fen took turns needing to be carried upstairs, and occasionally Ferntongue forgot as well. But there were only one or two accidents on the
bare, easily cleaned floor of the bedroom, neatly deposited in some corner, well away from the mattress Lissar had dragged off the bed so they
could all sleep on it more comfortably.

Her puppies were sleeping through the night by the time they were three months old. "That's extraordinary," Hela said, when, at three and a half months, Lissar told her this. "That's extraordinary," was also what Hela had said the first time she saw the puppy waterfall pouring down the stairs.

"They're extraordinary puppies," said Lissar proudly, trying not to grin foolishly, at the same time reaching over to pry Fen's teeth out of Pur's rump. But she looked up, smiling, at Hela's face, and there was that look again; the look at Lilac's breakfast table, the look the kennel staff had given her the first evening in the common-room. The look that had become almost palpable the afternoon she had told the story of Ash and her escape from the dragon. She had only even told it accidentally, uneasy as she was in the common-room, and not accustomed to lingering there. She was there because Ossin was, and because he obviously assumed that she would stay—that she belonged there, as the rest of the kennel staff did.

"No one can outrun a dragon," Jobe said.

"I know. We were lucky. It couldn't have been very hungry, not to have chased us." But she looked around at the faces looking back at her, and did not see "luck" reflected in their expressions; and she wished she had said nothing.

But Ossin smiled at her, meeting her eyes as the others had not, and said, "Yes, I remember once when Nob and Tolly and Reant, do you remember him? He ran afoul of that big iruku that long winter we had, when he was only four—we were out looking for the signs of a herd of bandeer that someone had brought word of, and we surprised a pair of dragons feeding on a dead one. They're slower, of course, when they're eating, and they never really believe that anything would dare chase them away from their prey, so they aren't all that belligerent, just mean by nature—but we got out of there in a hurry. I gave the order to scatter, so they'd have a harder time, I hoped, deciding whom to chase. I don't know if that's why they decided to leave us alone or not; the dead bandeer was bigger than any of us."

Twenty-four

There was much activity in the kennels during high summer. From midsummer through the harvest was the hunting season; winter began early here, and the snow could be deep soon after harvest. Sometimes the last ricks and bales were raked up while the snow sifted down; sometimes the last hunts were cancelled and the hunters, royal and courtier or district nobility and vassal, helped their local farmers, the snow weighing on shoulders and clogging footsteps with perfect democratic indifference. As often as not the stooked fields were turned briefly into sharp white ranges of topographically implausible peaks and pinnacles before the farm waggons came along to unmake them gently into their component sheaves and bear them off to the barns.

The hunting-parties went out as late in the year as they could; while the season lasted—so long as the weather threatened neither bliz-

zards nor heatstroke—Ossin rode out himself nearly every day. The in-
habitants of the king's court depended on the huntsfolk and their dogs
to provide meat for the table. The court held no farmland of its own,
and while the king could tax his farmers in meat, no king ever had. All
the wild land, the unsettled land, belonged to the royal family, who
leased it as they chose to smallholders, or awarded it to their favorites—
or took it back from those who angered or betrayed them. Their own
flocks were the wild beasts of the forests and hills; and wild game was
considered finer meat, more savory and health-giving, than anything a
farmer could raise. Rights and durations of royal land use leases were
very carefully negotiated; if the land was to be cleared for agriculture,
then cleared it must be; if it was to be kept wild for hunting, the king
had the power to declare, each year, how much game could be taken on
each leashold (the position of royal warden, and advisor to the king on
the delicate question of yearly bags, was much prized), and to name who
led and maintained any local hunt. (In practice, however, the latter
generations of Goldhouses were all good-natured, and almost always
said "Yes" to any local nomination.) This also meant that if any aristo-
cratic or royal tastes ran toward chicken or mutton, the noble bargainer
was in an excellent position to make a trade.

The prince hunted not only for those lucky enough to live in the
king's house, but also for all those that royalty owed favors, or wished to
create a favor in, by a gift of wild game, or a tanned skin; for wild leather
was also considered superior. The king himself rode with the hunt but
seldom any more, but the leather that he and his craftsmen produced
was very fine, and it was not merely the cachet of royalty that produced
its reputation. Potted meat from the royal kitchens was also highly
prized; no meat was ever allowed to go to waste, no matter how hot the
summer, and the apprentice cooks were rigorously taught drying and
salting, boiling and bottling.

There was always work to be done in the kennels at any time of
year; but as the summer progressed the pace became faster. Lissar initially

helped the scrubbers when some of the more senior of these were taken hunting in the hunting-parties. Hela told her in something like dismay and alarm that other people could do the cleaning—that if she wanted occupation they would use her gladly working with the dogs. Without anyone saying it openly, there seemed to be a consensus that she had a gift for it. It was true that her guess at Harefoot's promise of more than usual speed was already coming true; and it was also true that a nervous dog, in Lissar's company, despite the seven dogs that this company included, was calmer. This had been discovered when they gave her dogs to groom; after Ash, all the short-haired fleethounds seemed almost a joke in comparison, but the touch of her hands most dogs found soothing.

So occasionally they gave her a tired or anxious dog for a few days; and each of those dogs returned from its odd holiday better able to listen to its training and adapt itself to its job. This made no sense on the surface of it, since six of Lissar's seven dogs wished to play vigorously with every creature they met, and could be ruthless in their persistence (only to Ash did they defer); but somehow that was the way of it nonetheless.

Lissar herself did not know why it was true, nor could she explain why it was so clear to her that the small pudgy Harefoot would justify her name soon enough. She did acknowledge that dogs listened to her. It seemed to her merely obvious that the way to make acquaintance with a dog was to sit down with it for a little while, and wait till it looked at you with . . . the right sort of expression. Then you might speak to it while you looked into each other's face.

She heard, that summer, for the first time, the name *Moonwoman* spoken aloud. Deerskin they called her to her face; but Moonwoman she heard more than once when she was supposed to be out of earshot. She thought of the Lady, and she did not ask any questions; she did not want to ask any questions, and when she heard the name uttered, she tried to forget what she had heard.

She and Ash and the puppies, and occasionally one of her four-legged reclamation projects, often went to watch the hunt ride out. Particularly on the days when someone wealthy or important was being entertained—"Gods! Give me a sennight when we can just hunt!" groaned Ossin. "If we have many more weeks like this one, with my lord Barbat, who does not like riding through heavy brush, we may be hungry this winter!"—it was a grand, and sometimes colorful, sight. Ossin and his staff dressed plainly, but their horses were fine and beautiful, no matter how workmanlike the tack they wore; and the great creamy sea of fleethounds, most of them silver to grey to fawn to pale gold, with the occasional brindle, needed no ornament. A few scent-hounds went with them, brown and black and red-spotted, lower and stockier than the sighthounds; and then some members of Goldhouse's court attended, bearing banners and wearing long scalloped sleeves and tunics in yellow and red; and if there were visiting nobility, they often dressed very finely, with embroidered breastplates and saddle-skirts for the horses, and great sweeping cloaks and hats with shining feathers for the riders. Occasionally some of these carried hawks on their arms. Lissar had eyes mostly for the fleethounds.

Hela and the other staff left behind sometimes came out as well with half-grown dogs on long leashes. Lissar's puppies were loose (only once had one, Pur, bolted after the hunting-party; when, the next day, he was the only one of them all on a leash he was so humiliated that forever after he would face away from the hunters, and sit down, or possibly chase butterflies, resolutely ignoring everything else around him). After the party had ridden out, there were lessons in the big field, although occasionally these were shortened if there were visitors waiting to see available pups put through their paces. The prince's interdiction about Lissar's family continued to hold; but Lissar preferred to stay out of the way of these activities nonetheless, just in case someone who could not be said "no" to took an incurable liking to one of her puppies, or merely made the prince an offer he could not refuse, including perhaps half a kingdom and a daughter who did ride and hunt.

It was on one of her long afternoons wandering beyond the cultivated boundaries of the king's meadow that a woman approached her. Lissar had begun wearing her deerskin dress again of late; she found it curiously more comfortable for long rambles, for all the apparent practicality of the kennel clothing standard. She was barefoot, of course, and on this day she had three leashes wrapped around her waist, in case she should need them. The dogs had all registered a stranger long before Lissar could differentiate this human form from any other, the puppies bounding straight up into the air to see over the tall grass, and the other three grown dogs and Ash standing briefly, gracefully, on their hind legs. Ash, as leader, made whuffling noises through her long nose. Lissar was not worried, but she was a little wistful that her solitary day was coming to an end sooner than she had wished.

Ordinarily she would not have stayed away even so long; she had missed out on doing any of the daily chores. But she had the three extra dogs with her today, dogs that Ossin had said of, "These need only one or two of Deerskin's days; but they've been hunted a little harder than they should, and they need a holiday." These three had the usual perfect manners of the prince's hunting dogs, and were no trouble; each of them had looked her mildly in the eye almost at once when she sat down to make their acquaintance; and they showed a tendency to like being petted, as if in their secret hearts they wished to be house-dogs instead of hunters. "One day," she told them, "when you have retired, you will go on to live with a family who will love you for your beauty and nothing more, and if you're very lucky there will be children, and the children will pet you and pet you and pet you. Ossin has a list, I think, of such children; he sends his hunting-staff out during the months they are not needed for that work, to look for them, and add names to the list." The fleethounds stared back at her with their enormous dark liquid eyes, and believed every word.

She had spoken to each in turn, cupping her hand under their chins, and smiling at them; and then she had taken enough bread for her, and biscuit for all ten of her companions, for a noon meal. She took a few throwing-stones as well, just in case she saw something she wished to try, for she felt out of practice, and her eyes were still better for the crouched and trembling rabbit in the field than the dogs' were; their eyes responded to motion. Not that there was much chance of any honest hunting whatsoever, with the puppies along; but the three extra adults were helping to keep order, and it would be too bad if she missed an opportunity.

She was aware that she was getting hungry now as the shadows lengthened in the afternoon light, that supper would be welcome; and the two ootag she had in fact been able to kill today would be barely a mouthful each divided eleven ways. But she wasn't hungry enough yet, and there were still several hours of summer daylight. She sighed as the stranger came nearer.

It was a woman; Lissar could see the scarf wrapped around her hair, and then could recognize that the legs swishing through the tall grass were wearing a farmwife's long skirt. As she grew nearer, Lissar was teased by the notion that the woman looked a little familiar; but the thought remained teasing only.

The woman walked straight through the dogs, who were so startled at being ignored that not even the irrepressible Ob tried to leap up and lick her face. When she came to Lissar, who was standing, bemused, still hoping that the woman had made a mistake and would go away, she flung herself at Lissar's feet.

Lissar, alarmed, thought at first she had fainted, and bent down to help her; but the woman would not be lifted, and clutched at Lissar's ankles, her sleeves tickling Lissar's bare feet, speaking frantically, unintelligibly, to the ground. Lissar knelt, put her hand under the woman's chin and lifted; and Lissar's life in the last eight months had made her strong. The woman's head came up promptly, and Lissar saw the tears on her face. "Oh, please help me!" the woman said.

Lissar, puzzled, said, "I will if I am able; but what is your trouble? And why do you ask me? I know little of this land, and have no power here."

But these words only made fresh tears course down the woman's face. "My lady, I know you are here—just as you are. I would not ask were it anything less, but my child! Oh, my Aric! He is gone now three days. You cannot say no to me—no, please do not say no! For you have long been known for your kindness to children."

Lissar shook her head slowly. She knew little of children, to have kindness for them or otherwise; this poor woman had mistaken her for someone else, in her distraction over her child. "I am not she whom you seek," she said gently. "Perhaps if you tell me, I can help you find who—"

The woman gasped, half-laugh, half-choke. "No, you will not deny me! Destroy me for insolence, but I will not let you deny it! The tales—" She released Lissar's ankles and clutched at her wrists; one hand crept up Lissar's forearm and hesitantly stroked her sleeve. "I recognized you that day in the receiving-hall, you with your white dress and your great silver dog; and Sweetleaf, with me, she knew who you were too; and her cousin Earondern is close kin with Barley of the village Greenwater; and Barley and his wife Ammy had seen you come down from the mountain one dawn. And I would not trouble you, but, oh—" And her tears ran again, and she put her hands over her face and sobbed.

"Who am I, then?" said Lissar softly; not wanting to hear the answer, knowing the name Moonwoman murmured behind her back, knowing the truth of the Lady, ashamed that she, Lissar, might be confused with her. And yet she feared to hear the answer too, feared to recognize what she was not; feared to understand that by learning one more thing that she was not that it narrowed the possibilities of what she was; that if those possibilities were thinned too far, that she would no longer be able to escape the truth. Her truth.

"Tell me then," she said strongly. "Who am I?"

The woman's hands dropped away from her face, her back and shoulders slumped. "I have offended you, then," she said, dully. "I did not wish that. It is only that I love my Aric so much—" She looked into Lissar's face, and whatever she saw there gave her new hope. "Oh, I knew you were not unkind! Deerskin," she said, "if it is Deerskin you wish to be called, then I will call you Deerskin. But we know you, the White Lady, the Black Lady, Moonwoman, who sees everything, and finds that which is lost or hidden; and my Aric was lost three days ago, as your Moon waxed; I know you would not have missed him. Oh, my lady, please find my Aric for me!"

Lissar stared at her. It was her own wish to know, and not know, her own story, that had caused her to ask the woman to name her; even knowing what the answer must be, the false answer. . . . The woman knelt again, staring into Lissar's face with an expression that made the breath catch in Lissar's throat. She knew nothing of the finding of lost children; she did not know what to do. But she did know that she could not deny this woman; she could not walk away. A search was demanded of her; the search, at least, she could provide.

"I will go," she said slowly, "but"—raising a hand quickly before the woman could say anything—"you must understand. I am not . . . what you claim for me. My eyes are mortal, as are my dogs. Therefore I ask you two things: do not speak that other name to me or to anyone when you speak of me: my name is Deerskin. And, second, go to the king's house, and ask for a messenger for the prince, and tell him what you have told me; say that Deerskin has gone to look, that no time be wasted; but that I have no scent-hounds; the prince will know that these are what is needed. The prince, or someone for him, will send dogs after me.

"Now, tell me what village you are from, and where Aric was lost."

Twenty-five

In deepening twilight, Lissar and her dogs trotted across whispering grassland, for the village the woman named lay most quickly as the crow flies, and not by road. Lissar thought wistfully of dinner, but had not wanted, for reasons not entirely clear to herself, to accompany the woman across the field in the opposite direction, to the kennels and the king's house, even to eat a hot meal and pick up a blanket for sleeping. Bunt and Blue and Kestrel could be used for hunting, and Ash would hunt without direction as she had done during their long months on the mountain, so long as the puppies could be prevented from spoiling everything. There would have been more ootag, and rabbits, today, were it not for the puppies. And as for blankets, she had slept without before.

She was reluctant to remain in the woman's company. Though she believed the woman would keep her promise to use only the name Deerskin, there was no mistaking the reverence of her manner, and that reverence had nothing to do with Lissar. She had no wish to be embarrassed before Hela and Jobe and whoever else might be around; the lives of six doomed puppies, and the dragon she had escaped, was enough to read in their eyes.

Meadowsweet wore out the soonest, as Lissar had known she would; she had persistently been the weakest pup during the long weeks when Lissar checked the puppy-heap every morning to see if they were all still breathing. Meadowsweet still had the least stamina, although she was among the sweetest tempered. Lissar slowed to a walk, and picked her up; she weighed comparatively little, although her long legs trailed. Lissar heaved her up so she could hang her forepaws over Lissar's shoulder; she turned her head and gratefully began washing Lissar's face. Next to collapse was Fen, as Lissar also expected; he went over Lissar's other shoulder, and she and the dogs walked on, gently, while twilight deepened, till the Moon came out, full and clear and bright.

Ash began walking with the look of "food nearby" that Lissar knew well; and Blue and Bunt and Kestrel knew it too but looked, as if they had trained with Ash since puppyhood, to her for a lead. Then suddenly all four dogs were gone, so rapidly that they seemed to disappear before Lissar heard the sounds of their motion. They were out of meadowland now, and into crackling scrub. Lissar had been growing tired; even undergrown fleethound puppies become heavy after a while. She turned her head, listening, and smelling hopefully for water; and as she paused, something shot out of the low scrub row of trees at her.

"*Here!*" she shouted, and the puppies, startled and inclined to be frightened, all bumbled toward her, even Ob and Harefoot showing no inclination to disobey. Lissar slid the puppies off her shoulders hastily; they had woken from their half-drowse with her shout, and were glad to hunker down with their fellows. As she knelt to let them scramble to the ground she was feeling in her pocket for stones; no more than the time for one breath had passed since she had first seen the animal burst out of the thicket toward her.

She rose from her crouch, rock in hand, saw the teeth, the red tongue, the hanging jaw of the thing; saw a glint of eye in the Moonlight, let her rock go with all the strength of her arm behind it, readying the next rock with her other hand before she had finished her swing— what was it? And she had been thinking of how many rabbits they would need to feed all of themselves satisfactorily; this creature was big enough, the gods knew, if it didn't eat them first—

It shrieked, a high, rageful shriek, when her stone struck it; and it swerved away from her, less, she thought, from the pain than from the confusion caused by suddenly being able to see only out of one eye. She saw no other plausible target for a second stone, and paused, and as she paused became aware of three pale and one brindle long-legged ghosts tearing out of the forest after the creature. Three were to one side of her and the puppies; the nearest one, to the other side, was by itself. She recognized the silver-blue coat a fraction of a moment before she recognized the fuzzier outline of one of the other three ghosts, as Ash bolted forward, ahead of the others, and hurled herself at her prey's nose. The beast, half-blind, staggered, but it was dangerous yet; Lissar saw the long tusks in the Moonlight. It was too big, or Ash had not judged her leap perfectly, for it threw her off, and, as it saw her fall, lurched after her.

She rolled, leaped to her feet and aside—barely in time; but by then Bunt and Kestrel were there, seizing its cheek and flank; and then Blue, at last, bit into its other flank. It screamed again, bubbling its wrath, and Ash launched herself at its nose once more.

There was nothing for it, Lissar thought; it could kill them all still. She was already holding her slender knife in her hand; the knife that ordinarily cut no more than big chunks of meat into smaller chunks for the puppies' meals. The creature was thrashing itself around—Kestrel had lost her grip, fallen, leaped back again—Lissar stared at the great dark shape. You shouldn't tackle anything this big unless you were a hunting party, dozens of dogs and riders strong! she thought wildly; did Kestrel or Blue or Bunt—or, for that matter, her foolhardy Ash—notice the unevenness of this battle? Lissar might have more than one chance, for she did not doubt the dogs' courage; but their strength was limited, and they had already had a long day. A second chance they might give her, did she survive a miss; not a third.

She thought, It's a pity we cannot simply leave it and run, as we did the dragon.

And then there was a smaller pale flash streaking from behind her, and Ob valiantly leaped and caught an ear. Harefoot followed him, but grabbed badly at a thigh, and was kicked for her effort and yelped, but got up again at once. Not the puppies! Lissar thought. They will only get themselves killed! She felt she had been standing for hours, frozen in fear and indecision, and yet her heart had pounded in her ears only half a dozen beats; and then she threw herself forward as irrevocably as any hunting dog.

There was nothing to hang onto. She grasped with her free hand at the wiry, greasy hair, being bumped by her own dogs, grimly clinging to their holds. She needed the weak spot at the base of the skull, before the great lump of shoulder began; her small knife was not made for this. She scarred the back of the creature's neck enough to draw blood, but it only shrieked again, and threw her down. It tried to turn and trample her; but Ash rearranged her grip, and the blood flowed freshly out, and the thing seemed to go mad, forgetting Lissar for the moment. Its screams were still more of an anger past anger, that pain should be inflicted upon it, than of the pain itself. Bunt was shaken loose, and when he fell he did not bounce back to his feet but struggled upright and stood dazed.

Two more of the puppies had leaped for a hold; at least they were the ones she could see, and she was afraid to look too closely at the dark ground under the great beast's hoofs. Lissar ran forward again, seized the free ear, hooked one leg behind the creature's elbow as best she could, buried her knife to its hilt as far up on its neck as her arm would reach, and held on.

The thing paused, and shuddered. Lissar could barely breathe for its stench. She risked pulling her blade free, and plunged it in again, perhaps a little farther in, a little farther up, nearer the head. The thing bucked, but it was more of a convulsion. One last time, Lissar, half holding on, half dragged, raised her knife and stabbed it down. The thing took several steps forward; then its knees buckled. It remained that way, its hind legs still straight, swaying, for several long moments; and then it crumpled, and crashed to its side.

Lissar sat down abruptly; she was shaking so badly she could not stand, and there were tears as well as blood on her face. She put her head between her knees for a moment and then sat up again in time to see Ash walk slowly and deliberately over to Blue, seize him by the throat, and throw him to the ground, growling fiercely. Lissar was so astonished—and stupid with the shock of the scene they had just survived—that she did nothing. Blue cried like a puppy and went limp in Ash's grip, spreading his hind legs and curling his long tail between them.

Ash shook him back and forth a few times and dropped him, immediately turning away; she walked slowly over to Lissar and sat down with a thump, as if exhausted, as well you might be, Lissar thought at her dog, putting out a hand to her as she laid her bloody muzzle on Lissar's drawn-up knees.

Lissar looked into the brown eyes looking so lovingly at her, and remembered how the creature who now lay dead had burst out of the stand of trees, with Blue nearest it, as if driving it. Ash had just told him, "You fool, this was no well-armed and armored hunting party; this was my person and six puppies; you could have gotten us all killed." And Blue, now lying with his feet bunched up under him and his neck stretched out along the ground, his tail still firmly between his legs, was saying, "Yes, I know, I'm very sorry, it's the way I was trained, I'm not bred to think for myself." Kestrel and Bunt were still standing by their kill, and Kestrel was washing Bunt's face; Lissar hoped this meant that Bunt had been no more than briefly stunned. She knew that the first thing she had to do was count her puppies.

Ob came crawling to her even as she thought that, so low on his belly that she was heart-stoppingly afraid that he had been grievously wounded; but then she recognized the look on his face and realized that he was only afraid that he had done wrong and was in disgrace. My hunting blood was too much for me, his eyes said; I could not help my self. I know, she replied to him silently, and stroked his dirty head, and he laid his head on her thigh and sighed.

The other puppies followed, all of them with their heads and tails down, not sure what just had happened, and wanting the reassurance of their gods, Ash and Lissar; and for a few minutes they all merely sat and looked at each other and were merely glad they were all still there to do it together.

Lissar raised her head at last. Their kill, she thought. She stood slowly, tiredly, achingly, up. There was dinner—and breakfast and noon and dinner and latemeal for a week besides, if she were in fact a hunting party. But if she did not do something with it soon, the smell of fresh blood would shortly bring other creatures less fastidious. She'd never gutted anything so big before; she supposed it was all the same principle. She thought, I need not gut it at all; I can chop off enough for us for tonight, and leave the rest; we can camp far enough away that what comes for our kill need not threaten us. But even as she was thinking this she knew that it was not what she was going to do; she felt a deep reluctance to give up, without a struggle, the prize they had won so dangerously. She wanted the recognition that such a feat would bring—not her, but her dogs, Ash and the puppies, and even Bunt and Blue and

Kestrel. She could not fail them, by throwing away what they had achieved; she had to make her best human attempt to preserve it, as a hunting master would.

Pur crept forward and lapped tentatively at a trickle of blood; but Kestrel was on him immediately, seizing him gently but inexorably by the back of the neck. He yelped, and she let him go, and he trotted away, trying to look as small as possible. Ossin's hunting dogs were well-trained; and the dogs knew they ate nothing but what the lord of the hunt gave them. Lissar sighed. That was she, and no escape; there was a little wry humor in the thought that she owed it to Ossin not to put his dogs in the position of being tempted to break training. She took a deep breath, shook herself, looked at the creature and then, mournfully, at her little knife.

A long, hot, sticky, dreadful interval later, she'd let the dogs loose on the offal, and was experimenting with looping the leashes she had almost forgotten she had with her around the thing's legs. She thought perhaps she could hoist it into a tree far enough that it would still be there in the morning. As she dragged it, it hung itself up on every hummock and root-knob, but she found she was too tired *not* to go on; that she wanted something to show for the mess and the danger and the exhaustion. She had been irritated by Hela's insistence that she take the leashes, although Hela was quite right that if in their wanderings they inadvertently came too near a hunting party, Lissar could not depend on her authority to keep Kestrel and Blue and Bunt with her. If she had thought of it since, she would have dropped the leashes somewhere she could find them again as soon as she left Aric's mother; but she would not annoy Hela unnecessarily by losing them deliberately. And now . . . the leashes were excellent leather (from the king's workshop), and bore the abuse they were receiving with no sign of fraying.

Ash left her dinner to inquire if she could help. "You're not built to be a draught animal," Lissar said, panting; "but then neither am I," she added thoughtfully, and looped a leash around Ash's shoulders, threw herself at the end of her two remaining leashes, and called her dog. Ash took a few moments to comprehend that she had been attached to this great jagged lump of flesh for a purpose. She wondered, briefly, if she should be offended; but Lissar herself was doing the same odd thing, and Ash scorned nothing her person accepted. So she pulled.

Lissar didn't know if it was Ash's strength or the moral support of company, but they got it to the edge of the trees, and then Lissar used Ash as part of a snub to hold the carcass in place as she slowly hauled it off the ground. This was easier to explain, for Ash knew the command *Stand!*, and when the weight began dragging her forward, *No, stand!* made her dig her feet in, hump her back, and try to act heavy. It was not done well, but it was done at last.

Then Lissar started a fire, rescued a bit of the heart and the liver, stuck them on the ends of two peeled sticks, and fell asleep before they finished cooking.

She woke up to the smell of meat burning, rescued it, and stood waving it back and forth till it was cool enough to eat. The dogs were asleep as well, sprawled anyhow from where the creature had died, and she'd performed the messy and disgusting business of gutting it, to where she stood by the fire she had started, a little distance from where the monster now hung dripping from its tree. She nibbled tentatively at the heart, thinking, if the story is true, then let me welcome this creature's strength and courage while I reject its hate and rage. The meat burned her tongue.

She was as tired as her dogs, but this was not the place to linger; there would be other meat-eaters coming to investigate, and to try how far from the ground the prize hung. Besides, she wanted water, both to drink and to wash the sticky reek away. She chewed and swallowed, bit off another chunk; found that she was waking up against all probability; perhaps this was the fierceness of the creature's heart.

Ash, she said softly, and Ash was immediately and silently at her side (and cross that she had slept through an opportunity to beg for

cooked meat). Ob, she said. Meadowsweet, Harefoot, Fen. She whispered the puppies' names, waked them with a touch on neck or flank; a
few murmured a protest, but they rolled to their feet, stretched front
and rear, shook their heads till their ears rattled against their skulls with
a curiously metallic sound; then they came quietly. Dark eyes glinted in
the Moonlight; black nostrils flared and tails lifted. Lissar had the sudden, eerie sense that they all knew where they were going—and that
she knew best of all. Blue, she said. Kestrel. Bunt. But they were awake
already, their training strong in them: go on till you drop.

She set out at an easy trot, for they had some distance to travel, and
the puppies would tire soon again; but it was as if there were a scent in
her own nostrils or a glittering trail laid out before her, the path of the
Moon. It was like the directionless direction, the windless wind on her
cheek, when she and Ash had come down from the mountains, only a
few months before.

Fleethounds hunt silently; the only sound was the soft pad of many
feet. Lissar kilted her dress up around her hips that she might run the
more easily, and so they flowed across meadowland and poured through
one of the slender outflung arms of the yellow city, almost a town of its
own; and while it was late, it was not so late that there were no people
drinking and eating and changing horses, mounting and dismounting,
loading and unloading, at the crossroads inn, the Happy Man, that was
the reason the city bulged out so in this direction. And so a number of
people saw the tall, white-legged woman in her white dress surrounded
by tall silver hounds run soundlessly past, and disappear again in the
shadows beyond the road. Speech and motion stopped for a long moment; and then, as if at a sign, several low voices: Moonwoman, they
muttered. It is the White Lady and her shadow hounds.

Lissar knew none of this; she was barely aware of the crossroads, the
inn; what she saw and heard was in her mind, but it led her as strongly
as any leash. And so it was that when midnight was long past and dawn
not so far away, she and her dogs entered a little glade in a forest on a

hill behind a village, and there, curled up asleep in a nest of old leaves, was the lost boy.

The glamour fell from her as soon as her worldly eyes touched him; the glittering Moon trail, the mind's inexplicable knowledge, evaporated as if it had never been. The dogs crowded round her as she knelt by the boy, knowing still this much, that it was he whom she sought. He slept the sleep of exhaustion and despair, not knowing that he was near his own village, that his long miserable wandering had brought him back so near to home. She did not know if she should wake him, or curl up beside him and wait for dawn.

He shivered where he lay, a long shudder which shook the thin leaves, and then a quietness, followed by another fit of shivering. At least she and the dogs could keep him warm. She slipped her arms under him, and recognized her own exhaustion; the decision was no longer a choice, for the muscles of her arms and back, having carried half-grown puppies and wrestled a monster, would do no more that night. He nestled himself against her belly not unlike a larger, less leggy puppy, making little noises also not unlike a puppy's, and sighed, relaxing without ever waking up.

She slid down farther, not minding the knobby roots of the tree, and felt the dogs bedding down around her, spinning in little circles and tucking their legs into their surprisingly small bundles, thrusting noses under paws and tails. Some large warm thing—or a series of smaller warm things—pressed up against her back; and then Ash bent over her and breathed on her face, and settled down, tucking her face between Lissar's head and shoulder, her long hair shadowing the boy's face, and one curl touching his ear.

Lissar never felt her leave; but it was one sharp, crisp bark from Ash, standing watch at dawn, that brought the prince and his company to the glade.

Twenty-six

L issar heard the pause, after that, when anyone called her by the name she had given first to Lilac, Deerskin; and she could no longer refuse to recognize the whispers: Moonwoman. It was Ossin she asked, finally, wanting to know the story that others had given her, but not liking to ask anyone she suspected of calling her so. Even Lilac, straightforward as ever in all other ways, had a new secret in her eyes when she looked at her friend. Lissar wished she did not have to ask him; but he was the only one who still named her Deerskin without an echo, who still met her eyes easily—as, it occurred to her, she met his. Even his kennel folk, who had learned not to call him "your greatness," never quite forgot that he was their prince. Lissar wondered at herself, for she was . . . only an herbalist's apprentice.

"You don't have stories of the Moonwoman where you're from?"

Ossin said in surprise. "She's one of our favorite legends. I was in love with her"—he was grooming Aster as he spoke; Aster was standing rigidly still in the ecstasy of the attention—"when I was a boy, her and her coursing hounds.

"The story goes that she was the daughter of the strongest king in the world, and that all the other kings sought her hand in marriage."

The most beautiful woman in seven kingdoms drifted across Lissar's mind, but she could not remember where it came from, and she did not like the taste of it on her tongue.

"All the other kings sought her hand in marriage because the man who married her would become the strongest king in the world himself by inheriting her father's kingdom. Not a country," he added, rubbing Aster's hindquarters with a soft brush, "who believed in strong queens. My mother liked to point this out," he said, smiling reminiscently, "which annoyed me no end when I was still young, why did she have to go spoiling the story with irrelevancies? Anyway, this princess did not like any of the kings and princes and dukes who presented themselves to her, all of them looking through her to her father's throne, and she declared she would have none of them.

"She further declared that she would give up her position as royal daughter, and that her father could choose his heir without her help, without her body as intermediary; and she and her fleethound set off to find—the story doesn't say what she wanted to find, the meaning of life, one supposes, something of that sort.

"But one of the suitors followed her, and forced himself on her, thinking—who knows what a man like that thinks—thinking that perhaps what the girl needed was to understand that she could be taken by a strong man, or that rape would break her spirit, make her do what she was told. . . . She was beautiful, you see, so her attraction was not only through what her father would give her husband. And thinking also, perhaps, that her father would admire the strong commanding action of another strong man, like a general outflanking an opposing army by one daring stroke; or even that his daughter's intransigence was a kind of challenge to her suitors.

"But it did not turn out quite as he had hoped, for the princess herself hated and reviled him for his action, and returned to her father's court to denounce him. But in that then she was disappointed, and her father and his court's reaction was not all that she wished—some versions of the story say that her attacker did in fact follow her father on the throne; even that her father told her that she deserved no better for rejecting her suitors and running away from her responsibilities.

"Whatever the confrontation was, it ended by her saying that she did not wish to live in this world any more, this world ruled by her father and the other kings who saw it as he did.

"And so she fled to the Moon, and lived there, alone with her dog, who soon gave birth to puppies. And because of what happened to her—and because of her delight in her bitch's puppies—she watches out for young creatures, particularly those who are alone, who are hurt or betrayed, or who wish to make a choice for themselves instead of for those around them. And sometimes she flies down from the Moon with her dogs, and rescues a child or a nestling. Or a litter of puppies. The story goes that she has, over the years, become much like the Moon herself: either all-seeing or blind, sometimes radiant, sometimes invisible."

He paused, and his brushing hand paused too. Aster stood motionless, hoping that he would forget how much brushing she'd had already, and begin again. But he laughed, picking her up gently from the grooming table and setting her on the ground. She looked up at him sadly and then wandered off. "There's another bit to the story that occasionally is repeated: that our Moonwoman is still seeking a man to love her, that she would bear children as her dog, her best friend, did."

He looked at Lissar and smiled. "I liked that very much when I was younger and tenderer: I thought perhaps she'd marry me—after all, we both love dogs, and the Moonwoman's hounds are fleethounds, or something very much like them. Then I got a little older and recognized that

I'm only the stodgy prince of a rather small, second-class country, that produces grain and goods enough to feed and clothe itself, and not much else, and that neither I nor my country is much to look at besides. We're both rather dullish and brownish. I don't suppose my choices are any more limited than the handsome prince of a bigger, more powerful country's are; but I fancy that the princesses of first-rate countries are more interesting. Perhaps the duchesses and princesses of small second-class countries say the same about me. . . . I lost my hope for Moon-woman about the same time as I recognized the other. I was lucky, I suppose; if there had been any overlap it would have been a hard burden to bear. . . . I was tender for a rather longer time than most, I think.

"I'm sorry," he said, after a pause, while he watched her brushing Ash. He had groomed three dogs, while she went on working at Ash. Ash had her own special comb for tangles and mats, specially procured by Ossin, and hung on the grooming-wall with all the soft brushes; its teeth looked quite fierce in such company. "I'm sorry to go on so. I've been thinking . . . about myself, I suppose, because there's to be another ball, ten days from now, and I am to meet the princess Trivelda. Again. We met five years ago and didn't like each other then; I don't imagine anything will have changed." He sighed. "Trivelda's father runs what might charitably be called a rather large farm, south and west of us, and most of his revenues, I believe, go for yard goods for Trivelda's dresses. She would not stoop to me if she had any better chances; she thinks hunting hounds are dirty and smell bad."

"Probably many ladies from the grandest courts think the same," said Lissar, with a strong inner conviction of the truth of her words.

"Probably . . . I find myself determined to think the worst of my . . . likely fate. It's a weakness of character, I dare say. If I were a livelier specimen I would go out and find a Great Dragon to slay, and win a really desirable princess; I believe that's the way to do it. But there haven't been any Great Dragons since Maur, I think, and Aerin, who was certainly a highly desirable princess, didn't need any help, and the truth is I'm very glad that all happened a long time ago and very far away. You're smiling."

"Must you marry a princess? Can't you marry some great strapping country girl who rides mighty chargers bareback and can whistle so loudly she calls the whole country's dogs at once?"

Ossin laughed. "I don't know. If I met her perhaps I could rouse myself for argument. I think my mother would understand, and my father would listen to her. But I haven't met her. And so they keep presenting me with princesses. Hopefully."

"It is only one evening, this ball."

Ossin looked at her. "You have attended few balls if you can describe it as 'only one evening.'" He brightened. "I have a splendid idea—you come. You can come and see what you think of 'only one evening.'"

Lissar's heart skipped a beat or two, and there was a feeling in the pit of her stomach, a knot at the back of her skull; she was an herbalist's apprentice, what did she know of balls? Where were these sight-fragments coming from, of chandeliers, spinning around her, no, she was spinning, through the figures of a dance, blue velvet, she remembered blue velvet, and the pressure of a man's hand against her back, his hot grasp of her hand, her jewel-studded skirts sweeping the floor—jewel-studded?

"Are you all right?" Ossin's hands were under her elbows; she started back. "Yes—yes, of course I am. It's only—the fever hurt my memory, you see, and sometimes when memories come back they make me dizzy. I saw a princess once; she was wearing a dress with jewels sewn all over it, and she was dancing with a man she did not like."

Ossin was looking at her; she could see him hesitating over what he thought of saying, and hoped he would decide to remain silent. She concentrated on the fine fawn hairs of Ash's back. She put out a hand, fumbled with the comb, picked up the brushing mitt instead. Ossin moved away from her.

But that was not the end of the matter. The next day she was soaping and waxing leashes with the puppies spilled at her feet when Ossin appeared and said he had something he wished her opinion on. She assumed it had something to do with dogs, and went with him without question or much thought; Ash at her heels, the puppies shut up protestingly in their pen. Nob and Tolly, who had come with Ossin, were left with Hela.

Lissar was puzzled when he led her back into the main portion of the Gold House, the big central building from which nearly a city's worth of smaller buildings grew, like mushrooms growing at the feet of a vast stony tree. It was still easy for Lissar to get lost in the maze of courtyards and alleys and dead-ends into wings and corners and abutments. She knew her way from the kennels to the open fields and back, and to the stables, where she visited Lilac—but that was nearly all. It was going to be embarrassing when Ossin dismissed her and she didn't know where to go. But the house servants were almost without exception kind, she could ask one of them; perhaps she would even see one that she knew, Tappa or Smallfoot or Longsword the doorkeeper.

The hallways they passed through grew progressively grander. "The oldest part of the house was built by old King Raskel, who thought he was founding a dynasty that would rule the world. His idea of support for his plans was to build everything with ceilings high enough to contain weather beneath them. I used to fancy storm-clouds gathering up there and then with a clap of thunder the rain falls and drowns an especially deadly state banquet." He flung open a set of doors. "Or a ball. Not a bad idea, if I knew how one made a thunderstorm. Raskel is the one who first called himself Goldhouse, seventeen generations ago."

They were in the ballroom. Lissar didn't need to be told. There were servants in livery hanging long ribbons and banners of crimson and gold and blue and green around the walls; the banners bore heraldic animals, dogs and horses, eagles and griffins. Goldhouse's own badge, which hung above the rest, held a rayed sun with a stubby yellow castle,

a horse, a deep-chested and narrow-bellied dog, and some queer mytho-
logical beast, set around it. Ossin saw her looking at it. "Fleethounds are
in the blood, you might say. Or if there wasn't already one there, I'd've
put one in, although it would ruin the design. No, I would have taken
the elrig out; ugly thing anyway. It's supposed to be an emblem for
virtue, virtue commonly being ugly, you know."

Other servants were taking down plain drab curtains and hanging
up other curtains to match the banners. "What do you think?" Ossin
said, but it was a rhetorical question, and she only shook her head. He
set out across the vast lake of floor, and she followed uneasily, dodging
around servants with mops and buckets and polishing cloths; the smell
of the floor polish made her eyes water. "They lay the stuff down now so
the smell will be gone by the night," he offered over his shoulder. "And
the doors will be barred when they're finished, so that people like me,
who lack the proper attitude, can't tramp through and ruin the gloss."
His footsteps echoed; the servants all wore soft shoes, and if they spoke,
they spoke in whispers. Lissar's bare feet made no noise, but she had the
uncomfortable feeling of the floor polish adhering to her feet, so that
she would slide, whenever she set her foot down, for some time after,
leaving a sparkling trail like a snail's.

The left by another, smaller door, went up two flights of stairs and
down a hall of a more modest size, with a ceiling whose embossed flower
pattern was near enough to see in detail. Then Ossin opened another door.

Twenty-seven

T his room was small and, while it was obviously dutifully aired at
regular intervals, smelled unused. It was dim, the windows closed
and curtains drawn over them; light came in only from the hall windows behind them. There were a few paintings hanging on the wall to
their left as they walked in; they hung crowded together and uneven, as
if they had been put up where there were already nails to hold them,
without regard to how they looked.

The paintings were all portraits; the one which caught Lissar's eye
first was evidently very old. It was of a man, stiff in uniform, standing
with his hand on the back of a chair that might have been a throne,
staring irritably at the portrait painter who was wasting so much of his
time. "That's Raskel's son—first in a long line of underachievers, of
whom I am the latest." As he spoke, Ossin was sorting through more—

portraits, Lissar saw, which were smaller and less handsomely framed, lying on a table in the center of the room.

She looked up at the wall again; several of the other portraits were of young women, and looked newer, the paint uncracked, the finish still bright. "Ah," said Ossin, and held something up. He went over to the window and threw back the curtains; afternoon sunshine flooded in. He turned to Lissar and offered her what he held. She walked over to him and stood facing the windows.

It was a portrait, indifferently executed, of a plump young woman in an unflattering dress of a peculiarly dismaying shade of puce. Perhaps the color was the painter's fault, and not the young woman's; but Lissar doubted that the flounces and ribbons were products of the painter's imagination. "That's Trivelda," said Ossin with something that sounded like satisfaction. "Only one evening, you remember, eh? Looks just like her. What do you think?"

Lissar hesitated and then said, "She looks like someone who thinks hunting hounds are dirty and smell bad."

"Exactly." The prince sat down on the edge of the table, swinging one leg. She turned a little toward him. "What are all these—portraits?"

The prince grimaced. "Seven or eight or nine generations of courtly spouse-searches. Mostly it's just us royals—or at least nobles—very occasionally a commoner either strikingly wealthy or strikingly beautiful creeps in. There are a few of the little hand-sized ones of the impoverished but hopeful."

"I don't think I understand."

"Oh. Well. When you're a king or a queen and you have a son or a daughter you start wanting to marry off, you hire a tame portrait painter to produce some copies of your kid's likeness, preferably flattering, the number of copies depending on how eager or desperate you are, how much money you have to go with the package, and whether you can find a half-good painter with a lot of time to kill, and perhaps twelve or so children to support of his or her own. Then you fire off the copies to the likeliest courts with suitable—you hope suitable—unmarried off-spring of the right gender.

"The one my father hired kept making my eyes bigger and my chin smaller—I'm sure from praiseworthy motives, but that kind of thing backfires, as soon as the poor girl—or her parents' emissary—gets here and takes a good look at me.

"No one has come up with a good way of disposing of these things once their purpose is accomplished—or in most cases failed. It seems discourteous just to chuck them in the fire. So they collect up here." He lifted the corners of one or two and let them fall again with small brittle thumps. "Occasionally one of the painters turns out to be someone famous, and occasionally we get some collector wanting to look through what's in here, in hopes of finding a treasure. I don't think that's going to happen with Trivelda."

Lissar was smiling as she looked up, turning, now facing the wall, noticing the deep stacks of paintings leaning against its foot, the sunlight bright on the portraits hanging above. Second from the right, some little distance from the door, now on her left, that they had come in by, was a portrait that now caught her attention.

A young woman stood, her body facing a little away from the painter, her face turned back toward the unknown hand holding the brush, almost full-face. Her long pale gold skirts, sewn all over with knots of satin and velvet rosebuds, fell into folds as perfect as marble carved to clothe the statue of a goddess. Her face was composed but a little distant, as if she were thinking of something else, or as if she kept herself carefully at some distance behind the face she showed the world. Her mahogany-black hair was pulled forward to fall over her right shoulder. She wore a small diadem with a point that arched low over her brow; a clear stone rested at the spot mystics called the third eye. Her own hazel-green eyes gleamed in the light the painter chose to cast across the canvas. Her left hand, elbow bent, rested on the head of a tall, silver-fawn dog, who looked warily out of the picture, wary in that it believed the girl needed guarding, and it would guard her if it could. Its gaze was much sharper and more present than the girl's.

It was Ash she recognized, not herself. This painter was a better craftsperson than whoever had painted poor Trivelda; Lissar could not decide—her mind, during those first moments, floundering for intellectual details to keep the shock and terror at bay—if she would have recognized Ash anywhere, however bad the likeness, because she was Ash; or if it was the painter's cleverness in catching that wary look, a look Lissar had seen often in the last few months, as Ash stared at six eager, clumsy, curious puppies. It was only because she could not refuse to acknowledge Ash that she had to look into her own flat, painted eyes and aloof expression and say Yes, that was I.

Standing, for hours, it seemed, though she was allowed frequent rests; the young painter, very much on his mettle, anxious to please, too anxious to speak to the princess; the princess too unaccustomed to speaking to any stranger to initiate; court women and the occasional minister came and went, that the two of them were never alone together. It was the women, or the ministers, who decided when Lissar should step down and rest. She remembered those sittings—or standings; curious how her memory brought up something, carefully enclosed, that led nowhere, to stave off the worst of the recognition of her own past; she could remember nothing around those occasions of standing being painted. She remembered nothing of the decision to have it done; she had no memory of how many copies might have been made, who they might have been sent to; when all of this had been accomplished. . . . She remembered, looking into her poised, uninhabited face, the faint surprise she felt at the portrait's being commissioned at all. It seemed so unlike . . . unlike . . . she couldn't remember. But she was so unused to strangers, and these portraits would be sent out into the world, to strangers; she was unused to strangers because . . . it was not that she was shy, although she was, it was because . . . she remembered the ministers coming in, to see how the work was progressing, the court ministers, her father's ministers. . . .

King's daughter

King's daughter

King's daughter

The memory ended. Her legs were trembling. So were her hands, as she moved a stack of paintings and sat down, sideways, her body turned toward the painting, but both feet still firmly on the ground. But she turned her face back toward the window and raised her chin, closing her eyes, as if she were only enjoying the sunlight. "Who is the girl in the golden dress, with the fleethound? The hound might be one of yours." Her voice sounded odd, feverish, but she hoped it was only the banging of her heart in her own ears.

"That's Lissla Lissar," said Ossin, easily, as if the name were no different from any other name: Ossin, Ob, Goldhouse, Lilac, Deerskin. "And that *is* one of my dogs. Lissar's mother died when she was fifteen; I was seventeen, and still deeply romantic—those were the years I was dreaming of Moonwoman and, coincidentally, raising my first litters of first-class pups. I sent her one of my pups, the best of her litter; I thought it a fine generous gesture, worthy of the man Moonwoman could come to love. I named the pup Ash." Ossin's gaze dropped to Ash, who had raised her own at the sound of her name. "She was exactly the same silver-fawn color as yours—except, of course, she had short hair."

He looked back up at Lissar. Lissar could see him thinking, rejecting what he thought even as he thought it. She tried to smile from her new, thin face at him; for the old Lissar had been rounder, and there were no lines in that Lissar's face. And she knew what he saw when he looked at her: a woman with prematurely white hair, from what unknown loss or sorrow; and with eyes black from secrets she herself could not look at.

But she closed her black eyes suddenly; for she remembered again what she had known all along, the life that went with the name she had retained. She remembered what she had, briefly, remembered on the mountaintop, before the Moonwoman had rescued her; that she was . . . not an herbalist's apprentice, but a king's daughter, and the reiteration of *king's daughter* in her brain was battering open the doors that had closed, opening the dark secrets lying at the bottom of her eyes; it went through her like a physical pain, like the agonizing return of blood to a frozen limb. King's daughter, daughter of a king who . . . who had . . .

No, not blood to a frozen limb; it was the thrust of the torch into the tarred bonfire, and the lick of the fire was cruel. The memories flared into brightness, seared her vision, stabbed through her eyes into the dark protected space inside her skull. . . . She wanted to scream, and could not, could not breathe, even so little movement as the rise and fall of her belly and breast—the involuntary blinking of her eyes as ordinary sight tried to bring her back into the room where the only warm things were her and Ossin and Ash, surrounded by cool paint on canvas, and dust—even this much motion, reminding her that she still lived, stretched her skin to bursting. It was as well she could not speak, even to moan; any cry would drive her over the lip of the pit, the pit she had forgotten, though her feet had never left its edge, and now that she had looked, and seen again, she could not look away. There were some things that took life and broke it, not merely into meaninglessness, but with active malice flung the pieces farther, into hell.

She would die, now, die with the benevolent sun on her face, leaning against a table in the quiet store-room of a man who was her friend and to whom she had lied about everything, lied because she could not help herself, because she knew nothing else to tell. She remembered the last three days and nights of her life as a princess; remembered the draining away of that life, and the last violent act that she believed had killed her. Even now, her body's wounds healed by time and Ash and snow and solitude and Moonwoman, and six puppies, and the friendship of a prince and a stable-hand; even now the memory of that act of violence would shatter her; she could not contain the memory even as her body had not been able to contain the result of its betrayal.

"Deerskin," said her friend. "What is wrong?"

Silky fur between her fingers; the reality of one dog, one dog's life, bringing her back to her own, as it had several times before. Her fingers clutched, hard, too hard, but Ash only stood where she was, bearing what she could for her beloved person's sake. Lissar, looking down into those brown eyes looking up, thought, Who can tell what she remembers of that night? But she is here as am I, and if I am to die of that night's work, let it not be before this man who gave me good work to do, and who has tried to speak to me as a friend.

I did not lie to him about everything, she thought. I told him that I liked dogs. And without conscious volition, her fingers searched out the lump at the back of Ash's skull. Ash had not carried her head as if it were sore in many months, not since Lissar had woken up wearing a white deerskin dress for the first time; but the lump was still there, for fingers that knew where to look.

"Forgive me," she said; her brain, still stunned, could not come up with even a bad reason for her faintness; any reason, that is, other than the truth, which she could not tell him, even to change her habit of lying to him. "Forgive me. It is over now. Will you"—her lips were stiff, and she could not think what question she might ask, to lead him away from her own trouble, and so she asked a question bred of memory and confusion: "Will you marry Lissar?"

Ossin smiled. "Not I. Not a chance. I am far beneath her touch. Her father is a great king, not a hunting-master with a rather large house, like mine. She's his only daughter, and . . ." He hesitated, looking at her, seeing her distress in her face, but seeing also that she did not wish to speak of it, and trying to let her, as he thought, lead him away from the source of that distress. He did not want to talk about Lissar; but the fate of a princess in a far-away country should be a safe topic. "After his wife died, the story was that he went mad with grief, and when he got over it, he grew obsessed with his daughter, and believed that no king or prince or young god with powers of life and death was good enough for her. Had I wished to run at that glass mountain I would have slid off its slick sides even before I was banished for my arrogance in wanting to try."

Lissar thought he looked at the painting almost with longing; perhaps he was remembering the first-class dog he had lost in a moment's romantic whim. "But you were sent a painting," she said, her mouth still speaking words that her brain was not conscious of forming. "You must have been considered an eligible suitor."

The longing look deepened. "I have wondered about that myself. My guess is that it was part of her father's wealth and importance that he could send paintings to every unmarried prince and king in his world." After a moment he went on: "I quite like the painting—who I imagine the person painted to be. She is watching from behind her eyes, her princess's gown—do you see it?" But Lissar was watching him. "Her mother was said to be the most beautiful woman in seven kingdoms, and that her daughter grew more like her every year. She is beautiful, of course, the glossy hair, that line of cheekbone, the balance of features; but it's not her beauty that I keep seeing in that painting. It's her . . . self, her humanity. Or maybe I just like the way her hand rests on her dog's head, and the way the dog is looking out at us, saying, mess with my lady if you dare, but don't forget *me*. I like thinking that Ash is appreciated." He turned away, embarrassed. "Pardon me. Here I've just been telling you that these portraits are invariably fraudulent, and now I am spinning a fairy-tale about a woman I have never met as painted by someone whose whims and imagination I have no guess of." Another pause. "Perhaps I was sent a painting in acknowledgement of the dog I bred; who knows how great kings think? I received no other acknowledgement, except Mik, who delivered the pup, was favorably taken by Lissar as a potential dog-owner."

Lissar dared to turn around and look at herself once more. "It is a very handsome dog."

"Hmm?" said Ossin. "Oh. Yes. It is a very handsome bitch." He smiled a little, again, sheepishly. "Perhaps I give myself permission to believe in how this painter presents the princess because the dog is so well done by. She looks so like her mother; that same wary look, when I was asking her to do something she considered of dubious merit. She would certainly have looked just so had I required her to sit for her portrait."

There was a longer pause. Lissar thought that Ossin would stir from his reflections, and suggest they leave, and they would leave; although Lissar's ghosts would go with her. But then they had been with her all along; now, only, she had names for them. And was not naming a way of establishing a pattern, of declaring control? She remembered the Moonwoman's words to her, and she wanted to say, It is not enough. I am sorry to be one of your failures, but I cannot bear it. I still cannot bear it.

Lissar straightened a little, still sitting on the edge of the table. "Whom did Lissar marry, after all?"

"She didn't. Although it's rather murky what exactly did happen. Usually we get quite good gossip at this court—we all like hearing how the real royals live—but somehow this story never quite got to the circle of our friends. I think she is supposed to have died; there was this uproar, and the king went very strange again, like after his wife died. No one would say if Lissar had actually died or if so what of. There was even a story that a lion leaped over the princess's garden wall and seized her; as soon say a dragon flew off with her, I think. But it was definitely given out that the king was now suddenly without heir.

"I favor the story that she ran off with a farmer and is happily growing lettuces somewhere. And raising puppies, although I don't like thinking what she might find to cross Ash with. I'd offer her any dog in my kennel for the pick of the litter, even now, when she probably doesn't have too many litters left. Her mother had her last litter at twelve, her idea, I didn't mean to have her bred any more, and those last five were as fine as any puppies she'd borne in her prime. . . . I suppose the king will marry again. I don't believe he's all that old, even though this now happened, oh, must be five years ago."

The king will marry again. The words went through her like swords; she barely heard Ossin's final words, and did not at first register them. The king will marry again. But Ossin was still speaking, Ossin, her friend, and the sound of his voice staunched her wounds, and she found that she was not plunging into the chaos and terror after all. She had paused on the brink to hear what he had to say, trying to distract herself as she felt her strength running out; and now she found that she had regained her balance, at least, while she listened. She was still weak and shaken, but she could stand without straining; there was little further call on her diminished strength. She could still hear the roar of the fire demons at the bottom of the pit, behind Ossin's voice; but it was not now her inevitable fate to fall to her death among them.

She listened, half attending to the prince, half attending to the knowledge that her own skin still enclosed her, that she was alive and aware of herself, feeling her chest rising and falling easily with her breathing, newly feeling the elasticity of her skin, and the sun's warmth on it, and Ash's long hair under her fingers. Feeling herself, with all that meant: as if her consciousness were a gatekeeper, now going round to all the doors of a house just relieved of a siege it had not thought to win.

The king will marry again. . . . No, no, it could not happen; it would not happen; she could not think of it, she saw her mother's blazing eyes striking down any who stood before the king's throne, her mother's eyes burning in the more-than-life-size portrait that hung on the wall behind. It would not happen.

She would win out. She was winning; she was here and she was not mad, and she remembered. She supposed it was necessary for her to take her life back, even when her life had been what it was. She risked taking a deep breath . . . and raised her eyes to Ossin's face.

She could not tell him.

"Please?" said Ossin.

The sound of his voice had been her lifeline, but she did not know what words he had said. She smiled, glad to have him there to smile at, embarrassed that she did not know what he was asking; delighting in her own ability to decide to smile, to speak, to walk; afraid of the moment when she would turn too quickly, lose her balance—for the chasm was there. What had happened to her the night she had fled her father's court and kingdom was a part of her, a part of her flesh and of her spirit. It was perhaps better to know than not to know— she was not yet sure—but the knowing did not make the chasm any less real, the grief any less debilitating, it only gave it a name, a definition. But the fact of definition implied that it had limits—that her life went on around it. They were only memories. She had lived. They were now only memories, and where she stood now the sun was shining.

Five years ago.

The Moonwoman had said, I give you the gift of time.

Time enough to grow strong enough to remember. Maybe the Moonwoman had known Lissar well enough after all.

"It is, you remember, only one evening," finished the prince. "Let's get out of here; it's a depressing place, the vain hopes and dreams of generations of my family. You're looking a little grey—unless you're just trying to buy time to think up an excuse to say no."

Time, she thought. I have all the time in the world. Only one evening is . . . I lay four years on a mountaintop, till the shape of my and my dog's bodies had worn themselves into the mountain itself. If we went back there, we would still see the little double hollow, like two commas bent together in a circle.

One evening. "Do I need an excuse?" she said cautiously. She stood up, and found that she could walk slowly after him to the door; she did not look at the painting of Lissar as she passed.

"My mother and her ladies will be raiding their wardrobes anyway so that anyone who wants to come may, so you will have a dress for the asking. Camilla's old dresses are only for children, it will be a few years before she's much of a resource; although being who she is she has rather to be forcibly restrained from having dresses made to give away. She'll be a queen like our mother, I think; I hope she finds the right king to marry.

"So you can't beg off because you have nothing to wear. And I doubt that you've been invited to any other grand performances that evening; this is a small place, and we're the biggest thing in it."

Lissar finally grasped that he was asking her again to come to the ball. "Oh, no, I couldn't!" she said, and stopped dead.

Ossin stopped too, looking at her. "Have you really not been listening? Or did you only think I couldn't be serious?" Or did something in the portrait room disturb you that much? I am sorry, Deerskin, sorry, my . . . it was a rude trick to play, I had not thought. "I am serious. Please do come."

"I can't," she said again; she had only just remembered her last royal ball, remembered how it fitted into her new pattern of memory.

"Why can't you?"

She shook her head mutely.

"What if I order you to come? Would that help? Offer to throw you in the dungeon and so on, if you don't? We do have dungeons, I believe, somewhere, someone probably knows where they are, or we could simply put you in the wine-cellars—with no cork-puller."

She laughed in spite of herself and he looked pleased. This was a different ball they were discussing, she said to herself, she was not who she had been, and this was not the man who had led her through those old dancing figures. "Do you have many herbalists' failed apprentices at your royal balls then?"

"Then you've remembered!" he said, and her eyes were on him as he said it, and she saw the dreaded ball disappear from his face. "You've remembered!"

She had told him, those long nights with the puppies when she was too tired to remember what she could or couldn't say, should or shouldn't, that she had been ill, and lost much of her memory. She was both frightened and heartened by his interest now, and she said, smiling a little, "I don't know how much I've remembered"—this was true; the fire still burned, reflecting off surfaces she did not yet recognize—"but your portrait room, I'm not sure, it shook something loose."

"Looking at Trivelda makes me feel a trifle unsettled myself," said the prince. "I did think you were looking a bit green there; you should have said something to me earlier. But see, then you must come to the ball."

"I do not see at all."

Ossin waved a hand at her. "Do not ruin the connection by analyzing it. Come meet Trivelda, and rescue me." Impulsively he seized her hands, standing close to her. He was shorter than her father, she noticed dispassionately, but bulkier, broader in both shoulders and belly.

"Very well," she said. "The kennel-girl will scrub up for one night, and present herself at the front door. Wearing shoes will be the worst, you know."

"Thank you," he said, and she noticed that he meant it.

Twenty-eight

The next day when she returned from taking the puppies for a long romp through the meadows, despite a thick drizzly fog and mud underfoot, there were a series of long slender bundles waiting for her, hung over the common-room table. She dried her hands carefully, and loosened the neck of one, and realized, just before her fingers touched satin, what these must be: dresses for the ball. A choice of dresses: a wardrobe just for one night, like a princess. Even her fingertips were so callused from kennel work that she could not run them smoothly over the slippery cloth; there was slight friction, the barest suggestion of a snag. Not satin, she thought.

She dropped the bag, whistled to the puppies, and put them in their pen. They looked at her reproachfully when she closed the door on them. "Have I ever missed feeding you on time?" she said. One or two, convinced that she was going to go off and have interesting adventures without them, turned their backs and hunched their shoulders; the others merely flung themselves down in attitudes of heartbreak and resignation.

Ash, of course, accompanied her back to the common-room; Hela was there this time. "Queen's own messenger," she said, nodding toward the bundles on the table.

"Oh," said Lissar, a little startled; she had not taken Ossin's suggestion seriously that his mother would be willing, let alone prompt, to provide the kennel-girl with a ball-gown, and with a choice of ball-gown at that. The further thought intruded: anyone can go who wishes to: but they will not all be wearing satin.

"Better you than me," said Hela.

"Have you ever been to a ball?" said Lissar.

Hela shook her head. "I was a maid-servant up there when I first came to the yellow city, till Jobe rescued me. I waited on a few balls. I like dogs better."

"So do I," said Lissar feelingly, but she took her armful up to her room, and spread the dresses out on the seldom-used bed. After teaching the puppies to climb stairs she found she was more comfortable on the ground floor after all, unrolling a mattress in their pen which, now that they were old enough to understand about such things, always smelled clean and sweet with the dry meadowgrass the scrubbers bedded it with. From the ground floor also it was easier to creep out-of-doors in the middle of the night, seven soft-footed dogs at her heels, and sleep under the sky. It was late enough in the season that even the night air was warm; Lissar began to keep a blanket tucked in a convenient tree-crotch, and she and the puppies returned to the kennels at dawn, as if they had been out merely for an early walk. She did not know how many of the staff knew the truth of it. On the nights it rained she most often lay awake, listening to the fall of water against the roof, grateful to be dry but wishing to be away from walls and ceilings nonetheless.

The last time they had all slept in Lissar's room was the day after they had found the little boy. She had stayed awake long enough that morning to walk down the hillside to the village, where a royal waggon, much slower than the prince's riding party, lumbered up to them, and where Lissar was made intensely uncomfortable by the gratitude of the boy's mother—the woman who had found her in the meadow the evening before. The woman had ridden home in her husband's market-cart, having managed not to tell him where she had gone and who she had seen during her long absence from their stall; and when she got home again she had kept vigil all night. She had known the Moon-woman would find her Aric.

Lissar had not liked the longing, hopeful, measuring, cautious looks the other villagers, attracted by the commotion and the royal crest on waggon and saddle-skirt, had sent her when they heard the story, and it was a relief in more ways than one when she could climb into the wag-gon, well bedded with straw and blankets, and collapse. Ossin had of-fered her a ride behind him on his big handsome horse, when they had met upon the hillside; but she had preferred to walk to the village—though she found herself clutching his stirrup, for she was so tired she staggered, and could not keep a straight line. He, at last, dismounted too, but she would not let him touch her; and so the party had come slowly down to the village, everyone mounted but Ossin and Lissar and ten fleethounds; the boy lay cradled in the arms of one of Ossin's men, and the short-legged scent-hounds the prince's party had brought rode at their ease across saddle-bows and cantles.

She remembered the scene as if through a fever; the euphoria of the night before, that queer, humming sense of knowing where she was to go, had departed, leaving her more tired and empty than she could ever remember being; so empty that the gaps in her memory did not show. She had stayed awake just long enough to tell the prince how to find the thing in the tree; and then even the jerking of the (admittedly well sprung) waggon over village roads could not keep her awake.

She thought of all that now as she shook the dresses free of their sacks, thinking that the queen had sent the kennel-girl four dresses to choose from, dresses of silk and satin and lace. She had slept through the bringing-home of the thing in the tree; she had slept through the first conversations, first responses, to her adventure. She had been glad to sleep through them. But she wondered, now, with four ball-gowns fit for a queen spread out before her in the plain little room of a member of the royal kennel staff, what version of the story might even have penetrated to the heart of the court: wondered and did not want to wonder. Wondered what version of the story of the six doomed puppies might have been told. Wondered what the version of the kennel-girl's friendship with the prince might be.

Lissar found it incomprehensibly odd that a kennel-girl should pull the straw out of her hair and dust the puppy fur off her backside and put on a fancy dress and go to a ball. It was not how her father's court had been run. . . . "Not a hunting master with a rather large house," Ossin had said. Beech, the first huntswoman, was going to the ball. Beech, who, at the height of hunting season, stopped taking her leaders to her room, and unrolled a mattress in the pack's stall. During the winter, when everyone relaxed (and recuperated), she would go back upstairs again. All of the kennel folk slept with a few special dogs bestowed around them on their ordinary human beds; it seemed, upon reflection, that since Lissar had seven dogs special to her it was more efficient for her to sleep with them instead of the other way around. She wondered if the story of her sleeping most nights out-of-doors with her seven special dogs had travelled beyond the confines of the kennels.

The satin dress was very beautiful, a dark bright red with ribbons and cascades of lace around the neckline; but she did not want to wear it, with her rough hands going *shh ssshhh* every time her fingers brushed the skirts.

The second dress was blue, light as cobwebs, with insets of paler blue and lavender; but it was a dress for a young girl, whose worst nightmares contained fantastic creatures and undefined fears never met in waking life, and whose dreams were full of hope.

The third dress was golden, vivid as fire, with gold brocade, a dress for a princess to stand and have her portrait taken in, not for a kennel-girl to wear, even if she has combed her hair and washed her hands. Even if she had once been such a princess, with her soft uncallused hand resting on her dog's neck. Especially because she had once been such a princess.

The fourth was the one she would wear. It was silver-grey, a few shades darker than Ash's fur, and it shimmered like Moonlight in a mist. The skirt was very full, and soft; her hands stroked it soundlessly. The bodice was cut simply; no ribbons or brocade. It was, however, sewn all over with tiny, twinkling stones, colorless, almost invisible, but radiant as soon as the light touched them. This was the dress she would wear, although her hands shook as she held it up.

THE QUEEN'S MESSENGER WAS BACK IN THE MORNING, bowing as he accepted three dress-sacks, and with a roll of brown paper under his arm, upon which he took tracings of Lissar's feet and hands, "that my lady's shoes and gloves may be made to fit."

THE PRINCE MIGHT DECRY BALLS IN GENERAL AND a ball for Trivelda in particular, but the atmosphere through and around the yellow city over the next sennight took on a distinctive, festive cast, which Lissar now knew why she recognized.

Lilac, whose parents, it turned out, were not such small farmers after all, nor quite so angry with her for running off to the king's city, would be attending the ball in a gown not begged from queen or princess but bought with money they sent her, to purchase the work of a local seamstress. "Fortunately Marigold is a friend of mine," Lilac said;

"all the seamstresses are swamped, and my gown isn't nearly as grand a piece of work as the court women's. Indeed, you know," she added, showing an uncharacteristic hesitancy in her speech, "I'll have money left over, if there's anything you need and don't want, you know, to ask for; I don't need it, but if I send money home my parents will be disappointed."

Lissar told her, equally hesitantly, about the gloves and shoes. There was a barely noticeable pause before Lilac said, in her usual tone, "You are lucky. I've known one or two people who've shown up barefoot. Usually there's this terrific run on plain slippers just before a ball, for everyone who has borrowed or been given a dress from someone at the court, it's pretty simple to make a dress that doesn't quite fit do well enough, but shoes are much harder, especially if you are going to dance in them."

"What happens at a grand ball when someone comes barefoot?" said Lissar, fascinated, remembering the courtiers of her childhood.

"What happens?" said Lilac, puzzled. "I don't know, really, this is my first ball here too; I've just heard the stories. Their feet get sore, I suppose, and perhaps they're very careful to choose graceful dancing-partners. Ask Redthorn; his wife is one of them, though I don't see Redthorn as being that light on his feet."

Lilac, as usual, seemed to know everything that was happening in the city, as well as all the details about the ball itself. Lissar longed to ask her . . . why the queen might have sent four ball-gowns to a kennel-girl; but she did not. Surely the queen had better sense than to believe that Moonwoman might take a job in a kennel, even a royal kennel. Ossin had never said what his mother had felt about the whole tale of the Moonwoman; only that she noticed it had no strong queens in it. The king rode out in the hunting-parties occasionally, the princess too; the queen stayed mostly at home, on the ground. Lilac had said once, kindly but pityingly, that the queen found horses a bit alarming.

Lilac offered to dress Lissar's hair for the ball; Lissar remembered, suddenly, a neck-wearying headdress she had once worn, so heavy and ornate she had felt it would slowly crush her down, till she lay on the ground to rest her head. And yet it was far simpler than some she had seen on the other ladies' heads, structures pinioned to the crown of the skull, the hair scraped over them, with hairpieces attached, adding bulk and weight, if the hair growing on the head proved insufficient, as it inevitably did.

As Lissar thought of this, Lilac had untwisted the braid Lissar commonly kept her hair contained in, and was stroking a shining handful with a brush, saying, "I've wanted an excuse to do something with your hair, Deerskin, it's such an extraordinary color."

"White," said Lissar. "Nothing extraordinary about white."

"Old people's hair isn't like this," said Lilac, thoughtfully. "Yours is almost iridescent. It breaks light like a prism."

Lissar tipped her head up to look at her friend. "You're imagining things," she said.

Lilac took a fresh grip, gently moving Lissar's head till she faced front, away from her, again. "We call it—imagining things—following the Moon," she said. "Children are natural Moon-followers. Some of us grow out of it more than others. I'm not known for it, myself," she added.

There was a little pause. Lissar, with a small effort of will, relaxed against Lilac's hands and deliberately closed her eyes. "Just keep it simple, please," she said. "I want to know it's still my hair when you're done."

Lilac laughed. "You needn't worry! You'd need a real hairdresser for the kind of thing you mean. Trivelda was wearing a menagerie, the last time she was here—birds and deer and gods know what all—these little statues, worked into this net thing she was wearing on her head. It was quite extraordinary. It's become a sort of legend. The joke was that it was as near as she ever got to real animals . . . you can't count her lapdogs. No one has ever seen one walk on its own, and she has them bathed every day, and they wear her perfume.

"Veeery simple," she said after a moment. "All I have to do is decide what color ribbons." She opened the little bag she'd arrived wearing round her neck; a visual cacophony of ribbons poured out: ribbons thin as a thread, as wide as the thickness of three fingers, ribbons of all colors, ribbons woven of other ribbons, ribbons of silk and velvet, ribbons with tiny embroidered figures and patterns, ribbons with straight edges, ribbons with scalloped edges, ribbons of lace.

"Mercy!" said Lissar, sitting up.

"Oh, Marigold let me borrow these. I'll take back what we don't want. Now, your dress is silver, is it not? Burgundy in your hair, then, and black like your eyes, and . . . let's see . . . maybe the palest pink, to set off your complexion. The palest pink. If it weren't for your hair I'd say your skin was white. . . . Now hold still." Her hands began braiding. "Everyone thinks this is it, you see. That's why everyone is so excited about this particular ball. I don't think anyone will come barefoot to this one."

"This is it?" said Lissar, finding herself enjoying having her hair brushed, like one of the dogs on a grooming table, lulled by the motion and the contact. She ran her fingers down the smooth midline of Ash's skull, Ash's head being on her knee. "How do you mean?" she asked, only half attending.

"Oh, that Ossin will offer for Trivelda. It's no secret that the king and queen are impatient to marry him off; he's gone twenty-five, you know, and they want the ordinary sort of grandchildren, not the kind that bark and have four legs, and besides, there's Camilla, who will turn seventeen in the spring, and there's this very tiresome tradition that the royal heir is supposed to marry first.

"There's an even more tiresome tradition that all noble families are supposed to marry off their children in chronological order, but it's really only the heirs that anyone pays much attention to. Ossin knows this of course—so does Camilla. Cofta and Clem are afraid she's getting too fond of that pretty count, he knows so well how to be charming and she's so young, and if they sent him away it might just make it all worse. But they can't really do much about pushing her elsewhere till Ossin is officially done with. And Ossin's fond of his sister, and likes Dorl even less than his parents do."

Lissar found herself strangely dismayed by this news, and the long gentle strokes of the hairbrush, and smaller busyness of fingers plaiting, suddenly annoyed her. "But he doesn't like Trivelda."

Lilac chuckled. "How much do you think that has to do with it?"

"They don't want Camilla to marry Dorl."

"That's different. Dorl really isn't much except charm—and old blood—and neither of those, even, is laid very thick. There are very few real princesses around, or even wealthy farmers' daughters, and most of them have gotten married while the prince has been out hunting his dogs."

"Chasing the Moonwoman," murmured Lissar.

"Eh?"

"Nothing."

"It won't be so bad because they'll have nothing to do with one another. It would be much worse if she wanted to ride and hunt; she's an appalling rider, hates horses, and her idea of a dog . . . well, those things of hers look like breakfast-rolls with hair. And they all bark, if you want to call it barking. Anyway, she'll stay out of the barns—and kennels— and he'll stay out of the drawing-rooms. Knowing Ossin, he'll be glad of the excuse, come to that."

"It doesn't sound . . . very satisfying," said Lissar.

Lilac laughed. Ash pricked her ears. "Deerskin, I've caught you out at last; you're a romantic. I would never have guessed. Do you know, I think I want a shade a little rosier than the palest pink after all. I have a brooch, I'll loan it to you, it will look perfect right here," and she stabbed a finger at the side of Lissar's head.

"You're a wealthy farmer's daughter," said Lissar, still distressed that

Ossin should be thrown away on a princess with hairy breakfast-rolls for dogs.

"Hmm? What?" said Lilac, fingers busy. "Who, me? Marry Ossin? In the first place, he wouldn't have me. In the second place his parents wouldn't have me. My parents aren't that wealthy, and I'm still a stable-girl. And third, I wouldn't have him. I know he's admirable in every way and the country is lucky to have him to look forward to as their next king. But he's so admirable he's boring. I don't think he's ever been drunk in his life, or broken a window when he was a boy playing hurl-fast, or spoken an unmerited harsh word. He's so responsible. Ugly, too."

Lissar, stung, said, "He's not ugly."

Lilac, now working from the front, paused and looked into Lissar's face. There was a tight little pause, while Lissar remembered the nights together in the puppies' pen, guessing that that story would have been heard in the stables. Had she ever told Lilac herself? She couldn't remember.

Lilac, irrepressible, started to smile. "You marry him," she said.

Twenty-nine

Not only shoes and gloves arrived in the final package from the queen, but a cloak as well; and on the evening as Lissar was bundling everything up to meet Lilac in the room of the Gold House they had been assigned for their final toilettes (to keep the dog- and horse-hair down to a minimum, one short hall's rooms had been given over to those of the animal staff who wished to come to the ball), something else arrived: a small package, wrapped in a white cloth, left on the common-room table again, with only a slip of paper with her name, Deerskin, on it.

"This must be for you," said Hela, catching her as she came downstairs, explaining to Ash that she would be back soon and meanwhile wouldn't she prefer to stay with the puppies, nearly full-grown now and not puppies except by the glints in their eyes and their tendency to forget their training for no reason beyond sunshine, or rain, or the shadow of a bird's wing, or the fascination of their own tails, and of being alive and frisky. Ash was not convinced. Her back was humped and her tail between her legs as Lissar put her hand on her rump and pushed her through the half-door. The puppies were delighted to see their leader, and fawned at her feet, waiting to see if she would stoop to playing with them, or if she would demand they leave her alone. Lissar left them to it.

"I think this is probably yours," Hela said again, emerging from the common-room, and held out the parcel. The flowing hand that had written *Deerskin* was both graceful and legible.

"Yes," said Lissar, "that is my name on it."

"Ah," said Hela. "We guessed. The rest of us can't read, you know."

Lissar looked up, startled.

"What cause for us to learn?" said Hela, smiling at Lissar's expression, and returned to the common-room.

"We'll want to hear all about it," Berry called, as she went hastily past the door.

Lilac was already dressed when Lissar arrived. "Anyone would think you didn't want to come," she said, almost cross. "The rest have gone before us. We'll be late, and I want to see Trivelda come in. I want to see what she has thought up, after the menagerie last time. . . . What's that?"—as the bundle Hela had given her dropped from under Lissar's arm.

"I don't know. It was left for me this evening. Open it while I get my dress on."

"Ribbons," said Lilac. "Look." And she held up two handfuls of ribbons: pink, blood-red, black, dark green, silver-grey. "Who sent them?"

"I have no idea." There was one significant difference between these ribbons and the ones provided by Lilac; these were sewn with the same tiny bright stones as the dress Lissar was wearing.

"Hmm," said Lilac, staring at the card with Lissar's name and nothing else on it. "It was Ossin who invited you, wasn't it?"

"Yes," said Lissar shortly, not wishing to remember the end of their last conversation about the prince. "But his mother supplied the dress. Help me—ugh," she said, tugging futilely at her hair, which was caught on the tiny hooks that fastened the tight bodice together.

"Hold still. Stop pulling; I want all your hair still in your head for this evening. Now sit down. I may use one or two of my ribbons just for contrast. And I brought that brooch."

THEY WERE, AS IT HAPPENED, IN PLENTY OF TIME; for the princess Trivelda was very late. Whether she was late on account of the time it took her to finish dressing—her entourage had only arrived the day before, and much had been made of how tired she and her breakfast-food dogs were as a result of the journey—or because she wished to make a grand entrance, Lissar did not know; but make an entrance she did.

Her gown was green, and her hair, much redder than in the painting Lissar had seen, was dressed both high on her head and permitted to fall, in a questionable profusion of curls, down her back. She was both short and plump, and the hair already made her look a trifle ridiculous, for there seemed to be more hair than person; and to make her waist look small, her skirts were tremendous, flaring out as though she and they would empty the ballroom of everyone else. Her skirts were worked in some dizzying pattern, also, that shimmered as the light caught it, and made it difficult to look at for any length of time, with the result that watching her small arrogant figure march down the long hall gave a faint sense of sea-sickness.

Lissar had established herself near a long curtain hanging from a pillar projecting from the wall; she recognized several other people from the king's house similarly clinging to the scenery, looking awkward in their fine clothes but at the same time glancing around with interest, and too absorbed in the spectacle to be uncomfortably self-conscious. Lissar stood absently rubbing her fingers together. Her hands felt as imprisoned by gloves as her feet did by shoes; simultaneously both were a comfort: costume, not clothing, stage set for the evening's performance.

The prince's friends were not the courtier sort, so there were enough of them (us, thought Lissar, for she was Deerskin here, Deerskin in costume) that no one need feel lonesome or truly out of place. She looked around for the Curn of Dorl, whom she had seen the first time the day Ossin had offered her six puppies to raise; he was easily spotted among all the people not trying to be visible, for he was wearing yellow as bright as a bonfire at harvest festival; he seemed to glitter as he turned. He bowed with a grace that might almost match one of Ossin's dogs, and it was as if the entire ballroom of people paused a moment to watch him.

Certainly the princess Trivelda paused, and offered him a curtsey rather more profound than a mere Curn required, but Dorl often had that effect on people, particularly women: Lissar saw Camilla watching him, with an anxious, wistful little smile on her face, as if she wished she did not care, wished that she did not wish to watch him, though she was as poised as she had been on the day Lissar had first seen them both.

Then the prince moved forward to greet his guest; Lissar, though she had been looking for him, had not noticed him before. He too was dressed in green, but a dark green, the color of leaves in shadow; and he stepped forward with all the grace of an unhappy chained bear to welcome the woman most of those watching believed would soon be his wife. He looked like a rough servant, cleaned up for special duty, perhaps; perhaps the special duty of waiting on the scintillant Dorl: and both of them knew it, as did Trivelda, who smirked.

Lissar, sharply aware of her gorgeous borrowed dress, found herself forgetting her own discomfort, forgetting to notice the ghosts that encircled her, that whispered in her ears, that crept between the folds of her skirt; forgetting as she watched her friend walk stiffly down the ballroom floor and bow to Trivelda, still like a bear performing a trick he had learned but does not understand, like a bear performing in fear of

a yank on the chain if he does not perform adequately. He moved as if
his clothing chafed him; there was none of the careless grace of easy
strength and purpose that he had in the fields with his hounds, or on
horseback. Here he was bulky, awkward, overweight, his eyes too small
and his chin too large; he looked dazed and stupid.

For a moment her own ghosts dissolved absolutely in the heat of
her sympathy; she was but a young woman watching a friend in trouble.
Almost she forgot where she was and called out to him. She did not
speak aloud, but she moved restlessly out of the shadowed niche between column and curtain; and the prince's eyes, sweeping the crowd,
saw her movement, identified her; and his face lightened—as if it had
been she he was looking for—for a moment he looked like the man she
saw every day in the kennels, as if his real nature came out of hiding and
inhabited his face for a moment.

She did not know what to do; he was about to offer his hand to
Trivelda, his future wife, and a hundred people stood between him and
Lissar, her back to a pillar. She could not speak, say, "I am with you."
She could not rub the back of his neck as she had done once or twice
during the longest of the puppy nights, when four o'clock in the morn-
ing went on for years and dawn never came; she could do nothing.

And so she curtseyed: her deepest, most royal curtsey, the curtsey a
princess would give a prince, for when she had remembered who she
was, with that knowledge came the memory of her court manners. She
had not known that those memories had returned to her, nor, if she had,
would she have guessed they would be of any use to her; had she known
she might have wished to banish them, as one rejects tainted food once
one has been sick. She curtseyed, had she known it, as beautifully as
her mother might once have curtseyed, for all that Lissar had learned
her court manners mostly as a mouse might, watching her glamorous
mother and splendid father from her corner. And as she curtseyed she
moved farther out into the room, fully away from the shadowing curtain; and the tiny gems on her dress and in her hair caught the light

from the hundreds of candles set in the huge chandeliers, and she blazed up in that crowd as if she were the queen of them all.

Trivelda's back was to her, and so she did not know what had happened; but she felt that something had, felt the attention of the crowd falter and shift away from her: saw the prince look over her head and suddenly straighten and smile and look, for a moment, like a prince, instead of like an oaf in fancy dress. She was not pleased; more, she was jealous, that Ossin should look well for someone else. She stiffened, and drew herself up to her full, if diminutive, height, and prepared to turn around and see what or who was ruining her grand moment—and to do battle.

Ossin, who was well drilled in courtliness, for all that he had no gift for it, saw Trivelda stiffen, knew what it meant, and snapped his attention back to her at once. Lissar rose from her curtsey in time to see what was happening between him and Trivelda; and so by the time Trivelda had graciously accepted his proffered hand, and moved surreptitiously forward and to one side so that she could see in the direction that the prince's defection had occurred, there was nothing to see. Lissar had resubmerged herself into the shadow of the crowd.

She had meant to return to her pillar, but the prince had not been the only person who noticed her curtsey; and she found that there were abruptly a number of persons who wished to speak to her, and several young men (and one or two old ones) who wished to invite her to dance with them.

She glanced down at her jewel-strewn skirts, rubbed one soft-gloved hand over them; no one need guess her current profession by her work-roughened hands tonight. "Thank you," she said to the smallest and shyest of the young men, who flushed scarlet in delight, and drew her forward to join the line that the prince and Trivelda led. The young man proved to be a very neat and precise dancer, but an utterly tongue-tied conversationalist, which suited Lissar perfectly. She had not danced since—her old life; and the memories her body held, in order to use the knowledge of how to dance, how to curtsey, brought too much of the rest with it.

Her heart beat faster than the quick steps of the dance could explain, for she was fit enough to run for hours with her dogs; here she had to open her lips a little, to pant, like a dog in summer. But the young man held her delicately, politely at arm's length; and when she caught his eye he blushed again, and looked at her as adoringly as a fortnight-old puppy to whom she meant *milk*. She smiled at him, and he jerked his gaze down. To her gloved hands he muttered something.

"I beg your pardon?"

"I asked, what is your name?"

"Lissar," she said, without thinking; but she had spoken softly as he had uttered his first question, and the musicians were playing vigorously, to be heard over any amount of foot-tapping, dress-rustling, and conversation, including the stifled grunts of those trodden on by inept partners. In his turn he now said: "I beg your pardon?"

"Deerskin," she said, firmly.

"Deerskin," he murmured. "Deerskin—it was a Deerskin who found the little boy from Willowwood."

"Yes," she said.

"Yes—you were she?" he said, flushing again.

"Yes," she said again.

They danced a few more measures in silence, and his voice sounded like a small boy's when he said: "My cousin is a friend of Pansy, whose son it was was lost. Pansy believes this Deerskin is really the Moon-woman, come to earth again."

"I do not dance like a goddess, do I?" said Lissar gently. She took her hand out of his for a moment, and pulled her glove down her forearm. There were a series of eight small deep scratches, just above her wrist, in two sets of four. "One of the puppies from the litter I raised taught himself, when he was still small enough not to knock me down, to jump into my arms when I held them out and called his name. Once he missed. I do not think Moonwoman's dogs would miss; nor would she willingly wear scars from so foolish a misadventure."

The young man was smiling over her shoulder, dreamily; but he said no more. The dance came to an end; they parted, bowing to each other. As she rose from her curtsey he, obviously daring greatly, said, "Sh-she might, you know. To look ordinary. Human, you know." Then he bowed a second time, quickly, almost jerkily, the first graceless gesture she had seen from him, and walked quickly away.

Thirty

She danced steadily all evening. Once or twice her partners asked her if she would rather have a plate from the long tables of sumptuous food laid out at one end of the hall, but she declined; it would be harder not to talk, away from the noise and bustle of the dancing; she could not keep her mouth full all the time. Nor was she hungry; she was managing to keep her useful skills separate from her secret, but the secret was a weight on her spirit, and in the pit of her stomach, and she was not hungry; nor was she aware of growing tired.

She was too tight-stretched, alert to keep the old terror at bay, to keep herself from doing anything so appalling as blurting out her real name again; to keep her mind on what she was doing, dancing, and not making conversation. Some of her partners were more persistent than others. She made a mistake in choosing to dance with one old fellow, stiff and white-haired, thinking he would probably be deaf, and if inclined to talk, would want to talk exclusively about himself and, as she guessed from the metal he wore across his chest, his glorious career in the military.

But he surprised her; he was not in the least deaf, and very curious about her. "I have five daughters within, I would guess, five years on either side of your age, and I thought I knew every member of Cofta and Clem's court of their age and sex. You never came with Trivelda— you're not her type—so who are you?"

"I'm a kennel-girl who has slipped her leash for the evening."

He laughed at this, as he was supposed to, but he did not let her off. And so he extracted her story from her, piece by piece, backwards to her appearance in King Goldhouse's receiving-hall the day after the prince's favorite bitch had died giving birth to her puppies.

"And where did you come from before that?" the relentless old gentleman pursued.

"Wouldn't you rather tell me of your dangerous campaigns in the wild and exotic hills of somewhere or other?" she said, a little desperately.

He laughed again; it was impossible not to like him. "No. Campaigns are a great bore; they are mostly about either finding enough water for your company, or being up to your knees in mud and all the food's gone bad. Battles are blessedly brief; but you're sick with terror before, blind with panic during, and miserable with horror by the results, when you have to bury your friends, or listen to them scream. I'm glad to be retired. But you remind me of someone, and I'm trying to think of whom; I've done a lot of travelling in my life, and—"

She jerked herself free of his loose hold in an involuntary convulsion of fear. "My dear," he said, and they halted in the middle of the figure, whereupon four people immediately blundered into them. "Are you feeling ill?"

"No," she said breathlessly; and took his hand again, and composed herself to pick up the dance.

"I do not know what your secret is," said the old man after a moment; "I apologize for giving you pain. I have heard of Deerskin, and of what I have heard of her, and looking into your bright young face tonight, I can think no evil of her. If I remember who you remind me of, I will keep it to myself."

"Thank you," she said.

"My name is Stronghand," he said. "If you find yourself in need of a friend, my wife and I are very fond of young girls; come find us. We live just outside the city, on the road from the Bluevine Gate. The innkeeper at the Golden Orchid can tell you just where."

The dance ended then, and as she rose from her curtsey, he kissed her hand. "Remember," he said, and then turned and left her.

She was standing looking after him when Lilac came up to her. "Come away quickly, before someone else grabs you—you've been on your feet all evening, I've been watching you. You're one of the brightest stars of the ball. Trivelda is going to send someone to spill something on you soon, to get you out of the way. But don't any of these great louts ever think you might want something to eat?"

She smiled at her friend. "Several of them have asked, but I preferred dancing to having to sit down and make conversation."

"If that isn't like you. Conversation is much easier than dancing— I think," she said, a little ruefully.

"Don't try and tell me you don't dance beautifully; I've been watching you too."

Lilac wrinkled her nose. "It depends completely on who I'm with. Ladoc, my friend's cousin, is fun; some of these fellows, well, one or two, my feet may never recover. Come and see the lovely food. I'm starving. And you don't have to make conversation with me if you don't want to."

"'Don't any of these great louts ever think you might want something to eat?'"

"This is the *third* time I've been down to the tables," said Lilac, handing her a plate. "The servers are beginning to recognize me. Here, this is particularly good," she said, thrusting her empty plate under the appropriate server's nose, and seizing Lissar's plate away from her again to proffer it too. "And this."

A little later they looked up when a pair of messenger-clad legs paused in front of them as they sat at a tiny table tucked in with other tiny tables behind the grand display of food. The messenger bowed first to Lilac and then, more deeply, to Lissar.

"The prince's compliments, and if my lady would permit this humble messenger to guide her to him for a brief moment of her time?"

Lissar rose at once. "I'll see you back on the dance floor," said Lilac, licking her fingers and trying not to look unduly curious.

The messenger took her back across the long length of the dance floor, toward the far end, where the dais stood, bearing tall chairs for the king, queen, prince and princess of this country as well as the king, queen and princess who were their guests; the fact that this was a ball, and that none of them would sit in the chairs all evening, was beside the point. The latter king and queen were dowdy in comparison to their vivid daughter, but the king looked as if the court he found himself in did not live up to his opinion of his own dignity. He kept scowling at the chairs set out for his family, although they were quite as fine as the others. The queen looked like a frightened chambermaid expecting to be caught out wearing her mistress's clothes, which did not quite fit. She was small, like her daughter, but Trivelda's hauteur came obviously from her father.

Courtiers stood near the dais in groups so carefully posed Lissar found herself wondering if they had been set out that way, like flower arrangements. Perhaps there were marks on the floors, telling them where to put their feet. Trivelda's courtiers all seemed to be carrying— one each—a long-stemmed ariola in a vivid blue-green that set off, or collided with, the shade of the princess's dress. Cofta's courtiers, with the exception of the Curn of Dorl, seemed a poor lot by contrast, and they wandered about in an unmistakably individual fashion.

Trivelda, surrounded by her parents and courtiers, was delicately nibbling at various small dainties offered her from plates held by kneeling courtiers, whose other hands were occupied in grasping long-stemmed ariolas. The prince—my prince, Lissar found, to her dismay, herself thinking of him as—was standing with his back to this edifying spectacle, and his mother was whispering something, it looked rather forcefully, in his ear, which Lissar assumed was the cause of his looking increasingly sullen and stupid. Lissar wished the messenger would walk more slowly.

As the messenger stepped aside, the prince stepped forward. His mother, obviously caught mid-sentence, shut her lips together tightly, but Lissar thought she looked unhappy rather than angry, and the glance she turned on Lissar had no malice in it. Ossin bowed, and Lissar's knees bent in a curtsey before her brain told them to. She had barely straightened up when the prince snatched at her hands and danced away with her.

He was not a good dancer, but after a few turns through the figure he steadied, or relaxed, and Lissar began to think she had been initially mistaken, for he danced very ably, catching and turning her deftly, and she surprised herself by leaning into his hands trustingly instead of holding herself constantly alert as she had done with her other partners. She saw him smiling and smiled back.

"I am smiling in relief," he said, and he sounded just as he did when they had been scraping puppy dung off the floor together. "You have the knack for making your partner feel that he knows what he is doing. Which makes him rather more able to do it. Thank you. It has not been a good night thus far."

"You do yourself too little credit," said Lissar in what she realized was a courtly phrase; she knew exactly what he meant and was flattered but found herself shy of admitting it.

"Stop it," he said. "This is me, remember? We've been thrown up on by the same puppies."

She laughed. "I was thinking of cleaning up diarrhea, myself. Balls and sick puppies don't belong in the same world, somehow."

"Ah, you've noticed that, have you? I couldn't agree more, and I prefer the puppies."

"You have looked a bit like you'd be happier pulling a plough when I've seen you long enough to notice, this evening."

He sighed. "I swear, I was thinking about turning tail and running like a rabbit before hounds when I saw Trivelda advancing on me tonight. Your appearance saved me."

Lissar saw a courtier carrying an ariola in one hand hurrying down the long hall again, toward the banquet tables. Another was returning, laden plate in one hand, flower in the other. She wondered if they were allowed to lay their flowers down long enough to make handling plates a little more feasible—or perhaps they held the stems between their teeth as they served? She wanted to say something to Ossin, but could think of nothing.

She became aware that the prince was dancing them firmly away from the central knot of the figure. "Come," he said suddenly, and seized her by the hand. They left the hall almost at a run, down a corridor, and then the prince checked and swerved, like a hound on a scent, threw open a door, and ushered her out onto a small balcony.

It was a beautiful night; after three days of clouds the weather had broken, and now the stars looked nearer than her sparkling skirts, and the Moon was near full. The prince dropped her hand, leaned on the balustrade, and heaved a great sigh through his open mouth. "I feel like howling like a dog," he said, and then turned and sat on the railing, bracing his hands beside him, looking up at her.

Lissar felt a tiny tremor begin, very deep inside her, deep in her blood and brain, nothing to do with the chill in the air.

"Deerskin—" he began.

"No," she whispered. Louder, she said, "We should go back to your party." The tremor grew; she began to feel it in her knees, her hands, she twisted her hands in her glittering skirts.

"Not just yet," said the prince. "Trivelda will feel that my absence is more than paid for by your absence—she likes being the center of attention, you know, and you haven't even got a lot of courtiers dressed up like unicorns or vases of flowers or something for a competition she can understand." He stood up; stepped toward her; loomed over her. The Moon was behind him, and he looked huge; and for the moment she forgot the many hours they had spent together with the puppies, when he had never looked like he filled the sky. . . . She stepped back. Her trembling must be visible now, but it was dark, and he would not notice. If she spoke he would hear it in her voice. She tried to swallow, but her throat felt frozen, and she was sick at her stomach, sick with her own knowledge of her own life, sick at standing on the balcony with Ossin when the Moon shone on them.

"Will you marry me?"

There was thunder in her ears, and before her eyes were the walls of a small round room hung in a dark stained pink that had once been rose-colored, and the dull brutal red was mirrored in a gleaming red pool on the floor where a silver-fawn dog lay motionless; and there was a terrible weight against her own body, blocking her vision, looming over her, blotting out the stars through the open door, and then a pain, pain pain pain pain

Some things grew no less with time. Some things were absolutes. Some things could not be gotten over, gotten round, forgotten, forgiven, made peace with, released.

—she did not quite scream. "No!" she said. "No! I cannot."

The prince put his hand to his face for a moment, and dropped it. He was deep in his own fears; he did not see, in the darkness, either her trembling or the shadows in her black eyes; he heard the anguish in her voice, but misread it utterly. It did not surprise him that she could not love him.

She remained where she was, unable to move, unable with what felt like the same paralysis of the limbs and the will that had left her helpless on the night that her father had opened the garden door. But Ossin did not know this; and when she remained where she was, he let himself hope that this meant that she was willing to listen to him.

"I love you, you know," he said conversationally, after a little pause. Through her own fear she thought she heard a tremor in his voice, but she scorned it, telling herself it was her own ears' failure. "Trivelda would be . . . in some ways the easier choice; even my poor mother, I think, would not say 'better,' she merely wants me to make up my mind to marry someone. I might, a few months ago, have let myself be talked into Trivelda; I have always known that I would marry some day, and I would like to have children.

"I was beginning to think perhaps there was something wrong with me, that I could not fall in love with any real woman, any woman other than the woman of the Moon, whom I had dreamed of when I was a child. I know what they call you behind your back, but I do not believe it. Moonwoman would not raise puppies the hard way, staying up all night, night after night, till she's grey and snarly with exhaustion, and being puked on, and cleaning up six puppies' worth of vile yellow diarrhea. I believe you're as human as I am, and I'm glad of that, because I love you, and if you really were Moonwoman I wouldn't have the nerve. I have found out that I can love—and I won't marry anyone else now that I know."

Lissar heard this as if from a great distance, though she felt the sweet breath of the prince's words kiss her cheek; but they and he were not enough, and her own heart broke, for she loved him too, and could not bear this with that other, terrible knowledge of what had happened to her, what made her forever unfit for human love. Her heart broke open with a cry she heard herself give voice to, and the tears poured down her face as hot as the river of hell. "Oh, I cannot, I cannot!" She turned her face up to take one long last look at him, and the Moonlight fell full on her. Wonderingly Ossin raised a hand to touch her wet face; but she turned and fled from him.

He did not follow her. She did not know where she was going; she knew she did not want to return to the ball, and so with what little sense that had survived the last few minutes, she thought to turn the opposite way, down the long hall that led to the ballroom. She blundered along this way for some time, the pain of Ash's supposed death and her own body's ravaging as fresh in her as if she were living those wounds for the first time. She met no one. She knew, distantly, to be grateful for this. She felt like a puppy, dragged along on a leash by some great, towering, cruel figure who would not wait to see that her legs were too short and weak to keep up. She wished the other end of the leash were in better hands. Dimly she realized she knew where she was, which meant—like a tug on the leash—that she knew where to go, knew the way out.

The doors were unbarred, perhaps for the benefit of the late-comers; she bolted past the guards, or perhaps she surprised them, or perhaps she looked too harmless—or distressed—to challenge; for none did. She ran across the smooth surface of the main courtyard, and through the twisting series of alleys and little yards, till she came to the kennels. At some point she had paused and pulled off her shoes and stockings, and the touch of the ground, even the hard cobblestones of the king's yards, against her bare feet steadied her, and her head cleared a little of the smoke of old fires, when her innocence and her future had been burned away.

She crept up the outside stairs and into her room, holding the queen's shoes in her hands. She was still trembling so badly it was difficult to take the beautiful dress off without damaging it—the beautiful dress suddenly so horribly like the dress she had worn on her seventeenth birthday—but she did it, and laid it carefully across the bed she did not sleep in. Taking her hair down was worse; her numb shaking fingers refused to understand what Lilac had done, and she had a wild moment of wishing just to cut it off, have it done, have it over, cut her hair, just her hair, but the blood on the floor, running down her face, her breast, running from between her legs . . . the ribbons came free at last, and she laid them out next to the gloves, and Lilac's borrowed brooch.

Then she turned, and eagerly, frantically, pulled open the door of her little wardrobe, groping under her neatly folded kennel clothes, and drew out the white deerskin dress. Its touch soothed her a little, as the touch of the earth against her bare feet had done; her vision widened from its narrow dark tunnel, and she could see from the corners of her eyes again, see the quiet, pale, motionless walls and the ribbons against the coverlet that were not blood but satin. She snatched up her knife and the pouch that held her tinder box and throwing-stones, and then paused on the threshold of the little room, knowing she would not see it again: a little square room with nothing on its walls, kind and harmless and solid.

Barefoot and silent she padded down the front stairs, into the long central corridor of the kennels. The dogs never barked at a familiar step, but as soon as her foot hit the floor there was a rustle and a murmur from the pen where Ash waited with the puppies.

She meant to let only Ash out; but Ob was going to come too, for he knew, in the way dogs often inconveniently know such things, that something was up; and he was quite capable of howling the roof down if thwarted. She did not need to see the look in his eyes to know that this was one of those occasions. As she stood a moment in the stall door, holding back the flood, knowing that she had no real choice in the matter, she heard Ossin's voice saying, "They're yours, you know. I'll take a litter or three from you later, in payment, if you will, but they're yours to do with what you like otherwise. You've earned them."

Earned them. Earned as well the responsibility of keeping them. But it was too late now, for they too knew they were hers, knew in that absolute canine way that had nothing to do with ownership and worth and bills of sale. Their fates were bound together, for good or ill. Too late now. She let the door swing open. If Ob was coming, so were the others.

Some heads lifted, ears pricked, and eyes glinted, in other runs; but there was nothing wrong with one of the Masters taking her own dogs—for all the dogs knew whose masters were whose—out, at any hour of day or night. There were perhaps a few wistful sighs, almost whines, from dogs who suspected that they were being left out of an adventure; but that was all.

Seven dogs poured down the corridor; she unbarred the small door that was cut into the enormous sliding door that opened the entire front wall of the kennel onto its courtyard, where the hunt collected on hunting days, and where dogs were groomed and puppies trained on sunny days. Seven dogs and one person leaped silently through the opening, which the person softly closed again. Then the master and her seven hounds were running, running, running across the wide, Moon-white meadows toward the black line of trees.

Thirty-one

At first Lissar merely ran away; away from the yellow city, away from the prince whom she loved with both halves of her broken heart. But in the very first days of her flight she was forced to recognize how much care and feeding seven dogs required. If she had not been in the grip of a fear much larger than her sense of responsibility toward her seven friends, she might have let the lesser fear of not being able to keep the puppies fed drive her back to the king's city again. But that was not to be thought of; and so she did not think it. She allowed herself half a moment to remember that she did owe Ossin a litter or three in payment, but there was no immediate answer to this, and so she set it aside, in relief and helplessness and sorrow and longing. Then she set her concentration on the problem of coping with the situation she was in.

After two days of too few rabbits, they had a piece of extraordinary luck: Ash and Ob pulled down a deer. Much of Ob's puppy pigheaded-ness was the boldness of a truly superior dog trying to figure out the structure of his world, and he worshipped the ground Ash and Lissar walked on. His adoration had the useful result of making him preter-naturally quick to train (even if it also and equally meant that he had to be trained preternaturally quickly and forcefully); and all the puppies seemed to comprehend, after their first hungry night on the cold ground (and no prince and waggon to rescue them the next day), that some-thing serious was happening, and that they had to stop fooling around and pay close attention.

Ash focussed and froze first on the leaf-stirring that wasn't the wind. Lissar noticed how high up the movement was happening, and felt her heart sink; she hoped it wasn't another iruku, another monster such as Ash and Blue and Bunt and Kestrel had flushed, almost to dis-aster. She hoped that Ash could tell what it was, and that the fact she looked eager meant that it wasn't an iruku. Lissar gathered the puppies together, and they began to circle upwind; as they approached the point where the animal would scent them, Ash struck off on her own, Ob and Ferntongue following at her heels. Lissar and the rest kept their line.

It was beautifully done. The deer broke cover, and Ash and the two puppies flanked it. Lissar was astonished all over again at how swift her lovely dogs were; and they tracked the deer, keeping pace with its enor-mous, fear-driven bounds, their ears flat to their heads, without making a sound. The deer, panicking, tried to swerve; Ob blocked it, and Ash, with a leap almost supernatural, sprang to grab its nose; the weight of the dog and the speed at which they were moving flipped the deer com-pletely over. It landed with a neck-breaking crash, and did not again stir. Ash got up, shook herself, looked over her shoulder to find Lissar's face, and dropped her lower jaw in a silent dog-laugh.

Everyone's bellies were full that night, and the next. Ash woke up snarling the second night, and whatever it was that had been thinking of trying to scavenge the deer carcass changed its mind, and thrashed invisibly away through the undergrowth again. Lissar threw a few more sticks on the fire and put her head back on Ash's flank. She could hear the last murmur of growl going on, deep in Ash's chest, even after Ash put her own head down.

It was the fifth night after they had fled the king's city, during which time Lissar had merely headed them all for the wildest country she could find the nearest to hand, that she heard, or felt, that inaudible hum for the second time; the same subliminal purr that had led her to the lost boy some weeks before. She felt like an iron filing lining up to an unsuspected magnet: she thrummed with seeking.

She put her head down on her knees and thought to ignore it; but it would not be ignored. Then she breathed a little sigh of something like relief, for it had been difficult, even over no more than five days, not to think about what she was doing, not to know that she had no idea what to do next, where to go. Five days not to think of Ossin. She stood up and stamped out their little fire; turned to orient herself to the line of the call, chirruped to her dogs, and set off.

This time it was only a lamb she found; but when she set it in the young shepherd's arms—for the call had merely realigned itself once she'd found the little creature, and told her where to take it—the girl's eyes filled with tears. "Thank you," she said. "I am too young, and my dog is too old, but we are all there is, and we need our sheep."

A week later Lissar brought another little boy home to his parents; and four days after that she was bending over an odd little carpet of intensely green plants bearing a riot of tiny leaves when her hands, without any orders from her, began gathering them, at the same time as she felt the now-familiar iron-filing sensation again. The plants' roots were all a single system, so they were easier to pull up and hold than they initially looked; she plucked about a third, and broke off the central root so that it would repopulate itself. When she came to a small cabin just outside the village she had returned the boy to a few nights previously, she tapped on the door.

A woman somewhere between young and old opened the door and looked unsurprised at Lissar and her following; and then looked with deep pleasure at the festoon of green over Lissar's left arm. "Do your dogs like bean-and-turnip soup?" she said. "There is enough for all of you."

The prince's ball had been toward the end of the hunting season, the end of harvest, when the nights were growing discernibly longer, and the mornings slower to warm up. But the early weeks of the winter were far less arduous than the time Lissar and Ash had spent alone in the mountains. A large territory imperceptibly became theirs, and many villages came to know them, catching glimpses occasionally on Moon-lit nights of seven long-legged dogs and one long-legged woman with her white dress kilted high over her thighs, running silently through the stubbly fields or, rarely, bolting down a brief stretch of road before dis-appearing. It was an interesting fact that no domestic animal protested their passing; no guardian dog barked, no anxious chicken squawked, no wary horse snorted.

And Lissar came to welcome the sound that was not a sound, the iron-filing feeling, for this often earned her and her dogs hot meals of greater variety than they could otherwise catch, and many barns were permanently opened to them. Lissar saw no point in sleeping on the in-creasingly cold ground if she could help it; hay stacks were to be pre-ferred. The puppies learned to climb barn-ladders, not without accidents, none severe.

Lissar now also had hearths to drag her proud company's skills to; they did not have to guard their trophies from other predators any more, and between their increasing skills as hunters, and Lissar's finding of missing people, creatures, and miscellaneous desirable items, they rarely went hungry. No one questioned her right to hunt wild game any more than they questioned her right to the dogs at her heels; any more than anyone had ever asked her about the origin of her white deerskin dress. Everyone called her Deerskin to her face, and she established a semi-permanent camp for herself and her seven dogs, in a hollow of a hill, not too far from the herbwoman's village.

She waited for news of Ossin's upcoming marriage, but she heard none. She wondered if she would hear it; but how could her new friends not tell her, when they told her so much else, about their cows and their cousins, their compost heaps and their crop rotations. About their babies, their sweethearts and—occasionally—about the yellow city. Ossin's name was mentioned once or twice, and Lissar believed that she was not seen to wince; but no one mentioned Trivelda. It was hard to know what the farm folk knew or guessed; that they knew she had lived at court, and that six of the dogs that followed her had originally belonged in the prince's kennels, she assumed; for the rest she did not guess.

It did not occur to her that she was shutting out thought of Ossin, and of her—happiness—during the time she was a kennel-girl in a way too similar to the way she had shut out all memory of the pain and terror in her past when she and Ash had fled their first life. She had had no choice, that first time; this time . . . it had all happened too quickly, and she could not see if she had had a choice or not. The day in the portrait-room had been followed too soon by the evening of the ball. She had been beset by too much at once, and she could not think clearly. She still could not think clearly—but now it was because she did not think she could. It did not occur to her that she might. And so she did not try; and her forgetting began slowly to usurp her life again.

Lissar wondered sometimes what went on behind Fiena's measuring looks; Fiena was the herbwoman who had fed them bean-and-turnip soup on the first evening of their acquaintance. But Fiena never asked embarrassing questions, and evenings might be spent there in silence, but for the slurping sounds of seven dogs eating stew. It was Fiena who made Lissar a pair of deerskin boots, from the hide of one of the beasts Lissar's hounds had pulled down, so that by the time the first snow fell,

she was no longer barefoot, although the boots, like any ordinary clothing, showed dirt and wear, as her deerskin dress did not.

She travelled in a wide swathe; revisited Ammy and Barley, who
were glad to see her, quartered the towns in a larger and larger . . . eventually she acknowledged that she moved in a circle around the king's
city as if it were her tether and she on a long rope. She spiralled in—not
too close; she spiralled out—not too far. But circle she did, around and
around, restlessly, relentlessly, endlessly.

Autumn had been gentle and winter began mildly. The game remained in good condition and the puppies grew into an efficient hunting team; more than efficient, joyful. Lissar began directing them more
and more carefully, till they as often as not could make their kill near
their home-hill, or near one of the farms who would welcome them.
She was proud of them, and she knew that had they remained in the
prince's kennels they would have been taken only on puppy hunts next
summer, and would not be considered worth joining the real hunting-
parties till the summer after that.

But as the season deepened she found herself less at peace than
ever, roaming farther and farther away from the villages, with a buzzing
in her head like the iron-filing sensation, only without the comfort of
a direction to clarify it. At last she found herself in the wilder hilly region on the outskirts of King Goldhouse the Seventeenth's realm—the
northern boundary where she had come down last spring. She stood,
surrounded by dogs, staring up the tree-covered slopes, and in herself a
sudden great longing. . . .

She turned abruptly, and began a determined trot south and west,
to Fiena's village and their home-hill, composing a half-acknowledged
list in her mind. Onions; apples; potatoes; squash; herbs, both medicinal and for cooking; blankets; a bucket. A comb. A lamp. Something to
keep the rain off. An axe. With six more dogs to think of, more than
would be comfortable for her alone to carry. She cast an appraising look
at her proud sleek hunting hounds.

Ash felt her dignity very much compromised by the makeshift harness Lissar put together, useful but unbeautiful as it was. But, as ever, she was willing to perform any task Lissar asked of her so long as it was plain what the task was. She suffered having the harness put on, but once she realized that when the pack was in place it was heavy, she set about getting back out of it again. Lissar contrived to dissuade her of this and Ash reluctantly accepted the inevitable, standing in her characteristic pose of disgruntlement with her back humped, her feet bunched together, and her head low and outthrust and flat-eared, swinging back and forth to keep Lissar pinned by her reproachful gaze.

Lissar had accumulated much of the gear she wanted to take already at her camp; for the rest, after some anxious thought, she called in various favors from several different villages, that none need feel preyed upon—nor any guess her plans. Then she had had to devise a harness, and sew it together; this all had taken time, while the thrumming in her head went on, persistently, almost petulantly, as if it would snatch the needle, thread, and mismatched straps out of her hands and say, Go now. The puppies, who felt that so long as they kept Lissar under their eyes they had nothing to fear, had little reaction to Lissar's new activities. Ash, who had known her longer, was suspicious of the bits of leather and stiff cloth Lissar dealt with so painstakingly; but, her look said, when Lissar had hung the first results on her, she had never guessed anything as dire as this.

The puppies had watched the drama of the harnessing of Ash very intently, so when Lissar turned to Ob with another harness, he dropped his head and tail but did not protest. If the perfect Ash permitted this and the adored Lissar asked it then he could not possibly refuse. She had made only three harnesses, to begin with, for the three strongest dogs— Pur, still the biggest, was the third—and distributed her bundles among them, keeping the most awkward items, including the bucket and axe, for herself. But then the other dogs were jealous of the special favor of the harnesses, of the work these three were honored to perform: they knew that Ash was their leader, and Ob her second-in-command, and Pur the toughest. The remaining four sulked.

Thus it happened that seven dogs wore harnesses, and while this put off their departure, it meant Lissar could carry more supplies than she had planned; all the better.

The sky was an ominous grey the morning they set out; she hoped she had not delayed too long. But she shook herself, like a dog, she thought, smiling, settling the unwieldy pack on her own back—she had spent more thought over balancing her dogs' burdens—and as she did so, she felt the same orienting tingle that she had now so often felt. This time she knew, as she did not usually know, what it was that drew her: a small hut, high in the mountains, where she had spent one winter, one five-year winter. Where she had met the Moonwoman.

The dogs were all sniffing the air too, tails high, ready for an adventure, even if they had to carry freight with them. Meadowsweet sidled up to Harefoot, bit her neatly in the ear, and bolted—not quite fast enough. Harefoot's jaws missed her, but seized a strap of her harness, and in less time than a breath there were two dogs rolling on the ground, their voices claiming that they wanted to kill each other but their ears and tails telling another story entirely.

Lissar was on them at once, grabbing each by the loose skin over the shoulders, barking her knuckles on the packs to get a good grip. "*Shame* on you," she said. It wasn't easy, lifting the front ends of two ninety-pound dogs, whose shoulders were thigh-high on her to begin with, plus their packs, simultaneously; but she shifted her grasp to the harness straps, which had been laboriously made to withstand a good deal of abuse, and heaved.

She managed to shake the two miscreants two and a half times before her shoulders gave out; the big dogs hung in her hands as if they were still twenty-pound puppies. She set them down again and they stared at the ground, pointedly away from each other, while she resettled their packs. The other dogs were ambling around as if indifferent:

none would tease another being scolded; the scolding was enough, not to mention the possibility of the scolding being redirected to include more dogs. One or two were sitting, respectfully watching the show. She hoped they all in their own ways were paying attention. Pur was notorious for picking up nothing by example, no matter how closely he appeared to be watching; Lissar thought that too many of his brains had been given over to monitoring his astonishing physical growth and that there weren't enough left for intelligence.

Ash, on the other hand, whose back was deliberately turned, could be depended on to know and understand exactly what happened; she was merely being polite. Lissar guessed it was Ash's refusal to add to another's humiliation during the puppies' early training that had led to their all being so implausibly willing to leave wrong-doers alone instead of joining into the fray. One of the reasons puppies weren't hunted till their second year was because this restraint was not a general characteristic of the race; Lissar had helped, once or twice, sort out the mêlée in a back meadow when training turned into a free-for-all. Not, of course, that there had ever been any question that Ash would demean herself by puppy antics; her style, since she had ceased to be a puppy herself, was more in her refusal ever quite to remember that she was not supposed to put her paws on Lissar's shoulders and lick her face any time she chose, whatever Lissar might be doing at the time.

It began to snow mid-morning. They had been running across open land, but Lissar decided to cut back to the road, to make travelling a little easier. The haunted feeling behind her eyes that told her where she was aiming would keep them from going wrong; but there was no point in falling in snow-covered holes any deeper than necessary, and the holes in the roads were shallower. The snow began to come down heavily. Lissar halted long enough to pull her boots out of her pack, and reluctantly put them on. She felt half lost as soon as her feet were no longer in contact with the earth; but the snow was burning her skin. They ran on.

Thirty-two

T he road grew steeper, and the grey light became fainter as the trees crept closer and closer to the narrowing road. And then it was no longer a road at all, but a rough track. The dogs, with four long slender legs apiece, seemed never to have any trouble keeping their footing; she, two-legged and top-heavy, was clumsier. As the incline grew their pace slowed, and steaming pink tongues were visible. Ash, who originally led the way, dropped back to stay at Lissar's side; Lissar curled her fingers in the long ruff as she had often done before, although the physical warmth was the least she took from the contact.

They had to camp several nights on the way. It was hard to tell in the snow; one camp, it seemed to her, might have been the same shallow cave Ash and she had huddled in the night after meeting the dragon. Nor could she guess how long it would take them to get to the little cabin she remembered, for she and Ash had wandered for some weeks before she had made up her mind to come down to flat farming country again, and look for people.

The sun showed but rarely through the clouds during their journey, and the snow fell, sometimes heavily, sometimes gently, but fall it did, and went on doing. The clouds looked low enough, sometimes, as if there were a roof of snow solid and tangible as any other roof, with the trees as poles holding it up.

It was on the ninth or eleventh day that they arrived; Lissar had lost track. The increasing depth of the snow worried her; even the dogs were floundering, and she had to trudge, step by heavy, plowing step. There would be little game for them up here, less still that they could catch in this footing; fleethounds were made for running fast over bare ground. She hoped she had brought enough supplies after all . . . she hoped they would find the hut before the snow simply buried them. There were also two sores under the dogs' harness that she did not seem able to halt or ease, Fen's shoulder and Ferntongue's ribs, no matter how she padded and rearranged the offending straps. The one thing she did not worry about was where they were going; asleep or awake, the direction was plain to her, as plain as a beacon across the grey snow; as bright as a Moon-track across black water.

The hut looked just as she'd left it in the spring: small and empty, shabby and welcoming. She had not permitted herself to worry that it would be occupied. The wood-pile looked untouched; or if someone had visited since she left, he or she had replaced anything that was burned. The roof was still a firm straight line, and the window was still closely shuttered. No smoke drifted out of the chimney. She would not have known what to do if someone had been there; she was almost dizzy, now, with the intensity of the invisible beacon which had brought her here.

She fought her way through a snowdrift up onto the narrow porch and lifted the latch; the door opened, and seven dogs and one human being, plus a great deal of snow, fell indoors.

There was barely enough floor space for all the dogs to lie down; even so there was a good bit of overlap, heads on others' flanks, tangles of eight and sometimes twelve long skinny legs; the entire room looked, Lissar thought, like a large version of the puppy-box that they'd used to carry the puppies outdoors when they were still quite small; she remembered how Ossin . . . she stopped the thought.

By the time she had gone out to haul extra wood indoors the dogs had spread out so seamlessly that she had to dig under a dog with every step (frequently to the sound of aggrieved moans) to find a place to put her foot. Most were snoring by the time she got the fire lit; several of them could not even be awakened to get their packs pulled off, and she had to wrestle with the straps, lifting up bits of limp dog, to pull them free. There was this to be said of a dog-covered floor, came the thought in the back of Lissar's mind: she could not see the dark ugly stain on the floor near the door. She piled the bundles any way on the table, climbed back through the welter of bodies, and up onto the bed, which a still-wakeful Ash had been protecting from all marauders. Lissar stayed awake just long enough to hear Ash breathe a sigh as long as a winter storm-wind, and to feel the dog's head drop into the valley between her ribs and pelvis.

She woke up at last because there seemed to be something preventing her from breathing. There were now four dogs on the bed, and one of them was lying across her face. She pushed the hairy body aside, recognized that it was Fen, and observed that it was morning. And, sleepily looking around the familiar room, she finally noticed the one change: her note of thanks was gone from the table.

The first weeks were simple if strenuous. She had no time to think, and wanted none; her days were full of fire-tending, and of hunting and cooking food. They had brought much food with them, but seven dogs eat an enormous amount, especially short-haired dogs in winter weather. What time was left was spent in grooming them, checking for hidden splinters in the foot-pads, possible sores in tender places; and relearning how to bathe herself out of a bucket. She did allow herself a moment or two to regret the bathhouse; generally she kept careful watch against any thought of Goldhouse's country, city, or son.

The winter before there had been only the two of them, she and Ash; the occasional rabbit or ootag sufficed, even if both Lissar's and Ash's ribs had showed through their skin by spring. Fleethounds were not meant to hunt in deep winter; they floundered and shivered in the snow, and their feet were cut painfully by ice crystals, and they could not range far from the hut. None of the puppies showed any inclination to grow a heavy, curly coat like Ash's; and Ash and Lissar could not hunt for them all alone. Lissar sometimes left the puppies in the hut and went out on snow-shoes; but her average was not as good as Ash's, and she worried about her expenditure of energy against the amount of food she managed to bring home. There were fewer cattails this year, and even the marshiest places were frozen solid.

Ash disappeared occasionally—as she had done the winter before, although that recollection made Lissar worry no less—for several hours at a time, simply not being there when Lissar led her half-frozen charges back again to the fireside. Ash never failed to bring something home from one of her expeditions; but even the fattest ootag, rendered thriftily into soup, would feed them all but once, and that leanly; and as the winter wore on, the ootags grew thinner too. The snow had grown so deep and the weather so bitter that Lissar feared that they would not reach the lowlands before they perished of the cold if they left the hut and risked it; and she wondered that she had been so determined to come here, wondered at the call, which had always brought her to finding something lost, that had brought her here. Had the call drowned out the sense that should have told her how better to prepare? Should she have assumed that this winter would be that much harder than last? On what grounds should she have made such a guess? Why had the call come at all?

She tried to comfort herself by thinking that she did not know how fierce the winter was in the farmlands; that it had begun easily meant nothing. Vaguely she remembered stories of being snowed in, mending harness, stitching elaborate pillows or wedding-dresses, whittling new pegs or pins or toys for children or grandchildren, going outdoors only long enough to feed the beasts. Were those stories of ordinary winter, or of extraordinary storms? She did not know. Nor, if she did climb down the mountains again, did she know where she might go; she could not spend all winter in anyone's barn. She could not think of returning to the yellow city . . . and there her brain stalled, and threw her back once again to thinking of how to feed her own beasts on this mountaintop.

Some days the wind howled and the snow blew so that it was a struggle to go outdoors even long enough for necessary purposes. Lissar did not remember that there had been many days like that the winter before; nor had the snow against the wall of the hut facing the prevailing wind reached the eaves, as it had this year, and drifted over the roof till it melted in the warm circle the chimney made.

One afternoon when they had returned from a long, cold, fruitless hunt, and were all shoving at each other to get nearest the fire (there was a slight odor of singed hair), Ash suddenly left the rest of them and went to stand by the door. Several of the others turned to watch her, as they automatically watched their leader. Ob and Harefoot caught it, whatever it was; and then the rest of them did, and quickly there were seven dogs standing tensely facing the door.

There was no window in that wall, and neither Lissar's hearing nor smell was sensitive enough to pick up what the dogs were responding to. Ash rose to her hind legs and placed her forepaws, in perfect silence, against the door. The long slow exhalation of her breath carried with it the tiniest of whines; so faint was it that Lissar only knew it was there because she knew Ash. She made her way through the throng and set her hand on the latch. Ash composedly lifted her paws away from the door, balancing a moment on her hind feet as if going on two legs were as natural for her as it was for Lissar; and then she dropped to all fours again.

Lissar would have closed the door again if she could, but Ash was off at once, streaking through the gap before the door was fully open. "No!" Lissar cried; but Ash, always obedient, this time did not listen to her; silent but for the crisp sharp sound of her paws breaking through the snow between her great bounds, she ran for the enormous beast standing on the far side of the clearing the hut stood at the opposite edge of.

The puppies, alarmed and confused by Lissar's cry and Ash's extraordinary disobedience, and perhaps by the size of their would-be prey, hesitated, while Lissar, hardly knowing what she did, groped for the bag of throwing-stones that hung just inside the threshold, and then laid her hand as well on a long ash cudgel. Then she started across the clearing herself, gracelessly crashing through the snow, listening to her own sobbing breath.

The old buck toro that paused at the edge of the trees and turned to face the dog that charged him, ears back and teeth exposed in a snarl, was as tall at the shoulder as Lissar stood; his antlers spread farther than the branches of a well-grown tree. He had not attained his considerable age by accident, and he did not turn and run when he saw Ash, nor even when he saw Lissar and six more tall dogs break after her. He turned instead toward the most immediate threat, lowered his head a little, and waited.

But Ash was no fool either, and had all the respect possible for the points of the great toro's horns. She sheered off at the last moment, dashing in for a glancing nip at the shoulder, and darting away again. Lissar gave some terrified recognition to the dangerous beauty of her fleethound even in snow to her shoulders.

It may yet be all right, she thought, floundering through the same snow. He will lumber off among the trees where we cannot possibly come at him: "Ash, it is not worth it!" she said aloud, but she had not enough breath to shout; we will all be very hungry by spring, but we are not starving yet, I will spend all my days on my snow-shoes after this, there will be enough rabbits—"Ash!" she said again.

But Ash merely ran round the toro, keeping him occupied, giving him no chance to retreat among the trees. She swept in once more, bit him on the flank; the hoof lashed out, but missed; a thin trickle of blood made its way through the thick hair.

This was not a proper hunt. A pack of fleethounds ran down their prey; at speed they made their killing leaps, and the prey's speed was used against it. A cornered beast was always dangerous, and in such situations the hunting-party or -master was expected to put an arrow or a spear where it would do the most good—and save the dogs.

Ash made her third leap, flashing past the antlers' guard and seizing the toro's nose. It was beautifully done; but the toro was standing still, braced, his feet spread against just such an eventuality; and he was very strong.

He roared with the pain in his nose, but he also snapped his neck up and back, barely staggering under the weight of the big dog. Ash hung on; but while she managed to twist aside as he tried to fling her up and over onto his sharp horns, as the force of his swing and her writhe aside brought her through the arc and back toward the earth again, he shifted his weight and struck out with one front foot.

It raked her down one side and across her belly; and the bright blood flowed. This was no mere trickle, as on the toro's flank, but a great hot gush.

"Ash!" Lissar said again, but this time it was a groan. It had still been bare moments since Lissar had opened the door of the hut and Ash had bolted out; Lissar had not quite crossed the clearing, though she could smell the heavy rank odor of the toro—and now the sharp tang of fresh blood. Ash's blood.

"Help her, damn you!" Lissar screamed, and Ob charged by her, made his leap, and tore a ragged chunk out of the creature's neck; its blood now stained the snow as well, from its nose and flank and now running down its shoulder, and Ash's weight made the deadly antlers less of a threat; but Ash's blood ran the faster. The toro bellowed again and made to throw its head a second time; and Ash was built for running, not gripping with her jaws, and her hold was slackening as her heart's blood pumped out through the gash in her belly. . . .

Lissar, scarcely thinking what she did, ducked under the high-flung head, and the body of her dog; and as one foreleg lifted free of the snow as the creature swung its weight to its other side, Lissar took the ash-wood cudgel in her hands and gave as violent a blow as she could, just below the knee of the weight-bearing leg. Vaguely she was aware that the thing had stumbled as the other dogs made their leaps; the toro kicked violently with a rear leg, and there was a yelp; Ash, silent, still hung on.

The leg Lissar struck broke with a loud crack, and the creature fell, full-length, in the snow. In a moment it was up again on three legs, bellowing now with rage as well as pain; but Ash lay in the snow. The toro turned on her as nearest, and would have savaged her with its antlers, but Lissar got there first, in spite of the snow, in spite of having to flee being crushed when the toro fell, in spite of how the snow held her as one's limbs are held in a nightmare; weeping, she brought her cudgel down across the creature's wounded nose, careless of the antlers, shielding her dog; and the toro shrieked, and fell to its knees as its broken leg failed to hold it. At that moment Ferntongue and then Harefoot, with two slashing strokes, hamstrung it, and it rolled, groaning, across the bloody snow, the knife-sharp hoofs still dangerous; Lissar leaped over, and buried her small hunting knife in the soft spot at the base of the jaw, where the head joins the neck; heedless, she grasped the base of one antler, to give herself purchase, and ripped; and the toro's blood fountained out, and it died.

Thirty-three

T he blood's rush was still measured by the rhythm of a beating heart as Lissar turned to Ash. She sank down beside her, shivering uncontrollably with cold and shock. Ash's eye was half open, and her tongue trailed in the snow. But the eye opened a little farther as Lissar knelt beside her, and her ear tried to flatten in greeting.

She had fallen on her wounded side, so Lissar could see only the ugly end of it, curving under her belly. "Ash," she said. "Oh, Ash, I cannot bear it. . . ." She thought she might kneel there in the snow till the end of time, but there was a questioning look in Ash's one visible eye, and so, still shuddering, Lissar reached out to stroke the sleek, shining fur on her throat, and down across her shoulder; and then she staggered to her own feet.

She went back to the hut, seized a blanket off the bed, and returned to the battlefield. As delicately as she could she rolled Ash onto the blanket; the dog made no sound, but she was limp in Lissar's hands, and Lissar was clumsy, for her eyes were blinded by tears.

Slowly she sledded her sad burden back across the snow to the hut, ignoring both the toro's corpse and the six other dogs, who, their heads and tails hanging, crept after her. She eased Ash up over the step and the threshold, and skated her across the floor to settle her, still on the now blood-sodden blanket, in front of the fire. It seemed like an age since they had left the hut together, and that the fire was still burning high and the hut was warm surprised her. The puppies followed her in and lay down, anxiously, as soon as they were across the threshold, unhappily, submissively, and tightly together, no sprawling, no ease. Lissar had just the presence of mind to count that all six had been able to return without assistance, and then she shut the door.

And returned to Ash. The cut across her ribs was nasty, but not immediately dangerous, and the ribs appeared unbroken. But where the hoof had sunk into the soft belly. . . . Lissar, feeling sick, bent her head till her face nearly touched Ash's flank, and sniffed; there was no odor but blood, and a lingering rankness from the toro. Could such a blow have missed all the organs? For the first time Lissar felt the faintest stirring of hope. . . . Then she looked again at Ash's outflung head and the eye, glazing over with agony, and at all the blood . . . at least she must stop the bleeding.

"Ash, I shall have to use needle and thread," Lissar said aloud; she barely recognized her own voice, for it sounded calm and reasonable, as if it belonged to someone who knew what to do and could do it. She took out the little roll of leather where she kept her few bits of sewing gear, which she had last used to make harnesses for the dogs for the trek up the mountain; and she threaded her needle with steady hands. Like her voice, they seemed to have no connection with the rest of her, for she was still having trouble remembering to breathe, and her knees were rubbery, and her thighs painful with cramp.

The bleeding, she thought, had slowed, which she feared might be a bad sign rather than a good one, but she knelt so that the fire might give her as much light as possible, said, "Ash, I am sorry," and set the needle into the flesh, a little below the last rib, where the wound went deep.

Ash's head came up off the blanket with the speed of a striking snake's, and there was white visible all the way around her dark eye; but her jaws clashed on empty air, for she had not aimed for Lissar, who was easily in her reach. Lissar clamped her own jaws together, drew the thread quickly through the first stitch, tied it and bit it off; and then repeated the procedure. Ash twitched and her sigh was a moan; six stitches Lissar made, and knew the wound needed more, but knew also that Ash was already at the end of her strength.

She poured a little water down Ash's throat, and believed that not all of it ran out again. Then she wiped her as clean as she could, and put more blankets over her, and sat at her head, her hand just behind Ash's ear, listening to her breathing, willing her to go on breathing. . . .

Dark came, which she might not have cared for, except that the fire was dying, and Ash must be kept warm. The puppies followed her outdoors to relieve themselves while she carried wood; and she had regained enough of her awareness of the world to notice that two of them were limping, Harefoot badly, hopping on three legs. When they went indoors again, she finally remembered that she had a lamp to light, and by its glow she examined the puppies. Pur merely had a long shallow slash across one flank and upper thigh; Harefoot's leg was broken. She panted, anxious and in pain, while Lissar felt the break as delicately as she could, and tried to engage some emotion beyond numbness at the discovery that it was a simple break and that it should not be beyond her small knowledge, gained by assisting Jobe and Hela, to set it effectively.

She did so, her hands as little a part of the rest of her as they had been when she held the needle at Ash's belly; and at the end she said, "Harefoot, you're a good dog," and a little unexpected warmth crept out of its hiding place and moved into her voice. Harefoot looked pleased, and dared to put her head on Lissar's knee and look up at her adoringly; and all the other dogs were a little reassured and crept forward, away from the door, toward the fire. Ash still breathed; and Lissar, and six other dogs, lay down around her, to keep her warm, and to remind her of their presence, and of how much they needed her; Lissar blew out the lamp, to save her small store of fuel, and all but she fell asleep as dusk darkened to night.

The next few days were a nightmare version of the first days with the puppies, almost nine months ago. Lissar did not sleep; she dozed, sometimes, curled around her charge, achingly sensitive to any signal Ash might make. For while nine months before she had worked as hard as she knew how, and feared, every time she woke from an unscheduled nap, to find one of her small charges fallen into the sleep no one wakes from, it was not the same. If Ash died, a part of Lissar would die with her; a part she knew she could not spare.

She was bitterly lonely in the long watches of the night, listening to Ash's faint, rough, tumultuous breathing; for not only was Ash not there to comfort her, but she had lost Ossin as well, Ossin, who was so much of the reason why she had saved the puppies; so much of the reason why she believed she would save the puppies. And now she found she could not stop herself holding a little aloof from them, because of the ghost of Ossin that lay between them. She was lonelier than she had ever been, because she now understood what loneliness was.

Lost him. Run away from him; fled him; threw him away.

Once she woke, not knowing she had slept, with Ash's head in her lap; it was her own voice that woke her, murmuring, "Not Ash too. Please—not Ash too."

She left the fireside only long enough to fetch more wood; six dogs followed her, two limping, which reminded her that her body had the same functions. Her body seemed an odd and distant stranger, a machine she rested in, and pushed levers and pulled handles or wires to make function, lost as she was in a haze of pain and fear and love and loss, where the promptings of her own bladder and bowels seemed like the voices of strangers. For the first time since she had awakened on the mountaintop, this mountaintop, after meeting the Lady, she did not greet her Moon-blood with gladness, did not welcome the red dreams the first night brought. Her dreams were of blood already, and blood now to her was only about dying.

She hauled snow for water, which took more time than bringing in wood, since so much produced so little; and one morning, perhaps the second after Ash was wounded, she suddenly remembered the corpse of the toro, which they had killed at such cost. And at that she abruptly noticed she was hungry; that she had been hungry for a long time. The puppies had to be ravenous, and yet none of them had made any move toward the end of the rabbit-broth still simmering on the fire, which she poured drops of down Ash's throat as she could; nor had any of them made any move to investigate the dead toro when they followed her outdoors.

Suddenly, as she pried Ash's stiff jaws apart, the smell of the broth registered: *food*. There was little enough of it anyway; but it was as if it caught in her eyes and throat now, like smoke. She looked up, blinking, and found six pairs of eyes looking at her hopefully. Tenderly she laid Ash down and covered her closely with blankets. Then she checked that her small knife was in its strap at her hip. She stared at the bigger kitchen knife and, after a moment's thought, picked up both the small hatchet and the bigger axe she used for wood, and went to the door. The puppies piled after her, the four sound ones giving space to Hare-foot and Pur, although the latter's flank was almost healed already, thanks to the remains of the poultice Lissar had made for Ash.

The weather had remained unrelentingly cold; the carcass had not spoiled, although she suspected that, since she had not gutted it, she would find some spoilage inside—if she could get inside, for it was now frozen solid. Perhaps it had frozen quickly enough to leave little odor;

for no scavengers had been attracted to it, and the snow around it bore only their own footprints. Lissar recognized immediately the blood-stained hollow where Ash had lain.

The puppies were all looking at her. She looked at the huge crumpled body, chose what might or might not be the likeliest spot, and raised her axe.

THE RESULTING STEW WAS NOT HER BEST; IT WAS, to her human taste, almost inedibly gamy, but the puppies ate it with alacrity and enthusiasm. So much enthusiasm that she had to tackle the gruesome carcass again almost immediately, although her wrists and shoulders still ached with hacking the first chunk free.

After eyeing the thing with loathing she spent some time chopping it free of its icy foundation; it was in a shaded spot till late afternoon where it lay, and the sun, as the season swung back toward spring, had some heat to it by midday. It might make the thing stink without making it any easier to cut; but it was worth the trial, or so her sore bones told her. Meanwhile it also gave her something besides Ash to think about.

Ash did not die, but Lissar could not convince herself that she grew any better either. Lissar tipped as much of the reeking broth down Ash's throat as she could, till Ash gave up even the pretense of swallowing; even at that Lissar wasn't sure, looking at the puddle on the floor, how much had gone down her at all. Ash's pulse was still thready and erratic, and she was hot to the touch, hotter than a dog's normally hotter-than-human body heat. She never slept nor awakened completely, although Lissar took some comfort in the fact that her eyes did open all the way occasionally, and when they rested on Lissar, they came into focus, if only briefly.

But she lay, almost motionless; always a clean dog, she now relieved herself as she needed to, with no attempt to raise herself out of the way before or after, as if she had no control, or as if she had given up. Lissar cleaned up after her without any thought of complaint; it was not the cleaning up that she minded, but what Ash's helplessness told her about Ash's condition. The only comfort Lissar had was that Ash's wound did not fester; it was even, slowly, closing over; it was not swollen, and it did not smell bad. Lissar kept it covered with poultices, which she changed frequently; the air of the hut was thick with the smell of illness, spoiled meat, urine, feces, and the cutting sharpness of healing herbs. But Lissar cared nothing about this either. Lissar only cared that Ash should live, and if she died, she did not care what she died of, and for the moment, dying was what she looked to be doing.

Lissar hauled the vast frozen dead beast into the middle of the snowy meadow with all the savagery of despair.

One night, having soaked more meat soft enough to skin, she was boiling the noisome stuff. She tried not to breathe at all though the puppies all sniffed the air with the appearance of pleasant anticipation. She sat with Ash's head in her lap, running her hand down the once-sleek jowl and throat, now harsh with dry, staring hair. Don't die, she thought. Don't die. There's already little enough of me; if you leave me, the piece of me you'll take with you might be the end of me too.

She must have fallen asleep, and the fire begun to smoke, for the room became full of roiling grey, and then the grey began to separate itself into black and white, and the black and white began to shape itself into an outline, although within the outline the black and white continued to chase each other in a mesmerizing, indecipherable pattern, as if light and shadow fell on some swift-moving thing, like water or fire. And the Moonwoman said, "Ash is fighting her way back to you, my dear; I believe she will make it, because she believes it herself. She is an indomitable spirit, your dog, and she will not leave you so long as you hold her as you hold her now, begging her to stay. She will win this battle because she can conceive of no other outcome."

The Moonwoman's words seemed to fall, black and white, in Lissar's ears; she heard them as if they were spoken twice, as if they had two distinct meanings; and she recognized each of the meanings.

"Do not be too hard on yourself," said the Moonwoman, reading her mind, or the black and white shadows on her own face. "It is a much more straightforward thing to be a dog, and a dog's love, once given, is not reconsidered; it just is, like sunlight or mountains. It is for human beings to see the shadows behind the light, and the light behind the shadows. It is, perhaps, why dogs have people, and people have dogs.

"But, my dear, my poor child, don't you understand yet that healing carries its own responsibilities? Your battle was from death to life no less than Ash's is now; would you deny it? But you have not accepted your own gift to yourself, your gift of your own life. Ash is looking forward to running through meadows again; can you not give yourself leave to run through meadows too?"

Lissar woke, finding herself crying, and finding Ash, rolled up on her belly from her side, where she had lain for so many hopeless days, feebly licking the hands where the tears fell.

PART THREE

Thirty-four

Spring began to come quickly after that. Something—several some-
things—discovered the half-thawed remains of the toro one night;
Lissar, who still slept lightly, woke up to hear a growling argument going on outdoors. The puppies were all awake, ears cocked, but none of
them showed any desire to go to the door and ask to be let out. The next
day, amid the bits of fresh fur and blood, Lissar dismembered what remained of their kill, and hung it from a few branches at the edge of the
forest.

Pur's flank was healed; Harefoot's leg Lissar left in its splint perhaps
longer than necessary, in fear of further accidents. When Harefoot ran,
more so even than usual with fleethounds, it was as if some sixth or seventh sense took over, and she became nothing but the fact of running.
Lissar's belief in her had come true for all to see when the kennel staff

had set up an informal match-race between her and Whiplash, considered the fastest fleethound in the prince's kennels. And Harefoot, only seven months old, had won. Lissar remembered how the blood vessels had stood out in her neck and upon her skull, and how wild her eyes had looked, and how long it had taken her to settle down again—how slow she had been to respond to her own name—after this. She would not take care of herself—could not be trusted to take care of herself—so Lissar would take extra care of her. The leg was setting straight; but Lissar wondered if it would ever be quite as strong as it was before, if Harefoot might have lost that edge of swiftness she had been born with. She remembered Ossin's comment on racing: a waste of a good hunting dog, and she tried not to mourn; but she wondered how it would look to Harefoot.

This year there was a new urgency to her preparation to leave, to the impatience that spring infected her with. The year before she had known it was time to leave, time to do . . . something; her pulse was springing like sap, and she could not be still. But this year there was a strange, anxious kind of compulsion, an uncomfortable haste, nothing like the calm delight of the Lady's peace last year. Some of the discomfort too was because Ash was regaining her strength only slowly. Lissar wanted to believe that she was anxious about this only because she wished to be on her way; but she knew it was more that it troubled her to see Ash still so weak and slow and unlike herself. If Harefoot might have lost just the least fraction of her extraordinary speed to a broken leg, what debt might Ash have paid to recover from a mortal wound in the belly?

Days passed and became weeks. Lissar, half-mad now with restlessness, had even cleaned the eaves and patched the shutters, making do with what tools she had and what guesses she could make about a carpenter's skills. Her own slowness was perhaps a boon, for it gave her that much more occupation, doing things wrong before she got them somewhat right. As she had spent two winters in this small house, she thought, as she missed the shutter entirely on a misguided swing with her hammer and narrowly avoided receiving the shutter in her gut as a result, she perhaps owed it some outside work as well as inside. It was a pity, though, that mending roof-holes required more skill than scrubbing a floor.

Every sunny day Ash spent lying asleep, dead center in the meadow; the puppies played or slept or wandered. Lissar had salted the rest of the toro meat—the gamy flavor was somehow more bearable when it was so salty it made the back of her tongue hurt—so she did not take them hunting. They were all badly unfit after the long weeks' inactivity, and she did not want to distress Ash by leaving her behind, nor tax her by trying to bring her along.

The first wild greens appeared; with double handsful of the bitterest young herbs, the toro meat became almost palatable, although she noticed the puppies inexplicably preferred it plain.

The first day she caught an unwary rabbit with one of her throwing-stones, she permitted herself to have the lion's share of the sweet, fresh meat, which she ate outdoors, so that she did not have to be distracted by the smell of the puppies' dinner.

All the dogs were shedding; when she brushed them, short-haired even as they were, the hair flew in clouds, and made everyone sneeze. This occupation was performed exclusively out-of-doors, and downwind of the hut. It took about a sennight for Lissar to realize one circumstance of one spring coat: Ash's long hair was falling out. It was hard to notice at first, because she was in such poor condition, and her fur stuck out or was matted in any and every direction; Lissar had sawn some of the worst knots off with her knife, so poor Ash already looked ragged.

But as the long fur came out in handsful the new, silky, gleaming coat beneath it was revealed . . . as close and short and fine as any other fleethound's. The scar, still red, and crooked from too few stitches, glared angrily through; but Ash was recovering herself with her health, and when she stood to attention, her head high and her ears pricked,

Lissar thought her as beautiful as any dog ever whelped. And, what pleased Lissar even more, as she began, hesitantly, in tiny spurts, to run and leap again, she ran sound on all four legs, and stretched and twisted and bounded like her old self.

They began sleeping outdoors as soon as the ground was dry enough not to soak through Lissar's leather cloak and a blanket on top—Ash must not take a chill. Lissar watched Ash's progress hungrily, still fearing some unknown complication, still in shock from having believed she might lose her, still not believing her luck and Ash's determination to stay alive, still reliving in nightmare the fateful, unknowing opening of the door, seeing Ash streaking across the snow toward the toro, ignoring Lissar's attempt to call her back—and knowing, as she had not known at the time, how it would end.

And hungrily too with a hunger to be gone from this place. It felt haunted now, haunted with two winters of old pain; that they had, she and Ash, been healed of their pain here as well seemed less strong a memory under the blue skies—and even the cold rains—of spring. Lissar built a fire-pit in the meadow—near the small hillock with the bare top, the hillock crowned by a hollow shaped like two commas curled together. There was no longer much need to go in the hut at all, although it was convenient for storage, and for when it rained; she had hauled the remains of the toro away some time since, and a good torrential rain two nights later had done the rest to eliminate the traces of its existence. It existed now only in Lissar's dreams.

But as spring deepened and the days grew longer and the sun brighter, Lissar began to have the odd sensation that the walls of the hut were becoming . . . less solid. It was nothing so obvious as being able to see through them; only that the light indoors grew brighter, brighter than one small window and a door overhung by a double arm's length of porch roof could explain. Perhaps it was only that I am seeing things brighter now, she thought bemusedly.

She left the table, where she had been chopping that night's meat ration into smallish bits, to make it easier to divide fairly eight ways; she thought of dragging the table outdoors, since she still liked to use it, but decided that this was too silly, that furniture belonged indoors. But coming inside to use it made her skin prickle with the awareness that this was no longer home. She went to stand in the doorway, where Ash and Ob were playing as if they were both only a year old; Ash, in her eyes, glittered in the sunlight, and the corners of Lissar's mouth turned up unconsciously. Lissar looked up at the roof, which appeared solid enough. I have no other explanation, she thought, so it might as well be that I am seeing my own life brighter.

She looked out at the dogs again. Ob was licking Ash's face, as he — and the other puppies—had done many times before. But this time looked different. Ash did not appear to be putting up with the clumsy ministrations of someone she knew meant well; she looked like she was enjoying it. And Ob did not look like a child pestering his nursemaid for attention; he was kissing her solemnly and tenderly, like a lover.

Lissar went back to the table.

When Ash flopped down and put her head in Lissar's lap after supper, Lissar bent over her, lifted one of her hind legs, and looked at the small pink rosebud that nestled between them. It was bigger and redder than usual. Lissar gently laid the leg back again. Ash rolled her eyes at her. "Should you be thinking about puppies with a mortal wound less than two months old in your side?" Ob chose this moment to come near and lie down protectively curled around Ash's other side. "But then, what have I to say about it anyway, yes?"

Ash raised her head long enough to bend her neck back at an entirely implausible angle and give Ob a reflective, upside-down lick, and then righted herself, and heaved her forequarters into Lissar's lap as well, munched on nothing once or twice in the comfortable way of dogs, and settled contentedly down for sleep.

When Lissar opened her eyes the next morning, the first shadows under dawn's first light were moving across the meadow. *We leave tomorrow*, said the little voice in Lissar's mind. *Tomorrow*. It fell silent, and Lissar lay, listening to Ob's intestinal mutterings under her ear, and thinking about it. They could sleep under the sky at some place an easy walk down the mountain from here as well as where they were; they would simply stop as soon as Ash got tired.

Tomorrow.

Yes, yes, I hear you. Tomorrow. The season is well enough advanced that even if it rains it shouldn't be too cold; not with seven of us to keep her warm, and the leather is almost waterproof. And if she's about to be carrying puppies—or already is—the sooner the better.

Tomorrow.

The iron-filing feeling had never been so powerful.

There wasn't much to pack; little enough left to do. The remains of the herbs she had brought were the only perishables left, and they retained enough of their virtue to be worth saving. She had been glad enough of the medicinal ones, this grim winter. She fished out a few dark wrinkled survivors from the root bin to take with her, and then wrapped most of the herbs and stowed them in the cupboard for any other traveller.

The extra tools would stay here; except perhaps the hatchet. She would take a couple of the extra blankets that she—and the dogs—had brought with them. She made a tidy bundle of the things that they would take and left it, with the dog harnesses, just inside the door; she would do the parcelling out the next day.

Tomorrow.

A fairly short search through the smaller, neighboring meadows netted her three rabbits, already plump from spring feeding; despite seven dogs in the immediate vicinity the small game at the top of this mountain had largely remained fatally tame. Lissar would put some tiny young wild onions and the last of the potatoes in the stew tonight.

It was an unusually warm night; she left even the leather cloak rolled up inside the hut door. They sat and lay on the earth, grass tickling their chins and bellies, the occasional six-legged explorer marching gravely up a leg or flank. She thought the voice in her head might not let her sleep; even when it did not shape itself into a word it hummed through her muscles. But a strange, restful peace slipped down over her . . . like a freshly laundered nightgown from Hurra's hands so long ago . . . she shivered at the memory, waiting for the panic to begin, waiting for that memory to leap forward . . . but it did not come. She remembered the softness and the sweet smell of the nightgowns she used to wear when her favorite bedtime story was the one of how her father courted the most beautiful woman in seven kingdoms, and the nightgown was still a pleasant memory, and she could further spare the knowledge of sorrow for what was to come to that little girl without spoiling the understanding of that earlier innocence and trust. And so she fell asleep, with dogs all around her, and a full Moon shining down upon the warm green meadow.

She woke up smiling, feeling as refreshed and strong as she ever had in her life, sat up, stretched, and looked around. As she moved, so too did the dogs.

The hut had vanished.

Thirty-five

Their speed down the mountain was less hampered by Ash's weakness than Lissar had expected. She called a halt sometimes not because Ash looked tired but because Lissar felt she ought to be. It seemed as if spring were unrolling beneath their feet; as if, looking over their shoulders, they might see the last patches of snow tucked in shaded hollows, but if they looked to their vision's end before them, they would see summer flowers already in bloom.

Since Lissar's boots had disappeared with the hut and all their other gear, she was grateful there were no late blizzards; she was even more grateful that the game increased almost daily, till she could almost reach out and grab a rabbit or an ootag by the scruff of its neck any time she felt hungry. She and her seven dogs were coming down the mountain as bare of possessions as she and one dog had done a year before: she had her knife, tinder box, and pouch of throwing-stones.

But there was the urgency that she had not felt before. There was no thought of lingering this year, nor any thought of where they were going; she thought they all knew; they were going . . . the word *home* kept rising in her heart and sitting on her tongue, and yet it was not her home and could not be, not since Ossin had said certain things to her on a balcony during a ball given to honor another woman, the woman he was expected to make his wife.

Perhaps she would return his six dogs—for all that he had told her they were hers; for all that she knew that they believed themselves to be hers. Seven was too many, if she were to go wandering. She and Ash could slip away alone one night. No, but there were Ash's puppies to consider, for puppies there would be; they would not be able to travel while the puppies were young. Then too, Ossin said he wished to have choice of any pups from the six dogs she had saved; and once he knew that Ash was who she was. . . . Lissar felt she owed him this thing—this one thing she could grant—and he would be doubly pleased with Ash's puppies sired by Ob. Perhaps she might then keep Ob, for Ash's company, two dogs would not be too many—although that would also result in more puppies.

As her thoughts wound in such circles, her feet carried her straight on, down and down not much less rapidly than the snow-swollen streams she and the dogs ran beside, and camped near at night. The water's roar was no louder than the drumming of the blood inside her own veins. She slept less and less, and lay staring at the stars many nights, or listening to the rain drip off the leaves overhead, because she knew Ash would awaken and try to follow her if she moved. The night of the next full Moon she did not sleep at all, although there was nothing left to guard or disappear, except themselves; and the Moonwoman would not take her dogs away from her. This year, when they struck the road for

the first time, Lissar did not hesitate; and so they ran on, through the
thinning trees, and out into the lowlands, where farmlands began
emerging from the wild.

They struck the village where Barley and Ammy lived, and Lissar
hesitated outside their door, anxious as she was to go on; and Ammy, as
if she had been standing by the window waiting for their arrival, threw
open the shutters and called Lissar's name—Deerskin.

She left the window then, and opened the door; and Lissar soberly
lifted the gate-latch, and went up the little stone-flagged path. She noticed Ob looking wistfully at the chickens, though she knew he was too
well-mannered to disturb them—at least so long as he was under her
eye. Even young spring rabbit grows tedious at last.

"You are going to the yellow city, are you not?" said Ammy, as soon
as they were within easy earshot, as if picking up a conversation they
had begun last week, as if it were the most ordinary thing in the world
to have Lissar standing in her dooryard again. "Even Barley and I
thought of going, for the wedding will be very grand."

Lissar stood as if suddenly rooted to the scrubbed-smooth stone her
feet rested on.

"Did you not know?" pursued Ammy. "Did you go up into the
mountains again this winter?"

Lissar nodded dumbly.

"What a silly thing to do, child. Winter is long and lonely enough,
even here, where we all know one another—and hard, too. You're as
thin as you were last spring, although your dogs look better than you do.
In the yellow city it is probably quite merry, even in the worst of winter,
and you hardly know the season at all. Well, perhaps the wedding was
not set up till after you left, for it was well into autumn when the news
went out. But you'll want to go back now—for you had become great
friends with our prince, had you not?"

This time Lissar shook her head, not so much to deny it, but not
knowing whether she wished to acknowledge Ossin as a great friend or

not. Would it be more or less possible now to remain in the prince's kennels with the prince married, to Trivelda, as she supposed? She did not
know this either, only that her heart ached, and the words Ossin had last
spoken to her pressed on her like stones. Why should the prince not be
married? It was nothing to her, because she had made it be nothing.

No. It was not she who had made it nothing, but her father.

She turned away, but Ammy said, "Will you not stay? I know Barley would like to see you again too."

Lissar shook her head again, firmly this time, and spoke at last:
"There are too many of us to house and feed this year—and I do not like
how Ob and Pur eye your chickens. It has been a long winter—they
may have forgotten their manners. We are better off away from farmland. Perhaps"—she hesitated—"we'll meet in the yellow city, when
you come for the wedding."

Ammy was smiling at her. "You have been on your old mountain too
long if you think anyone will be able to find anyone else in the crowds
that the city will host for this wedding. But perhaps you will come back
here for a little quiet space afterwards. I do not believe any dog that trav-
els with you would stoop to eat a chicken if you told him nay.

"We are far enough out here you know that our countryside is not
much hunted; you could provide us with an autumn's game and spend
next winter here; we've missed having a hunting-master, there has been
no one willing to settle in so dull a place since Barley and I were children. But I do not like seeing you look so thin and pale. Spend the winter here; I will teach you to spin. Our weaver is forever complaining
that she has not enough work."

Lissar forgot the wedding for a moment, and smiled. "I thank you. I
will remember it. For your barn is by far the most comfortable I have
slept in." And my winter home has disappeared, she thought. My home.
For the king's city is no home for me. Not now. Not ever. How could she
have thought otherwise? "Perhaps you will see me again sooner than
you think." She wished she could push the voice, the directional hum,

away from her, as she might slap at a fly; for so long as it buzzed at her, she had to go to the yellow city whether she would or not. She would go, then, but she would also leave.

"Good!" said Ammy, and made no further move to stop them, but watched with her curiously bright eyes as they walked back up to the road again. Lissar felt Ammy's eyes as she dropped the latch back in place. She lifted a hand in greeting and farewell, and turned away; and she and the dogs picked up the slow, long-striding trot they used to cover distance.

There was more activity on the road this year; she heard the word "wedding" once too often, and struck out across the fields, her skein of pale and brindle-marked dogs stretching out behind her. This year she knew her way, for she had hunted all over this country, and need not keep to the road even for its direction; and the word she heard now, more than once, as they trotted through dawns and twilights, was "Moonwoman."

She did not herself understand the urgency; it was as if her feet hurt—not if she kept on for too long, but if she stopped. She kept one eye always on Ash, and half an eye on Harefoot, whose leg seemed perfectly sound no matter how she bolted ahead or circled around the rest of them. It became a habit, this watchfulness, like checking between the dogs' toes for incipient sores; like running her fingers down the long vivid scar on Ash's side and belly. But there was no heat, no swelling, no tenderness; Ash, Lissar thought, was amused, but she had never been averse to extra attention, and if Lissar's desire now was to stroke a perfectly healthy side several times a day, then that was all right with Ash. But as they passed through the last days in what had become not a journey to the city but a flight to the city, the dogs caught Lissar's restlessness, and seemed as little able as she to settle down to rest for more than an hour or two.

And so they came to a water-cistern at a crossroads after a night of no sleep, just as Ash and Lissar had done the year before, a crossroads at the outskirts of the city, not far from the city gates, where it had become inescapably evident that farms had given way to shops, warehouses, inns and barracks—the water-cistern where Lissar had met Lilac, leading two couple of the king's horses. And they stopped again to drink. Lissar was refreshing her face with handsful of the cold water when she heard, "Moonwoman," but she paid it no heed, for she never paid that name any heed.

Till a hand gripped her elbow, spinning her around; and it was Lilac herself, and she threw her arms around Lissar. "I am so glad you have come back! I have missed you so much. No one would say where you had gone or why—why could not you have sent me just one word?—No, no, I will not scold you, I am too glad to see you, and Ossin was cross and gloomy and silent for weeks after you disappeared, so I knew you must have left, somehow, about him, which made your just vanishing like that a little more—oh, I don't know, acceptable, except that I did not accept it at all. . . . I mean, I have spent so much time wondering what had become of you, but that's all . . . I just told myself, well, that's the way you'd expect the Moonwoman to behave. . . ." Lilac's voice suddenly went very high, and her voice broke on the last word.

Lissar found there were tears in her eyes. She blinked. Not knowing what else to say, how to explain, she struck on her usual protest, and said, "But I'm not the Moonwoman."

They had been standing there with their arms around each other, and Lissar's neck was wet with the shorter Lilac's tears. Lilac stirred at this, and backed half an arm's length away, bending back so she could look into Lissar's face. "Aren't you?" she said. She looked down at the dogs then, and Lissar could see her looking for the one shaggy one, and then anxiously counting, coming up with the right number, and then looking again. Ash turned toward her, her right side exposed, and Lilac's eyes widened. "Gods, what was that?"

"A rather large toro," said Lissar.

"A toro? You're mad. You don't tackle a full-grown toro alone with a few dogs."

"It wasn't my idea; it was Ash's; and she would not be called off. I might have found it under other circumstances reassuring that not all of Ash's ideas are good ones, but in this case . . ."

Lilac knelt by Ash's side, which was the signal for seven dogs to try to lick her face, and, unheedingly bumping dog noses away with her other hand, ran her fingers over the scar, just as Lissar herself so often did; Lissar could have sworn that when Ash raised her eyes to meet Lissar's her look was ironic. If a dog can have a sense of humor, as Ash manifestly did, could she not also have a sense of irony? Lissar knew that at heart she believed that a good dog was capable of almost anything: Ossin would understand because he agreed.

She thought of the days and nights when the puppies were only babies, and wished she had thought to ask if he believed a dog capable of irony, for she would not have another opportunity.

"I think you are lucky to be alive," said Lilac.

There was a little pause during which the friends thought of the many things they might say to each other and the many things they wished to say to each other. Lissar found that she wished so badly to tell Lilac everything—everything she knew, including that Ossin had said that he loved her and wanted her to be his wife, and everything she remembered, including the first winter she and Ash had spent alone on the mountain, and everything she . . . could neither remember nor not remember, but only feel in her heart and bones and blood and the golden guarded space behind her navel, like how it was she came to leave her old life—that she could not speak at all. There was a noise in her ears not unlike the roaring of the demons at the gates of her own mind, before she had learned what monsters they guarded. The demons roared no longer, but she dared not tell her friend of the monsters; and the despair that rose in her then was the same that had driven her from

Ossin last autumn, and her tears spilled over, and she stood in a silence she could not break, and thought, it is no use; I should not have come back. I should go, now, right away, away from here. What I owe Ossin does not matter, Ash's puppies do not matter; nothing matters so much as that I must take myself away from this place where I have friends who love me, because I cannot tell them who I really am.

Lilac, seeing this, thought only that she wept for Ash, for the memory of seeing her when the blow had just been dealt, when fear of her dying would have squeezed Lissar's heart to a stop; for she had some good guess, as a friend will, of what these two meant to each other, though she had no guess of why. And she knew too that Lissar could not speak, though she again guessed only that it was to do with Ash: and she cast around for something to break the silence. Anything would do. "What . . . you must have had to sew it together. What did you use?"

"Flax thread," said Lissar. "It was . . . awful. But she didn't mind when I pulled them out; O-Ossin," she said, stumbling over the name, "had told me that they don't hurt coming out, but I didn't believe it: I had been there when Jobe stitched up Genther's side, after he was struck by a boar." But her tears fell only faster.

"And her hair came out with the stitches," said Lilac, watching her friend's face worriedly, guessing now that there was some great trouble that was not healed like Ash's side. "An interesting side effect. She really is a fleethound now, you know. She even looks like one of ours— of Ossin's. I see the ones that people from Fragge or Dula bring, fleethounds, and your Ash looks like she was bred here."

There was another pause, and Lissar's tears stopped falling. "Yes," she said at last. She opened her mouth to say more, but knew she could not, and closed it again.

Lilac smiled a little. "I've been sorry, occasionally, that your tongue doesn't run on wheels, as mine does. It gives me more room, of course, and I dislike anyone talking over me! But I would know your history several times over by now, if you were a talker, and I can listen, I just think silence is wasteful when there is someone to talk to. I guess . . ." She looked into Lissar's face and saw the unhealed trouble there, and realized that she believed her friend would tell her of it if she could; and wished there were some better way to show her sympathy than only in not pressing her about it.

She said at last: "You've come back just this sennight rather than the next for the wedding, I suppose? Leave it to the Moonwoman to have heard of it even from the top of her mountain."

Lissar found she still could not speak.

"One would expect the Moonwoman to keep track of time well, of course," said Lilac, "even if your reappearance just now is a trifle melodramatically late. You should get used to it, Deerskin; they've been calling you Moonwoman since I first found you, and after you spent last autumn haring around—pardon me, Harefoot—silently catching toros and finding rare herbs and lost children, there was no more chance of your being spared. And Deerskin isn't your real name either, is it?" Lilac went on without pausing, without looking at Lissar. "And if you're not thinking of coming back to stay"—here she risked a look up, and Lissar shook her head. Lilac sighed before she went on. "Well, you have yourself and seven dogs to keep, and the Moonwoman will always be welcome."

"I will give the puppies back." But her voice was a croak.

Lilac looked down. When she had stood up from examining Ash, the dogs had rearranged themselves around Lissar, as integral a part of her as the spokes of a wheel were to the hub, even if the hub remained unaware of it. "Of course you will," said Lilac; "and I will fly over the rooftops to get back to the stables with these abominable streamers that simply must be attached to the carriage trappings or the wedding can't possibly come off. If you'll wait a little, I'll come with you to the city; they've got every seamstress working on it, they should be done before midday. And stay with me if you'd . . . rather not go back to the kennels."

Lissar found her voice at last. "I thank you. I—I don't know quite what I want to do. I hadn't thought that far ahead. Just—when I heard—"

"It will be pretty spectacular; gold ribbons on black horses, and a golden carriage—real gold, they say, or anyway real gold overlay. He likes showing off, that one."

"He?" said Lissar, slowly. "It's not Trivelda?"

"Trivelda?" said Lilac. "She's not getting married till summer, and it won't happen here in all events; the Curn has fallen on his feet there. The wedding Trivelda's parents will lay on for her should gratify even his vanity, though the country will be paying for it into their grandchildren's time."

"But . . ." faltered Lissar. "But I thought Ossin . . ."

"Ossin's not getting married," said Lilac, watching her closely. "Certainly not to Trivelda. He wasn't very nice to her at the ball, you know; went off in the middle of it and only came back at the very end with this really lame excuse about a sick dog. You could see poor Clementina turning pale even from where I was standing; and Trivelda's father turning purple. I found out what he'd said later, about the dog, I mean; my friend Whiteoak was waiting on Clementina that night, and just then standing very near.

"You might accept that excuse, or I, but not our Trivelda. She was furious. I gather she hadn't liked the ball very well anyway; there were too many low people there from places like the kennels and the stables. No, she's marrying the Curn of Dorl, who attended her beautifully all that otherwise unsatisfactory evening, blinking his long curling eyelashes and comparing his soft pink hands and smooth round fingernails with hers, I imagine."

Lissar barely heard most of this. "Then who—?"

"Camilla. Ossin's sister." Lilac frowned. "It's all been very quick; it's only two months ago his emissaries arrived, and he followed them . . .

well, I'm not the only one who thinks there's something a little too hasty about it; but there isn't anything anyone can point to about its being wrong.

"Camilla is willing; of course it's very flattering for her. I don't think she ever really loved the Curn, but it must have been a little hard on her, and she's so young; but I really think that it's not the flattery alone, but the feeling that she's doing her best by her own country by making so grand a match. She's like that, you know. Not much sense of humor but a lot of responsibility—and she's always been like that, since she was a baby.

"And it's flattering for the whole country, come to that. If the stories are right his palace is about the size of our city. Cofta and Clementina are a little dazed, I think, but Ossin would stop it if he could, because Camilla is so young; but he has nothing to work with, the rest of the family and all the court sort of smiling bemusedly and saying but it's such an opportunity for her as if marriage were a kind of horse race, where if you see a gap between the leaders you automatically drive for it. And Camilla herself has a will of iron, and she's decided that she is going to do this. It's not that she loves him; she's barely met him, and he's very stiff and proud."

"I—I thought the heir was supposed to marry first," said Lissar, wondering why she felt no relief that Ossin was not to marry.

"Ah, yes, that is sticky. But I think Cofta and Clem are a bit put out at the way he missed his chance—again—worse than missed it—with Trivelda, and are glad to be marrying anyone off. It's also why Ossin's not in a good position to try and stop it. And I think probably at least partly why Camilla is so set on it: take herself off her parents' hands and do it brilliantly as well. Because it is such a grand alliance, that works against everything too—or for it, depending on your point of view."

There was no reason for the rising panic Lissar felt; she should be feeling—guilty, embarrassed, crestfallen, relieved. But the question came up at once: why had she been drawn here so urgently for Ossin's sister, whom she barely knew; as it was not to show herself that she had done right—that Ossin had returned to his proper track—in fleeing him, six months ago, then why? She had thought she must be coming here to set that part of her life finally aside. She felt as if she were standing in a world suddenly strange, as if she had looked around and discovered the trees were pink and orange instead of green; her mind spun, and yet the directional buzz was as strong as ever. She had come to where she was supposed to be; but she had never come to the place directed before and not known what she was to do there.

The urgency boiled up all the higher, pressing against the inside of her ribcage, against her heart, feeling like a fist in her throat: she swallowed. "Who—who is it Camilla is to marry?"

"I can never remember his name. He's old—a lot older than Camilla—his wife died some years ago, and he went into seclusion for some time then, and then his only daughter died five or six years ago, and he withdrew again, but this time when he came out I guess he realized he had to marry again since he had no heirs, and I guess he decided to waste no time.

"I remember—he or his ministers sent Ossin, or Goldhouse, a portrait of his daughter not too long before she died, and everyone here wondered why, even us farmhands, because a big powerful king like him who can afford a golden coach for his bride was certainly not going to marry his only child to a tin-cup prince of a back-yard kingdom like ours—where a wedding coach is just the same as any other coach with a few posies tied to the rails, except that there's usually no coach at all. There was a whole swarm of courtiers who came with the portrait, the whole country knew about it. We thought he must just be puffing out his importance. And now it's him going to marry our princess. I still can't remember his name. Oh, wait—his daughter's name was Lissla Lissar. Funny I remember that, but it's such a pretty name. Her mother had been called the most beautiful woman in seven kingdoms and she supposedly took after her—I never saw the portrait. I've even heard a story that old Cofta paid court to the mother before he settled down with Clementina. Deerskin—are you all right?"

Lissar seized the arm held out to her. "They—they aren't married yet?" Lissar shook her head, failing to clear it, although the directional hum was gone, vanished with Lilac's words. "I don't even know what your marriage rituals are."

"Noo, they're not married yet," said Lilac, looking worriedly into Lissar's face. "But as good as, or nearly. They're taking their vows today, although the public show and the party for everyone who can walk, ride or crawl here is tomorrow—the one we can go to—the one the golden coach is for. They aren't really married till tomorrow. She sleeps alone with her ladies in the next room, one last time, tonight. She only turned seventeen a few days ago—but she forbid any notice to be taken of, saying it was her marriage that mattered. She's so young . . . Deerskin, what is the matter?"

"Where?"

"Where do they take their vows? In the throne room. Not the receiving-room, where you went your first day. The throne room is behind it, smaller, and grand. Very grand. It's not used much. Is it that you know something about him?"

Lissar's eyes slowly refocussed on her friend's face, but her own face felt stiff and expressionless. "Yes—I know something about him."

There was a tiny silence, a silence unlike any either of them had experienced before, as if the silence were a live thing, making space for itself, expanding, pushing the noise of the inn and the crossroads back, so that the two of them stood in another little world: a little world where it was known that this king was no fit husband for the young, kind, responsible princess Camilla. No fit husband for any woman.

"It is curious, I was so sure I would see you today, I kept looking out of the front window. I told myself I was just bored, that I was thinking of you because this is where we first met. But I was really expecting you. The ceremony will be read out at midday; you'll have to hurry. Do you want my horse?" Lilac's words dropped into the silence, echoing, al-most, as if they stood in a chamber with thick bare walls.

Lissar shook her head. "No; the dogs and I will make our own way quicker; but I thank you."

Lilac smiled a little. "It's true, it would look odd, the Moonwoman on horseback; they'll make way for you more quickly, this way."

"I am not the Moonwoman."

"Perhaps you are not, after all; would the Moonwoman not know what she had come for? But then the stories never say that she always knows what she'll find; only that she arrives in time. Sometimes just in time."

Lissar was already gone; Lilac touched her cheek where her friend had kissed it, knowing that she had done so and yet not remembering its happening. She could not even see Lissar on the road ahead of her.

Thirty-six

I t must have been true, what Lilac said, for Lissar found nothing but empty road spinning out before her. She was dimly aware of people lining the narrow clear way, dimly aware of the noise of them, but she seemed to move in the little world of silence that had been born in her last words to Lilac, silence undisturbed by the quietness of her bare feet striking the ground, and the dogs' paws. For they ran swiftly, the last desperate effort before exhaustion; but that last effort was a great one, and so seven dogs and one Moonwoman fled, fleeter than any deer or hare, and the people rolled back before them like waves, parting before the prow of a ship running strongly before the wind.

It was a long way from the crossroads to the last innermost heart of Goldhouse's city, and the woman and the dogs were already tired, for they had come far in a very short time. Ash ran on one side of Lissar, Ob on the other, and the other five ran as close behind as the afterdeck rides behind the bow. The wind whistled out of their straining lungs, and flecks of foam speckled the dogs' sides, but there was no faltering; and the people who saw them go would tell the story later that they moved like Moonbeams. Some, even, in later years, would say that they glowed as the full Moon glows, or that mortal eyes saw through them, faintly, as Moonlight may penetrate a fog.

But Lissar knew none of this. What she knew was that she had to get to the throne room before Camilla's vows were uttered; somehow, that Camilla should merely be bodily rescued was not enough. Those vows would be a stain on her spirit, and a restraint on her freely offering her pledge to some other, worthier husband; that Camilla should have that clean chance of that other husband seemed somehow of overwhelming importance to Lissar; that she was driven by her own memory of fleeing from Ossin on the night of the ball did not occur to her. But having lost her own innocence she knew the value of innocence, and of faith, and trust; and if she could spare another's loss she would.

What the people she passed saw was a look of such fear and rage and pain on the Moonwoman's face that they were moved by it, moved in sorrow and in wonder: sorrow for the mortal grief they saw and wonder that they saw it. For they were accustomed to the Moon going tranquilly about her business in the sky while they looked up at her and thought her beautiful and far away. They knew the new tales of the lost children, and the cool bright figure with her hounds who returned them, but the stories shook and shivered in their memories as they looked at her now among them, running the streets of their own city, and with such a look on her face. Their hearts smote them, for they had believed her greater than they. And some of these people fell in behind her and followed her to Goldhouse's threshold, hurrying as they could, with some sense that even the Moonwoman might like the presence of friends, mere slow mortals that they were.

"Tomorrow," said Longsword the doorkeeper, standing as if to bar the way. "Today is for the family, and for the private words; tomorrow is the celebration for everyone, and we look forward to seeing you all." But Longsword was not a strong swordarm only, and he remembered Deerskin, and read her face as had the people who followed her now; and the official words died on his lips, which turned as pale as the Moon. "Deerskin," he said, in quite a different voice. "What ails—?"

"You must let me pass," said Lissar, as if Longsword's duty were not to bar those from the king's door that the king had decreed should be barred; as if she had the power to direct him. But he stood aside with no further question, and she ran by him, her dogs at her heels, having paused for less time than it takes to draw a breath on the doorstep.

She did not remember the way, but the urgency guided her as clearly as any beckoning finger; as clearly as she had ever known, in the last year, where to find a missing child, or a cabin on a mountaintop. She burst into the receiving-room, where a number of grandly dressed people waited to be the first to congratulate the newly married pair. Their natural impulse was to recoil from so abrupt and outlandish an intrusion as that of a barefoot woman in a rough plain white deerskin dress, her wild hair down her back, accompanied by seven tall dogs. What was Longsword doing? Why had he not called up his guards?

And so Lissar was past them before they had any thought of what to do to stop her; none had looked into her face. And she flung open the doors to the inner sanctum.

The room was big enough to hold two hundred people, and the picture they made, in their richest clothes, against the backdrop of the finest possessions of Goldhouse's ancestors, was a spectacle to dazzle the eye; no evidence here of a tin-cup, back-yard kingdom, with precious gems and metals wrought into graceful forms and figures shaping the room like a chalice. But the company, as they turned, in horror, toward the crash of the doors striking the walls, were themselves dazzled by the sight of a woman, so tall her head seemed to brush the lintel of the door, blazing like white fire, and guarded by seven dogs as great and fierce as lions.

She was so tall that as she strode into the room, even those farthest from her could see her towering head and shoulders above the crowd, her flame-white hair streaming around her like an aureole.

The group on the dais at the far end of the crowded room turned also to look toward the door. Lissar saw five frightened faces turned toward her: Ossin, Camilla, the king and queen, and the priest, whose hand, which had been upraised, dropping stiffly to his side again, as if released by a string instead of moved by conscious human volition. . . . The sixth figure remained facing away from the door a moment longer: as if he knew what the sound of the crashing doors meant, that his fate and his doom had arrived.

And so Lissar's first sight of her father in five and a half years was of his broad back. He stood as tall and proud as he ever had, and he stood too as a strong man stands, his feet planted and his shoulders squared; like a man who feared nothing, like a man who might have brought a leaf from the tree of joy and an apple from the tree of sorrow as a bride-present to his truelove's father, and thought little of the task. And yet, staring at his back, what she remembered was the look in his eyes, the hot stink of his body, the gauntleted hands hurling her dog into the wall: and that he was also a tall handsome man was like a poor description by someone who was a careless observer. His golden hair was as thick as ever, though there was white in it now, which had not been there five years before.

Lissar glanced once, only once, at Ossin; she could not help herself. And she saw his lips shape the name he knew her by: Deerskin. She did not understand the fear in his face; anger she would have expected, anger for this intrusion, anger after their last meeting, to meet again after what had passed between them, in these circumstances: anger she would have understood and submitted to. She did not like it that Ossin should look at her with fear. But she could not deny her poor heart one more look at his beloved face; and her heart saw something else there, love and longing, stronger than the fear. But this she discarded as soon as noticed, telling her heart it was blind and foolish.

Then she turned back to the task she had come to do, and prepared
not to look at Ossin again, ever again. But she let her eyes sweep over
the rest of the group before the priest, and saw the fear in their faces too,
and wondered at it, and wondered too that in none of their faces was
recognition; it was only Ossin who had known who she was.

"Father!" said the blazing woman; and the doors slammed shut
again, but as they jarred in their frames they shattered, and through the
gaping hole a wind howled, and lifted the tapestries away from the walls,
and the great jewelled urns shivered on their pedestals, and the light
through the stained glass turned dull and faint and flickering, like a guttering candle, though it was a bright day outside. Several people screamed,
and a few fainted.

And the foreign king who was to have married Camilla turned
slowly around and faced his daughter.

"You shall not marry this woman, nor any woman, in memory of
what you did to me, your own daughter," said the blazing figure; and the
people in the receiving-hall heard the words, borne on a storm-wind, as
did the people who had followed the Moonwoman's race through the
city; as did Lilac, who sat, her head in her hands, on the edge of a water-
cistern at a crossroads where not far away seamstresses sat embroidering
streamers of gold and felt their fingers falter, and a chill fall on them, for
no reason they knew, and they suddenly felt that the streamers so urgently ordered would never be used. But Lilac, her head in her hands,
heard no storm-wind; the words Lissar spoke, over a league away, in
Goldhouse's throne room, fell into the silence around her, the silence
that had held her since Lissar had left her, and the words were as clear
as if Lissar had returned and stood before her.

Lissar knew she was shouting; only those few words made her throat
sore and raw, and she felt almost as though they had been ripped out of
her, as if it were not her tongue and vocal cords that gave them shape
and sound. She held up her hands, fingers spread; but curled them into
fists, and shook them at her father, and her sleeves fell backwards, leav-

ing her arms bare. Her father stood, looking at her, motionless, but as he might look at a basilisk or an assassin. Her own flesh seemed to shimmer in her eyes; but the blood was pounding so in her head that it was hard to blink her vision clear of it. Every time she closed her eyes, for however brief a flicker of time, the sight of a small round pink-hung room flashed across her vision and dizzied her.

He knew what she was there for, but he did not see her, his daughter, and his eyes were blank, as unseeing as they had been the night he had come through the garden door and flung Ash against the wall so hard as to break her skull, and then raped his daughter, once, twice, three times, for the nights that she had locked her door against him, for he was her father and the king, and his will was law.

But his daughter had been dead for five years; he had mourned her all that time, and was here now only because his ministers demanded it. He did not care for Camilla or any other woman. He had ordered dresses for his daughter lovelier even than those her mother had worn: one the color of the sky, one brighter than the sun, one more radiant than the Moon. But she had never worn them, she who was more beautiful than all these together. Camilla was dull clay beside her. His daughter! He missed her still. He closed his blind eyes in memory and in pain.

Father! screamed the figure, only half visible through the brilliance of the white light that surrounded it, brighter than sun or Moon or noon sky; but then as its fists opened, everyone saw hands, ordinary human hands, and bare arms beneath them. But there was blood running from the hollows of the cupped hands, as if the fingernails had gouged the flesh in some private agony; but there was too much blood for that, and it ran and ran down the bare white arms, and as the blood coursed down it put out the light around the figure, as water will put out a fire.

The mysterious wind died, and the company, silent with shock, now heard the terrifying soft sound of warm human blood dripping from outstretched arms and striking the floor, a sound as innocent as rainfall.

Lilac heard that sound, and she slid off her perch at the edge of the cistern, and sat on the ground, drawing her knees to her chin, laying her face down upon them, and wrapping her arms around her head.

Open your eyes! said the bleeding woman, her voice like a wound itself. *Open your eyes and look at me!*

The foreign king opened his eyes and looked at her. Lissar staggered as from a blow, and pulled her arms back to herself again, sliding the red palms down her white hair, and then dropping her hands to her sides where her fingers touched Ash and Ob; and she could feel them growling. They gave her strength, that touch of warm dog against her fingertips, the reverberation of their growls; and she let her hands rest on them quietly, reminding herself of her dogs, reminding herself that she was alive, and here for a purpose.

Deerskin, breathed the company. The blazing figure had dwindled as its fire was put out, and they saw her at last. It is our Deerskin. What is she doing here? How can she be the foreign king's daughter? She is poor and barefoot, as she was when she first came here, a year ago, when our prince was kind to her, and gave her a place in his kennels, because she liked dogs.

But the ministers and the courtiers who had come with the foreign king staggered as Lissar had when her father's eyes opened. Lissar! they murmured. For the blood was running down the long white hair of this wild woman in her wild deerskin dress, and it darkened and spread like dye through cloth, till her hair took on the astonishing almost-black of her mother's, Lissla Lissar's mother's hair, mahogany-black, red-black, like the last, deepest drop of heart's blood, brought to light only by violent death. And they recognized the face, for it bore the same expression as it had when their king had declared that he would marry his daughter, eons ago, eons during which they had wrought mightily with their king, to get him to this place that he might honorably marry again at last, and get his country, and his ministers, a proper new heir. And with this thought they grew angry: they all thought Lissar had died. She was supposed to have died! Why must she ruin their plans thus again, this wild woman in her white dress, spoiling the marriage of their king, the marriage they had worked so hard to bring about.

Our Deerskin would not lie, murmured Goldhouse's court, much troubled. Our prince and his dogs love her. The Moonwoman is here to rescue us, murmured those who had followed her. Rescue us and our princess, as she has rescued our lost children.

It was only a young woman of slightly more than average height, although with astonishing red-black hair, who stood before them now in her blood-spattered white deerskin dress, bright blood also on the floor before her, and in her face a haggard weariness that belonged to someone much older. She dropped her eyes from the figures on the dais, and with her gaze her head dropped also, sagging forward on her neck as if she could keep it upright no longer. So she stood, gazing at the floor, as if at a loss; and she began to look out of place, among the richness of style and dress, furniture and ornament, around her; and the blasted doors behind her were an embarrassment, as if a careless servant had dropped a laden tray, making a mess on the fine carpet, and spraying the dinner guests with gravy and wine-dregs.

Thoughtfully she knelt, and touched her sullied hands to the red shining pool; thoughtfully she raised one finger and drew a red line down her cheek. The room was utterly silent; no rustle of satin nor tap of shod foot nor gasp of indrawn breath. At her back Lissar felt the warmth and presence of her dogs; and Ash's whiskers brushed the back of her neck. "I remember," she said, in quite an ordinary voice, "I remember waking up, after you left me, the last night I spent under your roof. I thought I was dead, or dying, and I wanted to be dead."

She sprang to her feet. "I carried your child—my own father's child—five months for that night's work; and I almost died again when that poor dead thing was born of me. I had forgotten how to take care of myself. I had forgotten almost everything but a madness I could not name; I often thought that I would choose to die than risk remembering what drove me to madness, for I believed the shame was mine. For you were king, and your will was law, and I was but a girl, or rather a woman, forced into my womanhood." She gripped her hands together, and they began to glow, as she had glittered in the eyes of the company when she first strode through the doors. She stared at her glowing hands, and she felt her dogs pressing around her, offering her their courage, offering her their lives in any way she might ask of them.

In a new, hard voice, she said, "I was no child, for you and my mother gave me no childhood; and my maidenhood you tore from me, that I might never become a woman; and a woman I have not become, for I have been too afraid.

"But I return to you now all that you did give me: all the rage and the terror, the pain and the hatred that should have been love. The nightmares, and the waking dreams that are worse than nightmares because they are memories. These I return to you, for I want them no more, and I will bear them not one whit of my time on this earth more."

But she staggered again, and dropped to one knee, and loosed her hands from each other, and clasped her belly, and curled around it, and the glow curled around her, like a halo, or like the embracing arms of a beloved friend. "Ah, no!" she cried, in a voice like the sound of the executioner's axe; and Lilac huddled down farther by the cistern while hot tears ran from her eyes down her folded legs, digging her knees into her eyesockets as if to stop the tears, but they swelled and overflowed anyway, and ran down the insides of her thighs.

"No!" cried Lissar. "I cannot bear it again. I cannot!" And Ash turned, and sank her teeth into Lissar's shoulder, but only to bruise and startle; she did not break the skin, or perhaps the deerskin dress did not let her. Lissar's eyes flew open, and she gave one great cry, and a burst of blood flowed from between her legs, thick, dark blood, not bright blood as from a clean wound as had flowed from her hands. This was the secret female blood, heavy with mystery, and it mixed with the more innocent blood already shed; and the intermingled blood sank into the floor, leaving a pattern of arcs and spirals and long twisting curves that forever after seemed to move if any eye tried too long to trace them. In later years that bit of floor came to be declared an oracle, and persons who wished advice on some great matter came to look at it, and see where the pattern led them, and many came away comforted, or clearer in their minds, and able to make decisions that had seemed too hard for their strength. And the throne room became the oracle room, bare and plain, containing nothing but the glowing pattern on the floor, and the shadows of the stained glass, which moved less enigmatically.

"I give it back to you," said Lissar, panting, on her knees, marked with her own blood. "All—I give it all back to you." And suddenly she was again the blazing figure she had been when she stepped across the threshold into the throne room, but she was all the colors of fire now, no longer white but red and golden. She stepped up onto the dais.

But for some of those watching the woman made of flame was two women, and they were identical, except that they were inimical. Some who saw thought of Moonwoman, and how she is both black and white, but they rejected the image, for Moonwoman was still and always herself, and what they saw now was . . . water and salt, wind and sand, fire and firewood—but which was the water and which the salt? The watchers shivered, and wondered at what they saw, and wondered at themselves. Some of them remembered their own nightmares, and perhaps it was those who had nightmares to remember who saw the second woman: and they watched fearfully.

The two figures shimmered, red and golden, and there was no differentiating them, except that there were two; as if a mirror stood somewhere that no one could see, and none therefore knew which was the real woman and which the reflection. But a change came, though the onlookers could not have said what the change was; only that the balance of their fear shifted, and they were suddenly afraid . . . terrified . . . panic-stricken at the thought that the one red-gold shape and not the other might be left when the mirror shattered, and only one remained.

If any of the watchers had looked farther, they would also have seen that Ossin put out his hand toward one, toward one and not the other, though he was too far away to touch her. What those who watched did see was that one of the flame-women put out only one hand while the other reached out with both of hers; and in the moment before they touched the watchers saw that the beauty of the one who held out both her hands was the greater, but that the greater beauty was of the kind that stopped hearts and did not lift them or bring them joy. And it was she who was the more beautiful who suddenly was no longer there, and the flame-woman remaining opened and shut her single outstretched hand as if she could no longer remember what she was reaching for.

Deerskin, murmured the watchers who had seen the two women; we have our Deerskin. Their hearts lifted, in joy and not only in relief of terror.

And Lissar, dazed, knew that she had seen her mother, but did not remember how; and thought it was perhaps only a fragment of old nightmares. She shook her head; for she saw her father standing before her, but her vision was blurred and flickering, as if she saw him through a sheet of flame. Her father? Her mother? Her mother had been dead— dead—as dead as her daughter three nights after her seventeenth birthday; but no, her daughter had not died, but had lived . . . lived to see her mother again upon a mountaintop, a mountaintop covered with snow. . . . Nightmare. But nightmare was a word used to mean unimportant and not real; and she had seen her mother, then and now. Her hands trembled, with memory and with present pain: for both were burned, one as if it had been plunged in fire, or as if she had been hurled bodily into the fire but had miraculously escaped, all but her poor hand, which she had put out to save herself. The other felt burnt as if from a rope—as if a rope had been thrown, awkwardly and almost too late, a homely rope, meant not for such adventures but for the tethering of horses, the tying of ill-fitting doors shut, or shaken-loose bits back on waggons. Almost she had not noticed it, almost she had not recognized it; but she had grabbed it at the last, and her shoulder ached from the rough jerk, and her palm was lacerated with the coarse fibers of it. But her hands were only sore, and she was alive.

Alive: alive and here, not in her father's court, no longer on a mountain, but in the throne room of the Gold House, watched by the people who had taken her in, a year ago, taken her in only because she had asked it, asked for work to do and a place to stay. How dared she answer their generosity by destroying the triumphant marriage of their princess—was it not enough that she had destroyed her own place among them?

She blinked: for her mother's face briefly re-formed before her, swimming into existence from the dizzy golden-red blur before her eyes. But it was not her mother's face, but the face of the painting, the painting that had hung behind her father's throne since her mother had died. The painting was there before her, as beautiful and horrible as she remembered, as clear as though she could touch the painted canvas; she recoiled from the thought, recoiled from the painting, recoiled from her mother: No! she told it. No! And the golden-red blur thickened, but as she stared, wide-eyed, her mother's face began to blacken, her mother's eyes dimmed and became only cracked paint, and the smell of burning canvas was in her nostrils.

She blinked again: and knew where she was, and why, and that she came not to destroy Camilla's future but to save it. She saw who stood before her, and recognized him, and did not cringe, although she hated what must come next. And she strode forward onto the dais, and all cowered away from her, all but two.

Her father she seized, she knew not how, for she would not have touched his flesh willingly; nor could those looking on decipher how the flame licked at him; but a look of horror, of an understanding beyond the grasp of mortality, and beyond the profoundest guesses of the still living about the darkest pits of hell, ran fingers like claws over his face, and left a broken old man where a proud king had once stood. The entire dais was lit as if by flame, and all those that stood by heard a roaring in their ears, as if the entire city were burning down around them. Almost they felt the heat of it, and the air seemed too hot to breathe, and struck harshly on their faces; and outside the throne room the people looked through the shattered doors as if down the red gullet of a Great Dragon.

When the fire released him, the foreign king would have fled, but his own ministers stood in his way, as they tried to press as far from this unknown figure of fire as they could: there had been something about Lissar, but this was not Lissar; this was—something beyond their ken. This was some outlandishness from a barbarian country steeped no doubt in witchcraft; it had been chosen merely because it was the nearest with a marriageable princess. This had been a mistake. It had nothing to do with them. They coughed, and their eyes burned, as if from standing too near a fire. When the dreadful being that stood too near them spoke, they heard the snarl of a crackling fire; but they feared to turn their backs on it to flee to a safer distance because of the seven vast lion-like creatures that stood around it, their jaws a little parted so the white teeth showed, their brilliant eyes fixing at once on any sudden movement. The ministers shuddered, and one of them wept, and so they barred their own king's way in their fear they would not accept as fear. Yet the king could not have fled as he wished even had the way been clear, for he was an old man now, and weak, and slow.

Ossin was the other figure who had stood firm at the coming of the fire. He was the only one of all in the room who had both seen what all the others had seen and yet equally still seen Lissar. He did not think the fire would burn him, or perhaps he did not care. "Deerskin," he said. "Lissar."

She turned to him, and tears of fire and blood were spilling down her cheeks, and her eyes, draining of their blackness, were fire-amber. "Lissar," he said, wonderingly; for now he saw what once had been the girl in the portrait, although the woman before him was much more than the poor, proud, though undeniably beautiful girl in the portrait gave any promise of becoming. "Lissar," he said, with love and sorrow, and reached fearlessly out to touch her burning face.

But she flinched away from his touch, as she had flinched away from him on a balcony half a year ago, and he saw the stricken look come into her clear amber eyes, followed by yearning and despair; and then she turned away from him, and sprang down from the dais, and ran to the broken doors; and the long ribbon of lion-dogs uncoiled itself and ran after her. The way opened for her, like a silvery line of Moonbeam; but behind her it closed in again, like shadows. But more solid than shadows, for when he reached after her, bodies blocked him, as there was a rush for the dais from his courtiers, to catch the foreign king as he fell.

She had a long start on him, for he would not force his way through the shocked, bewildered crowd at the risk of hurting anyone, and it was some minutes before he won his way to the gaping doors. And he knew how swiftly she could go. But he refused to lose her again, and he set his teeth, and thought, agonized and hopeful, that she must be weary to heart and bone; she could not go far without rest. Not even to escape him. When she had fled from him the night of the ball it had been too dark to see clearly; but today he had seen her face, lit by her own light, and he had seen the yearning and the stricken look. He would not let her escape, and he thought he understood now how he might hold her—or he knew how he might try, and then hope and agony blinded him. If he had not needed to pursue her at once, he would have killed her father with his bare hands, he who offered a prayer that his shaft or blade might fly straight to the heart of every beast he caught hunting, to spare it pain and fear, and thanked its spirit after its death for giving him meat for his people. He could have killed this other human being with his bare hands.

In the stir of people talking, of people discovering that they could still talk, and move, he could hear nothing of her soft-footed flight; but when he reached the door and said to Longsword, "Which way?"

Longsword pointed without a word of query. Ossin ran on, aware of the slow heavy sound of his own footsteps. He thought he could guess that she would head out across the fields behind the kennels, through the little stand of wood beyond, and toward the crossroads where the Happy Man stood. It was a longer way out of the city's environs than through the Redvine Gate, but he believed that she would prefer the way that would give her bare earth under her feet, rather than the shorter way through the city streets.

He needed to catch her before she went beyond the crossroads, however, for the land began to turn emptier then, with farms biting chunks from the emptiness, but doing little to disturb the vast secrecy of the wilder hunting lands; and for the first time he cursed his own and his people's fondness for the life his dogs were bred to, that wild land should lie so near the king's city.

He was running out of breath, and a fine fool he must look, every unaccustomed step jarring his body, used as it was to riding not running. He bolted down the back streets of his city, mostly deserted on account of the grand doings at the king's house, where the front courtyard and the wide street that led to it were jammed so close that no one could easily move from the tiny foot-sized space of land where each stood. He could hear the babble of the crowd, and fancied he felt the reverbera-tion of so many hearts beating in the air, or in the ground under his running feet. He spun in his tracks at the sound of hoofbeats, and saw some small farmer, dressed carefully in his best clothes, dismounting from his young cob, and looking cautiously around him. "Sir!" cried the prince. "If I may borrow your horse!"

It did not occur to Ossin that one of his subjects might not recog-nize him, and fortunately this man had seen the prince at hunting more than once; though Ossin's court clothes—which in fact this particular prince spent most of his life avoiding—might well have suggested to this farmer that he would do best to say yes to this request, whether he recognized his supplicant or not. As Ossin swung into the saddle—

damning those same court clothes for their awkwardness for running or riding—his mind was frantically trying to calculate if he saved more time in commandeering a farmer's idea of a riding horse, or if he would have done better to have taken the long detour to the royal stables for one of his own horses. How much longer was the longer way through the fields after all? Might he have done better to follow the way she would have gone and hoped to catch sight of her? He convinced the cob, who was young enough to have retained a sense of adventure, that, unlike its master, he really did want to gallop. The cob put its ears forward and galloped.

But there were still people and alleys and obstacles; he even lost his way, once, in the labyrinthine, ancient backside of the Gold House, by not paying enough attention to the immediate three-dimensional twists and turns before him; and that made him all the more frantic.

He changed his mind halfway and ducked out a small side-gate, down a lane, and into some of the waste land below the city walls that was left unused as a buffer between city and farm. His heart sank, for no matter how he strained his hunting vision, accustomed to sighting the smallest indicative shivers in grass and leaf, he saw no sign of Lissar. But he set out across the field as if the crossroads were his certain target. The cob, though rough-gaited, was sound, and willing, and kept a good pace, but with every stride Ossin cried out silently at the slowness of it, and thought longingly of Greywing, standing idle in her stall. And then the cluster of buildings that heralded the crossroads loomed up before him, and still no sign of Lissar or her seven dogs.

But instead there was a figure riding out in such a direction as obviously intending to meet with him; and as he drew up, resenting the pause but hoping for news, he recognized Lilac, who, as soon as she saw him draw rein, dismounted, and held out her own reins. Lilac had lost what little fear she had had of him as the prince and king's heir after seeing him once or twice in the early morning after a long night with Lissar's puppies, months ago; and they respected each other, cautiously, without thinking about it, because each knew the other stood as a good friend to Lissar. "Take mine," she said now. "He is one of Skyracer's get, and runs in his stall if he is not given enough running outside it. Lissar went that way"—she said, and pointed, her hand a little unsteady, like her tongue on the new name—"but a few minutes ago. I lost her in the trees, but she cannot yet have gone far."

"My thanks," said Ossin, meaning it, accepting the reins she held out to him; she said no word further, but her face was a little less drawn than he felt his own to be. He would have said one word more to comfort her, could he have thought of one. But he could not, and he settled into the saddle and gave the horse his head. Trust Lilac to have persuaded Redthorn to let her take one of the most promising young horses in the king's stables on a page's errand. The colt seized the bit and flew.

And so he burst through the veil of trees into the first wide swathe of farmland, and there, at last, he saw what he sought; and he saw too that they were tired, weary nearly unto death, although he could not say for sure where his knowledge came from, for they were all still running, running as lightly as Moon on water.

But his heart was sick in him that she should run herself to death to escape him, for he was sure that she knew he would follow; and almost he took the bit from the colt and turned him away from their quarry. But he remembered the look on Lissar's face when she had turned away from him, and remembered too what else she ran from, what she had faced and broken by her own strength before the eyes of everyone in the throne room, and then he closed his legs around the colt's sides a little more firmly, and leaned a little lower over his flying mane. For he knew also that if he looked into Lissar's eyes now, now that the past had burned away, if he looked into those clear eyes and still saw a despair that could not be healed, he would return and kill her father; and he needed to know if he must do this or not.

The colt caught up with the dogs only a few steps before the first of the real woodlands began; the cob would never have got him there in time. But it abruptly occurred to Ossin that he did not know what to do now that he had come abreast of them. He could not hold them captive; they could, if they chose, duck around him and dodge into the cover of the trees after all; and he would not be able to follow them closely, a man on horseback, through the undergrowth. He could, he supposed, seize Lissar herself somehow. . . . But he would not. He hoped she would decide to stop of her own will.

She did. She stopped like a branch breaking, and stood swaying; several of the dogs flopped down immediately and lay panting on their sides.

Ossin dismounted, pulled the reins over the colt's head and dropped them; he'd had enough of running for one morning, and would perhaps stay as he was trained. "Lissar," said the prince.

"Go away," she said, between great mouthsful of air.

"No," he said. "Don't send me away. I let you leave me the first time because I thought that was what you wanted—that what you wanted didn't include me. But . . ."

"I do want you," she said, her voice still weak with running, and with what else had happened that day. And as she stood she began to tremble, and her teeth rattled together; and it was all Ossin could do to stand his ground, not to touch her. "I had forgotten that I have thought of you every hour since the night of the ball; I had convinced myself that I thought of you only every day. I remembered the truth of it when I saw you today, standing beside . . . your sister." She was too tired not to speak the truth; having him before her, himself, the warm breathing reality of him, struck down her last weak defenses; she thought she had never been so tired, and yet the strength of her love for the man who stood before her was not a whit lessened by her body's exhaustion. Her voice had dwindled away to little more than a whisper. "But it does not matter. I am . . . not whole. I am no wife for you, Ossin."

"I don't care about—" he began; but she made an impatient gesture.

"I don't mean . . . only that I have no maidenhead to offer a husband on our wedding night. I am hurt . . . in ways you cannot see, and that I cannot explain, even to myself, but only know that they are there, and a part of me, as much as my hands and eyes and breath are a part of me."

Ossin looked at her, and felt the hope draining out of his heart, for the red and gold were gone from her. Even her yellow eyes were closed, and her face was as pale as chalk, and nearly as lifeless. Only her glinting dark hair held its color. "Then you do not love me?" he said in a voice small and sad.

Her eyes flew open and she looked at him as if he had insulted her. "Love you? Of course I love you. Ask Lilac, or Hela or Jobe, or—or Longsword. Ask anyone I ever spoke your name to last summer."

"Then marry me," said Ossin. "For I love you, and I do not believe there is anything so wrong with you. You are fair in my eyes and you lie fair on my heart. I—I was there, this morning, when you—when you showed the scars you wear, and I accept that you bear them, and will always bear them, as—as Ash bears hers," for even in his preoccupation he had seen and, unlike Lilac, recognized what he saw of Lissar's seventh hound.

"It is not like that," she whispered. "It is not like that."

"Is it not?" said Ossin. "How is it not?" And in his voice, strangely, was the sound of running water, and of bells.

There was a little pause, while they looked at each other, and Ossin knew that it could go either way. He understood that she did not believe that last summer was more important than the truth he had heard spoken at such cost only an hour ago; and he could think of nothing he might say to change her mind, if his love could not reach her, if she counted the love in her own heart as nothing.

And then Ash moved forward from Lissar's side, and leaned against Ossin's leg, and sighed. And they both looked down at her. Almost Ossin held his breath, afraid that this was the last stroke, the final fragment that would produce Lissar's decision, whole and implacable and—the wrong one, the one Ossin feared. And so he broke into speech, saying anything, wanting to prevent Lissar from putting that last piece into its place and presenting him with his fate. But his tongue betrayed him, betrayed the fact that he could not think of life without her, now that he had her again, now that he had caught her when she had run away—now that he had heard her say that she loved him. "This is the Ash I sent you when your mother died," he said, "and some day I want to hear why she grew a long coat, as none of my dogs has ever done and as I as their arrogant breeder am inclined to count an insult to my skill, and why she then lost it again, and what happened since I saw you last that left this mark in her side."

Lissar's eyes were fixed on her dog, who had left her to lean against her lover; but then she lifted her eyes and her gaze met Ossin's, and he saw the hot amber was a little cooled by green, and the green was very clear and calm. Her tone was wondering as she answered: "Lilac asked the same thing. It was a toro—a large toro—and I did not set them on it, for I have more sense; but Ash would not be called back. I do not know myself about her coat. She protected me by disguising herself— protecting me as she has always done." As she believes she is protecting me now, she thought, and guessed that Ossin heard these words too, though she did not say them aloud. "The night I . . . ran away. . . . After my father left me, I waited only to die. And I only did not die because Ash lived, and because she wished me to live too." Will you desert me now, Ash, if I do not choose as you would have me choose, after all that has come before?

They both heard more unspoken words, this time Ossin's. What do you owe me, then, for Ash? Your life? What risk will you take for her risk? For me? But he heard her answers to the words he did not speak: It is not like that. It is not like that. You do not understand.

I do not have to understand, he said. I have seen the scars you carry, and I love you. If you and Ash cannot run quite so far as you used because of old wounds, then we will run less far together. "I was never a runner anyway," he murmured aloud, and Lissar stirred but made no answer.

Aloud he said: "There is another reason we should marry; for you are the only person I've ever known who loves dogs, these fleethounds, as much as I do; and therefore I suspect that I am the only person you have ever known who loves them as you do."

Lissar almost smiled, and a little color came back into her face, and her eyes were hazel now. "And I promised you puppies, didn't I? Ash is pregnant by Ob now, I believe."

"You did promise me puppies," said Ossin, trembling now himself, fighting to keep his words low and kind, as he would speak to a dog so badly frightened it might be savage in its fear; knowing that she wanted to come to him, not knowing if he could depend on that wanting, clamping his arms to his sides to prevent himself from seizing her to him as he wanted to do.

"Ossin," Lissar said, and sighed, and the sigh caught in her throat; and she held one hand out toward him, hesitantly, and he put his arms around her, gently. I cannot decide, she said but not aloud; and so I will let you—and Ash—and my heart decide for me. But I do not know if this is the right thing. She remembered the Moonwoman's words: Ash is looking forward to running through meadows again; can you not give yourself leave to run through meadows too? But she remembered also that Moonwoman had said, It is a much more straightforward thing to be a dog, and a dog's love, once given, is not reconsidered.

"It is not so easy as running and not running," she said, and found that she had spoken aloud; but she was in Ossin's arms as she said it, and knew that she would stay there—for now. And she promised, herself and Ossin, and Ash and the puppies, that she would try to stay there, for as long as the length of their lives; that she would put her strength now and hereafter toward staying and not fleeing. But I do not know how strong I am, she said. I cannot promise.

It is enough, said Ossin. For who can make such promises? No one of us is so whole that he can see the future.

Then she stepped toward him of her own volition, and put her own arms around him, and he heaved his own sigh, and bent his head, and kissed her, and she relaxed forward, against his breast. And the dogs closed around them, pressing up against their thighs, wagging their tails, rubbing their noses against the two figures who were holding each other so tightly that they seemed only one figure after all.